'If you have only a dim recollection of the Arthur legends, this is an opportunity to rediscover their variety. And Massie entertainingly adds his own, deliberately anachronistic, original ingredients: Virgil, Alexander the Great, even, at one point, Ezra Pound, which sustains the legend's vitality and will further its longevity'   Salley Vickers, *The Times*

'It is in the mists of sinister suggestion that Massie's skill truly glitters . . . you are held by the throat from beginning to end'   *Scotland on Sunday*

'Massie wears his enormous erudition lightly . . . This novel simply adds to my admiration for this absurdly underrated author'   Frank McLynn, *Glasgow Herald*

'A lively and colourful yarn, with some familiar episodes from British legend re-told with commendable freshness'
Max Davidson, *Sunday Telegraph*

'A colourful account, which brings a strong flavour of the period. The prose is peppered with earthy language and sharp humour. *Arthur the King* brings a fresh perspective, emphasising the private and public character of Arthur over romance and magic'   Kath Murphy, *Scotland on Sunday*

'With its humour and energy, its generous range and its sad music of humanity, the chronicle of Michael Scott recalls another, later Scot – great W. Scott himself'
Christopher Hart, *Daily Telegraph*

Allan Massie is the author of seventeen novels, including *The Evening of the World*, the beginning of an unconnected Dark Ages sequence, of which *Arthur the King* is the second. His Emperors Quintet (*Augustus*, *Tiberius*, *Caesar*, *Antony*, *Nero's Heirs*) have been translated into more than a dozen languages. He is also a prolific journalist, and has lived for the last twenty years in the Scottish Borders.

Arthur the King

A Romance

ALLAN MASSIE

PHOENIX

A PHOENIX PAPERBACK

First published in Great Britain in 2003
by Weidenfeld & Nicolson
This paperback edition published in 2004
by Phoenix,
an imprint of Orion Books Ltd,
Orion House, 5 Upper St Martin's Lane,
London WC2H 9EA

A CIP catalogue record for this book
is available from the British Library.

ISBN 0 75381 781 0

Printed and bound in Great Britain by
Clays Ltd, St Ives plc

First, for Alison, as ever;
then, for Claudia

Prefatory Note

The story of Arthur has been told by many authors in many different ways.

This version purports to be a translation of a narrative written by the medieval scholar and astrologer Michael Scott for his pupil, the Hohenstaufen Holy Roman Emperor Frederick II (1194–1250).

Complete in itself, it is also the second volume of my Dark Ages trilogy, published by Weidenfeld & Nicolson and Phoenix. Anyone interested in learning how and where Scott's manuscript is said to have been discovered will find a full account in the introduction to the first novel in the trilogy, *The Evening of the World*.

A.M.

BOOK ONE

I

The winter sea was grey and the grass was grey and the stone of the little chapel on the hill was grey. Towards noon it began to rain, but still the rocks resounded to the clang of mailed feet as the knights strode from the yard where they had tied their horses to the stretch of level ground before the chapel. That stood on an eminence. There was a shallow valley beyond it and then the ground rose sharply again towards the outer ramparts of the castle.

A bier had been placed in the Great Hall and on it lay the body of the King, Uther Pendragon, the face visible that all might see that it was indeed the King who lay there awaiting burial when the frost released its hold on the earth.

But the knights paid little heed to the King whom they had been accustomed either to obey or defy. A dead king is a dead lion, no longer to be feared; the divinity that hedged him in life fled. Uther Pendragon was no more, and all Britain was held in suspense till his successor should be known.

A stone stood before the chapel and from a cleft in the stone protruded a sword, the hilt encrusted with jewels: rubies, amethysts, topaz. Uther Pendragon's will was known: whoever should draw the sword from the stone was the rightful king. So all day long, knight after knight had made the attempt. Knight after knight had sweated and strained; and the sword remained fixed.

'It is as tight as a Jew's fist,' muttered Sir Kay whose hands were bruised and bleeding from his struggle to release the sword.

'Tight as a boy's arse,' growled his brother.

Trumpets sounded. The crowd parted and a squat, saturnine

I

man, with a thick black moustache and a lower jaw that stuck out beyond the upper so that the two did not meet, advanced towards the stone. He wore a circlet of gold on his helmet and, as he clanged up the rocky path, he wiped his hands, thick-fingered and hairy, on the skirts of his tunic.

'Who is it?' some asked, ignorant men.

But Sir Kay, doing the honours on behalf of his father, the castellan, who lay in bed suffering a tertiary ague, stepped forward to greet the newcomer. He looked him boldly in the eye, but could not hold the steely gaze directed at him, and fell to his knee and kissed the hairy hand that was demandingly extended.

'It is King Lot of Orkney,' one said. 'Surely he is the man will draw the stone.'

Others, now he was identified, nodded in agreement. King Lot's reputation as a mighty warrior, who had cleared the northern seas of pirates, was known to all. Moreover, he was the husband of Uther Pendragon's daughter, Morgan le Fay, she of the russet hair, eyes blue as cornflowers and figure of the pagan goddess, Venus Aphrodite.

King Lot looked neither to left nor right. He paid no heed to the murmurs of the crowd, which, however, now fell silent, in hushed anticipation, as when a champion of renown enters the lists. He brushed Sir Kay aside and approached the stone. He looked hard at the sword. He lifted his narrow black eyes to the heavens and his lips moved, as if perhaps he mouthed a prayer. He spat twice on his right hand and seized hold of the richly decorated hilt.

He pulled, but the sword did not move. He stepped back and frowned, then advanced a second time and resumed his grip. He tugged and heaved, and the sweat ran down his swarthy cheeks and his temples throbbed. He uttered a loud cry and, placing his left hand also on the sword, gave a sudden upward jerk. But there was no movement. 'This is some trick,' he said, 'some witchery' and turned, angry and disconsolate, away.

'If Lot fails, then the sword cannot be freed and we shall have no king in Britain,' a voice in the crowd was heard to say and a low murmur of dismay rose from the assembly.

But still other knights queued up to make the attempt. All in vain. For a moment it seemed as if the gigantic Sir Bedivere, a man built like an ox, had succeeded in causing the sword to shift position. But it was not so and he too fell back defeated. Another knight in black armour so strained and heaved that he dropped to the ground in a swoon and was carried lifeless from the stage.

A cold wind blew up from the sea, and it began to rain more steadily. The shades of night closed in. The crowd was commencing to disperse, when a quiet voice was heard to ask if one not yet dubbed a knight might nevertheless attempt to draw the sword.

The speaker was a youth, scarce out of boyhood. He was slight of build and pale-complexioned. His dark-brown hair was cropped coarsely short and his whole demeanour was modest. But he looked steadily at the stone from blue eyes fringed with long lashes, like a girl's, and his lips were parted as if in expectation, revealing one broken tooth. There was a V-shaped scar on his forehead and he was dressed only in a blue-grey tunic, girdled at the waist and rucked up to show slim but muscular thighs.

The crowd laughed to see one so meanly dressed and insignificant of figure offer to draw the stone, and Sir Kay called out to the boy to be gone and not to waste everyone's time. 'This is a challenge for noble knights,' he said, 'not for beardless boys who should be attending to their lessons or their domestic duties.'

But the officiating priest intervened. Uther Pendragon's will, he said, was clear: there was no limit to whoever should seek to draw the stone. The boy should have his chance.

So the youth stepped forward, amidst mocking laughter from the crowd. But he paid no heed to this. Instead, he looked composedly on the stone and on the jewelled hilt of the sword. The pink tip of his tongue protruded and he gave a quick lick to his lips. Then he placed his hand on the hilt and, without straining, drew the sword smoothly from the stone that held it and raised it high above his head. He lowered it to the ground and, resting his hands on the pommel, seemed for a moment to be abstracted in prayer.

A loud roar broke the silence of the gathering dusk.

'We have a king, we have a king . . .'

The priest said, 'What is your name, my son?'

The boy smiled. 'In the castle kitchen where I work, they call

3

me by many names, sometimes "Brat" or "Wat" or "Wart", but I was baptised "Arthur".'

'Then long live King Arthur,' cried the priest, 'Arthur, King by the Grace of God.'

The crowd took up the cry, but was silenced when, first Sir Kay pushed himself forward, saying 'this is tomfoolery, enough of it' and then King Lot strode forward. He looked the boy up and down, and spat on the ground between his feet. 'There is some devilry here,' he said, 'and madness too. Will you be ruled by some kitchen brat, got in a ditch of an unknown slattern? Will he lead you in battle against the Saxons? How he drew the sword, I know not, but that he did so by fraud, of that I am certain. You, boy,' he said to Arthur, 'come here.'

But Arthur smiled and did not move, looking calmly on the enraged King of Orkney, who, furious at this defiance (as he thought it) himself stepped forward and struck Arthur with his mailed fist, so that the boy fell to the ground and lay there, blood spurting from his mouth.

'There is your king,' Lot said, 'grovelling in the dirt. Know this, that if you take him as your king, there will be war in Britain. I shall not rest till I have destroyed him and exposed this deception.'

II

Now this is the story as it is commonly told. It makes – you will agree – a fine tale, and when I first heard it in my childhood sung by a minstrel in Newark tower on the banks of the Yarrow Water, I delighted in it and had no reason to doubt that it was true. For it is well-known, and of frequent occurrence, that great heroes are often obscure in their youth, and must prove their mettle and assert their right by mastering a test which baffles other men. And it is indubitably the case that the young Arthur was thought to be of no significance till this day that he is said to have drawn the sword from the stone. He had served latterly in the household of a knight who goes by different names, but who was first the seneschal of that King Vortigern who rashly invited the Saxon kings Horsa and Hengist to settle in Kent (called, by some, the Garden of England) and who then served as Master of the Horse to Uther Pendragon himself. And in this household Arthur, whose parentage was unknown, was but meanly regarded. He was treated as a servant, confined to humble duties – cleaning tack, sweeping floors and the like. Nobody thought that he would become a famous warrior. Nobody thought that he would make a warrior of any sort and Sir Kay, who was the castellan's son, often told him, between kicks, that he was fit only to be a servitor at table or a priest.

How he had come to that castle in the West, none knew or could remember. Though he had lived there, he had never lost the soft accent of the Scottish Borders; and, the Scots being regarded as rude barbarians, he was mocked and reviled for this reason too.

This, then, was the boy who drew the sword from the stone, though grown men, gnarled knights and mighty kings had failed. With your keen intelligence, my Prince, an intelligence which I am pleased to observe grows more sceptical by the month, you will doubt the story. It may, of course, nonetheless be true. Strange

5

things happen, inexplicable by reason. That is incontrovertible. Nevertheless, if you suspect some deception rather than merely dismissing the tale, you may be right.

At the back of the story lurks the mysterious figure of Merlin. (He was by some accounts lurking in the churchyard too.) And Merlin takes some explaining. Who was he? What was he?

Geoffrey of Monmouth, author of *The History of the Kings of Britain*, a scribbler of matchless impudence, gives this account.

But first, a word concerning this Geoffrey. There are some – fools – who regard his work with the reverence properly due to great historians such as Livy or even Julius Caesar himself. But I should draw your attention to the judgement delivered by my old friend William of Newburgh, a man of unimpeachable rectitude. 'It is very clear', wrote William, 'that everything this man Geoffrey wrote about Arthur and his successors, or indeed about his predecessors from Vortigern onwards, was made up, partly by himself and partly by others, either from an inordinate love of lying, or for the sake of pleasing the Britons' – by whom my old friend meant the Welsh, a goatish people, some say, who stole their best songs and histories from my own Scottish Borderland.

Well, then, this is the story of Merlin as Geoffrey tells it, and of how he rose to prominence.

It happened in the days of King Vortigern, a Roman citizen belonging to an old British royal family, who had raised a rebellion against the Emperor Constantius and established his own independent kingdom. Then, because his rule was insecure, he invited the Saxons (as I have already said) to settle in Kent that they might guard the shores of Britain against other invaders. This was foolish; as well invite the wolf to guard the sheep against other beasts of prey. So, soon, the Saxons, despising Vortigern, turned against him, seized him, bound him with ropes and compelled him to surrender large parts of his kingdom to them in exchange for his life. All this is well attested and we need not rely on Geoffrey as our sole witness or authority.

Vortigern was now greatly dismayed and at a loss to know what to do. So he summoned his counsellors, whom Geoffrey styles 'magicians', even though it is clear from his own account that these were ignorant and foolish men who knew nothing of

6

magic, which is an art or craft requiring deep study to be mastered. They advised him to build a strong tower into which he could withdraw if he lost all his other fortresses; and Vortigern, whose understanding of the art of war and of strategy was evidently poor, thought this advice good. He summoned his stonemasons and set them to work at the site he had selected in the mountains of north Wales. But, Geoffrey tells us, when they began to lay the foundations of their tower, however much they built in one day was swallowed up in the night, so that the work made no progress.

Vortigern then consulted his magicians again, as to what should be done. And they said he should seek out a lad without a father, then kill the boy, and sprinkle the stones and mortar with his blood. This being done, they said, the foundations would stand firm.

Now, though Vortigern was, by Geoffrey's account, a Christian who had been distressed to learn that the Saxons worshipped pagan gods, Wotan (whom some call Woden), Thor and Freya, he nevertheless found this absurd advice to be good and acted on it, sending messengers throughout the country to search for such a boy. In a town called Kaermerdin, now Carmarthen, they happened on two lads who were quarrelling over their play. One struck the other, crying out that he was insolent to argue with him, since he (the speaker) was of royal blood, while as for the other boy, 'nobody knows who you are, for you never had a father'. The messengers enquired further and were told that this was indeed the case, though his mother was a daughter of a Welsh king and now resided in a nunnery by the Church of St Peter.

So they fetched her, doubtless protesting, and brought her with the boy to Vortigern, who enquired of her closely how her son came to be born.

She replied, 'By the living God, my Lord King, I never had relations with any man to make me bear this child. But it happened that, in the nunnery I was sometimes visited in the evening, after dusk, by a being who took the form of a handsome young man with red-gold curls and a pleasing singing voice. Sometimes he held me in his arms and kissed me, and then he would vanish, though the door and windows remained closed. At other times, when I was alone, working on my tapestry, he would speak to me, though I could not see him. And, though invisible, his talk was all of love; and in this way he made me pregnant. So, my Lord King, you must decide in your wisdom who was the father of my son, for I swear to you, on the Holy Rood, that never otherwise, and in no other guise, did I have relations with any man.'

Vortigern scratched his head. (All the evidence suggests he was a man who was easily puzzled, a man out of his depth, who had assumed honours and a title that came his way by fortune and not merit.) He called on a wise councillor, a certain Maugantius, concerning whom Geoffrey knew no more than his name, who spoke as follows.

'In the books written by our sages and in many histories,' he said, 'I have read of such mysterious births. Apuleius, in his treatise *de deo Socratis*, asserts that between the moon and the earth there live spirits, incubi, whom we term demons. Their nature is divided, part men, part angels, and when they choose, they take on the shape of men and have intercourse with women who, being like all the daughters of Eve suggestible and open to corruption, yield and indeed welcome their advances. It is my opinion that one such appeared to this woman and begot the boy.'

Then, as Geoffrey has it, the lad Merlin approached the King and asked why he and his mother had been brought there. Vortigern relayed the advice he had received from his magicians, with some relish for he was, men say, one of those who delight in the infliction of pain. If, however, he expected the boy to display terror at the thought of his imminent death, he was disappointed; Merlin smiled, grimly we may suppose, and said, 'Call your magicians here and I shall expose their falsehood.'

So this was done, and when the magicians were assembled, Merlin spoke as follows.

'Because you are ignorant men and do not know why your tower cannot be built, you have told the King that my blood should be sprinkled on the stone and mortar. I wonder what nonsense you would devise next when you found that that remedy did not work. But I have a simpler question for you, which, if you

8

are in truth masters of magic, you must be able to answer. What lies beneath the foundations of your tower?'

To this they made no reply, for they did not know.

Then Merlin said, 'My Lord King, now call your workmen and tell them to dig deeper. They will find a pool. That is why the foundations are not stable and the tower cannot be built.'

Such was his assurance that the King did as he was bid; and a pool was discovered.

Merlin said, 'What, most learned magicians, lies beneath the pool?'

Again they were silent.

'Drain the pool,' Merlin said, 'and you will find two dragons sleeping on a slab of rock.'

'What dragons are these?' the King asked, amazed.

'The red dragon of Britain and the white dragon of Germany,' Merlin said.

Now Geoffrey does not tell us whether these dragons were indeed discovered. Instead, he embarks on a long account of what he styles 'the prophecies of Merlin', in which the fate of the dragons is made to conform to the history of Britain. There is much truth in these prophecies, as you discover when you penetrate beneath the surface of the language and the deliberately opaque style.

And this should not surprise you, since, like most prophecies, these were invented retrospectively.

Nevertheless, though much in Geoffrey's narrative is but sad nonsense, there is a substratum of truth and Merlin, as I shall relate, was a remarkable man and indeed, a worker of wonders and a cunning politician.

III

Some, ignorantly, term Merlin a mere magician, a practitioner of the most vulgar forms of the occult arts; and indeed, it is in this guise that the ridiculous Geoffrey displays him. Others, more imaginatively, state that he was a Druid, perhaps the last of the Druids, the priests who served the Britons at the time when the Roman legions first penetrated these isles. You have, my Prince, read the great Caesar's account of these priests, who assembled in oak groves, foretold the future and conducted human sacrifices at the two solstices and, as some authorities assert, at the full moon also. But it is well known that the Druids were driven to take refuge on the Isle of Anglesey, which the Romans called Mona, and there perished in a sinful act of mass suicide. Therefore it is absurd to suggest that Merlin, who flourished several hundred years later, was one of these deluded men.

The truth is other.

You will remember from my previous account* that when Marcus escaped from the prison in Constantinople where he was confined he came, by the advice of his loyal friend Sir Gavin, to Britain, where he was received joyfully by the dying king at a city called Winchester and then reigned in his stead, this being after the feeble and lascivious and cowardly Emperor Honorius had withdrawn the legions from Britain.

Now it so happened that three cohorts of the Twentieth Legion based at Chester to guard the Irish Sea failed to answer the summons, perhaps because they had either become detached from the main body of the legion, or had been sent further north and so did not receive the order, or, as some say, because they mutinied, the soldiers refusing to leave their British women and murdering the legate who tried to enforce the imperial command. Be that as

* *The Evening of the World.*

it may, they remained behind, and their centurions assumed full authority. Lonely and embattled, they survived with difficulty.

Marcus learned of this and sent Sir Gavin north to summon them to his colours. For these men, some by now gnarled and suffering from the aches and pains of advancing years, it was a great joy to learn that a true Roman was returned to Britain and established as Emperor. So they hastened south.

The boy Merlin was among them. He was the son of a centurion, by name Macro, and a woman from that part of what is now the Scottish Borderland called the Ettrick Forest. Some say the boy's true name was Myrrdin, which is cognate with the French *merde* and means shitty. But this is not so; that was merely the nickname given him by the other children of the camp, who found the boy strange, dirty and disagreeable. In truth, he was by nature a solitary, such as other boys habitually fear and resent.

Were this fiction I would tell you of the remarkable powers he displayed even as a child. But since I write nought but sober truth, I must refrain from such invention. The young Merlin was distinguished only by his awkwardness, his stammer, his aversion from sociability, and by having one eye blue and the other brown. Moreover, he was given to sudden spasmodic gestures, nervous tics and a quite unusual clumsiness. It was perhaps because he was conscious of his oddity that he devoted himself with an extraordinary ardour to the service of Mithras, God of the Soldiers.

It was Lycas, formerly the bedfellow and lover of Marcus, now his closest friend and most loyal follower, who brought the boy Merlin to Marcus's attention. He had noticed him soon after his arrival at the palace, and felt aversion, for he was a lover of beauty. But he also pitied him.

Then one day, descending to the courtyard, he came on a group of mean youths throwing stones at an aged mastiff which was chained there. He was about to reproach them when the boy Merlin, with a howl of rage or indignation, flung himself at the ringleader of the group who threw him off and then kicked him as he lay on the ground.

Lycas ran forward and struck the youth a sharp blow on the ear. He upbraided them as boors, rogues, wretches, so forcibly that all slunk off. Meanwhile the boy Merlin had crawled towards the dog and now cradled its bleeding head in his arms.

'We must see to the dog,' Lycas said, 'and then to you.'

The boy Merlin was uncouth. Lycas, whose tastes had been refined by his association with Marcus and Artemisia, could not be easy with him. He seemed to him like a wild animal, a creature of the woods, caught in a hunter's net, ready to bite even the hand extended to help him. And yet, as he said to Marcus, there was 'something there'. If the boy's blue eye was vacant, the brown gazed on the world with a passionate intensity. Days passed in which Merlin scarcely moved; he would lie on the rushes sucking his thumb or pressing himself against one of the mastiffs. The dogs alone seemed to understand him, to be at one with him. When, on other occasions, he spoke, in his awkward vulgar Latin, his words were gnomic.

It was blind Artemisia who took him in hand, insisted he be taught to read and write, corrected his Latin and had him instructed in the science of astrology. 'He has rare qualities,' she said, and in time others were compelled to assent. Moreover, she defended him from the priests who would have had him put to death as one who still honoured the pagan gods. But Artemisia said, 'Though you declare that you alone have knowledge of the one true God, and follow the one true Faith, wise men in other times and other countries have spoken with equal certainty and been rewarded by their gods with success in all manner of ventures. So I have come to believe that there are many paths by which we may approach the truth and attain knowledge.'

When they heard this the priests would have charged Artemisia herself with heresy, but Marcus forbade them.

Holy Church would, as you know, my Prince, be in accord with these priests who would have had Artemisia put on trial. But here in Palermo, you have Arab subjects who follow the rule of Mohammed, and hold Christ Jesus to be merely one of the prophets; and these followers of Islam, whom Christians style infidels, are faithful to their own faith and are often virtuous men abiding by your royal law. Therefore, be not swift in condemnation of those who take other paths, but judge men by their actions, not by the God or gods whom they worship.

Merlin adhered to the God of the Legions, Mithras, who is declared to be the Mediator between the unknowable God and the human race which suffers here below, the spirit of celestial light, who grants increase and abundance, watches over the flocks, and gives fertility and life.

And Marcus, listening to the boy's words, protected him, for they might be true and besides, he remembered conversations he had had with those who worshipped Mithras. And so Merlin grew to strength and wisdom, and Marcus, who had now, in accordance with the wishes of the British, assumed the purple, sought his advice concerning all great enterprises. But often Merlin vanished, into the forests or the waste places, for months or even years; for it was his nature to reinforce his spirit in solitude.

IV

Britain flourished under Marcus's rule. Great men lived contented on their estates. The corn was harvested in peace. White cattle grazed the meadows watched over not by armed guards but by a solitary herd boy. The hills resounded to the bleating of sheep. Trade revived, merchants travelled the road without fear and towns flourished. The Saxons, bloodily repulsed, no longer dared to raid and Marcus made treaties, forging bonds of friendship with the Scots and the Picts. Truly, it was a blessed time, and long remembered as such.

But Marcus could not forget that he was a Roman. There came a year when every night for a long week he dreamed of Italy and of white herds of mighty bulls washed clean in the sacred river of Clitumnus, being led towards the temples of the old gods of Rome, and he woke to memories of the city given over to the Goths. Surely, he thought, my work here is done, my nobler work scarce yet commenced.

Artemisia sought to dissuade him, Lycas also. 'We are grown old,' he said, 'adventures such as you purpose are for the young and indeed, we enjoyed our fill of them in our youth.'

Marcus felt the force of his words; and yet his restless spirit could not be appeased. So he sent out heralds to summon all his barons, knights and vassals to assemble at Dover. And when they were come together – knights from the deep shires of midland Britain, archers from the Welsh mountains, sturdy pikemen from the Scottish Borders, and two legions drawn from the eastern counties and drilled to fight in the antique Roman manner, with javelin, short sword and shield – he addressed them as follows.

'Soldiers, we are all children of Rome. I myself am a descendant of the great Aeneas to whom, as the poet tells us, the old gods promised empire without end. Those gods have departed; they live only in the dark forests of memory. That empire is now Christian, following the true faith in the one true God. And yet it has fallen on evil days. The wolf that was once guardian of Rome now despoils the city and litters in the places that were once holy. The successor to St Peter, assailed by barbarians, cries out to us for succour. The sword I now raise in his defence is the sword of the Lord of Hosts and Righteousness. I have therefore called you to a crusade, a holy war, to restore to all Europe the peace that is Roman, that Gaul and Italy and Spain may once again flourish as Britain now does. Whoever feels himself unworthy of this great cause, let him depart, for we shall be the stronger without him. But let all that remain resolve to march with me and do battle in a manner worthy of our ancestors and of Rome.'

When he had finished speaking, none departed, for all knew it were shame to abandon the Emperor. Yet Lycas felt that a bitterness was in the air, that there were poisonous weeds among the flowers. He knew a presentiment of doom, and that night Vortigern, Count of the Saxon Shore, slipped from the camp, and took with him King Lot of Orkney and all his men, for he saw that, with Marcus overseas, he could secure the throne for himself. And Lot went with him because Vortigern argued that Marcus was led astray by vanity and ambition to leave Britain undefended.

So some say the expedition was cursed from the first. Marcus, however, received the news of these desertions with equanimity. 'The fewer men, the greater share of honour,' he assured those who remained; and this satisfied many who were ardent for glory. But Lycas suffered, though he smiled in public.

They crossed over into Gaul and fought many battles against barbarians, and were victorious in all. Yet with each battle their strength was diminished, though their ardour grew. With each battle and with each mile that they advanced towards the mountains that lie between Gaul and Italy, Marcus seemed to his troops the more serene, as if he was carried on the wings of an unquestioning spirit.

Then, in an Alpine pass, with the army straggling in column of march, fierce mountaineers fell upon them, cut off the rearguard and destroyed it. The remnant descended into a fogbound plain, where they were stricken with fever, dysentery and plague. Here some mutinied and swore they would march no further, but Marcus kept his gaze still fixed upon Rome.

Some came to Lycas and said, 'The Emperor is sick'; others that he was mad and would destroy them all.

Lycas said, 'Whoever deserts him, I shall remain.'

They passed by towns and cities now empty of inhabitants, through fields denuded of their flocks and herds, by vineyards where no wine was made, by chapels falling into ruin, along roads made by the legions where coarse grass now grew. Somewhere – near Terni, it is said – Artemisia died and was buried. A cross was raised over her grave, prayers were said, but still Marcus pressed on for Rome. By now only a handful of men remained with him.

At last they came within sight of the city. They found cypress and ivy growing on the walls, weeds and wallflowers matted together. They saw columns fallen and broken, the great aqueducts shattered, temples without roofs and churches with doors swinging open to the winds.

'Rome is now Troy,' Marcus said and they rode slowly into what was once the Forum. There they rested, for the Emperor was very weary, and he sent to the Pope to tell him of his arrival. While he waited for a reply, he stretched out on what had been the Sacred Way, and gazed up at the sky in which kites and other birds that feed on carrion hovered.

In time the messenger returned to say that the Holy Father knew no emperor, for the keys of the city had been given to the Bishop of Rome by the great Constantine himself; but that if the self-styled Emperor had come as a pilgrim, he was welcome to find refuge in a tavern. Hearing this, those few soldiers who remained with Marcus laid down their arms and disappeared into the night. Lycas, left alone with his love and master, helped Marcus to his feet, and together they left the Forum by owl-light and crossed over beyond the theatre which Augustus raised in honour of his beloved nephew Marcellus, and there, in the street which bears the name of the Emperor's sister Octavia, they entered into a mean tavern.

Lycas said to the Jewish woman who kept the house, 'Let us have please a flask of the best wine that you have.'

'There is little good wine now,' she said, 'for there are few labourers to tend the vines as they should be tended. Nevertheless I have a barrel of Marino wine from the Alban hills, and it is good wine when it is fresh and drunk young as this is.'

'Very well,' Lycas said, 'then draw us a flask, and let us have bread and cheese to eat with it, for my friend is weak and much fatigued.'

So he sat down by Marcus, who did not speak but held his cloak pulled round his shoulders and over his head. The woman laid the wine and bread and cheese, which was that cheese made of ewe's milk that the Romans call *pecorino*, before them and a dish of black olives also; and she wished them good appetite.

Cajoled by Lycas, Marcus drank a little wine and ate a morsel of bread and cheese. He took an olive and said, 'How foolish we have been, Lycas, to live in a land where the olive does not grow.'

Then he fell silent again, for a long while, and Lycas did not dare to speak for he sensed that Marcus was pondering thoughts which were of great moment.

'We have fallen into misfortune,' Marcus said.

'True,' Lycas replied, 'but how often have I heard you say that so long as we can speak of misfortune, we may escape it.'

Marcus said, 'And what is there to blame but my irrational desire? It lifts me so high and flies up through the skies till it attains the sphere of fire which scorches its wings, as the wings of Icarus made of wax were melted by the sun; and then, unable to support me, it lets me fall, plummeting to earth. Yet this is not the end of my ordeal, for my desire, which some miscall ambition, sprouts new wings and is burned again, so that there is never, it seems to me, any end to my rising and falling.'

Lycas made no reply, for it seemed to him that Marcus had forgotten his presence and that the words he spoke were a meditation addressed to himself, perhaps in reproach.

But an old man who was sitting in a corner of the tavern with a bowl of soup before him, fish-soup smelling strongly of garlic and the sea, lifted his head when he heard Marcus's words and now approached them. He made a gesture as if asking permission to be seated by them and, when Lycas gave him the nod, being as ever friendly and hospitable, the old man, who was dressed in a woollen tunic such as shepherds wore in Arcady, settled himself and said, 'I hear despair in your words, the despair of one who longs for death and finds that he has always retreated round another corner. Has it struck you that the true image for the reality of the world is an artichoke, which is multiple, prickly and composed of many layers, each densely superimposed upon the other? From this it follows that nothing can be explained if one looks only for a single cause for every effect, since every effect is determined by a multiplicity of causes and each of these has many other causes lurking behind it, prompting it into being. Why you are in Rome and seeking death, I know not, but to ascribe the cause to an irrational desire is meaningless, since no desire can come into being, that is to say into your consciousness, without there being several causes, and each such cause being a reason, no desire can properly be termed irrational.'

Marcus said, 'It is not death I seek, but sleep.'

'And is not our sweetest sleep', the old man replied, 'that which most closely resembles death, in which we are free from dreams; whereas the sleep that disturbs us is light, restless and tormented by images, broken narratives and uncompleted adventures; which sleep, in my opinion, is a true image of life.'

'Where is your home?' Marcus said. It pleased Lycas to hear his friend roused into curiosity for the first time for many days.

'I am a native of Sicily,' the old man said, 'but my home is the open road.'

'I have heard,' Lycas said, 'that all Sicilians are in love with death and strive to make life as deathlike as they can.'

'At Cumae', the old man said, 'resides the Sibyl and, when asked what she desires, will answer, "I wish for death," which is denied her. In like manner, men on the point of death may wish for life to prolong itself. We are so made as to wish always that the coin falls the other way.'

But, though the Pope denied Marcus the imperial title that was his by right of birth and prowess, word of his arrival in the city restored the hopes of others, for there were still members of the old nobility resident in Rome, much fallen from their former high estate, yet still mindful of what their ancestors had been and of what they should be themselves. So when certain of these men heard tell that the Emperor was returned to Rome, they sought him out.

Three came to him in the tavern where he lay sick. It was winter now. The north wind blew cold from the mountains and snow lay heavy on the Alban hills. The three, whose names, Curio, Nepos, Metellus, recalled the great days of the Republic and early Empire, were all young, ardent and ashamed to live under a clerical dominion.

'It may be', one said, 'that our ancestors were pagans, following false gods, as the priests tell us. And yet, while they did so, and honoured Jupiter, Rome flourished. Now, under the successor to Peter, the vicar of Christ, all is fallen to ruin.'

'There is still an empire in the East,' the second, Nepos, reminded his friends.

'Indeed yes,' said Metellus, 'and I have visited Constantinople and can testify to its majesty. But there the Emperor is master of the priests and is indeed the Pontifex Maximus of old Rome. But here, that position has been usurped by the Bishop, and those whose duty it is merely to pray, as in the old days they conducted sacrifices and took the auspices, now exercise the imperium which belongs properly to men of birth.'

They were confused, these three brave young men, and this is not to be wondered at. They had been raised in ignorance of history, and what they knew of it was merely that which fragmentary memory retained and passed on to them. Nevertheless, they discerned more than they truly understood, and felt as iniquity and perversion the power to which they and their noble families had been compelled to submit. And so they sought out Marcus, whose renown had been transmitted to them, if but dimly.

When Lycas understood their purpose, he was afraid. His experience had freed him from all illusion and he understood that their vision of the world was vain, for it flew in the face of things as they truly were. He tried to explain this to the young men, and begged them to go home and live quietly. 'In any case,' he said, 'the Emperor whom you seek is old and ill. His hold on life is uncertain.'

The young men exchanged troubled glances.

Then, 'No matter,' said the tallest of them, who was Curio. 'We wish only to speak quietly with him and do him homage.'

So Lycas, who looked with favour on Curio, on account, perhaps, of the resemblance he bore to Marcus when they were both young, consented. But even as he did so, he warned them again that they could look for no help from Marcus in whatever undertaking they had in mind.

He led them to an inner chamber of the tavern. Marcus lay on a couch and, in the light of the lantern set beside it, his face was grey as if he had already crossed the portal into the shadow country of the dead. And when he spoke his voice was weak, and his Latin was that of a world that had passed away. They knelt before him and addressed him as Augustus. He heard the word and a weary smile like the sun breaking momentarily in a sky of thundery clouds acknowledged their intention and spoke of its hopelessness.

Then he spoke, with difficulty for he was short of breath and very weak. 'When I crossed the Alps into Italy, my dreams were such as you dream now. But then I woke, in the valley of the Tiber when what was once Rome reared up before me, and that which I had dreamed was revealed as vain. I commend your spirit, but you will not find men in Italy to stand by you in the battle. Rome will live, Rome will be revived. That is certain, for it has been promised and is ordained. But you must look to the north, to Britain and Gaul, and even, it may be, to Germany, for it is in these lands that a new spirit is to be born . . .'

Then he told Lycas to command wine for the young men and closed his eyes. They retired into the other room, and sat over their wine and broke the bread of sorrow. And, as they did so and debated among themselves what might next be done, there came a hammering at the door of the tavern, and when it was opened a detachment of the Papal Guard entered and the centurion in command told the young noblemen they were under arrest. Curio drew his sword and would have resisted, but two of the guard seized him from behind and another struck him on the head, so that he fell down. His friends were clapped in irons, and he was lifted unconscious from the floor and bound also. Lycas, too, was seized, and two other guards entered the inner room and dragged

Marcus from his couch, and fixed irons on his wrists. All were then carried to the mausoleum of the Emperor Hadrian, which served as the papal prison, and thrust into a dark cell.

Two days later the three noblemen were taken from the prison and, still shackled, thrust into sacks with, in each of them, a live cockerel and a viper, and these were then hurled into the river, from the bridge that leads from the mausoleum to the city. But Lycas was saved for the time being to be subjected to examination by the officers charged with the investigation of heresy. He was condemned as a heretic and a sodomite, and to be burned at the stake in the Field of Mars.

No record of Marcus's fate survives. It is assumed that he died in the cell to which he had been consigned, some say in the night before Lycas was carried off to the torture chamber where his examination was conducted.

And from this day, for many centuries, there was no emperor in Rome; but the imperial power was exercised by the Popes, in defiance of reason and tradition.

V

So Marcus slipped into the black night we call the past and Vortigern reigned in south Britain. A weak king and foolish man, he invited certain Saxon tribes to settle in that part of the country called Kent. He did so because he believed they would resist the incursions of their fellow Saxons more successfully than he could. Men said, 'He has called on the wolf to guard the sheep.'

The Empire Marcus had maintained did not survive him. It broke up into several kingdoms, and in the hill country between Humber and the Forth the King was Uther Pendragon, son of Marcus by the daughter of a citizen of York which the Romans called Eboracum.

Now you will find that Geoffrey of Monmouth tells us that Uther was the son of the Emperor-King Constantine, and the brother of Aurelius Ambrosius, who was for a time King of all Britain; and that the brothers fought against Vortigern.

There is some truth in this, but not much, for my researches have established beyond question that this Constantine never existed, but that, as I say, it was Marcus who fathered Uther by the lady I have spoken of, and that this Aurelius, who was certainly a notable general, was the half-brother of Uther, being the son of that citizen of York and not therefore of royal or imperial blood. And why Geoffrey should have pretended otherwise I cannot tell, unless he wished to make mischief. But it was probably ignorance, of which he had no lack.

When Vortigern learned that Uther had been hailed as King in the north, he resolved to destroy him, for which reason he admitted yet more Saxons to the kingdom and also made an alliance with the Picts. Furthermore, he promised King Lot of Orkney, who was then a young man and very ambitious, that he should have the northern part of Uther's realm if he joined him in battle. To this Lot agreed, though, being cautious, he sent also ambassadors to Uther to enquire what reward might be his if he abandoned Vortigern, whom he despised. Uther, prudent but timid and himself no man of war (which may be the reason that some have denied that Marcus was his father) consulted Merlin, who advised him that it would certainly be wise to make peace with King Lot.

'But I warn you,' Merlin said, 'this King is as treacherous as the adder that lies in the heather. Therefore it is necessary to find some means to bind him. Fortunately, he has a great weakness for women and can be governed only by a woman. Till recently he never acted but by his mother's advice, but she is now dead.'

'That is good advice,' Uther said. 'But where shall I find the woman who can govern him?'

Merlin smiled. 'This Lot', he said, 'has a nature that is so suspicious that he will reject any woman you offer to him, for his suspicion masters even his lust. He knows his own weakness and fears to be controlled. If you suggested any particular woman he would at once detect a plot. So it is necessary that he should seem to happen on the woman, and should suppose that she is alone in the world and with no connection to you or any other man of power.'

'What you say makes sense,' Uther replied, scratching his head, not because it was lousy but because this was his habit when perplexed. 'But where shall we find such a woman and how shall we contrive that Lot encounters her?'

Again Merlin smiled, but this time said nothing.

'She should be a virgin,' Uther said. 'That is certain. And yet I fear I should be committing a sin if I arranged that a virgin should be seduced by the King.' Uther was a godly man with a great fear of Hell; and this rendered him timid.

Merlin said, 'I understand your hesitation. So it is better that you leave matters in my hands.'

You will not be surprised to learn that throughout this conversation Merlin had no doubt as to where he would find the girl to be delivered as, apparently, a sacrificial victim to the libidinous King.

So straightway he left the court, after the King, Uther, had betaken himself to the basilica of St Peter of York to make confession and attend his third mass of the day. Merlin thought it was no great harm that the King should confess his sins, since he was ignorant of those committed in his name, to advance his greatness. It was not simply loyalty to the memory of Marcus and Lycas that made Merlin eager to thwart the plans of Vortigern and Lot, and in time to destroy both. He had suffered from their scorn, for they were among those who had taken him to be an idiot and had mocked him accordingly.

Now Merlin journeyed for many days, through rugged hills and by winding valleys, far to the north, till he came to a place where a three-headed mountain stands over a river. Lush meadows beautiful with the flowers of spring, cowslips, bluebells, primroses and golden lilies, lay alongside the water; and, for it was now evening, the bells of a convent tolled the summons to vespers. Merlin presented himself at the gateway and commanded that a message be carried to the prioress to say that he awaited her pleasure. He spoke with courtesy for, though he remained, in his innermost being, devoted to the God of the Soldiers, Mithras, in whose faith he had been raised, yet he had learned that prudence required him to be respectful to the True Church and those who served the Christ. And in any case it was in his nature to take delight in duplicity.

So, when the prioress advanced with stately dignity, he knelt before her as if to request her blessing. If you are surprised (as you may well be, knowing the arrogance of certain great ladies who order the affairs of religious houses in this kingdom) that the prioress had humbled herself to answer his summons instead of keeping him waiting till it was convenient he be brought before her, the explanation is that, being possessed of a formidable and awe-inspiring pride, this lady delighted in disguising it with a semblance of humility.

The prioress took Merlin by the hand and led him into the convent, to her day chamber, which some call by the French word 'boudoir', though that word was not yet known since nobody at this date spoke French. This chamber was furnished with an elegance then rare in Britain, according to the Byzantine fashion, and the walls were hung with tapestries, save for one which was decorated with icons richly painted.

'I have come for my ward,' Merlin said.

As if she had not heard him, the prioress summoned a maidservant, or perhaps a novice accustomed to perform the duties of a maid, and ordered her to bring them fish, bread and wine. 'You have travelled far,' she said to Merlin, 'and must be both weary and hungry.'

And till he had eaten of the river fish, which had been smoked and was accompanied by slices of lemon brought from Italy by traders who exchanged these fruits for a cargo of the local fish, smoked or salted, she refused conversation.

It seemed to Merlin that she remained silent because she was deliberating by which ruse she might cheat him of that which he demanded. Nevertheless, he ate and drank what was placed before him. 'I have need of her,' he said.

She took up her needle and resumed work on a tapestry that was stretched on an easel. The needle trailed blue thread and she worked on the Virgin's gown. 'She is too young.'

'Nevertheless,' he said.

'You brought me a child, ignorant of manners, of quick and violent temper. We have trained her in docility and duty. It were better she remain here in the service of the Lord and the Virgin.' She spoke in Latin and her sentences were well-formed.

'She has a part to play in the affairs of the world,' Merlin said and drained a goblet of the spiced wine.

'Here we abjure the world,' the prioress said, smoothing her velvet gown with the hand that did not hold the needle.

Merlin said, 'You cannot refuse me. My craft is more powerful than your faith.'

She flushed and found no words, but bent her head over her work. 'It were unkind to take her,' she said, 'and besides, I have a passion for the girl.'

'Sister,' Merlin said, 'like me you love none but yourself. I tell you again, I have need of her. Command that she be fetched.'

She gave way to sighs, short and infrequent, and a tear like the first drop of a thunderstorm rained down her painted cheek.

So the girl was brought and stood before them, awkwardly, twisting the long tresses of her harvest hair between slim, active fingers.

'You must go with your guardian,' the prioress brought herself to say. She did not look at the girl as she spoke, but at the Virgin's face as it had grown on her tapestry.

'I do not wish to go,' the girl said, 'for you have taught me that the world is evil.'

'Aye, so it is, and yet you must go.'

'And if it is my will to refuse?'

'Then I shall bend your will,' Merlin said, and he fixed the girl with a firm gaze before which she grew pale and her lips wavered. She tried to turn her eyes away from his, as one may from that which offends one; but she could not. She was compelled to be held by his eye as if by a basilisk's, and she cried out 'Mother', but even as she made to form the words which should succeed, her voice failed her. If she had had as many eyes as Argus, which were numbered at one hundred, she could not have averted a single one of them. Nor could she move, but felt herself to be as firmly rooted to the spot as if her foot, once so swift and eager in running, were planted in the stone. She felt as if her hair were being transformed into foliage and her arms were heavy as the branches of a laurel tree.

And when he saw that he had possessed her, Merlin gathered her up and departed, while the prioress was left to weep, till she was completely consumed by her own tears and the sky rained grief.

VI

For three days they journeyed north, sleeping at nights in the forest on a bed of pine needles. And for these three days the girl refused to speak. On the fourth day a cold wind blew and the air was heavy, threatening unseasonable snow. They looked to the mountains and their tops were hidden, veiled by clouds the colour of dark sandstone. At last the girl asked what purpose there was to their journey, and why Merlin had taken her from the convent where she had been happy and the prioress whom she had loved.

'When I brought you there as a child, you screamed and kicked and wept and swore, and cried out that you would not remain there. Do you remember that?'

'I was young and foolish,' she said. 'I was a child, thinking like a child.'

'And are you wise in judgement now?' he said.

She bit her lip and made no reply.

'You are a daughter of the Empire,' Merlin said.

'What of that? What is the Empire to me? I was not reared in a palace but was abandoned by my father, and condemned to live with my mother's man, who abused me sorely. At night I weep when I remember how he treated me.'

'Indeed yes,' Merlin said, 'you were harshly treated.'

'The thought seems to please you,' she said.

'It is to my purpose.'

Then they came to a river and there was no bridge. On the other bank they saw tents rising from the mist which clung to the banks of the river and hovered over the water. A boat was moored in the rushes and Merlin ordered the girl to seat herself in it. Then he told the ferryman who sat in the bows to carry her over to the other side. When she saw that Merlin was abandoning her, she cried out in fear, but he said only, 'Morgan, my child, it is your destiny to pass over to the further bank and mine to remain here.' And he stood and watched as the ferryman plied the oars.

He continued to watch as the boat nudged the other bank, and the ferryman took her arm and helped her out, and in the mist her legs were silver. Then he saw two horsemen pick their way through the bushes of broom and whin towards the river, and one lean down and sweep the girl up, so that she sat before him on the horse and was carried back to the camp.

Then, though he could see no more, in his mind's vision he saw the girl brought to King Lot, whose army it was there encamped, and received with wonder by the King in his pavilion. And he saw the King's rough hairy hands fumble her dress and push under her skirt, and his body bend as he forced her to his couch.

He turned away. 'I have yoked her to misery,' he thought.

VII

That year Aurelius Ambrosius commanded the army of Uther Pendragon in battles against Vortigern and his Saxon allies. Vortigern himself hid from the war and his army was led by his son, Paschent, a man treacherous as a serpent, treacherous beyond even his father.

Aurelius Ambrosius defeated the enemy in three great battles, one in the Vale of York, the second by the bridge across the Trent at the place now called Nottingham and the third by the Roman city of Silchester. Then, in desperation, Paschent sent to King Lot of Orkney calling for the aid he had promised. But Lot lay in bed with Morgan, his hairy hands caressing her smooth limbs, and would not stir. And this was as Merlin had provided, for he had given the maiden the power to bewitch her lover. Yet Morgan hated Lot even as she entranced him, and would have repelled his advances had Merlin not infected her also with keen lust.

Then, however, just as all was going well with the Romans – for so I choose to term those Britons who had retained the manners and mentality of Rome, and were true heirs of Marcus – Aurelius Ambrosius fell sick and lay at Winchester in the grip of fever. At this moment a man called Eopa came into Paschent's camp and asked what should be his reward if he rid him of his enemy.

Paschent was delighted by the offer and promised a thousand pieces of silver. But then he said, 'You are, as I perceive from your speech, a Saxon. How will you contrive to approach Aurelius, who has given orders that any Saxon who is taken should have first his ears clipped, and then his tongue torn out and his right hand cut off, unless indeed he be left-handed, in which case it is that hand that shall be struck off his arm?'

'Why,' said Eopa, 'though I am indeed a Saxon, I can speak both the British language and the Latin tongue also. Furthermore I am skilled in herbal medicine and have a deep knowledge of all poisons. I shall disguise myself as a monk and declare that I am sent by God to heal the general. You may trust me, my Lord King, for I have never failed in any undertaking I have attempted. And, to prove that you trust me, give me now but a hundred of the thousand pieces of silver you have promised.'

Paschent was so impressed that he did as he was asked, even though his wife, an Irishwoman who claimed the gift of second sight, told him he would see neither Eopa nor his money again. In which, however, she was mistaken, as in my experience the Irish often are.

Eopa indeed did as he had said he would. He submitted to the tonsure, garbed himself in a brown habit and approached the British camp, carrying on his arm a basket containing several pots of what he said were medicines. 'I have been sent by the Lord to heal the general,' he said.

Now, unfortunately Merlin was not then in the camp. Otherwise he would, doubtless, have tested Eopa and discovered the imposture. So Eopa was admitted to the general's tent, where he lay sweating and moaning, sometimes crying out, for he suffered evil dreams.

It was because the general's cries, whether of fear or anguish none could tell, so distressed those who waited on him and also his guards, that Eopa was made welcome. He prepared a draught, frowning as he did so, to make it clear that the task was one requiring great skill. Then he told the attendants to wake the general and, when he was roused, gave him the potion, assuring him that it would restore him to health and vigour. Aurelius Ambrosius swallowed it as instructed.

'Now,' said Eopa, 'you will sleep till the cock crows to announce the dawning of a new day and, when you wake, the fever will have departed and you will be strong.'

So the general drew the bedclothes about him and reposed himself. He soon slept and, as he slept, the poison coursed through his veins. Meanwhile his attendants, seeing the general at ease, as they supposed, were restored to cheerfulness and, thinking the crisis past, began to drink beer, mead and wine. When they were so engaged, Eopa slipped from the camp and hastened to Paschent to claim his reward. And indeed he had earned it, for when the cock crew, Aurelius Ambrosius was discovered to be dead.

When the news was brought to Uther Pendragon he grew pale as the winter moon and rent his clothes, cursing and lamenting. He turned in fury on Merlin whose arts, he said should have prevented this.

Merlin bowed his head, as the King pronounced his banishment. 'It shall be as you say,' was his only response and he prepared to depart from the court.

From this moment the fortunes of war turned against the Romans. Uther Pendragon, either because he was cursed by the Fates, or because he had no skill in warfare, was defeated in seven battles in seven months, and at length forced to take refuge in the northern mountains where the forces of Paschent and the Saxons did not dare to follow him. And there he survived for many years. Meanwhile the Saxons turned on Vortigern and Paschent, and confined the former to a dungeon, while the latter they took and thrust into a sack with a she-wolf to savage him, for, they said, the murder of Aurelius Ambrosius, though our common enemy, proves that this man is dishonourable and not to be trusted.

So for many years the Saxons ruled the land of Britain which they now called Angleland, or England.

VIII

When Merlin received the order of banishment he was tempted to curse the King, for he resented the injustice of his punishment. But then he remembered how Lycas had once spoken to him of justice and injustice, of how the former was found but rarely, while the latter was the common lot of men. 'There are those', Lycas had said, 'who respond by taking revenge for, they say, revenge is a kind of wild justice. But for my part I have found no satisfaction by that means.' Merlin brushed a tear from his brown eye which, incidentally, was the only one that ever wept, while his blue eye stared dully on the world. He was often moved when he thought of Lycas and now, thinking of Lycas recalled him to his duty towards the departed Marcus.

'Why', he said to himself, 'should I feel amazement or hurt to discover that this King Uther Pendragon is a fool and an ingrate, who believes he can help himself by banishing the one man who could be of aid in his extremity? I always knew he was an unworthy successor to the Emperor.' So reflecting, he took his staff and departed from York.

For seven days he travelled north, sleeping in the forest by night. Autumn and the leaves fell, and the dry leaves made a bed for him. By day the winds blew but when darkness descended all was still. It was a time for making ballads, Merlin thought, but words did not come easily to him and, when they did, declined to form themselves into verse. So instead, as he journeyed he chanted aloud lines from Virgil, which Artemisia had had by heart and had recited to him so often that they were imprinted in his mind. And every night before he sought sleep he repeated to himself lines which from the first had seemed to him to speak the true magic:

> Sunt geminae somni portae, quarum altera fertur
> Cornea, qua veris facilis datur exitus umbris,

Altera candenti perfecta nitens elephanto,
Sed falsa ad caelum mittunt insomnia Manes.

(There are twin gates of Sleep, one said to be of horn through
which true ghosts may easily pass, the other made of shining ivory
but through which the spirits send false dreams to the world
above.)

And each morning he woke to a cold, blue, shining day, and on
the fourth of these days knew happiness such as he had rarely felt.

After seven days he came to a narrow valley, the flanks of which
were deeply wooded with birch, alder, hazel and rowan. The track
ran alongside a tumbling stream and twisted obedient to the dance
of the water. It climbed, but slowly, until after some two miles the
valley opened out on a little plateau where there was a meadow,
in one corner of which stood a rude hut.

An old woman sat on a three-legged stool before it and a basin
of blackberries was by her side. She looked up as Merlin
approached. 'So it is time,' she said.

'It is time.'

She gestured towards the water beyond the cottage and Merlin
first followed her gaze, then betook himself in the direction she
indicated. Meanwhile the old woman picked up the basin and
withdrew into the cottage to prepare supper.

Merlin came to the river which here formed a pool beneath
overhanging branches. There was a ripple on the dark water, and
then a head rose up and Merlin saw it was the boy. He swam to
the bank and lightly lifted himself from the water, and stood
naked and unashamed of his nakedness before Merlin.

'You swim like a fish,' Merlin said.

'More like an otter I'd have hoped,' the boy replied.

He stretched himself out on a shelf of smooth stone, letting the
red sun of the late afternoon play on his gleaming legs. His smile
was open, frank, trusting. 'I thought you'd forgotten me,' he said.
'Hunting deer and swimming, that's happiness enough for me.'

Merlin smiled. 'Dry yourself. Put on your tunic. Your carefree
days are at an end. I have come, my son, to recall you to the duties
enjoined on you by your birth.'

'I don't understand what you mean by that,' the boy said, 'but at least there will be venison for supper.'

'How bitter is the reflection', Merlin said to the old woman when they had eaten and the boy slept, 'that we must kill the child to make the man.'

'What you mean by that', she replied, 'I can't tell, but then I have never understood your sayings and have often wondered how I could have given birth to one like yourself. Still, I'll thank you to remember that this is a good boy and a gentle, generous-hearted one.'

'I have a tenderness for youth,' Merlin said, 'having been cheated of it myself.'

She chewed on a knuckle bone and was silent, looking into the dying fire, till she raised her smokened face, looked at him steadily and said, 'You were born an old soul indeed, as I recall, but I'll thank you to remember that this boy, whom I have come to think of as my own bairn too, is one of the innocents of the world.'

'There is nothing', Merlin said, 'that is entirely good. We shall leave with the first light.'

For three years Merlin devoted himself to the boy Arthur's education. In the first year he taught him Latin and Greek without which, as he said, there is no understanding of philosophy. As it happened Arthur found little of interest in that subject: questions of essence and existence passed him by. He would frown politely, knitting his brows together in a manner that made him look younger than his thirteen years and say, 'What does it matter, sir? What does it really matter?'

'It has mattered, brat,' Merlin said, 'to men of greater intellect and virtue than you' and cuffed him round the head. 'Philosophy, brat, is the queen of sciences.'

'Perhaps that's why it doesn't matter to me. I take little interest in queens. Or perhaps I'm just stupid. Do you think I am stupid, sir?'

'I think you are lazy.'

'Is it stupid to prefer Ovid to Aristotle, sir? I don't think so. For instance, when we read Ovid, the stories seem to make it impossible that time could ever drag or lie heavy, as you once put it, on our hands. But when you thrust my face into Aristotle, doing it sometimes so hard I must say that I seem to bruise my nose and my eyes water, it is as if time could never move again. And that is impossible, isn't it? Which to my mind proves that Aristotle's philosophy is false.'

Even Merlin, for all his acuteness, was never certain whether at such moments Arthur was serious or was teasing him.

In truth, he was both, for teasing of this intellectual sort is a form of true seriousness, as when we debate whether the table at which I set you to study exists when we are not there to see or touch it.

Nor was Arthur enamoured of mathematics, even though Merlin took great joy in that subject and excelled (as he supposed) in expounding it. But when, one day, as he was setting forth Pythagoras's theorem concerning the size of the square on the hypotenuse, he observed the boy's right hand slip below his tunic and occupy itself in exercising his virile member, he threw the book at the boy's head and swore that he was unworthy of the feast of learning being set before him.

'I am sorry, sir,' Arthur said, 'but I had other thoughts and in that line of Virgil which you have taught me to love, I was practising a woodland muse upon my slim reed.'

So no more mathematics were taught that day, or any other.

It was chiefly poetry that delighted Arthur, and chief among poets were Ovid and Virgil. He delighted also in all stories of the Trojan War and in imagination was now Achilles, now Hector. He wept to hear of the conflict between them, and the image of Hector's comely limbs dragged in the dust as Achilles's chariot careered round the walls of Troy aroused in him mingled pity and terror, disgust and excitement. When Paris fired the dart that killed the hero Achilles, he knew anger that so feeble and frippery self-regarding a thing as Paris should have been permitted to triumph over valour.

'But that too often is the way of the world,' Merlin said.

Then Arthur delighted also in natural history, not only (as is proper) in stories of terrible beasts such as dragons and basilisks and griffons, and those more commonly encountered as wolves and bears, but also in birds and butterflies and flowers. When

Merlin directed his attention to the intricate beauty of a spider's web, glistening in sunlight after rain, he was entranced and forgot for the moment that it was a killing trap for the unwary fly.

Merlin drove the boy hard, for, as he said, 'The limits of your language are the limits of your world; and therefore the man whose language is narrow and restricted lives like one in prison, whereas he who has a wide command of language and can form pleasing mental visions in consequence may be free even when confined in the darkest dungeon.'

'That is at least a pleasing reflection,' Arthur said, 'though I wonder if experience such as I hope to avoid would prove it to be true. Isn't it perhaps the case that the dull and stupid may find imprisonment less irksome than the educated? I know that you have told me that your mind is a kingdom and that it is your intention to make mine one too, but I can't help observing that when the cattle are penned up for the winter they don't seem to suffer from their confinement, while the wolf that has been put in a cage grows thin and looks wretched. And in my opinion wolves are more intelligent than oxen. But I dare say, sir, that I am wrong and you are, as ever, right.'

'Sometimes', Merlin said, 'you irritate me more than I would have thought possible. Rightly are you called Brat.'

Yet even when exasperated Merlin could not keep a loving note out of his voice, which is as it should be for the teacher.

Nor did he neglect the necessity of instructing Arthur in martial exercises. Being incompetent to do so himself, he engaged an old knight to teach him the mastery of the lance and the sword. Unfortunately there was no horse available, but Merlin trusted that Arthur's affinity with animals would be sufficient to make him a notable horseman; which hope did not prove vain.

Meanwhile Merlin himself saw to it that the boy learned the arts of war from Caesar's *Commentaries* and Vegetius's manual. 'Read them well,' he said, 'read deeply, for the history of the world itself resembles the laws of nature and is simple, like the human soul. The same conditions bring back the same phenomena.'

Arthur obeyed and, because the books interested him to a degree he found remarkable, did not reply that at other times

36

Merlin had assured him that the human soul was dark, unfathomable, twisted as the ivy that twines itself round an oak tree.

And so his education proceeded till the day came when Merlin said that though there was still much he could teach, for the search for knowledge and understanding is endless as the ocean in which the earth swims, nevertheless, the time had come when Arthur must go into the world. 'Remember', he said, 'this above all: "every man has his appointed day; to all men a short and unalterable span of life; but by deeds to extend our fame, this is the task of virtue and courage".'

Arthur grew pale at these words, spoken so solemnly. He recognised them as Virgil's and it amazed him that he could once have read them lightly.

IX

It was Merlin's intention that Arthur should be constrained to make his own way in the world, 'for', he said, 'I have learned that hardship is the proper school of excellence'. For this reason he sent him forth, alone, mounted on a stout pony and with but two days' provisions in his saddlebag. So Arthur set childhood behind him and turned his face to the south, and it is not to be supposed that Merlin did not shed a tear as he watched the boy ride up the twisting valley and out of sight.

As for Arthur, his heart was filled with ardour. He lifted his face and smelled the wind.

Towards evening of the first day of his new life he came to a river and saw rude tents pitched on its bank. It seemed a modest encampment. Smoke rose from small fires, goats and sheep and cattle wandered loose, and three or four scrawny ponies were tethered to hawthorn trees. He heard the cry of children at play and saw women crouched over cooking pots. As he drew closer, with his pony picking its careful way on a loose rein down the stony track, a savoury smell came to him and he realised he was hungry.

A man with a grizzled beard stepped out from behind a clump of broom and presented a pike at him, commanding him to halt and account for himself.

'I am a traveller,' Arthur said, 'and I come in peace.'

The man, whom he took to be a guard or sentry, lowered his pike, took the pony by the bridle and led Arthur into the encampment.

There an old woman rose to confront him. She was very tall, taller than Arthur by a head, and her face, which was streaked with smoke and dirt, was strong-featured, the nose large and hooked, the mouth twisted, and her eyes black as a crow's feathers. When she spoke, her voice was harsh and the words unwelcoming.

But Arthur's mild demeanour and modest language persuaded her that he threatened no harm, so she indicated that he should dismount and stood by him while the man who had first accosted him took charge of the pony.

'I would wish', Arthur said, 'that you let it drink of the river and then feed, for we have journeyed all day and the beast is weary. I was brought up to believe that one should always see to one's horse before attending to one's own needs.'

So this was done, and then the woman told Arthur to be seated and served him with a bowl of stew from the cooking pot. It was a dish of wildfowl and herbs, and Arthur found that it was very good. While he ate, the company watched him and no one spoke.

He now saw that there were about a dozen of them, two men, five women and a handful of naked children. All the time the guard who had made him halt kept his hand on his pike. When he saw this, Arthur unbuckled his belt, from which his sword and a dagger hung, and laid it aside.

Then the old woman who seemed to be the chief among them enquired of him where he had come from and what was his purpose in journeying.

'To make my way in the world,' he replied.

'Why do you wish to do that?' she asked.

It was a question he had never considered and therefore he had no ready answer. So instead he did what wise men do in such circumstances and turned questioner himself, asking her what manner of people they were and how they lived.

'We are broken people,' she answered, 'and we live as we may. Once we were more fortunate, as men judge fortune. We had homes and farms which we worked and which provided us with abundance. But then men came from the sea and burned them, and destroyed our crops and drove us out, so that now we are landless and condemned to wander.'

'That is surely a great evil,' Arthur said.

'Why, so we thought ourselves at first,' she agreed, 'for we valued what we possessed and thought ourselves rich and blessed. But now that is all gone, all has been taken from us but that which

39

you see around you, and we live naked as we came into the world, exposed to wind and rain and all the extremities of weather.'

'And what have you learned from this?' Arthur asked, after a moment of hesitation, lest the question anger her.

She did not answer at once, so he continued, 'It seems to me that your sufferings prove that the world is ill-ordered.'

'And why should it not be,' she said, 'since it has always been so? Men and women go blind through their lives, and what they see when they are young as golden prospects are no more than idle dreams.'

'Yet', Arthur said, 'it need not be so, for I have heard that there was once a golden age and that, if we live rightly, it may be by our efforts restored.'

For the first time something like a smile shone in the old woman's face, and she stretched out her grimy hand, rough with hard work, and touched Arthur's cheek still ignorant of the razor. 'You are young,' she said, 'and therefore foolish. Time will cure you of that. Now you live in hope, which is a false friend, a shadow that goes before you, and which will be lost in the dark of night. I shall tell you, young man, what is the business of living. It is endurance, nothing more. We keep on going because, miserable as life may be, death, which awaits us all as a fierce beast attends the unwary hunter, offers only extinction. You think our life wretched and so indeed it is. We suffer cold, hunger, fear. Yet every morning the sun rises. In the evening we watch the dying light play on the waters and we know that the dead see neither. All has been taken from us and yet we go on, and I cannot tell you why, except that it is our nature.'

X

The next morning Arthur rose before the sun was up and, when he had drunk a bowl of milk which the old woman brought him, took his leave, regretting only that he had but a few mean coins to offer as payment for his lodging. But she refused them for, she said, they had no use of money and knew none that had. So he rode on his way, which led through a dark forest. Then a wind blew up and it began to rain, but he rode on doggedly and his mind dwelled on the old woman's words. He thought, 'I have found life to be good, but she who has suffered much sees it only as something to be endured. These people were wretched and poor. Yet they were kind to me. Merlin taught me that it is the duty of kings to care for the poor, but that enjoying all the pleasures of the world they frequently neglect that duty, which is why misery is so often to be found.'

The thought and the cold rain depressed his spirits. He felt for the first time since he had set out on his travels that he was lonely. He wondered why Merlin had cast him out in this manner and knew self-pity. Wolves howled in the depths of the forest. The rain had now soaked him to the skin. His teeth chattered. And he feared that he had lost his way, if he had ever been certain what it was. Then he remembered a sentiment Merlin was given to quoting: 'The worst is yet to come so long as we can say, "this is the worst".' 'It pleases him,' he thought, 'but brings little comfort to me.'

He journeyed all day till night fell early on the forest, which still seemed to extend endlessly beyond him. So he halted and tethered his pony to a hawthorn tree in a little clearing where there was rough grass for the beast to eat, and a gurgling stream from which it could drink. Since he had nothing with which to kindle a fire, and in any case the branches that lay around were all wet as his tunic and jerkin, he mixed a cup of oatmeal with water from the stream and made his dinner of that. Then he wrapped himself in the cloak which had been rolled up in his saddlebag and set himself to sleep, leaning against the trunk of an oak tree.

Perhaps he slept. Afterwards he was not sure. But if he did he was awakened to alarm. A wolf was howling, uncomfortably close. Arthur told himself not to be afraid: a wolf was only a species of wild dog and he had always been on good terms with any dog he came upon. All the same, he found that he was shivering and knew that he would not sleep again, if, indeed, he had slept. At least the rain had stopped and a thin moon danced in the sky, casting weird shadows as the topmost branches of the trees waved in the wind. The moonlight was cold on his face and then a voice addressed him.

He sprang up and his hand flew to his sword. But he saw no one. 'It is my imagination,' he said to himself; and did not believe his own words. He stood with his back to the tree and looked all around, and still there was no one to be seen. But the voice sounded again and this time he could distinguish the words. But they were in a tongue which he did not understand.

Boldly he called out, challenging the speaker to step forward into the clearing and make himself known. 'I am only a boy travelling on my own,' he said, with the intention of offering reassurance; and then regretted his words lest they make his invisible audience bold. 'But I have a sword,' he said, striving to keep his voice even. 'And know how to use it.'

Again there was no response. Arthur felt himself trembling. All his life he would remember this moment and the imperative he knew: that he must not reveal his terror. Often, in years to come, he would tell his young knights that it was natural to feel fear but that, if you once let your fear be seen, the wolves will attack and tear you to pieces. So now he pressed his back hard against the tree as if by exerting his force of will he could thus arrest the trembling.

At last a figure emerged from the shadows and for a moment his fear was still more acute: for it seemed that the cowl which shrouded the head disclosed the face of a dead man. But it was the pale moon that shone white on the visage that presented itself to him. The figure advanced, slowly, and Arthur saw that it was

42

slight, and sensed that it was in no way dangerous. His own body relaxed and he took a step forward. 'Look,' he said and, removing his hand from the sword hilt, extended his arms wide to indicate that his intent was peaceful. 'I am only a boy travelling on my own,' he said again.

And this time came the reply, in his own tongue, 'If you come in peace, you are welcome.'

Arthur smiled. 'Why should I not come in peace, since I mean mischief to none? But I am cold and wet and hungry, and if you can offer me shelter and food, I shall be grateful and shall pay you for them.'

'Shelter and food? Yes, I can offer these, but I must confess you disappoint me. When I saw you first, I thought you were an angel, and now I see that you are, as you say, but a boy. It was perhaps the moonlight that made a halo hover above your head.'

So saying, he led Arthur by a winding path through the trees till they came to a rude hut made of logs and mud. As they approached the man called out to someone within that they had a guest.

The moon had risen high and shed a silver light over the open doorway. In answer to the cry a girl now appeared there. She was perhaps Arthur's age, but shorter by a head, though he was not tall himself, and seeing her he did not wonder that his new companion's mind should have run on angels, for the girl was lovely beyond compare. She smiled at him but did not speak. Nor did she reply when Arthur addressed her, except with a grunt.

'My daughter is afflicted,' the man said. 'She is dumb and has been so since birth.'

Then he ordered her to fetch them bread and beans and beer, and settled himself on the earth floor of the house, indicating that Arthur should do so also. Then he stared at him, till Arthur felt that he was being deprived of his will, that he could not move his limbs and that he was being mastered by the other. But at that moment the girl laid food and drink before him, and her father's gaze wavered and Arthur was released from its hold.

Then the man spoke. 'What does the text mean,' he said, '"My kingdom is not of this world"? What does that signify?'

'That might depend on who spoke it. Forgive me,' Arthur said prudently, 'but I am trained as a knight and have no taste for theology.'

'Him they call Christ. But was he the celestial Christ or his elder brother whom some call Satan and others Samael, who, it is written, made this world and therefore all that is evil, and is lord and master of it, and of all fleshly things.'

'I am sorry,' Arthur said, 'but I am quite out of my depth' and he looked at the girl who smiled sweetly at him.

'Is it not the case', his interlocutor persisted, 'that the divine spirit is imprisoned in this wall of flesh, and that to attain perfection, we must renounce the flesh?'

At these words the girl drew nearer to Arthur, but subtly, so that her movement might not be perceived, and slipped her slender arm behind his waist.

'And did not Satan, or Samael, himself assume the shape of a serpent and seduce Eve who is held by all to be the mother of all mankind, and so entice her into intercourse, so that her desire glowed like an oven or a fiery furnace, at which moment he emerged from the reeds in the shape of a serpent and entered into her, so that she brought forth his children, all accursed?'

'Clearly,' Arthur said, allowing the girl to lay her head on his shoulder – an action which her father, bewitched by his own rhetoric, did not perceive – 'clearly you have thought long and deeply concerning these matters, but you are too learned for me and they are beyond my poor comprehension.'

And, saying this, he lowered his head and brushed his lips against the girl's young breasts, and kissed them, and knew her ardour and desire were great, and equal to his, which was swelling. So, while her father talked, abstracting himself from those whom he deemed to be his audience and elaborating his theological speculations, Arthur and the girl withdrew into a corner of the hut, and there fondled each other and pressed their lips against each other's. He searched her speechless tongue with his and she responded, and their tongues danced together. They grew more ardent till their desire could not be contained and all was consummated, to their great delight. So they rested in each other's arms, while the old man's discourse rolled on, unstoppable

44

as the river that lay beyond the meadows. And Arthur and the girl rested till it was light.

XI

Arthur woke, cold, wet and stiff. His back was pressed against the oak tree. A sharp wind from the east cut into his neck. Snell, Merlin would have called that wind. He tried to will himself back to sleep, to recover his dream and the taste of the dumb girl. But she had fled him. 'Why dumb?' he thought. 'Wherever dreams are sent from, we make them ourselves.' That was something else Merlin had taught him. 'So why did I give her no voice? And her father's talk? What, if anything, was the meaning of that? And where did I get it from? Merlin again?'

That day's ride was bitter. The wind still blew hard from the east. He was chilled to the bone, shivering cold. Clouds swelled up heavy with snow. He let the reins hang loose and allowed the pony to pick its way along the track, which now led them over a waste of moorland. It was all he could do to stay in the saddle. More than once he swayed and came near to falling off. Lines ran in his head, but made no sense.

As the light faded the snow began to fall, first lightly in small flakes, then more heavily. Arthur choked, then, blinded by the snow, found he was sobbing. He clutched the pony's mane, his hands twisting the coarse hair. He pressed himself forward against its neck, using it unthinkingly as a shield against the wind. But it was no good. He was so cold the wind cut through him, entering his body at one side and emerging at the other.

It was the pony, not Arthur, which saw the castle rear before them. The drawbridge was lowered and, as one heading for its stable, the beast quickened its pace and crossed the bridge at a trot. It was a weary trot, but it made it into the courtyard where the wooden walls sheltered them from the terrible wind. The pony halted, lifted its head and whinnied. Answering cries came from the stable block. At that moment Arthur slipped over its shoulder and fell senseless to the ground.

When he woke he was lying in straw. It stank and he knew he had fouled himself. His throat was dry as a miser's charity and his skin was hot as fire. He heard a shuffling of beasts, cattle or horses, and the scrambling of rats. He could move his legs and his arms, but the effort exhausted him and he closed his eyes, shutting out the dim light. As soon as he did so, fires danced before him and he heard the shrieks of devils. Then their talk: preparing torments for him. They were torments, he knew, which he had no means of escaping. Sweat, now hot, now cold, poured off him.

Someone was holding a mug to his lips and he felt an arm behind his shoulders raising him so that he could drink. The ale was sweet, nutty, with a bitter aftertaste. He swallowed and his throat hurt. He gagged twice and shook. The mug was withdrawn, then presented again. He took another swallow, felt stronger, opened his eyes. The light was dim, but he was looking into the thin rat face of a boy.

'We thought you was for it,' the boy said. 'Understand?'

Arthur nodded his head, just a little, couldn't yet bring himself to speak.

'But I said, let me try him with the ale. Good ale works miracles, that's what my gran always used to say. Drink again. You're lucky you found your way to the castle. Leastways, it's a sort of fortune. Course, there's many as comes here would like best to find their way out again and never does. But that's life, ain't it?'

In the days that followed Arthur slowly regained his strength. He was still too weak to walk and lay in the stable or cowshed. The boy, whose name was Cal (a diminutive of Calgacus, itself the name of a famous king who had led the Caledonians against the Romans), brought him food – ale, broth, bread and cow's milk cheese, hard, sharp and invigorating. (All his life Arthur would love cheese, and often said it would be no hardship to him to be deprived of beef so long as he had an ample supply of cheese and good bread or cakes made from oatmeal and dripping.)

Cal, two or three years younger than Arthur, was lively, alert, inquisitive. Arthur replied to his questions cautiously; he remembered that Merlin had instructed him to say as little about himself as possible. 'The more you reveal of yourself, the more you surrender to the power of others.'

'Who keeps this castle?' Arthur asked on the third day and saw a nerve leap in Cal's cheek.

'I don't know his name, only what we calls him.'

'And what's that?'

'Stoneface. He don't speak much, but when he does . . . as for his son, Sir Cade' – the boy lowered his voice – 'you don't want to get on his wrong side, not half you don't. He's a . . .'

'And what is he, boy?'

Cal leapt as if stung or pierced by the sharp point of a dagger. Arthur looked up and saw a tall, thickset, bearded man who now extended his arm and seized Cal by the hair, lifting him off his feet and holding him dangling and squealing in the air. Then he hurled the boy away from him so that he fell against the wall, striking his head and lying there moaning. Now the man turned to Arthur and commanded him to get to his feet. He obeyed, though with difficulty, for he was still very weak and his legs trembled.

'Who are you and how did you come here?'

'I am a wanderer who lost his way and fell ill in the forest, and my pony carried me here, and where this is I know not,' Arthur said.

'You speak our language at any rate. The word was, you were a Saxon spy. Are you a Saxon, boy?'

'No, sir.'

'And yet you have a strange tongue. From the north, I surmise. One of King Lot's spies perhaps.'

'Sir, I am no one's spy, and I do not know who King Lot is or where he is to be found.'

Arthur lowered his head, to show that he could not meet his questioner's gaze, and assumed an air of humility. But his legs still trembled on account of his weakness and he was afraid he would fall. This he did not want to do for he sensed that his questioner would despise a show of weakness. He guessed that this was the Sir Cade of whom Cal had begun to speak so fearfully.

The man stretched out his hand and took Arthur by the chin and forced his head up. 'A wanderer you say. To make yourself sound mysterious and important, I suppose. But' – he ran his rough hand over Arthur's cheek – 'if you were cleaned up, brat, you might be a good-looking boy. Such as I can make use of. You stink now, abominably.'

He thrust Arthur out of the stable and into the courtyard where a number of men stood by a pump. He handed Arthur to one of the soldiers – a fellow in a jerkin of hodden grey – and commanded him to strip the brat and hold him under the pump till he stank less of the midden. Arthur would have resisted this humiliation, but was incapable of escaping the soldier's grip and so submitted, though sore distressed to be presented thus as an object for the mocking laughter of the bystanders. When he had been swabbed down in the icy water, which came from a deep well, he heard Sir Cade order that he be provided with a tunic. 'Put the brat to work in the kitchen. He can turn a spit better, I dare say, than that feeble mollycoddle Cal.'

So Arthur was condemned to be a scullion and had no choice but to accept this role. And, though his pride was offended, he did so not entirely unwillingly, for Merlin had said to him that he must dwell some time in the Valley of Humiliation before he came into his own. What that was he did not know for certain, or when it might be, but Merlin's words sang in his head: 'Only those whose faces have been rubbed in the mire, and who have eaten of the bread of desolation, are fit to sit on high.'

So Arthur, the future king and emperor, was pressed into service in the kitchen, the butt of the cook and serving-maids, who called him Wart. When he served at the tables in the hall the men-at-arms treated him more rudely, sometimes tripping him as he carried a pile of dirty dishes and sending him sprawling, at other times belabouring him with blows or contenting themselves by hurling insults at him. And all this he bore with fortitude.

His only friend was Cal who attached himself to him with an eagerness and intensity that were almost frightening. Cal himself, though given at odd moments to outbursts of high spirits, existed much of the time in a state of fear. He had only to see Sir Cade cross the yard to begin to shake and seek somewhere to hide himself. As for Sir Cade's father, whom he called Old Stoneface, the mere mention of him sent the boy into an abject state: a nerve in his cheek would leap and his hands shake uncontrollably, while

49

he was well-nigh bereft of speech. When Arthur later questioned him, all he would say was, 'There are things goes on here as is better not talked about, believe you me, friend, I knows.'

Indeed, Arthur soon was given some understanding of what these things might be. One day a troop of Saxon prisoners, members of a raiding party who had found themselves separated from their fellows, were brought in. Arthur was curious; he had heard much of the Saxons but had never before seen one. They were mostly big awkward fellows with a dull look to their eye. But two were young lads, blond, blue-eyed, stocky boys who, even mud-streaked and bloody, with their tunics torn and their hair matted, seemed to Arthur to radiate vitality.

The prisoners were drawn up in the courtyard before Sir Cade and old silent Stoneface. Sir Cade smiled as he regarded them. 'There's gold here,' he said and drove his fist in its studded leather glove into the belly of one of the two handsome boys. The boy crumpled to the ground, holding his midriff, spluttering and gasping for breath. For a moment all was still. The boy struggled to his knees, whereupon Sir Cade planted his boot in the boy's neck, sending him tumbling into a pile of dung. 'Dirty beasts, Saxons.' The knight laughed. 'But these boys might one day fetch a good price at Silchester slave market.'

He lashed the other boy across the thighs with his whip. The boy said nothing and did not move or shrink from the second blow which followed. Instead, he raised his square chin and looked Sir Cade in the eye as if challenging him to repeat the blow. But the knight only laughed and ordered the boys to be taken to his chamber. 'To await my pleasure.'

Meanwhile his father was examining the other prisoners. Still without speaking he indicated that three were to be separated from the rest, and they were led to a corner of the yard and there thrust down the steps which led to a dungeon.

That left two Saxons.

'I know this one,' Sir Cade said, 'a notorious pirate. And the other, as I remember, is his brother. There's only one thing to be done with them.'

This remark was immediately understood or interpreted by the men-at-arms who had brought in the prisoners. Without further ado, ropes were hooked round their necks. They were led to the gallows, which stood in the inner court of the castle. The ends of the ropes were quickly tied to the gibbet and, at sword's point, the men were forced to mount a cart. It was abruptly pushed away and the two Saxons were left dangling.

'Unshriven,' Cal muttered to Arthur later. 'That means they go straight to Hell. I know they are pagans, but . . .'

'We are at war with the Saxons, I suppose,' Arthur said. 'All the same . . . I'm glad the two boys were saved. They can be only my age . . .'

'Saved, you call it,' Cal said. 'Saved for suffering . . .'

That night, as Arthur lay between waking and sleep, nestling against the flank of a rough-haired mastiff, for the warmth it offered and because of the comfort that contact with the dog brought him, he was startled by the sound of screaming from the tower where Sir Cade lodged with his father. Cal crept across the kitchen floor to join him. Arthur stretched out his hand and found that his friend was trembling.

'Now do you understand what sort of place this is?' Cal whispered.

Arthur put his arm round him and held him tight. 'It's better not spoken of,' he said; and felt ashamed, as if this made him an accomplice in horror.

He never saw the Saxon boys in the castle again. Perhaps they were indeed taken away to be sold as slaves, he told himself; but did not believe it.

One night Cal asked him, 'Have you ever wondered, friend, why there are so few women here?'

Arthur said, as before, 'These things are better not spoken of.'

Cal said, 'I've been . . . You think Sir Cade's a horror, but Old Stoneface . . .'

Some nights men came to fetch Cal, and he was absent for a day and another night. When he returned, he was paler and more given to trembling that ever, but when Arthur sought an answer to his questions he would only shake his head, bite his lips, mumble nothings, while his eyes filled with tears. Then, 'If it wasn't for you, Arthur, I couldn't go on living.'

The night came when the two who fetched Cal on other

occasions – burly fellows, the taller one-eyed and his comrade with a heavy limp, the result of a spear wound – walked straight past the boy and came instead for Arthur. One of them twisted his arm behind his back and the pair of them marched him to the tower. They thrust him into a room where Sir Cade and Old Stoneface were drinking wine.

'This is the one you've been keeping for me,' Stoneface said.

They were the first words Arthur had heard him utter. His voice was curiously thin and high-pitched.

Sir Cade nodded and drank more wine.

The two handlers led Arthur into the middle of the room where there was a bench some three feet high. They forced him over it and strapped his wrists to it. Arthur struggled but his efforts were vain. Then he felt his ankles being bound together and he was held there, like a trussed chicken. The handlers were then dismissed and for some minutes nothing happened. He could hear the glug of more wine being poured. There was silence. Nobody moved.

'I told you he would come on,' Sir Cade said. 'He was a pitiful wretch when we happened on him.'

Old Stoneface giggled.

Arthur heard one of them approach him. He felt his tunic being raised and a hand stroked his buttocks. And then the lash fell. Even the first stroke cut into his flesh. He bit his lip, hard, to stop himself crying out. But as lash followed lash, he could not prevent himself. His body convulsed at each stroke and soon he was screaming for mercy, but mercy was no more to be found there than milk from a lion; between lashes he heard once again the old man's high-pitched giggle.

'Now,' Sir Cade said and pressed himself upon Arthur, and the boy's buttocks were forced apart and he was entered. He howled, lost all control of himself and fainted.

You wonder, my Prince, why I write of such sinful and disgusting matters. They are not, I assure you, to my taste. But it is necessary that you understand to the full the wickedness of the world, and the perversions in which men indulge and with which, if they but knew it, they torment their souls.

This Sir Cade took his pleasure in cruelty, in the infliction of pain and humiliation, as many do. Some conceal the nature of their tastes from the world and even, it may be, from themselves by an assumption of virtue, and by declaring that they act in the name of the Lord and of Holy Church. Such are the learned doctors who serve the Holy Office, otherwise known as the Inquisition, who delight in torturing sinners that, as they say, their souls may be saved.

Understand therefore, my Prince, that whatever I set down, no matter how filthy and repulsive it may be for you to read, my purpose is pure and I seek only to enlighten you.

That being so, it behoves me to say more concerning this debauched pair, Sir Cade and his venerable father. Of the latter there is little to relate. Some years previously, leading his knights and men-at-arms to repel a Saxon raid, he had suffered the misfortune of being taken prisoner. For some reason of which I am ignorant, the Saxon chief had not chosen to have him killed, as was his usual practice; instead, he had commanded that he be gelded. Some say this was because he had seen the prisoner cast lascivious looks at the young Saxon prince who had been placed in attendance to him. But whether this was the case or not, none can now tell. The old man – already white-haired and white-bearded – was subjected to the mutilation and then cast out to make his way back to his castle, and to serve as an awful warning of the fate of those who fell into Saxon hands; for it is well known that men fear this mutilation more than death.

He survived and none dare mention his condition, for fear of his anger, which was celebrated. Henceforth, any Saxons whom his soldiers took prisoner could look for no mercy. Those who were hanged were the fortunate ones. Henceforth also the old man found the pleasure that was now denied his body in the lewd exercise of his imagination, stimulated by awful scenes enacted before his eyes.

As for Sir Cade, though it might seem that it was his purpose, as indeed he was wont to assert, only to please his father, and that he assaulted boys and young men merely from a sense of filial obligation – since only thus could his father obtain relief from his mutilated condition – yet this was not so. The fact was that Sir Cade, whatever his intentions when he commenced this course, was now in thrall to vice. He denied the existence of God, or even the old pagan gods. If He or they exist, he said, they take no interest in mankind, except to perplex us. In truth, he had concluded that there was no God, and that therefore everything was permitted to the man who dared. Yet it is the nature of vice, and in especial of the sexual vice, that what pleased at first no longer does; what were once vivid sensations became dull; what seemed daring and desperate becomes banal. More must be attempted, more done, and yet the return on this investment of effort is diminished. And how poor, how impoverished – which, I would have you note, is not a synonym for 'poor' as some suppose, but a word that signifies a transition from wealth to poverty, or from at least sufficiency to indigence – how impoverished is the imagination of the vicious. How dull, to those who escape their pleasures, is that which delights them; how dull and stupid. And in order to recapture their earlier sensation of daring and of pleasure they must, besotted creatures, press ever further on, devising new refinements or intensifications of what they do – and all in vain.

But I digress, for which I am not to be condemned, since the author who does not pause to gather wayside flowers or, more appropriately in this context, to reflect on his narrative, is like a man who hurries through a city in search of experience and never pauses to gather it, to look at girls gathered round a fountain engaged in idle talk, or at . . . but enough. It is time to return to Arthur.

But before I do so it is seemly to add that there be some authorities who would ascribe Sir Cade's indulgence in the grossest and most disgusting vice to another cause. They assert that he belonged to one of these cults, to which they do not deny their title to be called a religion, whose initiates seek to attain that union with the divine spirit (which is the highest aim of Man) by surrendering reason and satisfying all fleshly appetites, however obscene; for, they say, it is only by taking these beyond any limit that the soul may escape the dominion of the flesh.

Such practices were known in the Ancient World and especially among the followers of the god Dionysus.

But for my part, I consider this argument vile sophistry, and hold to the view that Sir Cade and his repulsive father were monsters such as should be expelled from the society of men, and driven into the waste places of the earth.

XII

Arthur crept back to the passage beyond the kitchen where he made his bield, sore, bleeding, distressed. To have been so used filled him with disgust, even self-loathing. He brushed aside the comfort Cal tried to offer. 'Is it the same for you?' was all he replied.

'The same? No, I think not. What he compels me to . . . I can't speak of it, even to you, even to you now . . .'

'I should like to kill him,' Arthur said. 'One day I shall kill him. I swear it. Meanwhile, since I cannot submit again to what was done to me tonight, we must make plans to escape.'

'We?'

'You don't think I would leave you behind, in this . . . this infernal pit . . .'

'If we are caught . . .' Cal said.

'Yes, if we are caught . . . So we must not be caught.'

'Where shall we go?'

'That is of no matter. The world is wide and . . .'

Arthur got to his feet and, taking Cal by the arm, led him to the end of the passage where there was a slit in the wall overlooking the valley below the castle. The moon had risen and all the valley was bathed in a silver light, flickering and uncertain as wisps of cloud drifted across the sky. 'Look,' he said, 'there is a world beyond this prison. The question is, how do we attain it?'

The question perplexed them for days. There were two gates to the castle, and both were heavily guarded night and day. Security was more intense than usual, word having been brought that a band of Saxons, thought to be seeking revenge for those taken by Sir Cade's men, had been seen in the neighbourhood. Arthur suggested they should dive from the topmost wall into the moat and swim to freedom. But Cal could not swim and, though he urged Arthur, if with trembling lip and broken voice, to make the attempt and so save himself, Arthur refused to abandon his friend.

And all the time both, but especially Arthur, lived in fear that they would again be summoned to Sir Cade's chamber.

Then, one afternoon, as dusk fell and a chill mist rose from the river flats below, the courtyard was filled with excited bustle.

'The mummers, the mummers have come.'

'The mummers?' Arthur said.

'Have you not heard of them?' Cal said. 'They stage a play, with sword fights. It's . . . oh how I should love to be a mummer.' He sighed. Arthur had never seen him so enthusiastic.

But he was soon diverted. The mummers went about the business of preparing their stage for the performance with an assurance that seemed to Arthur a play in itself. There were seven of them and one in particular, a gaunt lean man, held his attention. He was not the leader, for that was an old man, rather stout, with a gleaming bald head fringed by a mop of white hair, which hung in ragged locks. But the gaunt man had an air of utter authority. He spoke but seldom, and then in a tongue that was strange to Arthur, but whenever he spoke his fellows leapt, as it seemed, to do his bidding.

'It's because he plays the Goloshan,' Cal whispered.

'The Goloshan?'

'The evil one. They think or fear he has become what he plays.'

Then as the rising moon penetrated the mist, the play began.

First the mummers formed a ring, in the shape of a five-sided star, and the old bald man entered the middle of the ring, placed two swords on the ground, one lying across the other, and began to dance. He moved with a light agility that denied his years and, as he skipped ever higher, with his hands clasped above his head, the mummers who formed the ring chanted a refrain unintelligible to Arthur.

Then the gaunt man, the Goloshan, entered the ring. He wore a horse's head on his shoulders and, if Arthur had not remarked the manner in which his left foot was set at an angle to the leg, the result doubtless of an accident, he would not have recognised him. This disability caused him to move in a manner that seemed lethargic and yet now, when he began to dance, this clumsiness was transformed into disdain. This was directed at the first dancer and his swords, and aroused his anger. He picked up the swords and, holding one by the blade, offered it to the Goloshan. Twice he refused it, but on the third offering took it and assumed the on-guard position. The two men circled each other, making sweeping gestures with their blades which, however, did not clash. The song now changed to a marching rhythm and it seemed as if the singers were urging the two contestants to warmer efforts. The Goloshan responded by lunging at his adversary who skipped nimbly out of the way. This provoked the Goloshan. He charged, clumsily. As he did so he stumbled and received, as it seemed, a swingeing blow to his neck. Straightway he fell to the ground, as if insensible. The victor advanced, removed the horse's head and held the point of his sword against his defeated enemy's neck. With a loud cry he seemed to drive it home and all the dancers moaned. Then one of them broke from the ring and knelt by the fallen man, uttering shrieks of lamentation. This brought another dancer from the ring, who also knelt by the apparently dead Goloshan and passed his hands over his forehead, all the while muttering an incantation in a tongue still unintelligible to Arthur. As he did so the victor and the first mourner rejoined the dancers and all began to move, slowly, widdershins, their chant now a low murmur. After they had made the circle seven times the mummer in the middle took the hand of the Goloshan and raised him to his feet. Then both resumed the dance, while the chorus swelled to a song of praise rising to the listening moon.

Arthur, though not understanding the significance of what had been enacted, was rapt. Yet he did not forget the purpose he had formed as soon as he saw the players.

When the play was done the company supped, on a sheep roasted in the yard; and they drank ale, others cider, for they were on the fringe of apple country. Arthur hovered in the shadow of the players, seeking opportunity to speak; and Cal clung to him.

Then, as the moon rose high, the boy who attended on the mummers took a lute and began to sing:

> My love, he loves another love –
> The winds now wester blow –

My love plays false as fairy dice,
Alas, why does he so?

He came to me one summer night
Like dew upon the rose,
Enfolded me in all delight,
And stole away repose.

He left me in the morning clear
With never a backward gaze;
His heart is cold as devil's sperm,
Beware his pleasant ways.

Beware his pleasant ways, my lad,
Beware his honeyed breath.
He is unearthly, from the Shades,
And serves the Prince of Death.

When he had finished singing some, even of the men-at-arms, wept; and Arthur noticed this and thought how strange it was that music could so move men who had seen the cruelty of battles and that a song of unhappy love could seem to unman them. Yet these were fellows who, if their master gave the command, would have strung the minstrel boy from the gallows without hesitation. Even as he thought this, the boy caught his intent regard and winked. He was a dark boy, curly-haired, with eyes black as currants. When Arthur held his gaze and smiled in return, he came to him and offered his lute. 'Can you make music, my friend?'

'I can try.'

'Then do so, for my throat is as parched as the desert that lies to the east of Eden.'

Arthur took the lute and struck a few chords, for he saw in this offer a means of escape, if he could but take the opportunity thus afforded. He turned to Cal and said, 'Let us sing together. The Ballad of Lost Things.'

'Alas,' Cal said, 'I do not know the verses.'

'Then sing the chorus.' He leaned closer to his friend and whispered, 'Sing all you can. It's important, I tell you.'

So Arthur strummed the harp, and sang in a voice that was clear and sweet as the vespers' bell.

A true knight lay by a forest stream,
And the queen of the fairies knelt by him.
 She kissed him once, she kissed him thrice,
 Kissed him once, kissed him thrice,
Locked his heart in a fairy dream,
And pinned it with a silver pin.

His lady watched from the castle wall,
Watched and waited for her love's return.
 She'd kissed him once, kissed him thrice,
 Kissed him once, kissed him twice,
Watched and waited as the shadows fall,
Spiered her maids, 'Do you hear his horn?'

His horse's hoof never bent the grass,
His horn was silent as the moon.
 Fairy kisses stole his wits away,
 Fairy kisses stole his heart away,
He lies in the vale where no days pass,
And the fairies dance to a silent tune . . .

'Why', said the dark boy when Arthur had finished singing, 'do you call it the Ballad of Lost Things?'

'Because', Arthur said, 'it is the name I was given.'

'You make good music,' the man who had played the Goloshan said, 'you should be a player.'

'There is nothing', Arthur said, 'that would please my friend and me more than to travel with you and make music.'

'And you have more songs?'

'There is no end of songs,' Arthur said, quoting Merlin, 'and music soars as high as a falcon.'

'Well,' said the Goloshan, 'we must see what we can do. I have long thought that our repertory was too limited. The times they are a-changing, as I have often observed, and new manners demand new material.'

Then Arthur thought it prudent to take the curly-haired boy, whose name was Peredur, aside, not forgetting to include Cal in the conversation, and explain to him how they were situated and how eager they were to escape from Sir Cade's castle.

'It were as difficult, I fear,' Cal said, 'to escape the fairyland of our song.' For he was inclined to melancholy and therefore to project difficulties where Arthur, being sanguine, saw opportunities. Peredur, however, laughed. He was a child of the morning, and thought therefore that all things were possible and that desire, if sufficiently felt, could always be translated into action.

'Would it was so,' Cal said, 'but as my grandam, who reared me, used to say, "If wishes were horses, beggars would ride".'

'Leave it to me,' Peredur said, 'and you shall find your wish to be indeed a horse.'

XIII

Peredur lay with Arthur and Cal in the cellar below the kitchen. His talk delighted Arthur, and even Cal, morose and melancholy by nature, made more so by wretched experience, began to respond to their new friend's stories of the pleasures that belonged to the mummers' life.

'We are vagabonds,' the boy said, 'and, though this means that many men will raise their hands against us, and look on us as thieves and disturbers of such peace as may be found in this land, yet we also enjoy a freedom to range where we please, to work as we please, to live as we please, paying no heed to laws or to what passes for morality. For my part, there is only one moral law worth a docken: take and give such pleasure as you may. For who knows what the morrow will bring?'

And so he smiled on Arthur and on Cal, and taught them, Arthur most certainly and willingly, that he spoke truth.

It was still dead of night, in the dark valley that lies between the old moon and the new, when he roused them, and all three crept through the silent kitchen and into the courtyard where the mummers' cart awaited their departure in the morning. They paused in the doorway, listening to the tramp of marching sentries on the battlements above. When all was silent, Peredur stepped into the open yard and stood for a moment watchful as a fox. He stretched out his arms like one who wakes from sleep and yawns. Then, very gently, he raised the cover from the cart; and again paused, on the alert. But there was neither sound nor movement. He whispered 'come', and Arthur and Cal, lightfoot as the dawn, slipped from the doorway and mounted the cart. They concealed themselves under the mummers' equipment and Peredur replaced the cover over all. Then, with a swagger, he himself climbed the stairway that led to the battlements and, complaining of sleeplessness, fell into lively conversation, and perhaps more besides, with the sentry.

So the night passed and in the morning the mummers departed from the loathsome castle, and Arthur and Cal safely with them.

'I was never so pleased to be rid of a place in all my days,' Peredur said.

Arthur found the mummers' life to his taste. He delighted in the freedom of the road and was soon a valued member of the troupe. Cal, however, remained for a long time prey to the terrors which his experience had brought on him, and even when they were well away from the castle could not be at ease. Moreover, unlike Arthur, he had no talent for performance, the prospect of which made him sick to the stomach. And he soon grew jealous of Peredur and the easy friendship he had so quickly forged with Arthur. This jealousy grew more intense when Arthur and Peredur sang duets and were rewarded with the favour of the public in the towns and inn yards where they performed. The lame mummer who played the Goloshan and other dark and weighty parts observed this, but for the time being kept it in his heart and said nothing.

Arthur soon realised that the Goloshan, as he always thought of him, though not the nominal leader of the troupe, was nevertheless its animating spirit and the deviser of new entertainments. He was a man of mystery who never spoke of his past or his origins, and no one, indeed, knew where he had come from or what was his native language. He had travelled widely and delighted the boys, when the mood took him, with tales of far countries and strange peoples. He had even sojourned in the city of the Great Constantine, and when he spoke of its churches, palaces, bathhouses, libraries, its colonnades and miles of fortified walls, the boys' eyes grew wide with wonder. He told them of the great Emperor Marcus who had been compelled to flee Constantinople and had travelled the seas till he came to Britain, where he restored the glory of Empire for a season that was only too brief.

'But', he said, with a smile to which Arthur attached one of Merlin's favourite adjectives, sardonic, 'what have the likes of us, strolling players, to do with emperors? We are vagabonds and all the better for it, since this renders us a liberty which the dynasts,

63

as they call the men – and women, oh yes, women too – of power in the Greek language, can only dream of. Take it from me, no wise man seeks power and glory, but rather to enjoy the keen air of the morning and to sleep beneath the stars in the secure knowledge that his death would profit nobody. For kings and emperors live ever in fear of enemies and to tell truth, the greater part of them fall victim sooner or later to treachery or the insatiable ambition of others. Ask little of life and you will receive more than those who seek, vaingloriously, to dominate it.' So saying, he twisted Peredur's curls round his fingers and planted a wet kiss on the boy's mouth.

On other nights the Goloshan spoke of the art they practised; theatre he called it, using the Greek term. 'It is the true alchemy,' he said, 'for just as the magicians seek to transmute base metal into gold, so we, in what to the foolish appears only to be make-believe, present the reality of the world, of things as they are, when understood by the initiated. For what is this world of shadows which we inhabit but an amphitheatre in which no one appears in a true light, as himself, but all are disguised. Therefore, by displaying ourselves in disguise, we enable the discerning to receive an intimation of the nature of reality, which they do not possess the words to describe. Our fraternity plays comedies which serve as a mirror to nature. Just as in dreams men attain an apprehension of realities which, in waking, are beyond their ken, so too our theatre presents our audiences with a dream that furnishes their imagination with matter of great import.'

'But if we do not ourselves understand, as I am sure I do not,' Peredur said, 'what that which we do signifies, does this not mean that . . . I have forgotten what my question was going to be, so greatly have you confused me.'

'Let me try,' Arthur said, 'for I think I see the tendency of your questioning. If we do not understand any concealed significance of the comedy we play, is that significance real or not? Is it perhaps mere fancy that attributes to our comedy meaning which we, the actors, are wholly ignorant and unaware of? Can you answer me this?'

'Indeed I can,' the Goloshan said. 'Do we not frequently speak without forethought and surprise ourselves by the words we utter, the value, significance, or truth of which we come to understand only when the words have taken wing from our mouths?'

'Yes,' said Arthur, 'I suppose that is sometimes the case.'

'And does not this prove that we know more than we suppose we know, and are often moved to speak in a manner that seems to derive not from that which we have considered but from that which we have not considered, and from depths that we have not plumbed? And is it not the case that men then say, "He speaks with the tongues of angels," which is another way of saying that we have spoken more than we thought to speak . . . And is it not the case . . .'

Arthur pondered all that the Goloshan said and kept it in his heart, but Peredur scoffed and said, 'Once the old man starts talking, he blows ideas about as the autumn winds toss dead leaves and, if you ask me, friends, with just as much point.'

As for Cal, he frowned and said only, 'In my opinion he is wise enough that can keep himself fed and warm, and all this talk is but the chatter of one who wags a wand in the water.' Then he sniffed and said, with a fearful sideways glance, lest the Goloshan had heard him and taken note of his words, 'But who am I to speak of such matters who knows not his own father?'

One day they came to an inn in a flat country. The innkeeper, who had long expected them, welcomed them with smiles, and set meat and wine before them. He told them that their coming was fortunate, for a great lady, a princess indeed, was lodging there with her suite. They were weary of travelling and would be content to see a merry comedy. Therefore, as soon as the players were refreshed and the summer sun was low in the sky, he would be happy if they gave their performance. But what would they play?

'We shall play a marriage comedy,' the Goloshan replied, 'for that always pleases the ladies. Why this should be,' he added in an aside to Arthur and Peredur, 'I cannot tell, since the world knows that most marriages prove to be unhappy.'

The play was simple, as all plays were in these unlettered times. But, as the Goloshan had hinted, there was a hidden significance, suggested first by the title, which was *The Chymical Wedding*, and second by the display on the inn wall behind the carts on which they played of certain Biblical emblems, the four beasts of Daniel and the image of Nebuchadnezzar, magic-working king of Babylon; and these represented allusions to prophecy.

As for the plot, it unfolded as follows. On a sea coast (the setting being announced by Cal, for this was the only role he was found fit to play) an aged king, played by Sir Topas, the nominal leader of the company, found an infant (represented by a doll much battered by overuse and with one eye missing) in a chest washed up by the waves. His expressions of surprise, in deftly rhyming couplets, delighted the Princess and her ladies, who showed their appreciation by leaving off the eating of sweetmeats. Then, delving more deeply into the chest, Sir Topas discovered a letter, which he read aloud. This purported to come from the king of the Moors and informed all that he had seized the land of which this infant was rightful queen.

The second scene showed the infant full-grown into a lovely young girl, played by Peredur in a wig of black ringlets and with much fluttering of his naturally long eyelashes and rolling of his liquid black eyes. His performance, too, brought appreciative murmurings from the Princess and her ladies. Peredur then danced expressively and sighed for lack of love. At this moment the king of the Moors (the Goloshan) rose through a trapdoor in the cart, seized the lovely maiden in his arms and swept her off into the nether darkness. Peredur screamed for mercy, very movingly, for he was proud of his screaming; then all was silent but for the Moor's evil chuckling.

Arthur now sprang on to the stage, in breastplate, short tunic (which revealed his shapely legs) and carrying a sword. He looked around, for a moment, in mystification and then, hearing the Moor renew his chuckle, called out a challenge in a loud clear voice. The Moor answered this. They fought and Arthur was victorious, the Moor leaping from the cart in flight. Arthur then drew up Peredur from the cart and fell to his knees before her, swearing his devotion. She hailed him as her champion and fell into his arms, and for a little they billed and cooed and kissed, most lovingly.

They were interrupted by Silas, a member of the company

whom Arthur had learned to distrust, and who was dressed as a priest. He offered to marry them and, in preparation, pressed them to drink from a goblet of wine. When they did so, both fell into a swoon, and the Moor reappeared, gave gold to the priest, and made to carry Peredur the Princess off again. But at this moment Arthur awoke from his swoon, comprehended what was happening and, full of righteous wrath, dispatched first the priest, with a blow from the flat of his sword on the buttocks, so that he soared off the cart and landed on his face on the stone flags of the inn yard, to general merriment, and then ran his sword, cunningly, as it seemed, through the Moor's heart. At this moment the aged King entered, understood all that had taken place and announced the marriage of his beloved son (Arthur) to his ward the Princess. Whereupon everyone cried out *'vivat sposus, vivat sposa'*, and all went merry as a marriage bell while the company sang of love's triumph.

Simple, even crude, as the comedy was, it greatly pleased all, the Princess and her ladies especially. She presented gifts to the company, and gave roses to Peredur and Arthur, a yellow rose for one and a red for the other. Then there was feasting, on beef and mutton, and tarts made with apples, ginger and the essence of almonds. Wine, cider, beer and mead were there in abundance and all who would drank deep. But Arthur partook sparingly, for he was conscious that the eyes of the Princess were fixed on him, and he knew a strange trembling of the limbs such as he had never before felt and a quickening of the flesh.

Then, as darkness fell, one of the ladies who attended the Princess came to him, touched him lightly on the shoulder and beckoned him to follow her. She led him into the inn and up the staircase till they came to the chamber where the Princess was lodged, to which she had already retired.

The lady told him to enter and then left him, and he found the room, which had a low ceiling and was dimly lit by three candles in a stand, at first seemingly deserted. Then he saw that the Princess was resting in a window seat, and she rose and came towards him. She smiled and her smile was of a loveliness he had known only in his dreams. She drew him to her and kissed his lips, and her kisses were soft, fluttering and gentle as summer evenings.

Both sighed as for a moment they paused, while time stood still between them. Now he saw that she wore neither skirt nor petticoat, but only a light wrap of finest silk such as the merchants of Damascus sell for much gold. As soon as he embraced her, this wrap slid away and she was left only in a shift, which offered no more concealment of what lay beyond than clear glass does to roses or lilies. Arthur slid his hands under the shift and it slipped away, and her skin was whiter than new-fallen snow and smoother to the touch than alabaster or ivory. Her breasts were small, round and firm, and the space between them was like a little valley between gentle hills such as we see in early spring when snow lies on the slopes. For a moment he stood bereft of words, and then she drew him on to the couch and . . . and . . .

But I leave what ensued to your imagination, for it is not fitting that I put such delights in words, even did I not lack the words with which to express them. And indeed, neither Arthur nor the Princess found need of words. But their enjoyment of each other was perfect.

It was a moment – no, not a moment, but hours – of magic and delight such as he had never before experienced and which he would never forget. Yet, so bitterly runs the world, so sharp is the comedy we play, that this night was to prove grievous to him, for reasons which I shall explain in the ripeness of my narrative.

XIV

It was three days later that Arthur noticed Silas was no longer of the company. At first he hesitated to enquire of the Goloshan where he might have gone and why, for, ever since the morning after they had given the play in the inn yard, the Goloshan had been silent, morose, apparently troubled in mind. And indeed, now, observing how Arthur looked doubtfully on him, it was he who crooked his finger at the boy and bade him approach.

Three times he made to speak and three times broke off with a frown. At last he drew himself a mug of ale from the barrel against which he had been resting, passed it to Arthur, then drew a second for himself.

'Good ale,' Arthur said, as if to encourage him.

'That it is. If life were as simple and wholesome as ale, we would none of us have cause to complain. You'll have observed that Silas is no longer among us.'

'Yes indeed.'

'Damn him, I say, for a meddlesome, malicious, snivelling, sly, sneaking villain.'

'If you say so.'

'That I do.' He drank again of his ale. 'And you, my lad, will have to depart from us also.'

'Depart? But I have no wish to depart.'

'Nor I to lose you. I have grown fond of you, boy – not as fond as of my Peredur' – he kissed the tips of his fingers – 'but fond indeed. Yet you must go. The longer you remain with us, the more danger we are all in.'

Arthur shook his head, being puzzled, and doubtless, as men do in such straits, grew pale. 'But . . .' he said, then paused, not knowing which objection to raise.

The Goloshan sighed again, and then unfolded his reasons. Silas, he said, had discovered that the Princess was in reality

Morgan le Fay, the wife of the renowned King Lot of Orkney. In the belief that King Lot who was known to be a very jealous man would reward him for bearing news of his wife's infidelity he had set off to the King's court to be the first with the news.

'He is a fool as well as a knave. I warned him that the King would reward the bearer of such news by slitting his nose, tearing out his tongue, cropping his ears and blinding him, rather than with gold. But he would not listen. Or would not believe. Besides, he hates you, it seems, and hopes that King Lot will seek you out and revenge the insult which you have inflicted on him by making him a cuckold. There, I fear, Silas speaks truth; and so, dear boy, you must leave us and go into hiding. I have to say also that I order you to do this for our sakes as well as your own. And that makes me ashamed. But I can think of no alternative.'

Arthur saw the justice of his words, so, manfully, obeyed. Peredur wept as they kissed goodbye and each swore undying friendship for the other. So, with Cal as his only companion, Arthur turned away. Both boys dropped some natural tears, Arthur because he had been happy with the troupe of comedians, Cal because they were venturing again into the unknown. But soon they wiped them away. The world lay all before them, with the promise of adventure and the question only of where to choose their next lodging. So, with wandering steps and slow, commending themselves to the cares of such powers as might watch over them, they took their solitary way.

For days they journeyed, over hill and vale, through marsh and fen, meeting few, conversing with none, ever on guard lest King Lot's men might be scouring the land for Arthur. He, however, enlivened the dark hours of night, and the long hours of their journeying, by permitting his imagination to play with images of the delights he had enjoyed in his congress with the Princess; and resolved that he would not be deterred from seeking her out and putting himself in every way at her service. He could not tell how this was to be achieved but, with the gay confidence of youth, did not doubt that it should be. He desired it; therefore it must be.

On the seventh day they found themselves on a barren moor, where there was neither sight nor sound of beast or bird. The ground was heavy, the sky leaden grey and, though there was no wind, it was bitter cold. The stillness of the air and the silence of the world lowered their spirits; and as the light began to fail and there was no sign of any habitation, fatigue and hunger warred for ascendancy over them.

Darkness, like a stealthy foe, crept in on them. Lone trees and bushes assumed strange and uncanny shapes. The night-owl cried its warning to the world and, from across a valley, a vixen howled. Cal, his teeth chattering from cold or terror, or more probably both, took hold of Arthur's arm and whimpered his distress. Arthur sought in vain for words to comfort or embolden his friend; yet himself drew strength from Cal's weakness.

It was at that moment that a light flickered ahead of them, a light that moved inconstantly. Arthur directed Cal's attention to it and urged him on. Distant music sounded, a wailing of women and the slow beat of a drum.

'It may be they are devils,' Cal said, 'or the spirits of the dead, for this endless heath surely belongs to those who have passed before us.'

'I think not,' Arthur said and again urged him on.

So they followed the light and came to a chapel. Still Cal would have hesitated and drawn back, but Arthur, being strong of will, prevailed. He pushed open the door, which creaked on its hinges, and entered the chapel.

The body of a knight lay before the altar, and a maiden knelt by his head and smoothed the pallid brow, and lifted up her voice in lamentation. She herself was pale of skin, with long golden hair that lay over her back, and the fingers which moved on the dead man's brow were slim as willow wands. She looked up as she heard them enter and in the dim light her eyes seemed pools of darkness.

Arthur was about to address her when a figure in the garb of a priest emerged from the shadows. Therefore Arthur spoke to him instead, so as not to interrupt the mourning of the maiden. 'Who is this dead knight and what is this place?' he asked.

'This is the chapel of the damned, of those who have been cast out beyond the laws of men and gods,' the priest replied, 'and I myself am one of these. As for him you call the dead knight, he is the Caesar with falcon eyes.'

'What Caesar is that?' Arthur said. 'For, as far as I am aware, there is no Caesar now in Britain.' And he spoke in a clear voice, to disguise the fear he knew.

Cal pulled at his sleeve. 'This place is uncanny,' he said, 'let us go.'

'I have heard', Arthur said, paying no heed to Cal, but allowing him still to grip him hard, for comfort and assurance, 'that the illustrious dead such as Caesars are held to lie not in dim chapels, which smell, as this one does, of damp and decay, but in an open place that was luminous and high.'

'Why so it was formerly, in the days of the Empire,' was the reply, 'but the Empire has perished under the waves of the grass shaken by the horsemen's charge. Tell me thy faith, you who dare to invade this unholy place.'

'I believe in my own strength,' Arthur said.

Later he could not account for these words, which expressed what he had never thought, nor whence they came.

'Then surely you belong here,' the priest said. He smiled and his smile was the smile of a wolf. 'You belong here,' he said again, 'for man is the maker of his own doom.'

'You speak in riddles,' Arthur said. 'Speak plain.'

'There is no plain speaking', the priest said, 'that is not also a lie. If I speak in riddles, it is because life is itself a riddle and to speak otherwise were to deceive. When we are born we enter a strange house of the spirit, and the floor of the house is a chessboard on which we play a game that we can neither know nor avoid against an opponent who changes shape and appearance, and whom, if we have any wisdom, we go in fear of.'

Cal tugged again at Arthur's sleeve and whispered in his ear, 'Let us go and brave the wilderness outside, for this man is mad and frightens me more than the wildest night.'

But Arthur said, 'I would hear more. You say, friend, that this is the chapel of the damned. But the damned are held, as I have been told, in Hell, and this chapel is here on earth.'

'And should Hell be constricted? Should Hell be confined?' the priest replied. 'Is not man a creature of sufficient evil to construct for himself Hell here on earth? Why wait for death to lay his icy hand upon you before entering into the service of the Most High,

72

whom some call Satan and the wise dare not name. You gaze on that woman, mourning by her dead father, or, it may be, her lover, or – who can tell? – both father and lover, and you desire her, as my eyes inform me. At the very moment of desire you find yourself on the threshold of Hell, for you are like the thirsty man who in sleep wishes to drink, and takes great draughts of water that do not satisfy him or satiate him, and who dies burned up with thirst in the middle of a rushing stream. Even so the Goddess of Love whom the Romans named Venus, though that is not her name which may not be spoken of men, nor of women either, though they are her servants, whom she employs to be the lures and deceivers of men. Thus this goddess conjures up for those who would be lovers all desirable images, simulacra, to inflame desire and feed the eager imagination. For a little this vision satisfies, but must in time be translated into action. Hands, greedy yet indecisive, run over the body of the imagined love. The flesh yields and grows warm. A foretaste of delight is offered and it seems as if the goddess is about to sow the woman's field. The lovers entwine; then desire, panting like a dog, approaches the intensity of heat, so that in their amorous ardour they even bruise each other and teeth bite into flesh. And yet all is in vain, for they do not succeed in losing themselves one in the other and becoming, as they desire, a single flesh, a unity. So they fall apart and lie apart and know disgust. As grey morning succeeds the ardent night, so lust in action breeds only weariness and self-contempt. You, my brave young chevalier, are, I see, marked out to be a great lover, and what will your reward be? Disappointment, self-hatred and at the last a vacancy chill as the north wind, misery and woe. See now, in this Chapel of the Damned, her whom you desire, approach.'

Even as he spoke the maiden rose from beside the bier, her keening changed into amorous murmurs, and advanced on Arthur. As she drew near her features, which had seemed so lovely, appeared to freeze, her eyes looked on him with ravenous lust, and blood dripped from the corner of her mouth. She leaned over him, and in that moment darkness descended and he fell into a swoon.

When Arthur recovered from his swoon he was lying on the moor by the side of a brook and Cal was wiping his face with a cloth. 'Where have they gone?' he asked, but Cal made no reply.

Arthur pressed him, but he affected ignorance of all that had been done and said in the chapel, and would only say that Arthur had fallen to the ground and that he had been much afraid. And indeed, when Arthur looked around the moor, which was now clear-lit by a full moon that shone bright, as the rising wind had scattered the clouds, he saw no chapel and for a little wondered if he had dreamed all that I have related.

Yet he was certain this was not so and thought that fear had so taken possession of his friend as to persuade him that what had been had not.

The words of the strange priest remained in his mind and he pondered them as they resumed their journey. 'No doubt', he thought, 'there was some truth in his words, but my experience with the Princess at the inn goes some way to contradict them.'

Yet he could not forget what had been said and it perturbed him that he remembered Merlin speaking in like vein.

'Is the most intense of experiences one doomed to disappoint?' he asked himself. 'Are we condemned in this life to live as in a wilderness in which all pleasure is transitory and delusory, and no love is sure?'

XV

Towards evening they came to the summit of a hill looking to the west. The sky was red; yet it was not an angry red, but a red softened by gold and, as the light began to fade, streaked with a melancholy grey.

In the valley below there lay a town, and this cheered them.

'Surely there will be an inn,' Cal said, 'and a warm fire, and meat and beer and perhaps a fine cheese, for the fields we see suggest this is cattle country.'

So they descended the hill with light hearts, for both were hungry and weary, and the thought of food and a roof over their heads for the night pleased them. As the light failed, the cold sharpened, but they were not dismayed.

Then they came to a villa outside the town. It was fronted with fine columns, but grass grew between the paving stones and all wore the appearance of desolation. The door stood open. They entered, but there was no one there; and likewise the farmyard was deserted.

They pressed on to the town, their spirits lowered by what they had seen, for it was difficult to believe that the town flourished if what had been a noble villa just beyond its boundaries was fallen into such disrepair and decay. And their fears were soon justified. They encountered no one in the streets and the market square was devoid of life. There was indeed an inn, but its sign, which displayed an eagle, hung crooked and the eagle itself seemed to have lost its feathers. Still they pushed open the door which led to the taproom. Three men sat at a table and Arthur made to address them, then saw they were all three beyond address. He laid his hand on the shoulder of the first man, and it was stiff and cold as a frozen branch. He touched a second on the cheek and not a muscle moved. The third stared at him with the fixed indifference of death. Only a rat, which scuttled into the darkness at their approach, defied whatever had befallen them. Arthur lit a candle that stood on the table and held it to the faces of the dead, and they were black and swollen.

Then, with Cal, he searched through the town, entering houses which had no locks to bar the doors. Some were deserted; in others they found bodies, and in a pit at the limit of the town under the wall on the western side they happened on a pile of corpses thrown in, untended, lying there exposed to the elements, as if their fellows had been overtaken by calamity before they were able to complete their burial. Or it may have been that they were too oppressed by the disaster that had befallen them all to care about such decencies. They turned away and by the well in the market place came on the body of a child, a boy, by what remained of the dress, of seven or eight years perhaps, with flaxen hair, now filthy and matted, and his flesh torn by scavenging birds, which had picked out his eyes.

At that moment they heard the drumming of horses' hooves and started, in mingled expectation and fear.

They came through an arch, erected by some provincial governor, in emulation of emperors, to celebrate some petty triumph over a barbarian tribe. There were four of them and they rode at a measured trot. Three of the horses were black as a winter's night and the fourth white as new-fallen snow.

They paused, drawing on their reins, and then the first rider advanced into the market place. He sat tall on his steed and his face was marked with a livid scar. He bore a lance in his right hand and a long sword depended from his sword belt. He gazed around and it was as if his eyes saw nothing.

Arthur spoke a challenge; without intention, for it seemed to him as if the words were drawn from him, or another power spoke through him.

The knight fixed on him those indifferent eyes and said only, 'I am War.'

Then the second knight advanced, and he was pale and wasted as the winter moon. Again Arthur spoke and again the knight replied, 'I am Famine.'

He turned away and the third rider took his place, and his

countenance was swollen and marked with bloody spots. In answer to Arthur, he pronounced these words: 'I am Pestilence.'

Then all three pulled on their reins and turned aside, and their companion on the white horse came forward and they greeted him with acclamation as their lord. He pushed up the vizor of his casque, and Arthur saw that the flesh had fallen away from his face and only the bones and gaping teeth remained. This time he had neither desire nor need to utter a challenge, but was silent, and the skull spoke: 'I am Death, lord of all, he who holds the field which my companions have conquered.'

And with no other words the four horsemen put their spurs to their mounts and rode off to the west.

While Arthur and Cal stood amazed by what they had seen, and before they could debate what it might mean, they were joined by a third. To Arthur it seemed at first as if this were Merlin, for he closely resembled him; and yet it was not Merlin for he did not acknowledge Arthur, or greet him as had been his wont. When he spoke, moreover, though his accent was Merlin's and the tone of his voice Merlin's, yet his words were not Merlin's. 'These', he said, 'were the Horsemen of the Apocalypse who herald the end of time and the second coming of your Lord.'

'And is your Christ,' exclaimed Arthur with an indignation worthy of a pupil of Merlin and for the moment oblivious of his destiny as a Christian emperor, 'and is your Christ to appear only when this world, with all its delights, has been laid waste by war, famine, pestilence and death, the master of all? Is this to be the salvation that your Christian priests have promised mankind?'

'Peace, friend,' said the man who was not Merlin but yet so resembled him. 'Peace, and give ear to what I have to say. For, unless you do, then you to whom so much has been given and to whom so much more is promised will be reviled for all ages as a traitor and backslider, ingrate and renegade. But first, since what I have to impart is deep and of great moment, let us repair to that abandoned hostelry and see if its cellar will still furnish us with a bottle of good wine, for there is nothing that serves like wine to oil the wits and render argument agreeable.'

So they did and the cellar was well-stocked still with wine, and their new companion selected a wine from Burgundy which is, as is well attested, a wine of great body that fortifies the mind and spirit as no other, not even our fine vintages here in Sicily. Admirable as they are, my Prince, they lack the subtlety of the wine of Burgundy, just as our evenings here, though heavy with the odour of lemon blossom, cannot match the soft twilight of my native Tweeddale in which the scent of wet birch trees mingles with the tang of the heather and the whins . . . But I digress and must return to our tale. However, before I do so, let me state, lest any be offended, and you, my Prince, resent the partiality I display for my native heath (where, alas, no vines grow and no wine is made) that for everyday drinking there are no vintages to match those of Sicily, especially when the vines are grown on the lava-rich flanks of Etna. Nevertheless, for a combination of subtlety and body, I insist that there are no wines to equal those of Burgundy. And in any case it was Burgundy that Arthur and his companions found in the deserted inn, and therefore Burgundy which they drank. There is no doubt about that.

When they were settled at a table before the inn – for they chose not to drink within on account of the bodies of the dead and any infection they might carry – and had slaked their early thirst and recharged their cups, their new companion spoke as follows.

'The horsemen you have been privileged to encounter here this evening are unquestionably those of the Apocalypse, but whether that is now upon us, or whether you have been granted a premonition of what may be, is uncertain. The evidence of our senses suggests the former and yet the intellect, God's sovereign gift to man, asserts denial. We cannot tell which is true. What is certain, however, is that this world is a battlefield between Good and Evil, between the Forces of Light and the Forces of Darkness. Some insist that the balance is tilted to the latter, for they hold that all flesh is evil and that the world we inhabit is the creation of the Lord of Sabaoth whom some call Satan.'

He pulled his saffron robe about him, for the night had turned chill, and drank some wine.

'Be that as it may, all agree that the last stage of the world will see Armageddon, the final great battle. Some say the Antichrist will triumph, and that the last of your Christian emperors will then lay down his sceptre on the Mount of Olives so that the

Antichrist, as they call him, will establish the reign of evil as foretold in the Holy Scriptures . . .'

'Allow me,' Arthur said, with that perfect courtesy which is the mark of princes – or should be, for I have known princes who were entirely deficient in this gentle quality – 'allow me, pray, to interrupt you. When you first addressed us, and I am exceedingly glad that you did for I am fascinated by your conversation, I understood that you were yourself a Christian. Now your manner of speech persuades me I was mistaken. So would you mind telling us who and what you are, that we may understand you more perfectly?'

'Who and what I am is no great matter. You may consider that I am whoever you choose that I should be. Suffice only to say that I am a wanderer who has seen all that is good and evil, and who has journeyed to every corner of the Empire that was Rome, and may be again, and even beyond into the lands called barbarian, where I have dwelled in forests and traversed the plains over which the wind never ceases to blow.

'You have seen the Four Horsemen and yet live, while thousands perish. For some say, now, that the end of the world is upon us – which for my part would occasion no distress, things being as they have been. There are prophets who declare that it is first necessary that the Christian Empire be renewed, first here in Britain, which some call the Third Rome, and then in Jerusalem, ever blessed despite misfortune, and that this must be so that the Head of all Evil, the aforesaid Antichrist who would plant his imperial throne here, must have some nourishment of faith, some sufficient foe, that he may fight against. And these prophets insist that the victory of the Antichrist is inevitable . . .'

He paused and chuckled, and, to Arthur's astonishment, his laugh was like a fresh morning in spring. 'I distress you,' he said. 'I see your cheek grow pale.'

He took the bottle and filled their cups again. 'A sovereign remedy,' he said. 'Miserable as my long life has been, terrible as my doom has appeared, there are moments when I drink good wine that I cannot believe in the teaching which insists that evil rules the earth . . .'

'This wine', Cal said, 'is indeed good. If only we had some cheese to accompany it . . .'

Their new friend sighed. 'Indeed yes. But one cannot have everything.' He paused again, reflectively. 'Inasmuch as one thing sometimes excludes another,' he added.

'That is so,' Cal said. He nodded his head, a little drunkenly. 'Though it puzzles me to understand why our having wine should exclude our having cheese also.'

'Be that as it may, let me resume my eschatological discourse.'

'Escatawhat?' Cal said. 'I am lost to understand where cats come into it?' And he closed his eyes and fell asleep.

But Arthur prompted their acquaintance to continue. 'The Roman poet Virgil', he said, 'talked, as my teacher Merlin used to say, of the age of gold now vanished, which it was promised the Emperor Augustus would renew. But I never heard that he did.'

Dark had fallen, but there were no clouds in the sky and, below them in the valley, a trail of vapour, mist resting just above the abandoned fields, stretched out like a dragon crawling disconsolate to its glen.

'Wherever I have travelled I have come on those who shared this memory of the golden age of the world and sighed to think that it lay behind them, even while that memory also fortified their spirit. Yet I have never been certain myself, though I was reared in the assurance that our first parents had been expelled from Eden because Eve listened to the serpent and gave Adam to eat of the apple which she had plucked from the tree. Yet when I saw the courage which even the poorest and meanest of folk bring to the harsh business of living, of mere survival, I have thought, for brief moments that last as long as a sparrow may fly through a great hall, entering by one door and departing by the other, that it may be that this golden age is yet to come, that the battle of Armageddon may not be lost and that the golden age may be realised here in time to come, that it may, so to speak, lie within history, and not behind it.'

Saying this, he smiled and, stretching out on the ground, with his saffron robe pulled tight about him, composed himself to sleep.

It is meet to add, lest any suppose this mere wild speculation suited only to a Romance, that this personage anticipated the thought of the learned Doctor Joachim, abbot of the monastery that is to be found in the distinguished and beautiful town of San Giovanni dei Fiori in Calabria, famous throughout your realm, my Prince, for learning and deep study. This Joachim, whose fame and wisdom are such that, only a few years ago, the English king, Richard of the Lion's Heart, summoned him to attend him on his journey to the Holy Land, that he might hear from him his interpretation of things to come, likewise asserts that Armageddon would not be lost, but rather that the Antichrist, whom he identifies as the Infidel, should be defeated, which victory for the Forces of Light will, he writes, signify the dawning of a new era in which a reformed Church shall usher in the Age of the Spirit, which he terms the Perfect Society made manifest here on Earth ... Furthermore, he declares, with candid confidence, that each event in history corresponds to a like event in another dimension of Time and Space. For there are, he says, three ages: the Age of the Father, which is revealed in the Old Testament; the Age of the Son, revealed in the New, which is that which we presently inhabit; and the Age of the Spirit, which is to come.

To follow his argument is to plunge into deep waters, for which you, my Prince, are not yet prepared. So I say now only that there is good matter in it, though his dating be at fault, since there is no evidence now of a reformed Church, but rather of one immured in ever deeper corruption, from which we may pray to be delivered.

Arthur saw that his companions slept. He took a blanket and laid it over Cal, whose thin face lost in sleep the anxious look it wore in waking hours.

For a long time he remained wakeful himself, his mind racing as he sought to fix in it all that the strange unknown had said. He gazed at the stars where if he calculated right he might read his destiny. He heard the long searching cry of the barn-owl, and the distant barking of dogs.

'Truly,' he said to himself, 'when we are at peace, this world is marvel-stocked. Truly, if peace could be established, all would be good . . .'

Then he thought of Peredur and the pleasures he had enjoyed

with him, and of the Princess at the inn and the delight he had known there. And then he slept, and in his sleep, he dreamed.

He dreamed, as he often did, that Merlin had come to him and taken him by the hand and raised him from the couch of flowers where he lay. Merlin was dressed in a long robe that hung in folds like a carved garment on a statue; and for once Merlin was silent. Even in his dream Arthur remarked on the strangeness of this: that Merlin should not be busy instructing him. Instead, Merlin turned away and Arthur followed him. They were in an open space, bounded on three sides by a cloister; and the moon shone on them through the arches of the cloister. Then they walked, still silent, into open country and the moonlight dappled the fields. Now Arthur saw that the fields were alive with animals: horses, white cattle, lions, tigers, wolves, deer and foxes; and there was neither fear nor fierceness among them, and in a little hollow a lion cub lay with a lamb. All was still and silent as, in the east, the grey of night was touched with the pink and streaks of red of the rising sun. Then all the animals – and Arthur now saw that there were serpents and dragons there too – lifted their heads towards the sun, as if in adoration. It was as if they knew, like the sun, that the dark was behind them and the dark age of the world was passing away; and when, for a moment, all as one, they bowed their heads, it seemed as if they were acceding to its passing. So, again, they raised their eyes to the sun, which now stood like a golden ball above the eastern hills, and Arthur knew that they were offering a welcome to a new age of peace and abundance.

He woke and it was still night. But the owl was distant now, its cry dying away. And he thought, 'Merlin talked much and often of mysteries, but really there are only three: where we came from, whither we are going and, since we are not solitary but members of a family that, as my dream suggests, includes the animals as well, how we should live with each other.'

'The questions', he said dreamily, 'are easy, but the answers? Well, it is to discover the answers that we live.'

Then he heard once more the faint dying cry of the barn-owl and remembered what Merlin had told him: that the Greeks declared the owl to belong to the Goddess of Wisdom. 'The Romans called her Minerva,' he had said, 'but I cannot recall her Greek name.' Trying to do so, he fell at last soundly asleep.

And when he woke it was bright day, and he was alone with Cal in the ruined and deserted town.

BOOK TWO

I

If, my Prince, you take this pair of compasses and place one leg on London, the city of Caesar as some say, and with the pencil attached to the other inscribe an arc, you will find that the division of Britain thus effected leaves the high land to the north and west of the arc, and the rich lowlands to the south and east. And in those days the lowlands were surrendered to the Saxons, who were mud-minded and suited to the heavy soil, but the high country was free of them and still obedient to the rule of Uther Pendragon, whom some called emperor and others king. In truth, this obedience was in little more than name, for Uther Pendragon, though in appearance dignified and even noble, and to his immediate household overpowering, was of feeble character, infirm will and dull wit. Nevertheless, all those who thought of themselves still as Romans or free Britons acknowledged him and swore allegiance to him, even if in practice they paid little heed to his command, evaded the taxes which he tried to levy and went their own way, each petty baron exercising government over the hills and valleys which his castle commanded and which his own armed retinue could compel to obedience. In short, they enjoyed that perfect liberty which is possible only when there is no true monarchy.

It were wearisome to list their wars, which were little more than squabbles, or, in the manner of a tribal bard, to recount their genealogies, which were for the most part imaginary. But everyone knew the genealogy of Uther Pendragon, son of Marcus and descended from Caesar and Romulus and Aeneas, and some said also that Brutus, a cousin of Aeneas and, like him, a Trojan

Prince who had fled the burning towers of Ilium; and also, as some had it, Jupiter himself and Venus, Goddess of Love, and, as others insisted, the Archangel Michael.

And you are not to scoff at these genealogies, my Prince, for I must remind you that you yourself claim descent from Wotan, whom some call Woden, who is himself in the direct line from Noah.

Be that as it may, when the word came that Uther Pendragon was dead, it was as if a mighty hand had laid a pall of darkness over Britain.

In passing, I must also tell you that his great rival Vortigern, too, was dead. Having trusted in the Saxons whom he had invited into the land, he was fully repaid for his folly. The egregious Geoffrey of Monmouth tells us he was besieged by Aurelius Ambrosius and burned alive in the tower which he had built. But this was not so, for the simple reason that, first, Aurelius Ambrosius died before Vortigern and, second, that it was the Saxons who put him to death, because they suspected him of treachery. And the manner of his death was this: he was boiled in a cauldron of oil, after years of imprisonment.

Now at the time when Uther Pendragon died, Arthur, as I earlier related, had been living for some time in the castle in the West where none knew who he was or what his heredity. With Cal he had arrived there and taken service; and this he did on the instructions of Merlin who saw that it was necessary that he remain concealed for a time. Moreover, as Merlin said, 'It is meet that you learn what it is to be one of the humble' and cuffed Arthur on the head when the boy suggested that his time and Cal's, in the castle of Old Stoneface and his son, Sir Cade, had already given him sufficient experience of that. 'Experience', he added, 'such as I have no wish to repeat, but burn only to revenge.'

'There will be time enough for that,' Merlin said. 'Now do as you are told.'

So Arthur obeyed and, with his friend Cal, suffered slights and derision, kicks and cuffs and blows on the head, from Sir Kay and the knights who surrounded him. They were all, as Arthur soon understood, poor types: braggarts, bullies, louder in speech than bold in battle.

He said to Cal, 'I have a pattern of knighthood in my mind and these fellows have no place in it.'

'For my part,' Cal replied, 'I have yet to meet a knight who wasn't a brute and bitch.'

In Scotland, I must tell you, we do not restrict the appellation 'bitch' to the female sex, but apply it indifferently to men and women; and this was the practice throughout Britain in Arthur's time. Sometimes the word may be used affectionately between friends; but that was not how Cal employed it. He suffered more than Arthur at the hands of most of the knights because they saw that he was afraid of them. Yet Arthur's persecution was no less, for the stronger and most brutal of the knights resented his spirit and took all the greater pleasure in trying to break it. And none did this with more zest than Sir Kay himself. He took an especial delight in correcting Arthur and chastising him; yet occasionally Arthur saw in his face an expression of bemusement, as if it had occurred to him that he, Arthur, might not be what he seemed to be.

In these months, in a mean and sordid castle, listening in the hall to knights who boasted in their cups of the mighty deeds they had accomplished and of how they would drive the Saxons from the land, but who by day were as timid as they had been bold in the evening, and whose battles against the Saxons were all either in a past, which they transmuted and embellished, or in a future which never arrived, Arthur came to be a judge of men and their character. He learned to despise those whom he termed 'blowhards', who were strong only when their victims were weak. In truth, he came close to feeling contempt for the very race of Man, and might have succumbed to this temptation had he not been mindful of the heroes of antiquity to whom Merlin had introduced him in history and poetry. Moreover, he was saved from cynicism by his experience of the fortitude of humble people he had met on his travels and his awareness of the virtue he had found in such as Cal and Peredur, and also in the man he knew only as the Goloshan.

So he survived, bruised certainly in spirit as well as in body, wary and sceptical of much, yet retaining in his innermost being a sense of reverence for the world about him and the certainty that virtue would prevail. This certainty may be accounted a delusion, by those who have read widely in the annals of history which is, it often seems, little more than a record of the crime and follies of mankind; yet he may be forgiven it, for he was still young, and it is proper that youth should be innocent and hold to virtuous ideals.

When word came of the King's death, many feared civil war, others that the Saxons would seize the moment to complete their conquest of the island. It was on account of these apprehensions that men listened to the message that Merlin brought.

He pronounced the will of the dead King and, though there were some who recalled that Uther Pendragon himself had sent Merlin into exile, and though the bishops denounced him as a pagan wizard and necromancer fit only to be arraigned for heresy and burned at the stake (which is that agreeable means by which Holy Church maintains its monopoly of the truth and enforces obedience, forbidding free thought), yet Merlin's voice was so full of authority, and his device for settling the succession so ingenious, that his will prevailed. And it should be said that he declared that it was Uther Pendragon's will that his successor should be he who could draw the sword from the stone. Since every knight believed himself capable of doing so, none chose to dissent; and the only point of contention was the order in which the attempt should be made. But Merlin decreed that they should draw lots and all were eager for the contest to begin before the King of Orkney could arrive to try to draw the stone.

When all was settled Merlin sought out Arthur. He led him to the castle roof and bade him sit in the shadow of a turret by the battlements looking to the north. When he had ensured that there was none who might overhear him, he spoke as follows.

'Dear boy,' he said, 'the longed-for hour is upon us, that hour for which I have prepared you. It is now time first to reveal what I have kept hidden from you. You have often asked me to divulge the secret of your birth and I have declined to oblige. Do not blame me for this. In truth, I kept the secret for your protection. But now I must tell you that you are of royal blood and are indeed the son, and the only living son, of the King who is no more, Uther Pendragon himself. As such, you are destined to be his heir and King in his stead. It is therefore you who will succeed in drawing the sword from the stone.'

Arthur heard these words but made no reply. He raised his chin, as one who issues a challenge might, and looked beyond Merlin to the northern sky in which the first stars of night were appearing.

'Did you hear what I said, boy?'

'Oh yes, I heard you, Merlin. I always hear you. But this time your words make little sense to me. You know my position in this household, for it was by your command that I . . .' He paused and laughed. 'So what you say is ridiculous. There is no chance that I shall be permitted even to try to draw the sword. If I even present myself as a candidate, Sir Kay will cuff me and kick me into the dirt . . .'

'Nevertheless,' Merlin said, 'when all others have failed, you shall succeed.'

Now, as you know, my Prince, all unfolded as Merlin promised, and so Arthur was hailed as King. But since you are given by nature and also, if I may speak proudly, as a result of the education I have given you, to a speculative and sceptical turn of mind, which takes nothing on trust or unexamined, you will wonder how this could be.

For some the simple explanation – magic – would be sufficient. Most men believe in magic and are encouraged in this delusion by Holy Church, which teaches of miracles wrought by Christ and by the saints who, nevertheless, were but men as I am. Indeed, I am reputed by some to be a magician myself, which accusation is mere malice and slander, at least as the word magician is vulgarly understood. This you will understand, for I have often told you that I cannot transform a staff into a serpent, or perform any of these nonsensical acts credited to magicians who are all frauds when they are not only self-deceivers.

To say this is not to deny that what many ignorantly call magic is a science, such as I practise, that is of great antiquity and worthy of the most profound study. There is bad magic, which is mere fraudulent trickery such as is employed by conjurers and jugglers, and there is good magic which is otherwise termed natural philosophy. And this depends on the study of the mathematical and mechanical arts, and of learned books such as the Cabbala in which you may discover how to invoke the sacred names of angels to effect the transmutation of matter. Now Merlin, though it delighted him at times to dazzle the vulgar by childish tricks (which was shame on him, I say as a scientist and scholar), had nevertheless read deeply in the book of knowledge which is all creation and was a master of the mathematical arts by which the world is moved.

Those who think he cast a spell on the sword in the stone that might not be lifted till Arthur advanced to try it err deeply; for the notion is childish. But that he had by his mastery of mathematics and the mechanical arts ensured that it could not be freed from the stone but by one who had been admitted to the secret that retained it there is mere common sense.

Therefore, if you choose to believe that Arthur succeeded where others had failed only because he had been admitted to knowledge of what prevented its release, and that this was a form of that magic which is properly termed natural philosophy, you are wise in your judgement.

Nevertheless, to the general, among whom I include the ignorant and unlettered kings, barons and knights there assembled, as well as the common people, his triumph seemed magic of the most vulgar kind – that is, a miracle; and they were impressed and abashed. And if you ask why Merlin should have gone to such lengths to ensure that Arthur was eagerly accepted as King, by all save King Lot who was consumed by jealousy and therefore deprived of reason and those who followed him, the explanation is simple.

Merlin knew that men are governed by imagination and by their fears. And what could so certainly persuade them to accept a mere boy, unproved in battle, slim and unwarlike in appearance, springing as they thought from humble stock and certainly appearing as one of lowly condition, as the evidence of their eyes: that he was possessed of an unfathomable power, beyond nature and therefore terrifying? For Merlin knew also that most men are fools and that to win their minds you must play on their folly.

II

King Lot, having sent the young Arthur tumbling to the ground with one blow of his mailed fist and threatened war in Britain, spat at the boy, turned on his heel and marched from the churchyard. And not only his own retinue followed him, but many other knights also, either because they too were offended or disgusted by what seemed to them trickery, or because they had immediately, without reflection, judged that from any such war Lot must emerge victor.

Meanwhile Arthur was left on his knees in the dirt. Blood trickled from the corner of his mouth. He shook his head as one who is dazed.

The crowd watched him in nervous silence. He seemed to them mean, weak, defenceless. Some felt pity, others contempt. 'This, then,' the murmur went, incredulous, 'is our King?'

Very slowly he got to his feet and again shook his head. His hand went to his bruised lip and touched the blood that still dripped from it.

Then he smiled. 'A man who cannot govern his temper is not fit to govern a kingdom,' he said. 'King Lot will live to regret what he has done today.'

He called Sir Kay to him and looked him in the eye till that knight, who had been used to cuff him and chastise him, fell, subdued by that royal gaze, to his knees and Arthur held out his hand for him to kiss.

'I shan't ask you', Arthur said, 'if all is ready for the feast this evening to celebrate the election of the King, for I know it is, having myself been engaged in the humble duty of preparation. But I observe that some of those knights who were expected to attend have left us, and of course the King of Orkney and his retinue also. Therefore I command you to choose among the good people of the town who have hailed me as their King and select a number to take the place of those knights who have put themselves in rebellion . . .'

Sir Kay hesitated. He blushed till his face was red as a radish. He swallowed twice and then, in a voice choked with resentment mingled perhaps with apprehension, said, 'It shall be done . . . Your Grace.'

Arthur then retired to the royal chamber, taking only Cal with him.

When they were alone, Cal said, 'What does this mean?'

'That I have come into my right.'

Cal shook his head. 'I don't know as it makes sense to me. What do I call you now?'

'When we are alone, it is as it always has been. How could you suppose otherwise? In public . . . I don't know. What did Sir Kay call me? "Your Grace" was it? But I would guess you couldn't pronounce the words without laughing. Cheer up, Cal. It's not a disaster that has overtaken us.'

'Isn't it?' Cal said. 'Well, if you say it isn't . . . but if you want my opinion, we should get out of here and take to the road again before someone sticks a sword in your neck.'

'No one will do that. Not yet, anyway.' He put his arm round Cal and hugged him. 'It's still you and me against the world,' he said. 'And now I think I shall take a bath. For I am a Roman, as well as King.' He smiled. 'And we must get you some clothes suitable for your position as the King's friend and adviser.'

Before descending to the feast in the Great Hall, Arthur summoned Sir Kay.

The knight looked sheepish, began to offer stumbling apologies for his treatment of Arthur. If he had only known . . .

'Indeed,' Arthur said, 'we should all act more wisely if we knew more than we do. But since we don't there's no more to be said, except this: that I trust you will in future treat any boy or youth in my household more kindly than you hitherto used me. That and that alone – the need to curb your ill temper – will be your only penance. Now, to other matters. How many have deserted us and followed Lot?'

'A good half the company, I fear.'

'Then let it be known that we are well rid of them. The fewer we are, the greater share of honour we shall win. Tomorrow I shall hold a council where the war that will be forced on us may be considered. Tonight we feast. Tomorrow also you must tell me what plans are made for my coronation. In the circumstances, the sooner the better. Some who might be tempted to desert us may hesitate to rebel against a crowned and anointed king. Don't you think so?'

'As . . . Your Grace says . . .'

Sir Kay, though rude and brutal of speech, a braggart and bully, yet possessed one quality that is both rare and valuable; competence. His household ran smoothly, if oiled by fear rather than respect. So the feast planned to celebrate the election of the new King was a fine affair. There might be dearth in the land. The peasantry might labour under heavy burdens and suffer great hardship. The roads might be infested with brigands, broken men, ruined, many of them, by war. Widows and fatherless infants might beg for bread. But in Sir Kay's castle that night there was abundance. They feasted on swan and wild geese, haunches of venison, carp from the fish ponds, barons of beef from cattle carefully guarded from those who would steal them, fine pastries and cheeses, and tarts rich in apples and candied fruits. There was wine from Gascony, beer brewed in the castle brewery, cider from the west and mead from monasteries.

Yet for some time the mood was sombre. All felt the oppression of spirits which dread induces. All knew that the elevation of Arthur had placed those who had not deserted him in great danger. Fear of King Lot's vengeance was now allied to fear of the Saxons and indeed, many shivered at the thought that the King of Orkney was indeed likely to join himself to the Saxons and divide the land with them.

Cal, sitting at Arthur's left hand, sensed the apprehension in the hall. Unable to eat, he nibbled cheese, gulped wine and his eyes flickered over the company as if they sought out those who could not be trusted but might seek to win favour from Lot by bringing him Arthur's head. He glanced beyond Arthur at Sir Kay: the sweat stood out on his temples and he looked darkly. 'He fears he has backed the wrong horse in the race,' Cal thought. 'He cannot be trusted.'

A harpist sang of the great deeds of heroes long departed, yet his music could not banish gloom from the hall.

Then Arthur rose to speak and this is what he said.

'You know me for what I was, not for what I am and shall be. There was a land menaced by a fierce dragon and its Queen was imprisoned in a well-guarded tower by a necromancer. The land was laid waste by the dragon's breath and all feared that the Queen herself was in great danger, for it was known that the dragon was in the service of the evil magician. Word of this was brought to a noble knight, whose name was George. And so he rode forth braving all perils and came to the wasteland. At the edge of the forest he encountered the dragon, which breathed fire on him that he might be destroyed. But he raised his shield against the flame and, advancing with his sword in his right hand, struck the dragon a great blow on the neck and forced it to the ground where he placed his foot on its shoulders and cut off its head. Then he advanced to the bridge that led to the tower, where the magician would have denied him entry. But he defied his knavish tricks and beat down the door, and took the magician captive, despising his false magic, and set the Queen free. Now this knight who slew the dragon and rescued the Queen was St George and the land in which he did these noble deeds was Britain. And I myself, even Arthur, though I be but young, have dedicated myself to the service of St George and of Britain. And, in the Saint's name and with the help of the noble knights here gathered, I shall free Britain of the dragon that is the Saxons and take captive the false magician who is King Lot of Orkney.'

So, when he had spoken, all were comforted and encouraged, and raised a great cry of acclamation. And then they retired for the night.

When they were in the royal chamber, Cal said, 'Those were fine words, bravely spoken, but, as my grandmother used to say, fine words butter no parsnips, and in any case all I could think of was what a fine actor you showed yourself when we were in the troupe that played comedies. But what we are to do to get out of this mess is more than I can fathom . . .'

Arthur laughed. 'What would I do without you? Just when I was in danger of believing my own rhetoric, you throw cold water on it. Indeed, my dear Cal, this was, as I know very well, but the first step. But let me give you another saying, which Merlin told me is proverbial in Gaul: it is only the first step that counts.'

'That may be a proverb, but it still makes no sense to me. Once again, I say let's slip away while we can and take to the road. Any hardships and dangers we have known are nothing to what's like to be in store for us if we persist with this play-acting . . .'

'Play-acting,' Arthur said . . . 'talking of that, I am sending out messengers to seek out Peredur and the Goloshan and bring them here. We certainly need all the friends we have.'

Seeing Cal frown, he added, 'Now don't be silly. I know you are jealous of Peredur and I confess I love him. But you know well that I love you too, if in a different manner. And as for the Goloshan, he's the wisest man I know except for Merlin and I value his counsel.'

'Why shouldn't I be jealous?' Cal said. 'But I'm not silly. If you and Peredur carry on as you did before, what do you think these barons and knights will make of it? And do you think they will be pleased if you take a play-actor as your councillor. And as for that Merlin you speak of, where has he got to? He's responsible for this fine mess, if you ask me, and now he seems to have slipped away. Why? Answer me that, if you can.'

'You do fuss,' Arthur said. 'There will be no trouble about Peredur and the Goloshan. As for Merlin's disappearance, that's his way. Provoking certainly. But when he appears again, he'll tell me that he was setting me a test by leaving me to my own devices. Now let's go to sleep. We've a lot to do in the morning.'

III

It was a cold spring, depressing spirits. It rained for weeks. The land was awash with water. Rivers flooded. Mud choked even the roads that the Romans had built. The word came that King Lot had indeed made an alliance with the Saxons and that a mighty army was being collected. Sniffing the wind, more fainthearts deserted Arthur.

'How can you keep so cheerful?' Cal asked him.

'If I don't show myself cheerful we are truly lost,' Arthur said.

Cal shook his head. 'I'll die with you, but I'd rather have had a long life.'

Peredur and the Goloshan arrived. Arthur embraced them both.

'We met few coming this way, many hurrying to join your enemies,' the Goloshan said.

'And yet you came.'

'There's an old kind of theatre called tragedy. I've always had a notion to play it.'

Arthur recognised irony in his friend's tone. He said, 'You'll have to wait. I have a task for you. You are the most ingenious deviser of plots that I know. I want you to direct your intelligence to the situation we are in.'

'Intelligence is the right word,' the Goloshan said. 'In all the works of history I have read, failure of intelligence has been the chief cause of calamity. If you have read your Livy, you will know that it was failure of intelligence that led the Romans into the disaster of Cannae.'

'Precisely,' Arthur said. 'I want you here as my chief of staff. I think I'd better make you a knight.'

So the Goloshan knelt, and Arthur touched him on the shoulder with his sword and said, 'You'd better have a new name. What shall it be? Hector, I think. He was the finest of the Trojans who were my ancestors.'

'No,' said the Goloshan, 'for that would be ill omen, seeing how Hector died and Troy was burned. I'll take a Greek name and, in self-flattery, will be Nestor, if you permit it, for Homer always prefaces his name with the adjective "wise". And this amuses me.'

'As you will,' Arthur said. 'Arise, then, Sir Nestor.'

Then Arthur also knighted Peredur, because he loved him, and would have knighted Cal also, but he refused, saying it was foolishness and that, when they were defeated and had to flee, he would rather not be burdened with knighthood. But the truth was that Cal's jealousy of Peredur had been revived and was more intense because Arthur lay with him. Yet Arthur denied Cal nothing and would have granted him whatever he sought.

Though Arthur trusted much in the Goloshan, or Sir Nestor as I must now call him, he did not neglect to include other knights, and notably Sir Kay and Sir Bedivere, in his councils, for he knew how necessary it was that he should retain their support. And this was the more essential since knights continued to desert him and attach themselves to King Lot and even his Saxon allies.

Meanwhile there was no sign of Merlin, and this puzzled Arthur and dismayed others.

Cal said, 'It was Merlin got you into this mess and now he's buggered off. Fine friend you have there, if you ask me.'

When Arthur had taken counsel, he drew Sir Nestor, as now was, aside and said, 'It appears to me that nobody except us, and of course our dear Peredur, believes that we can defeat our enemies. They are certainly more numerous than we are. So what do you suggest?'

Sir Nestor said, 'As a boy I used to hunt birds. And I have often noticed that if a game bird has young chicks, she will pretend to have a broken wing and so lead the hunters to follow her as she scurries in search of cover, always drawing them away from her nest till they are so far removed that she knows her young ones are safe, and only then does she take wing.'

Arthur considered these words and understood their meaning. So he made his plans for the campaign accordingly.

The rains stopped and the wind blew hard from the east, drying the land, and word came that the army of King Lot and his allies was advancing.

One night, as Arthur slept, Merlin came to him and commanded him to rise. He said, 'You have done well, my son, and I have come with gifts for you and with advice.'

So he gave him first a shirt of mail which he had caused an elvish smith to fashion for him from steel mesh; and its name was Wygar. Then he put a sword in his hand, which had been forged in the lake isle of Avalon and which possessed, he said, magic powers; and its name was Excalibur.

And the advice he gave was this: that Arthur should trust in speed and not in strength; that he should ride the land as a ship glides across the waves, and they should travel in silence, with no words spoken, that the enemy might be surprised.

As Merlin spoke, Peredur too rose from the couch which he shared with Arthur and rubbed sleep from his lovely eyes. Merlin saw him and was seized with lust, for, as some say, his father was the Devil. So he cast a spell over Peredur and, when he departed, the boy followed him. But others say that he did this not on account of lust alone, but so that Arthur should not be distracted from his duty to wage war on his enemies, and so that men should not despise him because he seemed to prefer a handsome youth to the fairest of maidens. Be that as it may, from this day onwards Arthur did not lie again with a boy or a young man, though in time to come many handsome youths of surpassing beauty presented themselves at his court and sought his favour. Though the departure of Peredur caused him heartbreak, he understood the lesson that Merlin sought to impart: that to be a hero requires self-sacrifice and abstention from a vice that many brave men despise. Truly, as a wise and virtuous bishop has said, those wicked souls who indulge in that horrible sin of seeking carnal pleasure with boys and young men rather than with girls and women, who may be led into married bliss, will burn most painfully on the Day of Judgement, and suffer eternal torment on account of their lewd and foul practices.

IV

Before I embark on the time of Arthur's greatness, let me discourse briefly on warfare and the art of war. Though I have not myself borne weapons since I was a youth – happy days when I participated in cattle-reiving raids across the English Border, and would pass days and nights without sleep, riding my dark-grey Galloway for hours on end so that we seemed to be not man and beast, but a hybrid like the Centaurs of antiquity – but I digress. Let me return to the matter of my discourse.

Though, as I say, I have not borne weapons since I was a youth – once then, in a raid, carrying off, as I recall, a fat English abbot, a chest of gold, and a round dozen quaking monks, whose bodyguard we had put to flight . . . but again I digress, a slave to tender memories.

Where was I? Yes . . . though I have not borne weapons since I was a youth when on another occasion . . . but let that pass and let me say simply that, throughout my life I have never ceased to be a student of war, its causes, purpose and the manner of its waging.

Therefore it is meet that I should give you the fruits of my study, for an emperor is, as the word in its original Latin form makes clear, one who commands, especially in war. So, my Prince, gentle as is your nature, devoted as you are to your studies, you cannot escape your destiny, which is to command armies in battle and conduct campaigns.

And it is my earnest hope that you may learn something of the art of war from a study of the wars fought by Arthur, than whom you cannot in all history find a more fitting or more noble model, except as may be Alexander and Caesar himself. Nor in all heroic literature will you come upon one more to be admired than Arthur, for he excels even Achilles in ardour, outstrips him in constancy and is his equal in courage.

But first my reflections, which you will heed well, if you wish to please me.

Man, according to the great Greek philosopher Aristotle, whose works I have myself translated into our own learned tongue, is a political animal. If I may again digress, but only for an instant: it will be a fine day when the narrow-minded bigots in the papal curia come to understand this simple, and indeed self-evident, truth.

As a political animal, civilised man seeks to avoid war. We call the process by which he attempts this diplomacy. It is, by the way, a common error to suppose that diplomacy can be practised only between two civilised states or kingdoms. What I have to tell you of Arthur will demonstrate that this belief is a fallacy.

Nevertheless, diplomacy often fails. This is first because many men are stupid and unable to recognise where their own best interests lie. In almost all cases war is avoidable if both parties are intelligent and capable of rational thought. But of course this is a rare conjunction. Furthermore, there are other occasions on which diplomacy fails because two parties in a quarrel have opinions or interests which cannot be reconciled one with the other. In such cases there is no remedy save force. And this is why one may state that every society is founded on the death of men.

Being, as Aristotle – to whose works I shall soon introduce you when I have completed and revised my translations – being, as Aristotle says, a political animal, man is also a warmaker. For, in conditions such as I have described, war may be defined as the continuation of political argument by other means; and this is true even of such wars as have been dignified with the name of crusade.

War is then natural, man being by nature a warmaker. But herein lies a paradox, for it is not natural to fight war as men must; that is, to the death. It is not natural to be a Spartan.

Have I told you that story? Let me tell it again.

When the great King of Persia made war on the cities of Greece, it fell to the men of Sparta, a state which may most accurately be termed a republic in arms, to hold the pass of Thermopylae in Thessaly, which is also called the Gate of Eastern Greece. Though betrayed and taken in the rear after two days' battle in the course of which they had inflicted heavy losses on the Persians, the Spartans and their general Leonidas refused either to surrender or to attempt flight. Instead, they held their ground till the last of the three hundred men was killed.

And this is their epitaph, addressed to all who enter the pass:

> Go, tell the Spartans, thou that passeth by
> That here, obedient to their laws, we lie . . .

Fine stuff. Noble words, which I would have you learn by heart. The fortitude of these Spartans . . . my eyes fill with tears when I think of it. It was magnificent, but it was not natural.

What does nature prompt us to do when we are faced with mortal danger?

It prompts us to run away. Nature argues for flight, for cowardice, for self-interest, for what the real Romans of today, the inhabitants of the quarter called Trastevere, call 'looking after number one' – that is, yourself.

Such are the urgings of nature, as my hero Arthur was to discover in the first battles of his wars against the Saxons, and King Lot and his allies. Heavily outnumbered, Arthur's armies took one look at the enemy and turned tail. There was nothing he could do to prevent them. Your grandfather, the red-bearded Emperor, might have managed to halt such a flight, for he had the presence whence he derived an authority that caused men to freeze when he addressed them. But even this is questionable. There was one battle, I believe, in which he laid about, striking his fleeing infantry with the flat of his great broadsword and crying out, 'Dogs, would you live for ever?' As it happened, according to my witness, they did not stay to answer his question, but their actions were answer enough. They ran away as fast as their legs could carry them and, if some lived to fight another day, it's quite likely that if the battle turned against them they ran away again. Cowardice is a habit like any other.

Arthur, too, found this out, in the most painful way you can conceive.

It so happened that word was brought by scouts whom, following Sir Nestor's advice, Arthur had deployed at the furthest extremity of the small territory which he then controlled, and they reported that a band of knights and men-at-arms had been seen riding from the north, with the purpose, as it seemed, of joining themselves either to the Saxons or to the great army which King Lot was assembling in the east midlands. Arthur therefore gave orders that his men should ride out to intercept this band and disarm them. And he himself led the advance, with his crownlet on his helmet and riding a fine dark bay mare whose name was Jubilee.

They rode briskly and Arthur's men were filled with happy expectancy. All were pleased that after weeks of hard training, they should now be on the point of engaging in action.

They passed through a dark forest and came out on to a rolling landscape, what the English call downland, a place of grassy hills and gentle valleys, pastoral country, though in these evil times the peasants had abandoned sheep farming.

A hawk hovered in the sky above them and Sir Kay, riding at Arthur's right hand, hailed this as a good omen. They jangled along the floor of the valley by a bubbling stream and some of the younger knights began to sing to express their joy. It was as if they were riding to a carnival, not a battle.

But then, as the valley veered to the south, there came cries from the northern hillside, and a squadron of cavalry descended it at a smart sharp trot, their lances at rest and all keeping good order. There was no time for Arthur to deploy his men. The surprise was absolute. They were taken in the flank and first rolled backwards, then thrown into utter confusion. The terrible cry 'every man for himself' was raised. Some of the troop turned and fled. Sir Kay, who for all his faults of character lacked nothing in courage, pulled his horse's head round, lowered his lance and charged the advancing line. His effort was not in vain, for he broke through the enemy line but, having done so, found himself isolated and judged retreat – or rather, flight – the wisest if not the most honourable course.

As for Arthur, he sat for a moment amazed as if he did not grasp what was happening. One of the enemy seized his horse's bridle and would have led him off a prisoner. But Arthur, with a spurt of courage, first thrust at the man's chest with his sword, then brought it down on the wrist, cutting clean through the bone.

For a moment the severed hand retained its grip on the leather, while the knight screamed in pain. Alarmed, either by the blows or the noise, Jubilee reared up and Arthur, already thrown off balance, fell heavily to the ground and lay ignominiously in the stream. Dazed, he staggered to his feet, to see Jubilee disappearing in the direction of home. He looked around. All was confusion. Panting with agitation and – it must be confessed – fear, he did not even notice that he had lost his helmet and that the little crown that had surmounted it was lying in the mud by the side of the stream. He turned and ran, awkwardly, as men in armour must run. His breath came painfully. Once he had to dive into a gorse bush as a knight riding behind him tried to cut him down before being carried beyond him by a horse out of control. Then Arthur saw a mill ahead of him and made for it. It was cool and dark within. He threw himself behind a wall made of sacks of meal and lay there, biting his lip to prevent himself from betraying himself by the sound of sobs. These at last subsided. The noise of battle rolled away. How long he stayed there he could not tell, but as he recovered his breath, he surrendered to bitter self-reproach. His first battle, no more than a skirmish really, and he had shown himself a coward. He felt warm dampness between his legs and knew that he had pissed himself. How long he lay there he could never tell, but dark was beginning to fall when he crept out from behind his wall of sacks, and dared to return from refuge to the world.

As it happened, by great good fortune, he found Jubilee grazing at the edge of a wood, as if the world were at peace. She allowed herself to be caught and nuzzled his face. He mounted and rode warily back to the castle. The drawbridge was raised and he had difficulty in persuading the sentry to lower it.

Men sat around the courtyard, disconsolate, nervous, ashamed. There was no cry of greeting for the King. When Cal came to him in his chamber, Arthur was again weeping.

Cal said, 'Now will you listen to me? It's time to give up this play-acting and save our skins while we still have them.'

Arthur raised a tear-stained face. 'No,' he said, 'I am the King. I have disgraced myself today. Nevertheless I am the King.'

V

Arthur held a council of his chief barons and knights. Some were angry, others despondent. All knew that since the skirmish in the downs desertion had been rife. So now some argued that they should make terms with King Lot.

'I know Lot,' one, Sir Lucan, said. He was a grey-bearded knight, formerly a favourite of King Vortigern and, as certain rumour mongers had it, in his youth Vortigern's catamite; later, his pander. This first was, Cal thought, a charge which the knight's looks now made hard to believe. 'I know Lot,' Sir Lucan repeated. 'He's not one for parley. It's true he's crooked as an ancient yew tree, but he will never make an agreement that requires him to yield an inch. He wants to be King, and he will be King. In my opinion' – and he looked Arthur straight in the face – 'young feller-me-lad here should resign the crown to him. And if he does that, I'll use all my influence with Lot, whom, as I say, I know of old and have fought battles at the side of, to endeavour to persuade him to grant pardons to all who have accepted Arthur as King . . . And' – he nodded at Arthur – 'I'll do as much for you, though I'm bound to say, fearing no man as I do, that at the very least he will command that you be stripped of all the appurtenances of knighthood and that you withdraw to a monastery.'

Arthur did not drop his gaze, though all saw him flush either with anger or embarrassment. 'Perhaps', he said, 'you think that Lot will also order that I be gelded.' He paused, then looked around the company and was grieved to see how few would meet his eyes.

Then he spoke, very quietly and as if sorrowfully, and his voice was level. 'I am the King,' he said, 'crowned and anointed, the King to whom you have all sworn to be loyal. I drew the sword from the stone and did so after Lot, exerting all his strength, had failed. And now you would desert me . . .'

'We could not desert you if you had not first deserted your men in battle.'

The speaker was a young knight, Sir Cathal. He wore a blood-stained bandage on his forehead, for he had been wounded in the skirmish, and the harsh contempt in his voice brought a quiver to Arthur's lip.

'Nevertheless,' Arthur said, 'I drew the sword from the stone.'

In the silence which followed he heard the weakness of his argument and sensed the departure of sympathy.

'As to that, as to that.' The new speaker was the Archbishop, a man with the yellow eyes of a hawk and a reputation as a skilled equivocator. 'As to that,' he said again and drummed his bony fingers on the council table, 'I must confess that I never approved that test. Indeed, I argued against it. There was, I said, something pagan, something uncanny, about it. In a very real manner of speaking, it was not the way such things ought to be done. There was, if I may employ a vulgar colloquialism, something fishy about it.'

'Deuced fishy,' Sir Lucan said. 'That fellow Merlin had a hand in it, I'll be bound.'

'Merlin?' said the Archbishop. 'I fear you may be right. A man one could never trust, evasive, dishonest and either pagan or heretic. He has always had protectors in high places, but if I had my way, which I may yet, which indeed I may yet, the place he'll find himself in is the dock – the dock of an ecclesiastical court, that is. And the charge? The charge, my lords, would be witchcraft. This being so, as it most incontrovertibly is, why then it is my considered opinion that we may properly disregard the evidence of the sword in the stone and proceed accordingly.'

Arthur looked round the table. Some nodded, others, sensing his scrutiny, averted their eyes.

The Archbishop said, 'There is a very suitable monastery on the isle of Anglesey which some call Mona . . .'

Arthur said, 'I take the sense of the meeting and must consider it in private. Therefore I adjourn it till this hour tomorrow, when I shall deliver my reply. Come, Cal.' And he rose and quickly left the chamber, followed by Cal, Sir Nestor, and leaving the company surprised by the speed with which he had, as they thought, consented to his deposition.

Sir Cathal proposed that men be sent to put Arthur under arrest at once, but the Archbishop advised that this was unnecessary. 'The boy', he said, 'understands that he had been put, or has put himself, in a false position. It is my opinion that he is at heart happy to be relieved of it. There is no reason why he should not be suited to the monastic life. I do not despair of his reformation, provided, always' – he smiled a thin smile – 'he is subjected to the harshest discipline. I shall be happy to take charge of him myself.'

So the meeting broke up, and Sir Lucan drew Sir Cathal aside and bade him ride at once to King Lot's camp, to tell him that all would be well and the castle surrendered to him. 'As for the boy,' he said, 'let the Archbishop think as he will. It keeps him out of mischief. Besides, who knows? We may have a use for the boy yet. Fortune, my young friend, is fickle.'

Cal sat with his head between his knees. 'This is the end,' he said. 'You don't believe all that stuff about a monastery, do you? They're going to kill you. They're going to kill us. Aren't they?'

'Looks that way,' Sir Nestor, formerly the Goloshan, said. He smiled. 'I've died many deaths in the theatre, of course.'

'And lived to tell the tale,' Arthur said. 'Cheer up, Cal. This is the worst we've known, but I remember Merlin telling me that the great Marcus, my grandfather, used to have a saying, "The worst is not yet on us, as long as we can say this is the worst."'

'That's meant to be comforting, I suppose,' Cal said. 'Can't say it comforts me . . .'

'Let me think,' Arthur said.

He withdrew himself from them and retired to a seat in the window.

Meanwhile Sir Nestor poured wine and passed a cup to Cal also. 'Might as well,' he said and began to sing. It is a song that our German students now delight in and this may have been the moment of its first singing. *Meum est propositum, in taberna mori*, it begins and the former Goloshan sang it gently, melodiously, in a voice that was at the same time melancholy and defiant.

Arthur sat by the window, looking out at the hills, which were still touched with a golden light that was fading by the minute. His profile was turned to his friends and when Sir Nestor looked up from his drinking he saw that the young King's face was set, and it seemed to him as pure and beautiful as the dawn. Arthur watched the shadows creep darkly over the rolling landscape and bushes assume strange shapes. Jackdaws quarrelled on the battlements above, but beyond all was still when the last crows had settled in the treetops. He saw the emptiness of the land and thought, 'To some night is frightening and to others it represents the peace of God.' He sat there for a long time and looked on the darkening world as if he would draw its silence to his heart. Then the owl called and he remembered it was Minerva's bird.

He thought, 'It's not the end. I am not going to think it is the end.' Then he turned to the others, his two friends, and gave them their orders. He gave them like the King he was determined to be.

VI

In the howdumdeid of night they slipped from the castle by the postern let into the western gate. It was opened for them by a young guard named Dermot who had wept when Sir Nestor told him of the danger that threatened Arthur. 'Gelded and sent to a monastery.' He shuddered; so now, trembling with fear, he aided their escape and came with them, leaving his fellow guards asleep, drugged by the doctored wine with which they had been plied.

There was no moat on that side of the castle, for the rock on which it stood was there precipitous and the gate to be attained only by a winding track, more suited to goats then cavalry horses. Thorn bushes climbed almost to the gate, and the lower slopes were thick with broom and whin. Moving with infinite care, lest they dislodge a boulder and alert any sentries on the battlements to their escape, they descended the hill. Not until they had reached the pine wood below did they pause and listen for sound of any alarmed pursuit. But there was only the sighing of the wind in the topmost branches of the trees.

By dawn they had travelled seven miles from the castle and were weary. Fearing the light, they lay up in a thick wood and with the brackish water of a stream made little cakes from the oatmeal which Sir Nestor carried in a pouch. Then, taking turns to watch, they lay down to rest.

But Arthur could not sleep, or, if he slipped into a half-sleep, words yet ran in his head and strange imaginings disturbed his mind. The land is dragon-ridden, came the message, from where or whom he could not tell. What is the condition of men, he asked himself, or rather heard the question posed. And the answer came, inexorable, harsh: all are prisoners bound in chains, who gaze in misery or bleak indifference on their fellows, some of whom are daily condemned to be killed in the sight of the others.

He remembered, as a man may seek landmarks in thick mist,

how Merlin had spoken to him of the ordeal of Philoctetes, marooned ten years on an inhospitable isle, reduced to rags, dragging his wounded and gangrenous foot, shrieking in wordless misery. 'That', said Merlin, his eyes clouded, 'is the ultimate image of man. Yet we must endure, yet we must strive to . . .'

Strive to what? Arthur could not remember.

'And it is this to be a king?' he thought; for in that moment, while his mind dwelled on horrors, he saw stretched out before him still more horrid reality . . . To be a king, to immerse himself in bloody pitiless war.

Then the thought: 'Am I man enough to be a king?'

When night fell they prepared to move again. They journeyed in silence, uncertain of a destination, alert as wolves for hunters.

And so it was for many days and nights, all the time moving as if guided by a spirit, towards the refuge of the hills.

Throughout these days, grey days on which a cold wind blew, Arthur was denied true sleep even while his fellows sank into the deep slumber of exhaustion; but, now half wakeful, now half dreaming, he turned his mind to questions which ever seemed to slip away from him. It could not be otherwise, for he was young and ignorant of the world, unpractised in philosophy. Yet, dimly he glimpsed, now at the nadir of his fortunes, what was to be his guiding principle: force without reason falls of its own weight; force that is mastered is favoured and advanced by Heaven. The thought came to him and yet he did not, could not, understand its import.

On the seventh night, as dawn broke, they emerged from a forest and stood on a ridge overlooking a valley in which a river lay with mist above the quiet water. A village nestled on its southern bank and, as the light grew, for the first time since they had set out on their travels the sun broke through, as if in welcome.

Arthur said, 'Let us descend and make ourselves known to the people of the village, for we have come to the end of this stage of our journeying.'

The others looked at him in amazement and uncertainty. But he smiled and said, 'Come, we shall be among friends.'

'That's easy to say,' Cal replied. 'But what reason you have for saying it is beyond me.'

'I have dreamed often of this village,' Arthur said and smiled.

So they went down the hill and entered the village, and, as they did so, they were all aware of watchers in the little huts, which were made of branches with mud packed between them.

Arthur, however, paid no heed to the watchers, but advanced with steady stride through what seemed to Cal to be, or to have been, the market place, and he came to the end of the village where the road forked and offered him a choice of paths. One went uphill again, so that Cal sighed to see it; the way was rough and by the stone which marked its beginning there stood a woman. Her face was of a grave and even stern beauty, and she made no sign, neither spoke a word. The other road led, as Cal could see, to a meadow in which many flowers grew and on which the sun shone benignly. Here, too, a woman stood by the stone. When she saw Arthur she lay down on the grass and beckoned to him, and the chestnut tresses of her hair fell over her white shoulders. Her mouth was red as the reddest rose and her eyes were deep pools, blue as the summer sea. She smiled on Arthur and gestured that he should rest by her side, and, as she did so, she drew up her skirts.

But Arthur turned aside and took the other path, and the woman who stood there as sentry gave no sign that she had remarked him. Reluctantly, with many glances at the reclining beauty, and many sighs and heavy hearts, for the meadow beyond was pleasant and fruitful, the three friends followed the King. As they did so, and mounted the rugged path, a chant as if of praise or thanksgiving rose from the village now behind and below them.

So they came to a castle, the gates of which stood open. There were knights and men-at-arms in the courtyard who, when they saw Arthur, hailed him as the King who had returned. And in this way he got himself an army.

VII

Of all the great men whose histories Merlin had made Arthur study, none impressed the boy more than Alexander, King of Macedon and known to all antiquity as 'the Great'. Everything he learned of Alexander filled him with admiration; he loved his audacity and unchained ambition. When he first read Arrian's biography, in a Latin translation, he sighed with longing. 'To have fought by Alexander's side,' he said, 'what supreme happiness.'

Merlin smiled sourly, for in truth he had neither love nor admiration himself for world conquerors and indeed, regarded all military men as belonging to a lower order than philosophers like himself.

In this, I may say, as a philosopher myself, he had doubtless some reason on his side, for the jewels of philosophy are imperishable, while the laurels that crown a conqueror's brow wither. The battles and triumphs of distant ages are like a wind that has blown fiercely, but leaves only a murmured memory behind when it dies away. Alexander and Caesar are in the grave, and their light no longer shines upon men. But the words of the poets and philosophers speak to ages that never knew their authors. Theirs is a fame that conquers time.

Nevertheless, Merlin was wrong to despise the sword and those who bear it; and in his heart he knew this. Moreover, he was fully aware that Arthur, as the grandson of Marcus to whom was handed down the task of restoring Rome in Britain, must be trained in war and in the study of the art of war, poring over Caesar and Arrian and Vegetius, and all those who have written on the subject. It was indeed Merlin who first declared that Arthur must be a second Alexander and taught him also what is the true purpose of war: the establishment of an empire, like that of Augustus, whose people shall be liberated from the fear of war. And yet, so twisted was his nature, on account doubtless of his uncertain birth and wretched childhood, that even while he urged his darling pupil to emulate Alexander, he could not resist the temptation to sneer, and to disparage all conquerors.

Arthur, being wise beyond his years, took what was valuable to him from Merlin's lessons and discarded what was not as dross.

So now, established in this castle, which stood on the site of a Roman camp, by name Trimontium, overlooking the lovely valley of the Tweed, he bethought him of Alexander and of how he might put his knowledge of that great King to present use.

He said, 'We are few and our enemies are many. If they were to join together in one mighty army, we could not resist. They must overwhelm us by sheer weight of number. Therefore we must prevent them from coming together, and attack them severally.'

He said, 'Alexander surrounded himself with armed knights whom he called his Companions. They were united to him in a bond of brotherhood and, while Alexander was pre-eminent, all the Companions were equal, each one to every other. So shall it be with my Companions. And that they may be identified in battle, each will wear a surcoat with the emblem of the rosy cross, over their breastplate of chain-mail.'

'Alexander', he said, 'had also Greek infantry, accustomed to fight at close and deadly quarters in the formation called the phalanx. I lack such men. Therefore I cannot engage in pitched battles such as Alexander fought. But the art of war, as I have learned, consists in adapting method to the means available; and it is in his ability to do this that Alexander may still serve as my model. In the war I have to wage, mobility and surprise must be my watchwords.'

Having come to this conclusion, Arthur chose his Companions, who numbered no more than two hundred; and to each Companion were attached three men-at-arms, whose weapons were the bow and the short stabbing sword, such as the Roman legionaries carried. And so he set smiths to work to forge swords in great numbers and assembled a store of them; and fletchers to make arrows.

Then he summoned leather-workers to him and said, 'I have heard that in the East, where the horse soldiers reign supreme, they have devised an attachment to the saddle which they call the stirrup and this allows the mounted soldier to have a firm seat, bestriding his horse from a high saddle, and so to employ weapons more skilfully.'

Therefore he set the leather-workers to fashion stirrups and the high saddles such as he described; and the smiths to forge body armour, coats of chain-mail, and shields to be worn on the left arm, and lances and sharp-edged swords. Moreover, he had each knight wear a dagger on his belt, that he might have a weapon with which to defend himself, should he be unhorsed.

Arthur himself drilled the Companions in the tactics of sudden war which he intended to employ, and he did this because he alone understood what he wanted. He made the Goloshan, or Sir Nestor as he was now called, his quartermaster, which is a post that many young knights ardent for glory despise, thinking it one that brings its holder no renown. But Arthur said, 'I have learned from Caesar and Vegetius that a single victory rarely decides a war, but that success is determined by the management of a campaign and that this requires that supplies be always available.'

In this he was wise beyond his years, understanding that an army marches on its stomach, and that an archer who exhausts his stock of arrows and is unable to replenish his quiver is of no more use to an army than a knight without a second horse to replace a dead, wounded, or worn-out lame beast.

In the armed camp to which his kingdom had been reduced Arthur inspired all with the means of grace and the hope of glory. Tireless himself (as it seemed, though only Cal knew how the shadow of intense fatigue would cloud his face at night), he drove all hard throughout the winter months; and, when spring came, his little army was ready to take the field. Even Cal, despondent by nature, ever fearing the worst, since that was all he had known, caught something of Arthur's exhilaration as he set his face to the future.

VIII

Yet if Arthur was confident, others were less so. Few seasoned knights had rallied to his standard. One among them was Sir Bedivere, a man of many battles and wise counsel. Nevertheless, though he had joined himself to Arthur, on account of the oath he had sworn to Uther Pendragon, he did so gloomily. 'All the chivalry of Britain', he said, pulling at his long moustaches, 'has assembled under King Lot's banner . . .'

'All, that is,' Arthur said, 'save those who are with us here.'

'Meanwhile,' Sir Bedivere resumed, as if Arthur had not spoken, 'the Saxons sweep across the country like the tide that covers the sands. We cannot fight both Lot and the Saxons. Therefore, it is my advice that you seek to come to an accommodation with one or the other. For my part, as a patriot, I urge you to approach Lot and offer to divide the kingdom between the pair of you. Then, together, we may expel these murderous barbarians.'

Arthur smiled. 'King Lot', he said, 'has promised to hang me from the highest tree and if you ask him what land he might grant me he will reply "six feet of British earth." There is no peace and no alliance to be had – not, at any rate, till we have defeated him in battle. Courage, my friend, courage and daring will see us prevail.'

'Enemies surround us and press hard upon us,' Sir Bedivere continued to object.

'Very well,' Arthur said, 'I shall attack them.'

In the summer months that followed it seemed as if Arthur had devised a new manner of war. Lot marched against him, secure in his panoply of power. Arthur withdrew into a remote valley. Lot, expressing scorn for his cowardly adversary, pursued. Arthur drew up his knights behind a ridge on the south flank of the valley, above the river which is now known as the Yarrow Water. He chose a point above a spot where the stream ran shallow and which Lot must cross to gain the level ground. When a third of the army was over the water and struggling to regain order, Arthur launched his knights in a close-order attack. They rode the slope with lances at the ready. Meanwhile, from the shelter of dead ground, Arthur's bowmen let fly volleys of arrows at that part of the King of Orkney's force which had not yet crossed the water and threw it into disarray. The force of the knights' charge, with Arthur in the van, the sun glinting on the jewels of his royal helmet, struck the disordered enemy in the flank, rolling them up and sending many tumbling in the water. All was confusion. The sound of Arthur's trumpeters mingled with the screams of the wounded and the dying; and then, as Lot struggled to restore order in his army, which outnumbered Arthur's by at least ten to one, the note of the trumpet changed, sounding the retreat, and Arthur's knights, obedient to the drill he had taught them, wheeled round and regained the hills, while the archers, from their place of concealment, now fired their arrows into that part of Lot's army which had sustained the attack of Arthur's knights and so inhibited any pursuit.

This was the pattern of the weeks that followed. Lot, with the sullen determination of his nature, followed the trail which Arthur, as if mockingly, laid before him. Keeping the higher ground, travelling and sometimes attacking by night, Arthur inflicted a succession of defeats on the King of Orkney. With each of these onsets his men grew in confidence, and Lot's entered into deeper dismay and knew a paralysing fear. It was a new sort of warfare, which baffled them and which, apprehensively, they came to call lightning-war. Each of these rapid battles left scores of his knights and men-at-arms food for wolves, foxes and those birds that feed on carrion; and with each, more knights deserted Lot in despair and the King's temper waxed more terrible, as he struggled to deny his impotence.

IX

Now Merlin had watched all these things from afar, and heard of what was beyond his vision from the spirits, elves, foresters and other mean people who served him. So now, having first ascertained that Lot was still absent with his army, much bloodied and depleted as it was, he betook him to the castle of Roslin where Lot had sent his Queen, Morgan le Fay, and their sons.

The Queen greeted Merlin coldly, for she had not seen him since he delivered her to Lot; and this was something for which she had never forgiven him. She said, 'If I were to act now as it would please me to act, I should have you whipped like a dog and thrown into a dungeon to starve to death. For you yoked me in marriage to a man I detested from the first moment when he undressed me with his eyes and then took and ravished me. And I recall that you told me I must submit to my destiny because I was a daughter of the Empire.'

'Why,' Merlin said, 'we must all submit to destiny, and now you are a queen and the mother of five fine sons.'

'I am the mother of four sons,' she said, 'and three of them are fine, and yet they are Lot's sons, conceived in hatred and disgust . . .'

'And the other?' Merlin said.

'He was conceived in love's most ardent passion; and yet he is a cripple. Can you unravel me that conundrum?'

'And what is his name?' Merlin said. 'Tell me that first.'

'His name is Mordred, for he is bitter fruit.'

'And who was his father?'

'Why do you ask, since I have no doubt that you know the answer. His father was a player-youth, a slim and gentle lover whom I encountered at an inn. There – you know my shame with which my darling husband has never ceased to reproach me.'

Her words were bitter and yet, when she spoke of the player-youth, her voice was sweet as honey and her eyes brimmed with tears.

'I would have prevented that, had I been able,' Merlin said and stroked her long hair as a tender father might.

'Then you would have prevented the sole night of happiness I have enjoyed since you took me from the convent where you lodged me as a child, and where I was truly loved and cherished.' And at this thought she surrendered herself to grief, to copious tears and choking sobs.

'I must tell you', Merlin said, 'that this player-youth with whom you coupled is now the King, the young Arthur himself.'

But he did not add 'and your brother also', for it did not seem fitting to him to tell her that their union had been incestuous. There might come, he thought, a time when it would be expedient to reveal this.

Morgan le Fay still wept, more bitterly indeed than before; and the reason was this: that her husband King Lot, on learning that she was with child, had put her servants to the question and ascertained that the likely father was a low-born player-boy. He had reproached her for her infidelity and rebuked her for preferring low company to his royal person. 'You might as well', he said, 'have lain with the scullion, the dirty stinking kitchen-boy, who by some devilry has usurped the throne of Britain that is mine by rights, fine company for a daughter of Rome and the wife of a king of noble lineage such as I am.' He continued in this vein for hours and frequently struck her. Moreover, when the child was born deformed, he first crowed in exultation and then would have had it exposed on a winter hillside that it would perish. But she cheated him by confiding the babe to a woman of the village and only retrieving it when the King went to the wars. So now she was overcome by a mixture of emotions and took refuge in tears.

Having wept for a half-hour by the clock, she turned and reviled Merlin, partly because she held him responsible for her misfortunes, and partly because there was no one else to hand on whom she could vent her temper and distress. Merlin heard her in silence, knowing that when a woman is so angered there is no reasoning with her.

When she was done, for even the most impassioned woman

must subside and come to quiet in time, he told her to fetch the child Mordred. So she sent for him and his nurse brought the boy to her chamber.

Merlin examined him and saw that he was indeed crippled, being lame of his left leg, and that the left side of his mouth was pulled down; and this, as Morgan, now trembling and exhausted by her temper, told him was because her husband had struck her in the stomach with his mailed fist when she was with child.

Merlin made a cat's cradle of his fingers, and the little boy laughed merrily and his black eyes sparkled.

'And now,' she said, 'I am with child again, three months gone, and my lord has been on campaign for six months that I have not seen him. When he returns he will surely kill me.'

'King Lot', Merlin said, 'has troubles enough. His army has suffered many defeats. He will soon be a broken man. Every day more knights desert him and seek out Arthur to serve him. Lot's day is done. That cannot grieve you, I think.'

'And yet,' she said, 'our eldest son, Gawaine, the apple of my eye, my heart's darling, is with his father.'

Then Merlin told her that he had come to take her, for her own safety and for other reasons which he did not divulge, to Arthur. But, he said, Arthur must not know of Mordred, that he was his son, and so for that reason he himself would take charge of him and be responsible for rearing the boy.

She assented without argument and this puzzled her since Mordred had been conceived in love. Yet she could not look on him without unease and was uncomfortable when she held him in her arms. Once when she suckled him he had bitten her breast and drawn blood. 'There is', she said, 'something uncanny about him. He was born with a full set of teeth and I am told that this signifies that he is evil. When he bit me he laughed as if he had done something clever.'

X

Concerning what I recounted in the last chapter, there is much that I find puzzling.

The conversation I reported is well-authenticated. Certainly it does not appear in Geoffrey of Monmouth's *History of the Kings of Britain*, but Geoffrey, as I have told you, was ignorant, a liar and mythomaniac. Its absence from his narrative is neither interesting nor remarkable. But it is vouchsafed for by certain older and previous chroniclers, and besides, in the monastery of Montsegur, in Occitania, there is a manuscript said to have been copied from one which is reputed to have been dictated by Merlin himself; and in this a version such as I have, more racily, given you may be read. Unfortunately the original manuscript from which the monastic one was copied has disappeared. Some say – and there is no reason to disbelieve them – that it was destroyed when the castle of Montsegur was burned by the Moors during their retreat after a great battle in which they were defeated by your illustrious predecessor and ancestor, Charlemagne.

Be that as it may, it is not the provenance of the story which I find puzzling.

It is rather Merlin's behaviour.

Why did he choose to take charge of the infant Mordred? Why did he carry Morgan le Fay to Arthur, knowing as he did the relationship between them, suspecting, as he must have done – or more than suspecting, for he was a wizard gifted with foresight – that they would resume their incestuous coupling? Why, indeed, did he not inform Arthur that Morgan was his sister? Is it possible that in his twisted heart Merlin was jealous of Arthur, whom nevertheless there is reason to believe he also loved?

Such a possibility will surprise you, my Prince, for you are young and yet innocent, therefore ignorant of the insidious ways of the affections and of how what I call the sexual impulse provokes duplicity.

For it happened as might have been foreseen and was, as I say, in my view previsioned by the mage.

As soon as Morgan arrived in Arthur's camp and stood there in her beauty – desolate and unhappy beauty, which was therefore the more enticing – and Arthur saw her with her dusky ringlets spread like tendril-trailing ivy over her magnificent and naked shoulders, he fell in love with her all over again. It is true that for a moment, the light being dim and her demeanour so changed, he did not recognise her as his Lady of the Inn; but when he did so, his ardour was redoubled. He knelt before her, took her pale hands in his, covered them with kisses and then, his lips advancing up her arms, smooth as monumental alabaster – but soft, yielding, exquisite – attained those naked shoulders and approached her lips, meanwhile his restless hands, bearing the scars of war and rough from the leather of his horse's reins, fondling her breasts – those breasts that were the delight of all who saw them, breasts candid as mozzarella made from the milk of patient buffaloes. Oh, to see the young King at that ecstatic moment was to see one whom the god Eros had taken joyful prisoner.

Now Merlin, as I insist, had foreseen this. How could he not have, being what he was?

There is one explanation that occurs to me. I advance it tentatively, having no evidence; and as you will have remarked, I never in this narrative say such-and-such was, unless the assertion rests on indisputable testimony, but only, such-and-such may have been.

You will recall that Merlin by his arts had lured the lovely boy Peredur from Arthur, having been consumed by lust the moment he set eyes on him. Now, though old men steeped in vice might wish it otherwise, it is inconceivable that Peredur should willingly have preferred Merlin, who stank of goats and had never been well-favoured, to Arthur, slim and lovely with long-fringed eyes and lips devised, as it were by gods, for kissing. To capture him, Merlin had had recourse to magic arts, but in time, the spell weakened, Peredur languished lovelorn, sighing for Arthur. So now, by presenting him, perhaps by means of magic mirrors – for there is no evidence that Peredur was now in Arthur's camp and it is unreasonable to suppose that Merlin would have risked an encounter between his unwilling catamite and the King – by presenting him, then, by some means or other, with the vision of Arthur enraptured by the Queen, Merlin hoped to dissolve the enchantment which Eros had woven round Peredur and Arthur; and so bring the recalcitrant boy to heel, despairing.

Yet I confess this explanation does not entirely satisfy me. For, since Merlin was a master of the magic arts, he would have found no difficulty in creating for Peredur images of Arthur in thrall to any number of loves, sufficiently compelling, ugly, monstrous or grotesque to have filled the boy with disgust, and killed whatever love of Arthur, or desire, he still felt. I remember, for instance, that a certain Jewish necromancer and conjurer of my acquaintance delighted the Archbishop of Salamanca by presenting to him the illusion of an ape deflowering a virgin of very tender years. In his defence, for he was a learned man and a good friend of mine, I should say that he performed this disgusting trick only to save his own young and much-adored daughter from suffering a like fate in reality at the hands (and worse) of that wicked cleric.

It may be that Merlin feared that Arthur would himself seek to recover Peredur and so sought to distract him by restoring Morgan to his arms.

Or it may be that he acted thus for sheer love of mischief, or because it delighted him to display his powers and order the lives of others.

With such as Merlin there is rarely one simple explanation or one pure and single motive to be identified.

Does this amaze you, that Merlin should prove so duplicitous, or that Arthur, before all his knights, should have abandoned himself so utterly to the expression of passionate desire? Then know this: that love resembles the middle part of Heaven which we call the Milky Way, which is a shining road composed of tiny stars. In love, poets and scholars have identified and described innumerable shades of emotion, each tumbling over the other, inextricable and as hard to recognise as any of the stars on that milky road. So Arthur surrendered all else – his renown, his kingdom, the leadership of his army – to this single moment of existence, which seemed to him then perfect happiness. And, being young, he could not know that the manner in which a passionate man lives changes ten times a day, even by the hour; that his soul which, as he embraced his recovered love, felt that this moment belonged to eternity, would become sated, for perfect happiness is transitory, sadness follows coition and the man who has fed well forgets what it was to be hungry.

But now, for the flight of a sparrow, the world stopped for Arthur, as he fixed his lips on Morgan's and she, though at first firm, dissolved into love which ran through them like a rushing stream down a mountainside. Then, with a cry that echoed to the hills, she tore herself away, as a great wind tears branches from a tree, and fell to the ground, sobbing.

But Arthur, murmuring words of love, sweet as honey, raised her up gently and led her to his tent where, with many kisses and trembling fingers, he unloosed her gown and, as it slipped to the ground, admired her skin whiter than new-fallen snow. So he took her to his couch and there . . . but I desist, for it is not seemly, my Prince, that I should elaborate what followed, save to say that in that hour Arthur knew the most intense delight of which sinful man is capable, as they came together, and it is enough to add that the acanthus that winds in flowing circles round the columns of a Greek temple is not more wonderfully bound together than were these lovers' legs and arms; while no traveller journeying through an unknown land ever made happier discoveries than Arthur and Morgan that summer night.

If you ask why Morgan first submitted and then, in full and eager surrender, sought to give as great delight as she received and urged Arthur to new displays of passion, even though she feared that any union blessed by Merlin was perilous, so grievous had been her experience of his intervention in her life, then I must tell you that my sources offer two explanations.

The first relates only to Morgan herself. Because, in years to come, as I shall relate, she was accused of witchcraft, some writers condemn her as immoral, twisted and evil in her nature. Therefore, they say, she being in league with the Powers of Darkness was drawn to any destructive course as a moth is to a flame; and so the belief that their coupling would, as the wheel turned, inevitably bring Arthur to his doom, in some manner or other, rendered it more pleasing to her. And they add that her initial show of reluctance was insincere and designed merely to draw Arthur on, for it is well known that a woman who feigns unwillingness is to men of ardour all the more desirable than one who shows herself eager for the sport.

But others, while not denying this, merely remark that she was a daughter of Eve and that women incline ever more to Satan than to the Lord. They are created by the Evil One to lead men astray, as Delilah did Samson, Helen Paris and Cleopatra great Antony himself.

This, however, I do not believe, for I have known many chaste and virtuous women, and, if I may imprudently confess, have had occasion to regret their chastity and virtue. But that is nothing to my tale.

For my part, speaking as I do from an experience of life that is both wider and deeper than that of most clerkly moralists, and also from a far more profound underfanding of human nature, I reject both these explanations.

In their stead I offer two of my own.

First, I deny that Morgan le Fay was at this time what is called a witch, no matter to what lengths she may later have been driven. On the contrary, I believe that Morgan was then a follower of the Perfect doctrine, which holds that man and woman are one, each having been reincarnated many times while held in this envelope of flesh. For the Perfect, according to their teaching which Holy Church terms heresy, ultimate reality is the divine, immanent self which is neither man nor woman. But if, in this world of matter, two people come together, man with woman, man with boy, woman with woman, thus prolonging their existence in this world of flesh, it is – if you excuse the pun – no great matter.

This explanation I have offered is cogent. Yet I draw back. It is perhaps too metaphysical for the times in which Arthur and Morgan lived. So it seems to me probable that both were in thrall to Eros, the boy-god of love, to whose powers the Ancients bear witness. Eros, though a boy, is a mastering and possessing deity. Those into whose hearts he enters lose all free will; they become his slaves. They are blinded to the consequences of their love, as

Paris, enamoured of Helen, carried her away from her husband Menelaus, back to Troy and so let loose terrible war which saw the towers of Ilium burned and all its heroes, even Hector, slain. And for all this Paris cared nothing; mastered by Eros, he had eyes only for Helen and she likewise for him.

Moreover, those whom Eros has enslaved forget all other natural affections, take no thought for codes of morality or for what the priests denounce as sin. Till Eros releases them they are powerless to act other than as he chooses.

So it was with Arthur and Morgan.

I am aware, of course, that Holy Church has abolished the gods of Greece and Rome, saying they are false gods, vain imaginings, and do not truly exist. This may well be so. But in another sense no one who has observed mankind can doubt the reality of Eros. He may have no existence in the sense that Almighty God and Christ Jesus exist. Unlike Christ, he may never have put on fleshly apparel. Yet he is there in the minds and spirits of men and women; and no one but a dullard can doubt his power, his capacity to seize, blind and even madden those he has chosen. To deny Eros may be the path of wisdom and the road to salvation; but to deny his power is folly, a flight from the true reality, things as they are.

That is all I have to say on the matter. For the time being, anyway.

XI

Throughout that summer Arthur felt himself to be two men opposed to each other. The first was the prisoner of Eros, for whom the world was well lost so long as he might lie with his love. The second was the King, the general of an army engaged in bloody war.

You ask how this might be. I can answer only that Arthur was remarkable. There is, in my opinion, one test of the superior man, whom a German poet of my acquaintance, a great scholar and a man of extraordinary penetration (though he died of drink, in a low tavern in Bohemia) called the *vir ulterior*, he who goes beyond his fellows; and this is the ability to hold two conflicting ideas in his head at the same time, to see both steadily and to continue to function. So it was with Arthur.

And there are two other features, my friend said, of the higher man, he who goes beyond his fellows. The first is his lightness of spirit, his 'gaiety', his unwillingness to be chained to the dull clay with which most men are content. And the second is his scepticism, his refusal to be bound to dogma or doctrine. His life, my friend said, is a perpetual search. It was sad that his own search was cut off untimely. But I believe the wine was bad and, some say, poisoned.

Cultivate these qualities, my Prince, gaiety and scepticism, and you will truly be the wonder of the world. Which, however, will also revile you, for it fears and detests that which is superior.

Even in Arthur's camp, even then in his marvellous youth, there were murmurings, mutterings, grumblings. His superiority was resented. Chief among the murmurers were Sir Kay and Sir Bedivere. Old allies, boon drinking companions, for whom no ale was ever too strong, who were never – or only rarely, not more than twice a week – mastered by wine, they found cause for complaint in Arthur's very grace. His body, slim and taut as a drawn bowstring, rebuked their own gross flesh. There was something, they muttered, of the girl in his face; those long eyelashes were not a warrior's. Sir Kay, moreover, remembered the time when Arthur had been a humble serving boy and how he had then often laid the flat of his sword across his buttocks; and in truth he longed to do so again, but dared not. As for Sir Bedivere, despite the victories Arthur had won, he said roundly that Lot would have his revenge for the insult Arthur had done him by lying with his wife. He did not dare say this to Arthur for, though Bedivere and Kay might secretly call him 'the boy', there was that in the steady gaze of the King's dark-blue eye which unnerved them. So it was only Cal who warned Arthur that his affair did him no credit and would end badly.

'What would I do without you, Cal?' Arthur laughed.

'Since you never take my advice,' Cal answered, 'your fate will be the same whether I speak out or keep silent. But you ought to know, there are some as says the lady has bewitched you and others as is certain that she's been sent by Lot to unman you. Either way, the gossip has it, you're fucked.'

'Poor Cal. I do believe you're jealous.'

'That's as may be.'

Arthur put his arm round his friend and drew him closely to him. 'Cal, Cal,' he said, 'we have endured much together. Believe me, you have a place in my heart from which you can never be dislodged. You are part of me, Cal, and I of you. Believe that, I pray you.'

'Fine words,' Cal said. 'Fine words, as is well said, butter no parsnips. I might have known you wouldn't listen for you're as wilful and wayward as an unbroken colt. Well, when things come unstuck . . .' He spread his hands out wide.

'You'll have the satisfaction of saying, "I told you so".'

'Laugh as you like. And another thing. Don't suppose that these two curmudgeons, Kay and Bedivere, have any love for you.'

Arthur frowned. 'I don't doubt what you say, but I can't think why they shouldn't have.'

'You think everyone should love you, you're so wonderful. Well, they don't. You don't hold the treatment Kay meted out to you when you was nobody against him. Well, he can't forgive you for having forgiven him. All right, all right, I'll say no more seeing as you're in no mood to listen. And now I suppose you're off to her Ladyship . . .'

XII

Arthur might be enslaved by Eros, but he was still the King, and one part of his mind was devoted to his royal duty and the war against King Lot. So now he resumed the campaign. Lot had retreated to a strong castle in a pass that guarded the road to the northern mountains, near where the Roman general Agricola defeated the Caledonians and their king Calcagus. The castle was strongly fortified and had never been taken in a hundred wars.

So Arthur, who wished to spare as many lives as possible, sent a challenge to Lot, inviting the King to meet him in single combat, with the castle as the prize. When Lot received the challenge he was roused to anger. At first he thought of accepting because he was sure that the boy Arthur was no match for him. Then he was not so sure; he thought of the battles in which he had been defeated, and he remembered that his back was bad and that his joints were stiffer than in his youth. And this angered him still more. Then he thought of his wife in Arthur's arms (for these things are never kept hidden), and he tore at his moustache and swore that he would have the boy's head and serve it on a platter at his victor's banquet. He smiled at the picture this presented and was about to send word that he accepted the challenge when he was seized by fear: if he lost, all was finished; he was disgraced, even if not slain. So he hesitated like a man standing on a high rock from which he must leap to cross a rushing river, now stepping to the edge, now drawing back as he pictures his body being dashed against the rocks. So, caught between desire and fear, Lot struggled as a fly struggles in a spider's web.

While he was so perplexed his eldest son Gawaine came to him and asked whether he should set out his armour; for all in the castle knew of the challenge. Lot frowned and said, 'Not yet; I shall not fight today. I am sick to the stomach and unfit for war. Tomorrow I shall answer this impudent challenge.'

So on the day following Gawaine came to him again and asked whether he should set out his armour.

Lot sighed deeply, shook his head and said, 'Not yet, for I am suffering from an ague as I think, and am unfit for battle. Tomorrow I shall answer this impudent challenge.'

So on the third day, for the third time, Gawaine came to him and asked the same question. And it seemed to him that each day his father the King looked darker and was diminished; and indeed, his body shook as if he did have an ague. So Gawaine felt pity for him. But he said, 'As we stand on the battlements gazing to the south there comes to us carried on the wind the sound of laughter.'

He thought, 'The ague that afflicts my father goes by the name of fear, and the word even among our knights is that Lot lurks in his chamber and dare not do battle with Arthur. And the hills are alive with the sound of laughter from the camp of the enemy. And I am ashamed of my father, which is indeed a terrible thing to be.' He thought all this but he did not dare speak these words for, in truth, though he was ashamed of his father and was right to be so ashamed, he still feared him also.

So, instead of speaking as he thought, he turned away and was about to leave the chamber, when he heard his father's voice.

'I cannot fight,' Lot said. 'I sit here remembering my many battles and my prowess in them of which our minstrels have sung, and yet I cannot fight. I wear a cuckold's horns and cannot avenge myself. Truly, I am the most miserable of men, the most wretched of kings.'

When he heard his father speaking as he had never heard him speak before, Gawaine was again filled with pity. He said, 'Father, the challenge must be met. Since you are sick, then let me take your place and do battle in your stead.'

Lot lifted his head. His weary eyes gazed on his son, then shifted away. He rubbed his stubbled cheek with a hairy hand. There were blotches of brown among the hairs. He looked at Gawaine again. He was still a boy, but sturdy and well-built. His hair was blond, cut short and his usually pale face, lightly freckled, was now flushed with eagerness. He stood with his legs planted apart and they were still soft boy-legs. All his beauty was in his youth, but he looked like a fighter. Lot said, 'Your mother is his whore. Will you still fight him?'

Gawaine flushed more deeply. He could not speak, but his eyes remained fixed on his father.

Lot said, 'Very well. Go arm yourself and let the herald carry the answer to the usurper. The throne he occupies is mine by right and will be yours when you have killed him and I am dead. Take my blessing, my son, and do your duty.'

If Gawaine had chanced to look round as he left the chamber he would have seen a sly smile cross his father's face.

But he did not look back. He descended to the Great Hall, and summoned Arthur's herald and told him to carry the message to his master that the challenge was accepted, and that Arthur would be met and should prepare for battle to the death in the meadow below the castle at noon on the morrow. And he said, 'Tell him that since he has issued the challenge, ours is the right to choose the weapons. So the fight will be on foot, and each will be armed only with sword and shield, and there shall be no squires in attendance, but all shall keep two bow-lengths distant. Should he not agree to these conditions, then let him storm the castle.'

'He will agree,' the herald said, 'for he understands and will abide by the rules of combat.'

When the herald had returned to Arthur, Gawaine went to the chapel and knelt in prayer. He was now very pale and felt chill, for he knew this might be the last night of his life. And he maintained his vigil in the chapel throughout the hours of darkness, and was shriven at dawn.

Then he went to put on his armour, a coat of mail made by the finest smiths in furthest Spain, and a helmet with a golden plume. He tested several broadswords and chose one that was well-balanced, and his squire sharpened its edge. And so he prepared for combat.

It had rained, lightly, in the hour before dawn, but now the sun climbed in the sky and there were no clouds. Its rays caught the young leaves of the beech trees that fringed the meadow beyond the castle moat and made them sparkle. Jackdaws swooped to and fro from the battlements, and from the woods below sounded the mocking note of a cuckoo.

Cal helped Arthur buckle on his armour and said, 'Mind you, now, this Lot is a right bugger. The only thing you can trust him to do is to play foul.'

Towards noon the trumpets sounded and the knights from both armies stationed themselves at either end of the meadow, all watchful lest either should breach the conditions of the truce on which the challenge depended.

Arthur advanced with a step that was light and eager, over the springy turf. He had not yet lowered his vizor and all could see that his visage was serene.

As he approached the middle of the field Gawaine crossed the drawbridge from the castle. He stepped off it and stumbled, and a groan rose from his army, but he quickly collected himself and, as he did so, lowered his vizor, for it was not his intention that Arthur should know it was not King Lot who advanced against him. But Lot himself looked from a casement window high in the castle at the two champions, looked briefly and turned away as if to hide his shame. And truly he was much ashamed, since he could no longer pretend even to himself that it was not fear which held him from the field. He slumped to a couch and bit his nails, then drank deeply from a goblet containing the strong wine of Bordeaux, and dashed the goblet to the floor. He called out to his page to fetch him more wine and drank again. But the wine brought him no comfort.

Arthur took up his stance in the middle of the meadow, awaiting his adversary, who now approached with firm step. He drew near and Arthur saw that it was not the King, for Gawaine was a head taller than his squat father and, moreover, moved with a lighter stride. So Arthur said, 'My challenge was to King Lot and you are not he.'

And Gawaine replied, 'I am his champion.'

'Is the King afraid that he dare not meet me according to my challenge?'

'King Lot fears no man, but he is sick and has made me his deputy. Come, let us finish with this idle talk and set to.' Saying this, he assumed the on-guard position and showed himself ready to fight.

But Arthur stood still at ease, with his sword point resting on the ground. He said, 'Tell me your name that I may know whom I am fighting and whose mother's son I must overcome today.'

'My name is of no matter,' Gawaine said, for so King Lot had instructed him to reply if this question was put to him.

'Then raise your vizor that I may see what manner of man has met my challenge.'

Then Gawaine, eager for battle, did as Arthur requested, and when he saw him Arthur took a step backwards. 'You are but a boy,' he said. 'Does King Lot still affect to despise me, though I have defeated him in seven battles, that he sends a boy to do a man's work. Has he no grizzled knights to fight in his stead?'

These words angered Gawaine, and with reason, seeing that he was no more than two years younger than Arthur. So he lost control of himself and cried out, 'Come to, for I am of royal blood, being the King's eldest son. I am Gawaine and fit to fight any man, even you, Arthur. Are you afraid that you still hold back?'

Arthur smiled a sad smile and shook his head. 'I am not afraid,' he said, 'or no more afraid than is natural when one is on the point of deadly combat. Nevertheless, I cannot fight you, Gawaine. Return to the castle and tell your father that it is not fitting that he should send you to a battle that he dare not fight himself.' Saying this, he made to turn away.

Now Gawaine had a quick and unruly temper, even from that childhood which was not long behind him, and these words roused him to fury. He understood why Arthur would not fight him; that it was on account of his mother. And this he took – with reason as you may think – as a stain on his honour, that Arthur should lie with his mother and for this reason decline to do battle with him. Then Arthur had accused his father of cowardice and this enraged him further, for the King had put in words the suspicion which he himself entertained but had not dared to admit.

So, as Arthur made to turn away, refusing battle, Gawaine uttered a loud cry, swung his sword, caught Arthur on the side of the neck just below the right ear and sent him tumbling to the ground. A great roar went up from both armies, Lot's men yelling with joy and excitement, Arthur's with shock. This was succeeded by a low angry rumble from them, as they sensed treachery, and for a moment it seemed as if, forgetful of the truce, and without command, they would surge forward eager to join general battle.

But Gawaine himself did not move to follow up his attack. Instead, he stepped back, as if amazed. Meanwhile, Arthur on the grass raised himself on his elbow, shook his head twice to clear it and struggled to his feet. He looked at Gawaine and saw uncertainty on his face. Then he said, 'I did not wish to fight you, but now . . . now you have made it impossible that I should not. But first, give me your hand in token that this shall be a fair fight and then lower your vizor.'

Gawaine extended his hand hesitantly, as if fearing a trick. But there was no trick. Then both, having shaken hands, lowered their vizors and set to.

They were at first evenly matched. Arthur was the older and more experienced in the use of weapons in real conflict, but Gawaine was a hand taller, heavier, more sturdy, if less nimble. So for a long time they exchanged blows, many cleverly parried but some ringing against armour, and some so heavily struck as to cause the other to stumble. And meanwhile both armies seemed to hold their breath, so compelling was the contest between the two young heroes.

They swakked their swords till both were panting and sweating, and both received wounds so that the blood ran down like rain. Then at last a mighty sweeping blow from Gawaine caught Arthur on the head and sent his helmet flying, and caused him to stumble again and almost fall. Gawaine rushed forward with his sword raised high to strike him down, but at that very instant Arthur recovered, stepped inside the arc of the descending sword and thrust at Gawaine. He found a chink in the armour, or it may be that the thrust was so powerfully made that it pierced the armour even where there was no chink. Its force was carried right through and Gawaine fell, wounded in the shoulder, with Arthur's sword still embedded. And his own sword fell harmlessly to the grass.

Then Arthur leaned forward and took Gawaine by the hand, and raised him to his feet and embraced him. Very gently he drew out his blade and held Gawaine up so that he did not fall in a swoon. He said, 'That is enough. You have done your father

proud and proved yourself a noble knight, worthy of all honour.'
So, very slowly and still supporting his wounded foe, he led him
back to his camp while both armies stood in silent amazement.

Morgan le Fay descended from the palanquin from which she
had watched the duel, with a mixture of emotions which you may
imagine more easily than I can describe them. Arthur surrendered
her son to her care and she retired with him into the camp to dress
his wound. And in this while, neither she nor Arthur said a word
to the other, for their feelings were too deep for speech.

Then Arthur sent to Lot by way of a herald requiring him to
surrender the castle by noon the following day. But he added that,
in recognition of Gawaine's courage and honour, he would not
require Lot's men to lay down their arms, but that those who
wished might withdraw with Lot, who was granted permission to
retire inviolate to the Orkney Islands, while those who so chose
would be welcome in his army, doing homage to him as the King
of Britain and, by right if not yet in actuality, Roman Emperor.

It was to be two days before Lot, with sour reluctance, accepted
the terms Arthur offered him. In these two days he had seen his
knights desert him, first in a trickle of ones and twos, and then in
droves. Among those who crossed over to Arthur's camp were
Gawaine's younger brothers Agravaine and Gaheris, who both
preferred their mother's embraces to their father's cuffs and
curses. So Lot, nursing his wrath, conscious that he was disgraced
in the eyes of all true knights, for few doubted that it was
cowardice that had kept him from the field, departed to the
windswept Orkneys where he built himself a palace with many
subterranean rooms in which he dragged out his bitter existence,
while his stewards fleeced the native Orkneymen, hard-working
farmers and fishers.

The night of his departure Arthur held a feast in the Great Hall
of the castle. He set Morgan le Fay on his right hand and Gawaine
on his left; and it was hard to say which he made more of, or
which gave him more delight. At one end of the long high table
Cal observed all that passed with a smile, now bemused when he
thought of how he and Arthur had come so far and of the dangers
they had encountered, the pain they had suffered, the humiliations

they had endured, now loving and almost cheerful when his gaze turned on Arthur, himself resplendent with happiness.

'You too must be a happy man,' a young knight who respected Cal's devotion to the King and, unlike so many, neither mocked nor despised him, remarked.

'Indeed,' Cal replied and raised one eyebrow, 'provided it lasts.'

When they had eaten of salmon from the silver Tay, haunches of venison, hill lamb, barons of beef, pasties filled with brains, sweetbreads and mushrooms, ewe's milk cheese, jellies, syllabubs, apple tarts, rhubarb creams and other kickshaws, and drunk well of Rhenish and claret, with beer, mead and heather ale for those whose taste ran to native drinks, Arthur called for silence.

Conversation died away, the minstrels and musicians in their gallery laid aside their instruments and then Arthur spoke in praise of all those who had fought with him in the wars, promised those who had fought against him but now joined themselves to his army that their past was forgotten, and then, turning to where Gawaine sat, laid his hand on his shoulder, hailed him as the bravest of adversaries and swore that from this day onward they should be as brothers; and then declared that it was his especial pleasure this evening to confer on Gawaine the honour of knighthood.

'I have in mind', he said, 'to create a new order of knights, who shall be, God willing, the goodliest brotherhood of noble knights the world has ever seen. What form this order takes I have not yet determined. But this is certain: Gawaine has proved his manhood, and thus I dub him knight and name him first and foremost in this new order.'

So saying, he took his sword, even Excalibur, and laid it gently on Gawaine's shoulder: who blushed and smiled, and looked shy and amazed and joyful.

XIII

Arthur had now established his authority over the Romans and the British, whose petty kings hastened to acknowledge his supremacy and do him homage. He received them all graciously, but investigated the manner of their rule, praising those who governed their people with justice and kindness, and chiding or chastising those who treated them harshly. 'They are your sheep,' he said, 'and you must guard them and care for them as a shepherd cares for his flock.'

Nevertheless, he was not yet King of all Britain, for in the south and east of the country the Saxons had established themselves. They were governed by their own kings and they called the British over whom they ruled 'Welsh', which in their language means 'foreigners'. Naturally the British, who had inhabited the land before the Saxons came, did not think of themselves as foreigners, quite the contrary; but they were a subject people, many of them indeed no better than slaves, and had no choice in the matter.

More important, the Saxons Kings were ambitious to extend their rule and conquer new territory, and they cannot be blamed for this, since such ambitions are natural. They had held both Vortigern and Uther Pendragon of little account, and they had allied themselves with Lot because his challenge to Arthur ensured (as they thought) that the British would remain weak and divided, and hence easy prey. So now they were dismayed to find Arthur triumphant.

You, my Prince, are yourself German, on your father's side, and in our modern world we can see for ourselves the many virtues of this great people. There is no need for me to elaborate them. Indeed, if I have read rightly, many in imperial Rome discerned in the German tribes who lived across the Rhine, beyond the boundaries of the Empire, admirable manly qualities which had disappeared, or were disappearing, from Rome itself. They approved the Germans' love of freedom. The power of their Kings was neither arbitrary nor absolute; the tribes, it was reported, made decisions collectively in popular assemblies and Kings must attend to the deliberations of their councillors. The Romans of the Empire – those, that is, who remained in their hearts secret Republicans – contrasted the decadence of Rome, its love of luxury and its effeminacy, with the vigour and virility of the Germans, who avoided all extravagant display; and one great historian, whose work unfortunately I have not been able to read, though excerpts from it are preserved in the books of other men, warned his contemporaries that a free Germany offered a greater threat to Rome than the despotic kingdoms and Empire of the East. And so, indeed, in the centuries when the tribes began to move, that time which in German is called that of the *Volkerwanderung*, it was the brave peoples of Germany who swept through the frontier defences, not to destroy but, as they hoped, to occupy the Empire and share in its blessings.

Certain of the tribes, as I have already written, invaded Britain and came to an agreement with Vortigern whom, however, they despised. They established themselves in the south and east of the island, so securely that eventually they would give their name to its southern half, which is now styled England, or Angleland. But at the time the Romans and the Britons who still governed the rest of the island regarded these Germans as invaders and oppressors, and hoped still to drive them out, to their ships or the cruel inhospitable sea.

These Germans, whom they called indifferently Angles or Saxons, though they had many virtues as the Roman historian had recorded, nevertheless seemed to the British frightening barbarians. They viewed them with both fear and contempt. The Germans were unlettered. They were pagans worshipping strange and warlike gods. They were uncouth in dress and speech. Their habits were said to be filthy. They raped British women and boys. They enslaved prisoners when they did not murder them. And so on. Such accusations are always levelled at those whom a people fears. Finally, and worse, there were many Britons who believed that the Germans could not be defeated in battle. That had been Vortigern's view. Scratching his ugly face (for he suffered from an irritating rash), he was wont to say, 'There is no choice but collaboration. Only by collaborating with the Germans can we hope to moderate their behaviour and build an enduring peace.' These words were not foolish. They seemed foolish only because Vortigern was afraid of the Germans.

But Arthur had no such fear. He said, 'The Saxons have settled here. It may be impossible to expel them from the island. Indeed, that may not be desirable. I have read that for many years Germans served in the imperial army and were loyal defenders of the Empire. So may it also be here in Britain. But it is necessary that the Saxons be first subdued, that their career of conquest be arrested and that their kings acknowledge our authority. I look forward to living at peace with the Saxons but, if we are to have peace, we must first have war. It is only by defeating them, and defeating them soundly, that we can persuade them of the virtues of peace. You tell me that Vortigern spoke of collaboration. But his perspective was false. There can be no good collaboration with an invader bent on conquest. We are ready to live alongside the Saxons in happy collaboration, but only when they have learned to submit to our imperial rule.'

'Do you think I convinced them?' he said to Cal when they were alone.

'I don't know. Happen you should have remained an actor. It was a mighty fine theatrical speech. Did you believe a word of it yourself?'

'Quite a bit,' Arthur said. 'I don't think we can drive the Saxons out of Britain. From all I hear they are now too well established. But if we defeat them often enough, then I think they may accept the terms I shall offer them.'

'It's a big "if",' Cal said, 'and I can tell you that precious pair, Kay and Bedivere, were looking as happy as if they had each swallowed a toad.'

'You can't blame them,' Arthur said. 'They have both been in too many battles against the Saxons and lost them all. Nevertheless, I need to consult them. They know how the Saxons fight and I don't.'

'You'd get more encouragement from a bear with a sore head.'

But Arthur persevered. He had, as you will by now realise,

many great qualities. He was, indeed, at this stage of his life, a knight beyond either reproach or fear, the perfect pattern of what would come to be called 'chivalry'. But perseverance was not the least of his virtues, though it is one which the world values too little.

There are two kinds of courage, my Prince. There is the courage which flares up in moments of danger, the courage which appears without reflection, as a mere natural response to the urgency of the moment. Though I say 'a mere natural response', you must not think that I wish to diminish this sort of courage, for many men lack it and the man who is brave in the hour of peril is justly admired.

But the other sort of courage is still more rare. This is a cold courage, which allows a man to look reality in the face, to contemplate adversity and not be daunted. It is a dour, level-headed sort of courage, that enables a man to hang on by his teeth when all around him crumbles. And this courage, too, Arthur possessed.

His war against the Saxons went badly from the start. His knights were brave – none braver – but they wasted their strength and courage in vain attacks against the Saxon axe-men who were protected by their shield-wall. They battled against it as the sea strikes a cliff face. And soon many were disheartened. Sir Kay and Sir Bedivere came again to Arthur and urged him to yield more land to the Saxons and, submitting, come to such terms as might be possible; else, they said, all is lost, Britain is utterly conquered and we are dead men.

They said this again in council and many knights hung their heads for shame, because they believed that Kay and Bedivere spoke truth.

'Let us be practical,' Kay said. 'We have now been defeated in four great battles. Our strength is wasted. Every day we are fewer. If we lose another battle, we shall have lost everything, for there will be no army remaining, and the Saxons may come and go where they please, settle where they please and enslave the British as they please. It is folly to continue the struggle. Let us make peace while there is still time and while we yet may make a treaty which will allow us to live as free men in an unoccupied zone.'

He sat down and for a little there was silence. All eyes were fastened on the King, and it seemed as if he were unwilling to meet them, for he looked beyond the gathering towards the hills as if he were contemplating the possibility of withdrawing there.

Then Gawaine got to his feet. He was flushed and looked nervous. 'I am only a young knight,' he said, 'and have no experience of speaking in public. So I ask you to forgive me if what I say seems muddled and ill-prepared. But maybe because I'm young I see things differently and what we have just heard seems to me to be rank defeatism. We have lost four battles and that is bad. But we haven't lost any territory, and we haven't lost the war, and also – and I think I can speak for many of the young knights here – we haven't lost heart. We are fighting for freedom and, though I'm no scholar, I have read that freedom is a noble thing, which no good man surrenders save with his life. So what I say is . . . what I say is to give up the struggle now is to surrender our birthright. And that's wrong.'

Many of the young knights cheered, but Sir Bedivere silenced them by thumping the flat of his sword on the table. 'What we've just heard is sheer sentimentality,' he said. 'The facts are as my colleague Sir Kay has stated them. We are defeated and our only course is to salvage what we can. I always said this war was a mistake and it gives me no satisfaction to have been proved right.'

Again, all eyes were turned on Arthur and what they saw surprised the company. For Arthur was smiling. It was a slow smile that lit up his face and, when he spoke, his voice was gentle. 'Everything that's been said has reason behind it,' he said. 'Nobody has spoken dishonestly. But, if you look, you will see that it is raining, raining quite hard. Now I've consulted with the wise men who watch the weather, and they tell me these autumn rains will last for weeks and will make campaigning impossible. And then winter will come. So we have time on our side. That's one thing, and the other is this: we have been fighting in the wrong way. I take responsibility for that. But we can change our tactics and we are going to have weeks, even months, to learn new ones, which we shall employ when we resume the war in the spring. That's all, I think.'

XIV

'I wish I knew where Merlin has got to,' Arthur said.

Cal sniffed.

'I need him,' Arthur said. 'I miss his advice.'

'It's not Merlin you're missing but Peredur you're sighing for. I've heard you of nights. I don't know why. There are plenty of pretty boys who'd be happy to be the King's bedfellow, prettier, some of them, than Peredur indeed. Young Geraint, for example. I've seen him make calf's eyes at you, and he's certainly got a shapely leg and nice rounded arms.'

'Stop trying to irritate me, Cal. It's not Peredur I'm missing. I've got over that. Anyway, you know perfectly well I lie with Morgan le Fay and she wouldn't thank me for . . . never mind. As for Geraint, well, if you admire him so much . . . I've sent for Merlin and my messengers have returned saying he's not to be found.'

'So what do you want him for? From what you've told me, half the time his advice has led you into trouble . . . Not that you need leading. And if it's military advice you seek, well, let me remind you that you told your council that you know how to beat the Saxon devils . . .'

'They're not devils, but men. If they were indeed devils, I would be less confident.'

'Oh, confident are we now? So what do you need Merlin for?'

'Reassurance.'

'Reassurance? Fancy that now . . .'

This is just a sample of the conversations Arthur and Cal had that winter. They bickered like an old married couple, which in a sense they were, having been through so much together. There were many at court who despised Cal, many who resented his intimacy with the King and put the worst construction on it, some who befriended him because they thought him the means by which they might curry favour with Arthur, many who could not understand why Arthur reposed so much trust in him.

But the answer to that was simple. Kings and emperors, my Prince, are ever surrounded by flatterers who tell them what they suppose they wish to hear, or what will be pleasing to them. The wise king recognises that this is dangerous. He remembers the reply a philosopher gave to a Roman emperor who enquired of him what was the most deadly poison: 'Incense,' said the philosopher. Arthur knew this story, and knew that Cal would never offer him incense. Besides, Cal was the only person with whom he could be a boy again and joke with as an equal. And he knew that Cal loved him and would never betray him. He knew too, by the way, that Cal would never attempt to seduce the young Geraint as he had jestingly suggested, but would be content to love and admire him from a distance. (There was indeed much to admire, for the lad had an angel's face, dark-blue eyes, a mass of golden curls and a smile like the sun of a spring morning.) Cal's sufferings in the castle of Old Stoneface had given him a horror of the flesh. Arthur pitied him on this account, even while understanding that it made Cal yet more trustworthy.

Still Arthur fretted because he could not find Merlin. It was not that he lacked confidence in his plans or that he doubted whether his analysis of the manner in which the Saxons should be fought was false. Indeed, he could not say why he needed Merlin. But he was sure he did.

When he spoke of this need to Morgan le Fay she upbraided him, for she could not forgive Merlin for having delivered her to King Lot. Moreover, though at the time she had been happy to give the infant Mordred to his charge, now that she was free of Lot and united with Arthur, she regretted this.

You must not suppose, my Prince, that these questions were uppermost in Arthur's mind that winter. On the contrary, he was immersed in the task of training his knights and the men-at-arms and archers in the new manner of warfare he had devised.

This was to be summed up, he said, in one word: mobility. 'We have learned', he said, 'the strength of the Saxons' defence when we meet them in open field. Their shield-wall and their axe-men have been too much for us in each encounter. So, when the war resumes in the spring, we shall feign retreat. We shall draw the Saxons on to a spot of our choosing, from which our archers will launch volleys of arrows to throw them into disorder and weaken the shield-wall. Only then will our knights attack, and our men-at-arms follow up on foot.'

And this manner of fighting proved successful. In a succession of encounters the Saxons were worn down. Their strength was diminished and their hearts grew first weary and then fearful. At last they were drawn into a hollow place which the hills surrounded, so that it seemed like one of the great amphitheatres built by the Romans.

It was a night of full moon, never dark, being the height of summer towards the day of the solstice. Arthur moved through his camp in the moonlight, praising and encouraging his men, while below them the Saxons lay round their campfires and some raised their voices in drunken song as men do when they seek to ward off despair.

In the night also Arthur dispatched a troop of horsemen under the command of Gawaine to take up position at the head of the valley behind the Saxons, and so deny them their line of retreat. And his archers were stationed on the fringes of the forest that coated the hills above the Saxon camp. Then he drew up his men-at-arms across the track that led up the valley, while he himself with the main body of his knights commanded the Saxons' line of march.

So when the Saxon King, whose name was Ethelbert and who was a man of great courage proved in many wars, woke in the morning he felt fear run through his army as a rumour hurries through a great city. He sent out a band of men under one of his sons, whose name has been lost or at any rate escapes me – for, as you know, I pretend to no knowledge which I do not possess – to seek a way out of the trap in which they were caught; and before the sun was high in the heavens came the noise of battle; and then silence, and his son and his axe-men did not return. For in truth, Gawaine had fallen on them as, losing order in their terror, they broke ranks, disobeying the King's son. So many were cut down and the King's son taken prisoner, to which he would not have consented, being brave, had he not had his hamstrings cut and was therefore disabled. The chivalrous Gawaine commanded that his wounds be treated, which was indeed done, but to no avail, for his leg rotted and the young man died.

So the morning advanced and the Saxons put themselves in battle order to resist the attack. They did so resolutely, but mournfully, being fatigued and many suffering from fever.

Now the Archbishop, whose name was Eugenius, came to Arthur. He had but recently attached himself to the army when he saw that the war went well. 'The Lord has delivered the heathen into our hands,' he said. 'Therefore, as the prophet Samuel commanded King Saul, I command you to descend into the plain and smite the Amalekites, and let not a man survive, for they have done evil to the faithful, and have burned and destroyed many churches and monasteries.'

Arthur looked at him and saw a sleek man with a round red face that sweated, perhaps on account of the warmth of the day, but also with holy zeal. Arthur smiled and said, 'Is that truly the wish of the Lord you serve, that we should slay those whom we have at our mercy? Yet these men will fight to the death, for that is their custom, and in the battle many noble knights and honest soldiers, fathers of families, will be killed. I shall win glory, and women and children will weep.'

Saying this, he then called to him two squires, Geraint and Agravaine, who was the second son of Morgan le Fay, and also Cal whom he trusted above all others, and, putting his spurs to his horse, rode down the hill towards the Saxon army. He carried no lance, and had unbuckled his sword and given it to his armour bearer, and the two squires had done the same, while Cal wore only a tunic and breeches, with no coat of mail.

So Arthur approached the Saxon army who watched him in amazement.

When he drew near he called out and asked if there was any there who spoke Latin.

A grizzled warrior, his face marked with sword cuts, stepped out of the ranks. 'As a young man,' he said, 'I served in the legions. My sword shines but my Latin is rusty. Nevertheless, I understand you and can make myself understood.'

Arthur then said that he wished to speak to the King, the noble

Ethelbert, and waited while the message was carried to him and the Saxons debated whether the King should accede to the request. Arthur sat his horse serene as one who waits for a day's hunting to commence. He was bare-headed and all could see that he was calm as a deep lake on a windless day. A smile played on his lips. He looked up at the sky where a falcon hovered.

At last the Saxon ranks parted and the King appeared, in the company of the old legionary and five of his officers. When he saw the King and knew that it was he, Arthur dismounted and handed the reins of his horse to Geraint, and came to the Saxon King, who overtopped him by a head.

But Arthur saw that he held himself with difficulty and surmised that he was weak from hunger. 'I am Arthur the King,' he said. 'Greetings.'

Ethelbert looked him up and down, and saw a slim boy who smiled at him as if he were a friend or comrade.

'For the moment,' Arthur said, 'we are equal. I have put myself in your power. But your army is doomed. I know that it is weak on account of hunger and fever, and you can neither advance nor retreat.'

He paused and looked to the old legionary so that he might translate what he had said. But to his surprise Ethelbert himself answered readily, speaking a Latin which, though not grammatical, for the case endings were lopped off, was easy to understand. 'What you say is true, Arthur. You are in my power. I could kill you with one blow of my sword.'

'Indeed, yes,' Arthur said and still smiled.

'And my army is indeed weak. But it is the custom of my people to fight the more bravely as the odds against victory grow longer. It is good to die as a warrior.'

'But better to live in friendship.'

Ethelbert was silent. He looked back at his army. He looked up to the hills where the army of the Romans stood in battle array. 'Is friendship possible between the Saxons and the Romans?' he said.

'There can always be friendship between brave men,' Arthur replied. And he stepped forward and placed his hands on Ethelbert's shoulders, and drew him to him, and the two Kings embraced. For a moment it seemed to Arthur that Ethelbert resisted, but then he relaxed, as one who no longer struggles against fate. And a cheer rose from both armies, and its echo resounded from the encircling hills.

Arthur heard the cheer and drew back from Ethelbert, and said, 'It appears that the brave men of both armies have given the answer to your question.'

So then Arthur proposed that they should make a treaty between them, to which Ethelbert assented. And that night they dined together, though the feast was meagre, on account of the exigencies of the campaign, but the men of both armies mingled, and exchanged memories and tokens of friendship. The moon rose high in the summer night, and all was still and at peace.

In the morning Arthur with his councillors met again with Ethelbert and his chief noblemen, who in the Saxon tongue were called Earls, to discuss the terms of the peace and how they should all, Romans, Britons and Saxons, live peaceably one with the other from that day on. Ethelbert acknowledged Arthur as Emperor of all Britain, and by right also of Rome, and swore allegiance to him. They agreed, moreover, that in those parts of Britain where the Saxons had settled and made their homes, the laws of both the Saxons and the Romans should be observed and obeyed; and that Ethelbert should rule his own people, but that Arthur should appoint a proconsul to guide him in the government of the Romans and the Britons who dwelled there.

When this was agreed, then all were content save the Archbishop Eugenius, who upbraided Arthur and reproached him for having made peace with the heathen and for having refused to exterminate them. 'You have forgotten', he said, 'the words of the Lord who declared that he came not to bring peace, but a sword, and you have defied the commands of the Lord of Hosts.'

Truly, my Prince, that text is a stumbling block to many, but you are not to suppose that it was Christ's intention to bring a sword and condemn men to warfare, merely that he understood that this would be the consequence of his teaching, as the state of the world and the battles against the Infidel in the Holy Land prove.

So the Archbishop cursed Arthur and would have torn the crown from his head, on account of his disobedience, but that he saw how Arthur was loved and therefore he feared to act. But he nursed his wrath, keeping it warm in his heart, with the consequences that I shall in time unfold.

Then the noble Ethelbert, being deeply moved by the generosity of spirit which Arthur had displayed, came to him and said, 'My Lord Emperor, I'm a plain man and have no taste for flowery speeches, but what we have done is good. Friendship between peoples is better than conflict, though war is always to be preferred to servitude. Yet, human nature being what it is, friendship is fragile and it is good to yoke people together with bonds of love. Now I have a daughter, whose name is Guinevere, who is as loving as she is beautiful, and her beauty shines like a field of ripe corn in the summer afternoon. I would that you take her as your wife that she may serve to hold us together, one to the other, and hold our peoples in union in like manner.'

When Arthur heard these words he understood that they were wise, but at the same time they grieved him, for he thought of Morgan le Fay, whom he truly loved.

XV

Arthur stretched out on his belly, his legs kicked up behind him, and chewed a straw. Cal watched him, waiting for the moment when his friend would choose to speak and knowing that it were vain to prompt him. The King frowned and looked like the boy whom Cal had come upon in the stable in that terrible castle.

'Why is it', Arthur said at last, 'that just when everything is going well . . .'

'Someone kicks away the bucket and you land in the shit,' Cal said.

'Just that.'

'Mind you, I've had reports of this Guinevere. People tell lies, of course, all princesses are beautiful. Nevertheless if half that's said is true . . . well, for those who like that sort of thing – and you do, don't you, nowadays – she seems what the stable boys would call a bit of all right.'

'That's not the point,' Arthur said and threw away the straw. 'Life was easier before I became King. Sometimes I wonder if it's worth all the trouble.'

'I believe you, of course.'

'No, you don't, but all the same it's true . . .'

'All right, let's throw it up and go on the road again, singing for our supper as we did before.'

'Don't tempt me,' Arthur said.

The next day Ethelbert sent for his daughter, that the King-Emperor might inspect her. ('He speaks of it as if he were trying to sell me a horse,' Arthur said. 'All the same, he's an honourable man and there's no question but that a marriage with his daughter would help promote the friendship between us and the Saxons, which I want to encourage.'

'Oh, so it's duty is driving you on,' Cal said.)

Actually, though Cal teased the King in this way, he favoured the demission of Morgan le Fay. There was, he thought, something uncanny about her.

Guinevere arrived at the castle of Camelot above the river that is called Tweed, where Arthur was then residing, and all men marvelled at her beauty. Her hair was the colour of ripe barley, her eyes were blue as the cornflower, her mouth was generous – though some thought her lower lip too thick – her skin was white as the whitest rose, her breasts were perfect apples, her legs, though a trifle short, were agreeably plump and well-fleshed, and her walk was slow and graceful as a cat's. In brief, she was the apotheosis of beauty such as my poor pen cannot render. It is true that some said that in repose her face was blank as a sheet of paper – Morgan le Fay would always assert that it resembled a scone. But as to this, there are two things to be said: first, that beauty is more desirable when there is a flaw – and in any case when she smiled, the sun emerging from behind a cloud was not more radiant – and second, Morgan le Fay was jealous and had never in any case been known to praise the beauty of another woman.

So it is not surprising that when Arthur saw this paragon, he was seized with desire. Indeed, he fell in love at first glance, all the more completely because there was no coquetry in her manner and indeed, she seemed utterly indifferent to the impression she made on him.

Cal thought that she looked bored. 'And probably boring too,' but he kept that thought to himself.

That evening Arthur said, 'If it were left to me, if I were permitted only to consult my own wishes, then, lovely as she is, I would send Guinevere away and remain faithful to Morgan le Fay. But it is my destiny to bind the peoples of this island in union, for it is only thus that I can advance to the restoration of the Empire of Rome. Therefore I must submit.'

'Very nicely argued,' Cal said. 'I won't swear to it, though, that you will convince Morgan of your destiny as easily as you have persuaded yourself.'

That thought chilled Arthur. Fearless in battle, he yet hesitated to tell Morgan of what he must do. He knew temptation: simply to send her away, under armed guard, back, if need be, to her husband Lot, or alternatively to some secure fortress. But he shrank from such cowardly cruelty. And yet he hesitated. Perhaps he could send Cal to tell her of what he must do. He looked at Cal and sighed . . . That would not serve either.

While he was so debating, Morgan herself entered his chamber. She ordered Cal to depart, which in some anxiety he did, though concealing himself behind a curtain. Then she turned to Arthur, and with words that bit into his heart like a whip into flesh, spoke as follows.

'Traitor and coward! Did you believe you could disguise your intentions and discard me without a word? To cast me aside for this chit of a girl, this Saxon milkmaid? And can nothing restrain you or deter you from this treachery, not the memory of the love tokens we have exchanged, nor even the thought of what will become of me, your Morgan le Fay, abandoned and shamed? Or is it indeed from me that you are trying to escape? If so, then pause, think and relent. Gaze now on the tears I shed – for, poor fool that I am, I am bereft of any other argument to sway you. Think of our union, of the marriage that was to be. Recall what I have surrendered for love of you; the respect due to a married woman and a Queen. It was for love of you that I left my husband, as Helen left the trusty Menelaus for love of Paris – lovely weakling as he proved to be. For your sake I permitted myself to be dishonoured, branded an adultress, condemned by the priests. I used to call you husband. Will you now throw me off to wed another? My sons have fought for you loyally. And is this to be their reward, to see their mother spurned and disgraced in the eyes of the world?'

She continued in this vein for as long as a man may take to walk the length of the seafront of Palermo and paused only when the sobs which she could not contain drowned her words.

Arthur listened to all she said, and struggled to master the agony which her words and reproaches aroused in his tender heart. So, at last, in a voice gentle and low, he replied, 'Morgan, Queen of Orkney and loveliest of women, I shall never deny that I am deep in your debt on account of your many kindnesses and the hours of love we have enjoyed. As long as I have breath in my body and retain the faculty of memory, I shall never tire of recalling what you have been to me. But let me make no more such protestations, but speak to the facts. I had no intention of disguising from you what I must do, or banishing you from Camelot without an explanation. Do not, pray, imagine that. If my destiny had allowed me to guide my life as I would wish, and solve my problems according to my own preference, then I would have had us live and love together till the end of time. But that cannot be. I am charged with a great duty, the restoration of the Empire. Whenever night shrouds the earth in its moist shadow, whenever the fiery stars shine in the heavens, then the anxious spirit of my grandfather, great Marcus, hovers over me in my sleep, and calls me to this duty. And now a spirit who seems to me to be the messenger of the All-Highest – that is, an angel, one of the heavenly host – has come before me, flying swiftly through the empty air to deliver the divine command. Cease therefore to dismay yourself, and me also, with your pleas, which must be vain. It is not by my own choice that I marry Guinevere.'

When she heard this speech, she did indeed cease her sobbing, and broke out in savage and scornful laughter. 'So,' she cried, 'I am to believe that the Higher Powers exercise their minds about the matter of which woman you couple with and allow such a concern to trouble them. How I have been deceived in you! I thought you gentle and good, noble and honourable. Now I see that you are a man as other men are, mean, selfish and cruel. Oh, I am not holding you. Far from it. Go, marry your Saxon milkmaid, sail the waves of the world in pursuit of your destiny. But do so with my curse: that she brings you naught but heartache and that you are deceived in your destiny, as you have deceived me in my love. For I still believe, and trust, and hope that, if there is any power of righteousness in the heavens above, if the God or gods care what becomes of us, then you will drink the cup of punishment and remorse to the dregs and, as you suffer, call out my name. For I shall ever be near you, how you cannot tell. And even when death's dark chill has parted my body from my breath, even then wherever you go my spectre will journey by your side. And I shall hear your despairing cry, and the news of your punishment will reach me, even deep in the valley of death . . .'*

*Readers well-versed in the classics will observe that in composing this

With these words she broke off sharply and hurried away, trapped between grief and anger; and she left Arthur in misery, anxious and hesitant; but now irrevocably fixed on the course that was his destiny.

exchange between Arthur and Morgan le Fay Michael Scott has borrowed freely from Virgil, and that this dialogue reproduces almost verbatim, though in prose, that scene in the *Aeneid* in which the hero bows to the will of Jupiter as conveyed to him by Mercury, who accuses him of forgetting his destiny while he dallies with Dido. In our day this would be called plagiarism and would be condemned. But the practice of medieval authors was different and Michael Scott's readers would have understood this borrowing (or theft) as an act of homage to Virgil. His intention undoubtedly was also to draw attention to his hero's significance by identifying him with Aeneas, father of the Roman people and therefore, at several removes, of the Empire. A.M.

XVI

So Morgan le Fay departed the court in great anger and there were many who held Arthur guilty of having wronged her. That, however, is the way of the world. Men will ever wrong women and there is no remedy. But before she departed she sent her son Gawaine to Arthur, not to plead her cause but to repeat her vow or threat of vengeance.

Gawaine was greatly embarrassed, for he loved his mother and Arthur also, whom he regarded as the greatest of Kings and to whom his loyalty was absolute. So now he said what had to be said, as his mother had commanded him, and then he wept, being so divided in his heart. Arthur did not reproach him for bearing his mother's message, but instead offered him comfort.

Gawaine dried his tears and said, 'For my part, I understand that you have done what you have done on account of necessity, and I pray only that you do not come to regret it, but that this Saxon Princess proves a good wife. And yet I cannot believe that she will love you as my mother has loved you and that she will be faithful to you as, perforce, you have not been faithful to my mother.'

Arthur commended him for his honesty and promised that he would not forget the courage Gawaine had shown in speaking as he did. Meanwhile Gawaine resolved to serve Arthur faithfully all the days of his life and, though he kept this to himself, to have nothing to do with women, having learned that love brings more anguish than happiness. It was on account of this resolution, which, however, circumstances determined that he could not always keep, that in years to come many regarded Gawaine as a boor; and indeed, he was often heard to say that love was a snare set by the Devil to deprive men and women of judgement and so to deliver them into his power. Which some thought cynical. The apostle Paul wrote that it is better to marry than to burn, but Gawaine did not agree.

As for Morgan le Fay, she refused to return to her husband, King Lot, but retired to a castle in the northern mountains, with her infant son Gareth; and there she devoted herself to study.

She also sent out messengers to seek for Merlin, whom she held responsible for her misery. In time he came to her one evening in autumn after the setting of the sun, in the half-dark which is owl light.

Morgan accused him of being the author of her misfortunes for, she said, 'My life has been wretched since you removed me from the sanctuary of the convent where I was happy.'

Merlin said, 'It was not by my will that you seduced Arthur who is your half-brother, being your father's son. Had I foreseen that, I should have summoned the great wind of the world to keep you apart. But I was prevented from such knowledge till it was too late, and all I could do was remove your son Mordred who is, as you know but have never confessed, Arthur's son also, and take him to school him in ignorance of his heredity.'

When he said this Morgan le Fay grew pale as the icy hand of death. At first she denied the truth of what Merlin had said and cried out that it was a plot of his invention to taint her memory of her love for Arthur, but he laid the proofs before her and then she wept, for she knew that there could be no reconciliation. So she wept tears bitter as a poisonous herb, and then she cursed Merlin as truly the author of all her misfortunes.

As she did so a cock crew, three times, though the twilight was that of evening and not dawn. Darkness fell and the chamber was cold. For a long time they remained there in silence. Merlin knew apprehension and could find no words with which to answer her. Then she said, 'I have seen in the mirror of the future what shall be. The woman for whom I have been rejected will betray him, and make him a cuckold and an object of mockery. And this will be your work too, Merlin.'

Then she called her guards and told them to take Merlin and bind him fast, and carry him to the dungeon below the castle, and she sent others to enquire of him closely where her son Mordred was lodged and then to fetch him. This was done and Merlin was held in chains, fastened to a pillar. And in time his wits wandered, and he howled like an abandoned dog.

BOOK THREE

I

The greatest of poets, Virgil, master of those who know, heralded in his *Fourth Eclogue*, loveliest of poems, the return of the Golden Age, and in the *Aeneid* declared that it would be Caesar Augustus, son of a god, who would establish that age of gold in Latium over fields that once were Saturn's realm. In truth, my Prince, men have ever looked back to a time, real or imagined, when all was peace and plenty, and will forever look forward to its return. But there are only a few moments, fleeting years, when the longing is translated into reality, and it seems as if Eden has been regained. Such a time was now inaugurated in Britain when Arthur reigned.

His magnanimity had conquered the Saxons whom the sword itself could not subdue. Friendship blossomed with peace. The marriage of Arthur and Guinevere reconciled Romans and Britons to the Germans who had invaded the island, and persuaded the incomers to make ploughs of their broadswords and pruning hooks of their spears. Law, and not violence, governed all, Arthur and his judges dispensing impartial justice. Men who had despaired of profiting from the fruits of their industry now gathered their crops without fear of pillage, and their flocks and herds had no need of armed guards to protect them. In short, it seemed to those fortunate enough to be his subjects that they had exchanged the worst for the best of times.

All this was as I say, and is well attested to by poets and chroniclers. But it is not the nature of sinful man to rest content with what is good, but instead many men are driven on in search of that which they think better, which, however, they interpret as being the establishment of their own superiority. So it happened now.

Arthur was keeping Christmas in London, holding a feast in that great tower which was built first by Julius Caesar. People had come to honour him from his dependencies, from all over Britain, from the northernmost tip of Scotland to where the land ends in the grey ocean in the West. They had come from Ireland and Iceland, and from Gaul, which is now France. There were seven kings come to do homage to Arthur, and many sons of kings and noble knights. There were Saxon earls and chevaliers from Brittany. Never, indeed, had there been such an assemblage of men of prowess. Food was plentiful and the wine flowed freely as autumn rain. The tables were covered with golden bowls and the minstrels sang of heroic deeds.

Then Arthur retired to his chamber with Guinevere his Queen. They lay together and made love, for at this time they never tired of each other's kisses and took deep delight in each other's bodies. Which is as it should be, though there are priests, mean men, ready to condemn all carnal delights. In which context may I say that, while chastity such as the Church commends may raise some to spiritual bliss, it is in my opinion wrong to say with St Paul that there is a law in the members which brings us into captivity and that to be carnally minded is death. For this is not the common experience of man. Nor of woman, either. So it was, to my mind, proper that Arthur and Guinevere should take such delight in the act of love, seeing as in their mutual passion each gave as much as received. And in any case, how could it have been otherwise, since both were young, beautiful and vigorous?

However, it so happened that on this occasion their sudden ardour, which caused them to withdraw from the feast, had evil consequences. A quarrel broke out in the absence of the King. How it started I do not know. There are many different versions and none may be relied on. Some say it erupted by chance. Some of the younger knights were amusing themselves by throwing loaves of bread. These were followed by goblets of wine. One caught a young man on the cheek and angered him. (It's said that he was a Wendish knight from the far east of Germany, but whether this was so or not, again I can't tell.) In any case this young knight, or perhaps another, was angered and picked up a carving knife and thrust it into the neck of the knight who, he thought, had hurled the goblet in his face. That knight had a brother, or perhaps a friend, who now seized another knife and attacked the aggressor. Soon there was general confusion, pell-mell. Tables were overthrown, knights scuffled and wrestled on the floor. There was much shouting and banging, there were cries of treachery and shrieks of pain. Blood mingled with spilt wine. You never saw such a brawl. A battle in the field was regular in comparison.

The noise of battle was carried to Arthur in his chamber. He leapt off Guinevere, briefly adjusted his dress, ran down the spiral staircase and burst into the hall. He jumped on to one of the few tables that was still standing and, seizing a horn from a musician, blew it loudly. Then he shouted, 'Sit down, all of you, at once, or you will lose your lives. Sit down on pain of death.'

Such was his authority that the tumult subsided. Men looked around, amazed by the confusion they had created. Some were ashamed, others afraid, others still glowered defiantly. Arthur ordered that the wounded be attended. Then he commanded all to retire to their chambers or their lodging in the city, and promised that the cause of the violence would be investigated on the morrow.

When all was quiet, and the hall deserted, except for the serving boys who were engaged in clearing up the mess, he took Cal aside and asked him if he knew how the fighting had started.

Cal said, 'Your guess is as good as mine, for if you were absent in the flesh, being engaged with Guinevere, I was absent in mind. I won't say I was asleep because the noise of the knights, all shouting their heads off as they boasted of their prowess and their importance, would have made sleep impossible. But I may have closed my eyes, I was so bored by the conversation on either side of me. As you know, this sort of great feast is not to my taste, and conversation that is all boasts and vain assertions, or challenges and gibes, which seems to be the only sort of conversation that your knights are capable of, is to me as agreeable as the chatter of village women round a pump. Less agreeable, actually. So I don't know, but if you want my opinion, which is only what I might call an educated guess, then it is that it all probably started because some young idiot was jealous because another young idiot had been placed in what seemed to him to be a more prominent or important position. That's the sort of fools they are.'

Though Arthur did not care to hear his young knights so abused, even by Cal, his trust in Cal's judgement was absolute. He scratched his nose and thought for a long time. 'You're probably right, Cal,' he said. 'Well, something must be done to prevent a repeat of this disgraceful scene.'

And this was what led him to conceive the idea of the Round Table at which no knight would occupy a position superior to any other.

II

That winter Arthur devised the qualifications, rules and ceremonies for his new Order of the Knights of the Round Table. And, though in his time Arthur did much that was memorable, there was no other action he performed that was to have greater significance for the history of Christendom than this, for it is from his definition of the character and duties of a knight of this Order of the Round Table that all the laws and customs of chivalry are derived. Now that we live in degenerate days, when selfish wilfulness governs men's temper and when chivalry itself is fallen into disrepute, it is good to be reminded of its noble origins.

There were, he determined, to be two degrees of knighthood, though one was not to be held superior to the other, but rather each was to be consecrated to different duties. But for both that word – duty or devoir – was to be paramount. All knights must submit to its discipline, for Arthur understood that a knight who is not subject to discipline is but a wild beast. 'There is', he said, 'no being more reprehensible, more menacing to the peace and virtue of the commonwealth, than a knight ungoverned who gives free rein to his own desires and heeds no will but his own.'

This he said formally in council, and later Cal said, 'You were thinking, weren't you, of those monsters, Sir Cade and Old Stoneface, and the horrors we knew in their castle.'

Arthur flushed; he hated to be reminded of the humiliation he had perforce endured there and would never speak of that experience, even to Cal. So now he bit his lip till the blood started and then turned away.

But Cal persisted. 'To think', he said, 'that these monsters may still . . . I mind you were once determined to be revenged on them. . . .'

Again Arthur said nothing.

'To think', Cal said, 'the other poor innocent boys may be enduring what we endured.'

'Do you know', Arthur said, 'who that Stoneface is? He is King Lot's brother and so that piece of ordure, Sir Cade, is our Gawaine's cousin. And he was also in his youth the foster-brother of our Sir Kay, whom I have heard speak of him with warm affection, though he was, of course, ignorant of my dealings with him. Yes, I wish still for revenge, but I will not have him killed in combat which would be to do him too much honour.'

'Then what?' Cal said.

'Do you think that I have not passed sleepless nights trying to resolve that? I would wish to see him arraigned and his iniquities exposed before a court of law, but . . .' and his voice trailed away.

'But that would give him the chance to humiliate you before all the world by confessing how he had used you . . . It would be better to hit him on the head and throw him into a ditch.'

They argued this matter, often and at length, and could not yet arrive at a conclusion.

Before the council the King elaborated his plans for the Order.

The first degree of knighthood was that of the knights bachelor. They were not to be condemned to chastity but, while they held this rank, were to eschew marriage. The reason for this require-ment was clear in Arthur's mind. His knights bachelor were to be dedicated to war and his service; they were his elite cavalry force. Moreover, they must be available at all times for any assignment which he might send them on, alone or in small bands. They must not be constrained by domestic affections and, while they were in the degree of knights bachelor, they should hold neither castles nor land even in trust as his vassals; for he understood that in time those who hold fiefs of the crown come to consider such as their own estates. In short, the knights bachelor were to be a species of monks of war, but considering their youth, their ardour, their virility, Arthur thought it wrong to impose on them, as is imposed on monks, a vow of chastity which, it was probable, they would be unable to keep. And in this he displayed his wisdom and his understanding of men. But he thought it proper to deny them, and that they should vow to deny themselves, attachments which bound them by law, and not merely by honour and sentiment.

Those who wished to form such attachments would, if they persisted, be removed from the order of knights bachelor and would enter into the second order, which was that of the knights territorial. To these knights Arthur assigned castles and lands to be held directly from him. They were to secure the peace of the countryside, hold law courts and, in times of general war, supply the King with a fixed number of archers, men-at-arms and auxiliary troops. It was their duty to collect royal taxes, apprehend evildoers, guard against incursions or civil strife. Though they were knights of the Round Table, they were excused, indeed forbidden, attendance at court, save at the great feasts of midwinter and midsummer. To each Arthur assigned learned clerks to assist them in their judicial and fiscal duties. But these clerks remained royal servants, owing their first loyalty to the King, who paid their salaries, and not to the knights territorial. Furthermore the knights territorial were required to send their sons to the royal court when they attained the age at which they might bear arms; and some were employed there as pages while the most suitable became novices in the order of the knights bachelor.

So Arthur provided for the good government of the realm; and it will not have escaped your intelligent eye, my Prince, that he had devised a judicious system of checks and balances to secure this. For, on the one hand, the knights bachelor served as his personal bodyguard and were free of the divided loyalties which barons who hold land from the King naturally and commonly come to feel; their ambition was centred only on pleasing the King and winning his approbation. At the same time, should any of the knights territorial come to be driven by personal ambition and seek to defy the King, even to the point of rebellion, or neglect his interest in favour of what they deemed to be his own, then the company of the knights bachelor, being free of the impediment of property, was at the King's disposal to suppress rebellion or call the errant to order. And, on the other hand, the knights territorial were established on their estates to ensure that the King's law ran throughout the land and order was maintained. That all should be safe and secure was in their interest too. Finally the requirement that they should send their sons to be reared and trained in the

King's court, where their employment would be determined according to their abilities, ensured that there should be no hereditary interest in the estates their father held from the crown and the castles they occupied. In this way Arthur hoped to avoid the consequences of family ambition that have weakened so many monarchies, as fiefs become hereditary and the interest of the family, which, as a philosopher, I term a sectional interest, is found to take precedence over the interest of the King, which is national.

In so devising these orders of knighthood and the form of the state – that is to say, the public thing, or republic, for a commonwealth that is well-ordered is a republic, whether it have one head or several – Arthur displayed his wisdom. He drew on many perfect examples, inasmuch as perfection may be attained in our disordered world, which indeed is to no great extent. He understood, as few rulers have done, that the science of constructing a commonwealth, or rather renovating it, since no commonwealth is constructed out of nothing precedent, is an experimental science, not to be taught a priori.

And yet, sadly, one may reflect that, admirable as his construction was – so admirable, indeed, as to be a model for all ages and one of the wonders of the political mind – yet it could not but partake of the common experience of mankind, could not escape that bitter law which decrees that very plausible schemes, devised with the utmost intelligence, may often have shameful and lamentable conclusions. For history demonstrates that things which appear of little moment may assume horrible shape and lead in time to adversity.

III

One morning in spring, a lamb-bleating morning with the sky woad-blue and the breeze gentle as a mother's smile, Gawaine came to Arthur. He stood solid before him with his legs planted wide and said nothing, till Arthur sighed and put aside his book, which was as so often Virgil's *Aeneid*, for he never tired of it, and lifted his eyes enquiringly to Gawaine.

Gawaine, having come to speak his mind, could not. Arthur gestured to a chair, and Gawaine sat and opened his mouth, and still kept silent.

'You look', Arthur said, 'as if you thought I would not care for what you have to say.'

Gawaine said, 'I'm bored' and flushed as if he had spoken an indecency. 'I'm not alone,' he said. 'Many of the young men, your knights bachelor, suffer the same infliction. We are soldiers, knights, and there is no war. It's not good, not for us. Peace . . .' and his words now came in a rush, though he was no orator and ordinarily silent, which was one of the qualities Arthur valued in him, saying, 'Gawaine speaks only when there is need. He never prattles.' So now: 'Peace is good for peasants, for the farmers. They get their crops in, and their beasts are safe in field and fold. Peace is good for priests and clerks. But peace means our occupation's gone, denied us.'

'There will not always be peace,' Arthur said.

For a moment he thought of telling Gawaine of his intention that, when he was assured that the whole land of Britain was truly at peace, he would lead his army across the sea and restore the Empire of Rome. 'No,' he repeated, 'there will not always be peace, though the imposition of peace is the duty of kings and emperors. It is always easier to make war than peace, but the art of government is to impose the custom of peace, to spare the conquered and subdue the proud.'

'Be that as it may,' Gawaine said, 'for us young knights peace is bloody boring.'

'I suppose it may be,' Arthur said. 'But I cannot conjure up an invading army to relieve you of boredom. Nevertheless, what you say disturbs me. We shall talk of it tomorrow when I have thought upon the matter.'

'How I wish', he thought, 'I had the Goloshan to advise me.' But the Goloshan was no more, death having come upon him like a thief.

He consulted Cal, who sniffed deeply and said the young knights were all fools. As for him, he said, he had known enough misery and fear to be content to lie in bed in the morning thinking that he would eat well that day and return to the same bed in the evening without having encountered any danger while out of it.

'Not everyone is as sensible as you, Cal,' Arthur said.

He took his trouble to Guinevere, who rested on a couch in a shift; her languorous attitude distracting him. He lay with her and they toyed with each other pleasurably, and when they had known delight, she stretched out a soft white arm and took a sweetmeat and bit into it, and put the other half in his mouth.

She said, 'They don't have this and you wonder that they are bored.'

Arthur believed her, for already, so early in their marriage, Guinevere too had complained of boredom and therefore was accustomed to recognise the condition which was foreign to him.

'It's all right for you,' she said. 'When there is no action you stick your nose in a book and it seems to satisfy you, why I'm sure I can't tell. It's not very polite to me, I must say.'

'Well,' Arthur said, disregarding the querulous note in her voice, 'few of my young knights know how to read. So that recourse is denied them.'

'They're none the worse for that,' she said.

Arthur pondered the question through the dark hours of the night, and in the morning called Gawaine to him and spoke as follows.

'You were right to come and speak to me as you did, and I was wrong not to have foreseen, or even observed, how peace and inaction chafe you and the other young knights. You are warriors and though it is necessary that at all times the greater part of the Order to which you belong resides at court, for one can never tell when a striking force will be needed, to respond at once to invasion or rebellion; and though it is also necessary that regular military exercises are held, so that my knights remain competent to undertake any task that may present itself, yet I see there must also be some relaxation. Therefore I have resolved that my knights bachelor should be free to seek out adventures of their own, and respond on their own initiative to any appeals for help made by those in distress, always provided that they act in a manner fitting their station, under penalty of dismissal should they not do so, and also that there is always a quorum of knights resident at my court, ready and able to respond to any emergency.'

When he heard these words, Gawaine knelt and kissed the King's hand, and his heart was full of joy. He asked for immediate leave to set forth in search of adventure and his request was granted.

And it was on account of this wise decision that so many noble knights enjoyed great adventures, of which so many stories are told.

IV

There are many stories told of Gawaine's adventures and it may be that some of them are true. But it is strange: in the years after Arthur established himself as King and Emperor in Britain, it is as if a veil falls over history. What I have already related is fact, questionable doubtless in detail, indisputable in outline. But now, in the stories concerning the adventures of his knights, it is as if we enter into legend. There are many details, vivid, entrancing, moving, so much so that one is tempted to believe that the story they illuminate must be founded in fact. Yet some of these tales have clearly been devised to entertain. They are the work of poets, not historians. I grant you that poets reveal truth. In this narrative I have often had occasion to mention Virgil and will doubtless speak of him again. Now, though it is in the highest degree improbable that the story of the *Aeneid* recounts events as they actually occurred – and indeed, in a whisper I might suggest that neither Aeneas nor Dido may have actually existed – yet who can doubt that the poet speaks with authority; speaks, indeed, a species of higher truth? But this is because Virgil draws on myth, which has meaning, not on legend, which is all too often merely the chatter of silly women and idle men.

So, for example, we have the story of Gawaine and the Green Knight. It is a good story, as you shall hear.

Arthur was holding court at Camelot. It was the last night of the old year and some knights looked back with pride or regret to the year that was dying, while others looked forward eagerly to that which was to be born. And some boasted of the mighty feats they had performed and others of what they would achieve. Some were merry and others quarrelsome; and in truth there was in the hall an undercurrent of anxiety, why none could be certain, save that the new moon which should have risen seven nights before had not yet appeared, though the nights were frosty and the stars shone bright in the skies. It is an ill omen, many said.

Then, though Arthur held court as was his duty, it was known that for some weeks past he had been troubled in both mind and body, suffering from fevers and sleeping ill at night. Many a knight that evening had glanced at the King as he sat, with Guinevere his Queen on his right hand and Gawaine his nephew on his left, at the High Table which stood raised on a dais at the western end of the hall; and they observed that he did not eat, but merely crumbled his bread, and that when he drank wine, the sweat stood out sparkling on his brow. And this disturbed them, for they feared that the sickness of the King was as a mirror foretelling the coming sickness of the realm.

None dared speak such fears but many minds were oppressed by them. As for Guinevere, she sat in silence and made no effort to urge Arthur to eat. She looked heavy, despondent, sulky.

Then, with a mighty crash, the outer doors of the hall were thrown open. All were alerted. All turned to learn the cause of this disturbance. All fell silent.

They saw a knight in green armour, taller by a head than the tallest knight of the Round Table. In one hand he carried an axe, such as the Saxon warriors wield in battle, and in the other the branch of a holly tree. Indeed, he was green from head to toe, and in the candlelight of the hall it seemed that his face was green also. He wore a straight coat that fell over his shining emerald breastplate.

Behind him came a squire, also dressed in green, and he led a noble horse such as we now call a destrier. The pendants of its breast harness, the fine crupper, the studs of the bit and all the metal fittings were also green, and so were the saddle bows, and the skirts of the saddle that were richly ornamented with emeralds and burnished gold. Even the horse itself seemed to be green.

The knight was handsome, no doubt about it, and the hair of his head matched that of his horse. It was beautiful, fanning out to lie on his broad shoulders, and a great green beard like a bush in spring hung over his chest.

Such a rare horse and such a knight were never seen in that hall before, and many of the knights took him for an ogre, despite the beauty of his countenance, for it was also a stern countenance and, it seemed, a cruel one. Of course, you, my Prince, belonging to an enlightened age and having also the benefit of my teaching, which is founded in experience and reason, know that ogres, man-eating monsters, belong to fairy tales, or the stories devised by old wives to frighten little children (which is not to be despised, for it stimulates their imagination). But Arthur's knights were more ignorant, and many of them believed in ogres and some swore that they had done battle against them. So it is not surprising that many at once judged that this extraordinary knight was such a being.

Now, holding his axe aloft, the Green Knight advanced towards the dais, as one who knew no fear but was accustomed to inspire it in others. 'Who', he said, 'is master of this company, for I would have speech with him?' And his eyes searched the hall as if he were looking to see who there was of the highest renown.

No one immediately replied, but all gazed on him with wonder, for they had never before seen a knight and horse that were green as the grass of early summer. Some took it as illusion and magic, and so even the boldest knights held silence, as though all had slipped into sleep and waited for Arthur himself to give the knight answer.

Which, though he was sick in body and mind (as I have said) he now did, and bade the incomer welcome. 'You are a stranger,' he said, 'and as such I invite you to be one of our company and partake of our feast, this last night of the old year.'

'No, so help me God,' replied the knight, 'that is not my intention. I have travelled here, from a far country, to deliver a challenge. I lay down before any knight here who is bold enough a goodly wager: that we exchange stroke for stroke. Here is my axe. I offer it to whoever will pick up the glove and I shall withstand the first blow, without returning it now. But I challenge whoever is bold enough to meet me to allow me, in my own castle, to return blow for blow, stroke for stroke, one twelvemonth to the day from now. Therefore speak out, he who dares.'

Then he rolled his eyes about and swung his green beard from side to side, seeking to see who would rise from his seat and meet the challenge. But no one moved, and he coughed very loudly and it seemed to some that he belched fire out of his mouth. But this could not be, though his glance shed lightning. Then he laughed. 'What, do all cower in fear without a blow being struck? What manner of knights are these?'

Arthur was offended by this mockery and, rising from his seat with such strength as in his weakened state he might muster, he approached the Green Knight and said, 'Give me your battleaxe now, and I shall satisfy your demand and grant you the boon you have asked for.'

But the knight held fast to the axe and would not yield it. 'Rare knights you have,' he said, 'that not one of them will take up my challenge but it must be left to their King and master.'

All the company felt his scorn and flinched to hear him speak in this way.

Then Gawaine, provoked and ashamed, came forward and said, 'This boor speaks truth. It is not fitting that you should take the burden of this challenge upon yourself. Therefore grant me the right to accept it, for this business is so foolish that it is not proper for you to concern yourself with it.'

So Gawaine took the axe from the Green Knight who, after enquiring his name and being satisfied that he was a man of birth and sufficient honour, extended his neck and bade Gawaine strike. And when he did so he cut clean through the bone with one mighty blow so that the blood spurted forth, crimson over the green flesh and the green garments, and the severed head tumbled to the floor.

All the company cheered, but were soon silenced, when they saw the knight lean forward and pick up the head by the green hair, and hold it towards Gawaine. Then the lips moved and it uttered these words: 'You have struck boldly, Sir Gawaine, and must, according to our bond, receive as boldly in your turn.'

Gawaine grew pale, to think of what this meant. He trembled, as any man, however brave, might in these circumstances. But he said only, 'And where shall I find you, a year from today?'

'Many men know me as the Knight of the Green Chapel and if you ask there, then you will not fail to find me.'

Then he mounted his horse, gave a tug to the reins and galloped out of the hall, his head in his hand; and flint sparks flew from the horse's hooves. None knew where he had gone or whence he had come, but Gawaine was left gazing after him and the blood lay about his feet.

When the season of Yule was over and snow lay deep on the ground, so that there was no hunting but all were condemned to idleness, there was, as you might expect, much talk of this strange encounter and of the terrible challenge which Gawaine had accepted. Arthur himself was disturbed because his nephew had put himself in such jeopardy. He said often, to Guinevere and also to Cal, that he wished he had Merlin with him, to consult as to what was best to be done. But Merlin had vanished and none knew where he was to be found.

Guinevere, who was displeased that Arthur in his perplexity seemed to neglect her, and who did not in any case value Gawaine as highly as the King did, pouted and said that, to her mind, Gawaine was a fool to have accepted the challenge and would be a greater one to keep his side of the bargain.

Arthur sighed. 'It is a question of honour,' he thought, 'such as you, my dear wife, being both a Saxon and a woman, do not understand.' In this judgement, which he prudently kept to himself, he did her some wrong, for the Saxons had, and have, a sense of honour as fine as that of other people. But it is true that women understand such matters differently from men.

Cal too was unimpressed. 'Honour', he said, 'is a fine word, doubtless, but it is only a word, and those who choose to be guided by their understanding of that word are mostly fools. I don't deny that there is such a thing as I too would call honour, but my understanding of it is different, being founded in common sense. To my mind, to keep an agreement that will result in you having your head cut off is quite simply grotesque. Besides, honour presumably, even in your code of chivalry, is something which can exist only between equals, which is why your knights will refuse to engage in single combat against men of low birth who are not eligible for knighthood. Now it's perfectly obvious that this Green Knight, whoever and whatever he may be, is not Gawaine's equal. There is something uncanny about him. Indeed, evidently he is not a mortal man. If he had been, he wouldn't have been able to pick up his head and ride away. He is some sort of spirit who had assumed the appearance of a knight. Which is not to say that he will prove incapable of dealing with Gawaine as Gawaine dealt with him. Only the result will be different.' He turned to Gawaine and said, 'Do you really suppose that when this Thing – which I call him since he is evidently no mortal man – has cut off your head in turn, you will be able to pick it up and thank him as he thanked you. It's too daft for words and if you want my opinion, you would be sensible to treat the whole episode as a bad dream.'

'I agree that what you say is improbable,' Gawaine replied. 'Nevertheless I gave my word and must keep it.'

So it was that at the time of the next winter solstice Sir Gawaine took his leave of the King, and of his brothers Agravaine and Gaheris, who wept to see him set off, fearing that he was riding to his death. There had been hard frost and his horse's hooves clattered as he rode over the drawbridge; but the sky was now heavy with snow and the air was still as the grave.

He rode for three days through a lifeless land, with gloomy Saturn in the ascendant, though the night sky was covered and by day the firmament was overcast with dull clouds. On the first day he asked an old woman to direct him to the Green Chapel, and when she heard his demand she crossed herself and turned away. On the second day he saw birds fall dead from the trees and on the third it began to snow. He rode over brown moors and followed the course of a frozen stream. Then the wind blew, and he set his face against it and rode on till he came to a castle rising up before him as the snowflakes bit into his face. He urged his horse into a trot and they crossed the drawbridge, and he hammered with the pommel of his sword on the gate.

He struck three blows but received no answer. He called out three times and only the echo of his voice returned to him. He beat again upon the gate, but his efforts were vain. 'Either this castle is deserted,' he said to himself, 'or those who occupy it are inhospitable beyond reason, or afraid of even a lone traveller.'

So he pulled his horse's head round and rode again into the night. He had travelled scarce a mile when he saw a light gleam in the forest on his left side. A track led towards it. Several times as he advanced along it he lost sight of the light and wondered if it was one of these wills-o'-the-wisp which, as all know, lead travellers astray and often to their death. The wood grew thicker, the track narrowed and he was surrounded by silence. Sometimes briars trailed across his path and even tore his face so that it seemed as if no one had come this way for some time past. A more fearful knight would have abandoned the quest, but Gawaine had the courage of a mastiff and was also deficient in that disturbing imagination which conjures up terrors. So he persevered.

At last he came to a clearing and the light flickered before him. It came, it seemed, from a little chapel and, dismounting, he led his horse forward and tied its reins to the overhanging branch of a tree. Then he pushed open the door and entered.

He now saw that the light within the chapel was green and it was so because the walls were covered with hangings of green silk, which reflected the light that came from a candelabrum that stood on the altar and changed its colour. A figure in a green robe knelt there as if in prayer, but when he heard the sound of Gawaine's foot upon the stone flags he rose, advanced towards him and, in a harsh voice, demanded to know his purpose.

'I am a knight in search of the Green Chapel,' Gawaine replied, 'and I think this must be it.'

'This is the Chapel Perilous,' was the reply.

'Why then,' Gawaine said, 'if this is not the Green Chapel, I must journey further. But first I shall rest here.'

'There is no rest to be found here. This is the Chapel Perilous, which is why I am condemned never to desist from prayer that I may keep myself safe from the danger that threatens.'

'And what danger is that?' Gawaine said.

'Some name it Possession, and now I must return to prayer.'

So Gawaine first tended to his horse and then lay down to sleep. But all night he was assailed by demons who came to him in the form of beautiful women who sought to seduce him. Many times he came close to yielding, for the temptation was great when they danced before him and leaned over him and pressed against him and kissed him on the lips, seeking to thrust their tongues into his mouth. And some stroked him and others lay across him, and all murmured endearments while two dark-skinned girls played on lutes and sang.

But he resisted for he said to himself that these were trials to deflect him from his mission; and therefore he denied them and subdued desire. And in the morning a chill wind blew through the chapel and the demons vanished. So Gawaine saddled his horse and rode on his way.

He had not journeyed seven miles when he came to a river and rode downstream till he found a ford. A knight sat on a roan horse on the further bank, and Gawaine called out to him and enquired whether he could direct him to the Green Chapel. The knight invited him to cross the water, for he had, he said, been sent to act as his guide. When Gawaine heard this he was filled with joy, for it was great satisfaction to him to think he had arrived at his goal, and had proved himself worthy. It is true that he felt also a shiver of fear, but that is not to be wondered at.

Then the knight invited him to accompany him to his castle.

They arrived there and Gawaine found a feast prepared. He fell to eagerly, for his appetite was sharp and healthy. A squire stood behind his chair and urged food upon him, cuts of cold beef and a rich pie of blackcock, partridge and venison. There was Rhenish wine to drink and the knight toasted Gawaine, who replied, 'I am pleased to find that my word was not doubted.'

'The feast was prepared whether you came or not.'

Then he took Gawaine by the hand and led him to a chamber, and said, 'I shall leave you here, for I must seek instructions, and also I must hunt, so this night and the next night and the one after, when we meet, we shall exchange gifts.'

So Gawaine was left puzzled, but not distressed. At the same time he felt obscurely cheated. It had taken courage to make this journey. He had nerved himself to meet the ordeal that awaited him. And he had eaten well and drunk good wine, and was now resting on a comfortable couch. Indeed, it was so comfortable that he fell asleep.

When he woke he was no longer alone. There was a scent of violets and on the adjacent couch there reclined the most beautiful woman he had ever seen. That was his first impression and the longer he gazed on her the more certain he became. There was something of Guinevere in her blondeness, pale skin and generous breasts, something of her also in the bow-shaped mouth. Yet she excelled Guinevere as the Arab steed excels the finest draught-horse. There was fire and nobility in her eye, and, whereas Guinevere's legs were a little too short for her length of body, so that she showed to best advantage when seated (or so at least Gawaine thought), no such disproportion marred the beauty of this lady. Indeed, since her robe was fashioned with a slit running from ankle to her hip, and the garment had fallen away as she lay on the couch, he could see that her legs were long and lovely as hyacinths.

(I become lyrical. Forgive me. It's weeks since I had a woman.)

The lady smiled at Gawaine, but did not move. Gawaine felt a surge of lust, but restrained himself. Meanwhile sweet music sounded from a minstrel's gallery and the winter sun sank in the sky. Then, as it dipped behind distant hills and pine trees stood black against a paling yellow and gold shot with streaks of crimson, the lady rose from her couch, leaned over Gawaine, kissed him once on the lips and left him.

That evening the knight returned from his hunting and gave Gawaine his trophy, and asked what he had to give in return.

Gawaine found himself blushing. 'A single kiss,' he said; and the knight extended his cheek to him.

On the second day, when the knight had departed to the forest, the lady again lay by Gawaine, and this time let pale fingers touch his brow. And when she left him as the evening sun slid from the sky, she kissed him twice.

And that evening the knight and Gawaine exchanged their gifts for the second time.

On the third day the lady was dressed in gold, and when the gold faded in the sky, she kissed Gawaine three times and then, stepping out of her slit skirt, she slowly and with an undulating motion unhooked her girdle and held it out to him. He opened his mouth to speak but she pressed herself down upon him and they found no need of words. All that Gawaine had ever dreamed was given freely to him. And when she left, without a backward glance, his hand fell on the girdle and he clutched it to him and smothered it with kisses.

The knight came to him with the spoils of the chase, and Gawaine gave him three kisses in exchange, but said nothing of the girdle or what he had received when it was loosed.

In the morning a page came to him and said he had been sent to guide him to the Green Chapel where his adversary was waiting. 'For', he said, with a simper that spoke of his embarrassment, 'I am charged to tell you that you will be deemed a coward if you do not come with me.'

'I am no coward,' Gawaine said, 'and if you are a servant of the Green Knight, as I suppose, then I must tell you that I have been awaiting this summons for three days now and was ready to question whether your master would keep his word.'

But, though he spoke boldly as befitted his station, he trembled, for it is an awful thing to prepare to have your head cut off, as, my Prince, you may well suppose.

So Gawaine commanded the page to wait a moment while he put on a second shirt, that he might not be seen to tremble on account of the cold. The page took him by the hand and led him from the castle to the chapel, which stood not far distant, and as they marched he spoke merrily as if to divert him from the ordeal that awaited him.

The frost was hard and Gawaine's mailed feet clanged on the icy ground.

In the chapel Gawaine knelt and commended his soul to the gods he worshipped (for I am not certain that he was a Christian) and the page knelt beside him and said some prayers, perhaps for his soul.

There came a sound as of a mighty rushing wind, such as the apostles heard, we are assured, on the Day of Pentecost. The door of the chapel flew open. Green leaves, as if it were summer and not dead winter, trailings of ivy, branches of holly, swirled through it, spiralled upwards towards the angels diving, as it seemed, eagerly from the roof. All whirled and swirled, and birled in the wild laughter of that mighty wind.

Then there was stillness, and the leaves and twigs and branches floated downwards and lay over the stone flags like a green carpet. Gawaine rose to his feet, turned to the doorway and saw there the Green Knight, tall as a pine tree and broad as an ancient oak.

He advanced towards Gawaine and did not speak till they were within arm's length of each other. 'This is genial,' he said. 'I'm bound to tell you, old sport, that I was surprised to find that you have kept your word.'

'And why should I not? Honour compelled me and in my turn I may tell you that your surprise does me dishonour, grave dishonour.'

'No need to mount your high horse,' the Green Knight said and laughed. 'If I were to tell you the number – aye, and the names – of the knights who first accepted my challenge and then reneged on it, being what I call chicken, you would not wonder at my surprise. In my experience, which is considerable, for I've lived in six countries and what I say is the truth therefore, there are many knights who are bold in their blustering talk, but shy away when it's a question of looking reality in the face. So I congratulate you, and don't think, young man, that in doing so, I am guilty of patronising you. Not my intention at all, I assure you, and would swear to my respect for you if this were my dying day and these my last words.'

Gawaine was pleased to hear this praise, though he blushed somewhat, to his embarrassment, and thought also that, in the circumstances, the Green Knight's last words were not happily chosen. 'In my opinion,' he said, 'a true knight must do what a knight has to do.'

'Absolutely my opinion too,' the Green Knight said. 'So let's get on with the business in hand, shall we? Kneel down, and I promise you it won't take long.'

Gawaine knelt and the page bit his lip to restrain his tears, for he had never witnessed such bravery as Gawaine now displayed, and was seized with admiration and smitten with love. 'This', he thought, 'is true nobility' and now he could not prevent himself, but gave way to weeping.

The Green Knight raised the axe, swung it once round his head and brought it down heavily on Gawaine's neck.

The blow drove his face to the floor so that his nose bled, but there was no other wound.

Again the Green Knight struck with the axe and again Gawaine's nose met the stone; but again there was no other wound; and he shook his head as if dazed or astonished to find it still attached to his body.

A third time the Green Knight struck, the mightiest of the blows he had delivered; and this time blood gushed from Gawaine's neck, but still his head remained attached and the page cried aloud for joy.

The Green Knight extended his hand, raised Gawaine to his feet and embraced him. 'Never', he said, 'have I come upon a knight who withstood this ordeal so bravely. From this day on we are brothers.'

Saying this, he released Gawaine and, raising both hands to his own head, removed it, shrugged twice and another head appeared from below, and Gawaine saw that it was the knight who had been his host at the castle.

He laughed to see Gawaine's amazement. 'Come,' he said, 'you didn't really suppose you had cut off my head last year in Arthur's court and then watched me walk out of the hall? It's an old trick but what I believe is called an esoteric one. I learned it on my travels, from one of the shamans, wise men, who dwell among the frosty Caucasus. They know a trick or two, I can tell you, and it's said that some of them have discovered the secret of immortality. But that's as may be, I'm not convinced. Fact is, old boy, these shamans talk a lot of cock. It fools some people, but I'm a plain unvarnished Englishman or Brit, and you can't pull the wool over my eyes. Now I think we could both do with a spot of beer. It's been a thirsty morning for the pair of us. Boy,' he said to the page, 'fetch us beer. Off you go. He's a good boy,' he said, lowering his voice, 'and a sweet one, but a tad soft, you know, a bit of a mollycoddle. Why, he was in tears now – you wouldn't have seen it, but he was – even though he knew you wouldn't come to any hurt.'

'I don't know about that,' Gawaine said, putting his hand to his neck, which was bleeding freely.

'That's nothing, just a flesh wound. Take this.' The knight handed him a linen cloth to stanch the bleeding. 'Should explain,' he said. 'But, by the bye, I've been remiss, haven't properly introduced myself. Sir Tobias, but I answer to Toby.

Where was I? Oh yes, that neck wound. That's because you cheated me.'

'Cheated you?'

'Yes indeed. When we exchanged gifts you held back on me. What about my lady's girdle? Eh, what about that?' And he laughed uproariously, and dug Gawaine in the ribs. 'Bit of a dog, aren't you.'

The boy returned with a jug of beer and two horns, and they drank each other's health. Then they repaired to the tavern and drank more beer, and were merry as larks.

V

For seven days Gawaine continued with Sir Tobias, hunting and feasting, and every day he found his company more pleasing. Over the wine, which was the richest vintage of Burgundy, his host spoke to him of his travels and adventures, of how he had journeyed in northern regions where the snow never melts and where, he assured Gawaine, women when they are widowed couple with wolves, and bring forth male children who are boys by day and, when it pleases them (which is, however, but infrequently) wolves by night.

'Furthermore,' he said, 'once, when attacked by a wolf as I sought a lodging for the night in an inn deep in the pine forest, I drew my sword and slew it, and found that at my feet there was only a pelt, with neither flesh nor bones nor blood, but when I entered into the inn parlour I found the landlord lying across the hearth with his throat cut. And yet there are some who assert that these werewolves, as they call them, may be killed only with a silver arrow.'

'Then,' he said, 'on another occasion, I journeyed into the mountains that lie beyond the great rivers to the east. And I came to a castle perched on a rocky cliff. The lord of the castle received me hospitably and fed me well, and gave me a strong liquor to drink, which he called vodka, or something similar. Firewater it was, if the truth be told. But not unpalatable. Not unpalatable, when served with strong ale as it was. The habit is that you chase the ale with the vodka – or is it the other way round? Damned if I can remember. No matter, all went swimmingly, though my host neither ate nor drank all the night long. But he told stories of the savage tribe known as the Huns, whom, however, he called the Wild Horde, who had driven his father from the plains where they had lived for generations rich in cattle and horses, to this mountain refuge, where he pined for what he had lost. And so, he said, he had become one who thought only on how to avenge himself on mankind and recover what fortune had cheated him of. He treated me kindly,' Sir Tobias said to Gawaine, but then shook his head and added, 'nevertheless, I was happy to escape that castle, for there was one uncanny morning when I went in search of my host and found him apparently asleep in a coffin, with dried blood at the corner of his mouth. And when I slipped away early one morning and descended into the plain and came to a village, they stoned me when they learned whence I had come. Indeed, I was lucky to escape with my life. Yes, indeed, I have had adventures . . .'

He took a pull of his wine, then told of how he had visited Byzantium, the great city where the floors of the imperial palaces are covered with precious stones, rubies, sapphires, opals and topazes. 'The Emperor', he said, 'keeps such state that no man may, if presenting a petition or seeking justice, address him in person, but must do so by way of intermediaries, passing the message and the response from room to room, so that the reply which is at last received is neither the answer to the question you proposed, nor, indeed, in all probability the answer which the Emperor delivered to the mangled question that he heard. And this, in my opinion, accounts for the failure of policy which afflicts the Empire.'

Gawaine could have happily listened to Sir Tobias till the seasons changed and spring arrived to refresh the land. There seemed to be no end to his stories. He had, for example, been taken prisoner by pirates in the northern seas and escaped death only because the pirate chief discovered that he played chess, for which the rude Northman had conceived a passion while serving in the imperial guard in Byzantium.

'He swore, jovially, that if he checkmated me in fifteen moves he would hang me from his topmast, but I held him off and he found me so well-matched an adversary that I do believe he would have kept me with him for ever if he had not toppled drunk into the sea one night . . .'

'And how did you escape, then?' Gawaine asked.

'Why,' said Sir Tobias, 'that was no easy matter, but I dived into the water as if to rescue him and swam towards land, which I should not have reached, for it was far distant, had I not happened upon a dolphin which carried me on its back.'

At last Gawaine, after many weeks of listening, determined that he must return to Camelot, for that was where his duty lay. But before he departed he made bold to enquire of his host why he had embarked on the masquerade as the Green Knight.

Sir Tobias pulled at the corner of his moustache and for some minutes huffed and puffed. Then he said, 'I had hoped you wouldn't ask that, old cock, for the truth is that I dislike exceedingly to be asked a question to which I don't know the answer. I could invent one, of course. I can invent anything if I please. But since you withstood my stroke so boldly, more boldly than any other knight that ever dared accept my challenge, I owe it to you to try to be truthful . . . And that is not easy, for you must have observed that men prefer lies to truth. Be that as it may, I can say only this: one day, in November, a dank, misty, moist afternoon, with the sun lying blood-red on the marshes, I was fishing in a sluggish stream and catching nothing, and I thought to myself, "Has the time come when I must abandon knight-errantry, which is a fool's game when all is said and done, and instead set my lands in order?" And at that moment a figure rose from out of the marsh, and before my eyes shed the muddy garments which it wore and was revealed as the most beautiful of women, but for one flaw. And this was that her heart had been torn out and her breast shed blood. She accosted me and spoke in a low voice, and a foreign tongue which I could not well understand. Despite her wound I would have lain with her, for I desired her greatly. I have to admit that. But she would have none of it and refused me. Instead, she took my hand and placed it in her wound where the heart should have been, and then she spoke again, and I understood her to say that she had been cruelly deceived by a knight who had pledged her undying love. She laid a spell on me. No question of that, for her will subdued mine and I was hers to command. And what she commanded was the charade which I have ever since been compelled to perform, and from which I now dare to hope your courage and constancy have set me free.'

Saying this, he wept, which Gawaine had never seen him do

before, so that Gawaine would have comforted him, had he known how.

But the Green Knight rose, shook himself and laughed. Gawaine read bitterness and longing in that laughter, and was afraid.

'But this may have been a dream,' Sir Tobias said, 'and sometimes I believe it was, and that it was I myself who devised this game, and that merely because I was bored. Which is the curse of our age, and one that afflicts especially knights such as me who have travelled the world to its bounds, seen much, too much, and found nothing left worth the doing beneath the visiting moon . . . It is the tedium of life that afflicts me with a longing for death which I can find no means to satisfy. So I play out this parody of the death that is denied me. Does that make sense, old cock?' he finished with a rueful smile.

'None to me,' Gawaine replied, 'for in my experience, my friend – as I trust I may truly call you – death comes easily to most men and often before they are willing to be quit of the flesh. I fear you may be bewitched.'

'That thought, believe me, is not foreign to me.'

'And yet,' Gawaine said, 'when you speak of the tedium of life and your wish for death, what you say strikes a chord in my innermost being, even though I am accounted a man who takes joy in life and has won great renown. Is it possible that this world we inhabit is not what it seems, but one in which we enact a ghostly drama ordained by fate?'

'That is as may well be,' his companion said. 'These are mysteries. And now I think we should drink some beer. If you ask me, my friend, we are doomed to trouble and must endure it. There's no remedy, but beer assists.'

The next morning Gawaine took his leave and rode back to Camelot, and as he rode, he thought, 'That is the bravest thing I have done in my life and yet now it seems meaningless. Sir Tobias called it a charade. Perhaps that is all it was. Yet we must go on, and the great thing is to make a good show and act as if there were a meaning which we cannot understand . . .'

VI

So Gawaine rode back to Camelot and, because his mind was busy with the marvels he had seen and heard, he mistook his way and found himself in a forest of mighty oaks and beeches. It was very still in that forest. No birds sang and he saw neither habitation nor wild beasts. Night fell and so he lay down to sleep with his back against an oak.

The moon rose and he woke from a fitful slumber, and heard music. Having ascertained that all was well with his horse, he followed a path that seemed to lead him to the music. It was beset with brambles and he walked warily, but in a little he came upon a clearing in the forest, and there he saw the musicians and those who danced to their tune.

They were beings such as he had only heard tell of – fairies – and their dance was light and elegant as any he had seen at court. For some time he stood, entranced, for he had never seen anything so beautiful as these slight little people who wore iridescent garments that seemed to him insubstantial as spiders' webs. And indeed, it is the practice of fairies to spin the clothes they wear for ceremonies such as their midsummer dance from such webs, though first they dye them all the colours of the rainbow.

Then one who seemed to be their Queen, for she wore a crown formed from honeysuckle on her brow, approached him, giving no sign of surprise at his presence, and addressed him as if he were a long-expected guest.

Then she led him into the magic ring, and the fairies danced around him and pleased him mightily, for Gawaine was rough and simple as he was honest and, there being no duplicity in him but only innocence, did not suspect that they might intend him harm. So there came another fairy, but of human size and riding on a white horse, and she gestured to Gawaine that he should mount behind her, which, nothing loth for she was lovely as the lilies in spring, he did obediently. And she rode off with him and carried him to her bower, and there made love to him. She kept him seven nights and seven days, and pleasured him continuously, till he was weak with love and well-nigh exhausted. So he submitted to her will and became her slave, and was content in his servitude.

Nor did it occur to him that his conduct was unmanly. On the contrary, it appeared to him that he experienced the highest bliss, as indeed he did, with the consequence, which she intended, that never again could he enjoy the love of mortal beings.

But fairy love is fairy gold, no true metal. From this day forward, Gawaine was less than he had been and would wander disconsolate through life. He had tasted, as he thought, the wine of Paradise and despised all lesser vintages.

After many days Gawaine was led by his lady to a great lake which lay on the edge of the forest, and which was enclosed by dark hills on the three other banks. Here she sounded a call on the flute and in a little another fairy figure rose from the waters of the lake and advanced, by no corporeal motion that Gawaine could observe, to the bank whereon they awaited her. And this was Vivian, the sister of the lady who had led Gawaine thither. The two fairies embraced and then led Gawaine to a rude hut that stood among rowan trees.

A knight lay there as if asleep. In truth, Gawaine did not realise straightway that he was a knight, for he was dressed only in a short tunic.

This knight was Lancelot and his history was curious.

He was the son of Ban, Duke of Brittany and his wife Helen who was the elder half-sister of Morgan le Fay, but not of Arthur, for while he and Morgan shared a father, Helen was the daughter of Morgan's mother. She was as fair as a field of standing corn and famed throughout the Empire for her beauty, so that many knights sought to be her lover. But she was virtuous and true to her husband the duke. He, however, was a man of little capacity and rash also, and doomed to misfortune. So he was driven by rebels from his duchy and fled to Britain, where he and Helen sought aid from Morgan's husband, King Lot of Orkney. But Lot declined to hear his pleas, so Ban and Helen wandered for many years in misery, until their son was born in a woodcutter's mean hut. Then Ban fell sick of a fever and died, and Helen, fearing for her infant son, whom she loved dearly, heard that the fairy Vivian was possessed of powers which could render a knight invulnerable in battle. So she carried the babe Lancelot to the lake and begged Vivian to employ her powers on his behalf. Now, when Vivian saw the babe, she had a vision of the handsome knight he would be, excelling all others in beauty, and she was enamoured of this vision. Accordingly she told Helen that she could indeed grant her son the invulnerability that she sought for him, but that, were she to do so, Helen must surrender the boy to her and never see him again. For a little Helen hesitated, but her love for Lancelot was such that she consented. So Vivian took the child and carried him into the lake, and sank with him beneath the black water. Helen followed the pair with eyes misted with tears till they disappeared from her sight. She wept and the tears did not cease for seven days and seven nights, and when at last they stopped flowing Helen was left blind. So she wandered in the forest, lamenting her fate and the choice she had made, and mourning her son (whom she feared drowned) till she herself fell into despair and died. Meanwhile Lancelot was reared in a cavern at the bottom of the lake, guarded (men say) by dragons, till he came of age and knew himself (none knows how) to be a man.

So he determined to return to the world of men and prove himself a mighty knight. For many months Vivian resisted his pleas, till she saw that he in his turn was falling into a decline and she feared that he would die; for, being a fairy, she had a great horror of mortality. So she consented, and this was why her sister had seduced Gawaine and brought him here, that he might escort Lancelot to the court of King Arthur, and teach him what alone she could not teach him: the duties of chivalry, which fairies do not understand, and the rules of knighthood, which mean nothing to them.

Gawaine was immediately delighted by Lancelot. From the first he loved him like a brother. It was a mark of his nobility that he was to be in no way envious of Lancelot even when he led him to court and saw how Arthur doted on him from the day of his arrival. Yes, even though Lancelot supplanted him who had previously held the highest place in his esteem, Gawaine never wavered in his love and admiration for his friend.

And indeed, Lancelot was wonderfully gifted. For a start his beauty surpassed that of all other knights. He was tall and well-made, long-legged and soft-skinned. His hair was yellow and his eyes a dark, soulful brown. His lips seemed to every lady – and, I fear, many men – to have been formed for kissing. His nose was straight and his chin firm. In short, he was the most perfectly formed knight that could be imagined. His voice, too, was low and gentle, even soft. He laughed rarely but his smile was like the sun emerging from behind a cloud.

Then it was soon seen that he excelled all in knightly exercises. From his first tournament he was the champion of the lists, and in battle he proved himself the bravest of the brave. There was no horse he could not master, and though he had never flown a falcon before he came to court, he soon surpassed all others in that art also.

With all this he was without vanity. Indeed, he appeared to be quite unconscious of his own excellences.

Arthur, as I say, was charmed. Men soon observed that he would introduce Lancelot's name into his discourse, no matter what the topic under discussion. It seemed as if he did so merely for the pleasure of speaking the word. Others behaved likewise, Gawaine's brother Gaheris, for example, could not conceal his infatuation with Lancelot. Men said that, for Lancelot's smile, Sir Gaheris would have stripped naked and rolled in nettles. That certainly expressed his devotion, for Gaheris was known to be fine and delicate to the point of being charged with effeminacy.

In short, Camelot had never seen such a prodigy before.

Only Cal had reservations. He admitted Lancelot's charms and even confessed to himself that they aroused his desire. He acknowledged that Lancelot made a far finer figure than Arthur, who had lost his boyish vivacity, whose face was now worn by anxiety and responsibility, and whose dark hair was receding at the temples and turning grey. Arthur stooped, now, and walked stiffly, sometimes with a limp when the wind was easterly. His appetite was poor and he was compelled to abstain from wine. Cal saw how Lancelot eclipsed the King-Emperor, how he attracted from him the devotion of the young knights and how his vitality seemed a reproach to Arthur's air of fatigue.

Moreover, Cal saw, before anyone else, how Guinevere looked on Lancelot. He knew that she now bored Arthur and that whatever she had felt for him was withered. 'Saxon cow,' muttered Cal to himself. He knew what was concealed from the court: that though Arthur went every night to the Queen's bedchamber, he did not remain there, but passed through it and slept on a camp bed in the tower room beyond. The marriage, undertaken for political reasons, had followed the course of most such marriages. The King and Queen did not yet dislike each other, but they approached that condition; and Cal sensed that Arthur now knew disgust for the body which had formerly excited him, and reproached himself for this and experienced guilt. Truly, this is common even among those who have married for love, which is but rarely permitted to princes. But on account of Arthur's high sense of honour, he did not take to himself a mistress or concubine, which (he thought) would have been to shame the Queen. So he dwelled in misery and Guinevere in discontent. She had her maidens read her romances of knights-errant and the ladies to whom they professed devotion, and she ate sweetmeats and, in the manner of Saxon women, grew fat. Moreover, there were no children of the marriage and for this the people blamed the Queen.

So, from the moment she first saw Lancelot she was infatuated and determined to seduce him. Hitherto she had been faithful to Arthur, but her fidelity grew irksome and she was ready for adventure. And, because she was now eager to betray Arthur, she formed an antipathy towards him; and this, my Prince, is often the way with women, who must always find justification for what they do and so be forever, in their own opinion, in the right. She told herself that Arthur insulted her by his neglect. She dwelled on the rumours she had heard concerning the love he had formerly borne the lovely Peredur and now suspected him of enjoying carnal relations with some of the young knights. For this she blamed Cal, whom she had loathed from the start, and whom she thought the King's pander and wished to destroy.

She made advances to Lancelot. At first he hesitated, for he was mindful of the lessons Gawaine had given him in honour. But, though he understood the concept, he did not feel it; and this on account of his fairy education. So it was not long before he responded and became the Queen's lover. He brought her delights she had never known; in love he was tender and imaginative as he was lustful. But he was soon bored. It was his misfortune – the curse which Vivian had wished on him – that he could inspire love in others but not experience it himself. It could not have been otherwise. So he is not to be condemned; he was the victim of the fairy distortion of his nature. He sought, found and gave pleasure in love-making, but was incapable of constancy, being also incapable of surrender. Dim awareness of his condition brought him misery. Whereas true lovers delight (so I am told) in resting in each other's arms after they have made love and find deep pleasure in waking together, Lancelot knew only emptiness and a profound sadness, which nevertheless drove him to try to prove the love, which he could not feel, ever more ardently. And yet those he loved felt his deficiency.

Meanwhile, Sir Gawaine observed the course of the Queen's love for Lancelot and was dismayed. He understood the shame it brought upon the King, and because he feared that Arthur, if apprised of the affair, would repudiate Guinevere and that this would be great offence to the Saxons, he urged Lancelot to depart from Camelot, so that in his absence the Queen's love might cool. To this Lancelot agreed, for he had no desire to bring shame upon the King whom he revered and wished to serve loyally.

So he rode away from Camelot in sadness and sought to bury his wretchedness in waste places. He crossed the seas to his native Brittany, where he was seized by his uncle, the duke who had usurped his father's place, and thrown into a dungeon. His uncle, who both feared and hated him, commanded that he be fastened to a pillar by an iron chain. And there he languished, and his wits fled him and he raved in madness.

At Camelot all was confusion. The Queen fell into a decline. Arthur himself was dismayed by what he took to be Lancelot's desertion and would not be comforted, though Cal told him it was for the best. Gawaine, too, was wretched, though he told himself also he had acted for the best. It was as if bleak winter had fallen on the court and extinguished its joy. Arthur sent far and wide to learn what had befallen Lancelot, but no word came of him for many months. No one dared tell the King how Lancelot and Guinevere had deceived him, and Guinevere herself kept her own counsel, being afraid of his wrath.

At last a knight, by name Sir Bors, who had been journeying in France, which was then still known as Gaul, heard tell of how the Duke of Brittany had taken a mighty knight, who laid claim to the duchy, and imprisoned him in a castle called Douloureux, and that it was said in its environs that the knight's name was Lancelot.

When he heard this Arthur rejoiced, and at once gathered all his knights and led them, a mighty army, across the sea into Brittany, and there gave battle to the duke. Never (men say) was such slaughter seen and many noble knights were slain. The battle was fought over three days, and each day more grievous than the one before, until at last both armies were exhausted, and the duke sent to Arthur offering truce. Some advised him to reject the proposal and renew the battle, but Arthur, saddened by the loss of so many of his companions, accepted the duke's offer on condition that Lancelot be released and surrendered to him. And, if this was done, he said, he would again retreat across the sea to Britain and leave the duke in possession of his duchy. So the duke consented because he knew Lancelot was mad and believed that he could no longer threaten to supplant him and regain the duchy that was his by right of inheritance.

So Sir Gawaine and Sir Gaheris entered the castle, rightly called Douloureux, to carry Lancelot forth, and when they saw him and the condition he was in, both wept. For he did not recognise them, but was wild-eyed and emaciated, and his beard had grown, and he whimpered as if with fear when they approached. They freed him from his bond and very gently brought him forth, and mounted him on a horse behind Gawaine, seeing he was too weak to ride unaided. So they brought Lancelot back to the army and then to Britain, and all men were horrified at the sight.

Guinevere herself was torn between pity and disgust when she saw the condition of her lover. For a little, indeed, she could not understand how she could have loved one who was now reduced to so piteous a state, and believed she could never love him again. And, since she held Cal responsible for Lancelot's flight, though for no reason other than the enmity she bore to him, she accused him before the King of having betrayed Lancelot to the duke. Cal denied this charge and was tempted to tell Arthur how the Queen had betrayed him with Lancelot. Yet he kept silent because he knew how this would cause Arthur distress. Then the Queen brought forward a witness, a knight whose name history does not record, though it is unusual that the name of one so iniquitous should be forgotten. This knight declared upon oath that he had overheard Cal plotting with an emissary of the duke to deliver Lancelot to him. Arthur hesitated to believe him, saying he could not think so ill of Cal. But Guinevere insisted on his guilt and said she would retire into a nunnery if the King did not believe her. Therefore, with great reluctance, he banished Cal from the court and commanded that he go into exile across the sea.

Meanwhile Sir Gawaine sent to the fairy Vivian to acquaint her with what had befallen Lancelot and to beg her to heal him of his madness. So she appointed a place in the forest where Gawaine should bring him and deliver him to her care.

VII

While Sir Lancelot was being healed of his madness, Arthur himself fell into depression. It seemed to him that the blithe morning of his reign had turned murky. Dark clouds hung over him. The wind blew and the rain was chill. Attempts to repair the shipwreck of his marriage failed. Guinevere turned away from him, spoke little, and then coldly. Meanwhile the Saxons were restless, ripe for rebellion, and this caused him yet again to postpone the war he intended that would restore the Empire of Rome. Even though the Pope himself, now oppressed by barbarian tribes, Lombards and Vandals, sent to seek his aid, he could not – did not, indeed, dare – depart from Britain where in every quarter disaffection and disorder loomed. Even his old enemy King Lot of Orkney raised his head again and was said to be in league with the rebellious Saxons. At the same time pirates roved the seas and fierce warriors from the North made inroads up the eastern rivers.

He felt himself to be alone. He missed Merlin. He missed the Goloshan. He missed Peredur. Most of all he missed Cal. So, deprived of both comfort and counsel, he passed uneasy months.

The knights caught his mood, were infected by his anxiety. Quarrels were frequent, blows were exchanged. The fellowship of the Round Table was broken.

It was at this inauspicious time that there occurred a strange event, which some deemed a miracle and which for us today sheds a glorious light upon these dark times. It was to lead to the Quest for the Holy Grail.

Concerning the Grail many stories are told and many explanations offered. It were rash to assert which of these is true. Nevertheless, inasmuch as I have undertaken to recount these matters to you, my Prince, I now give you the version of the story as I heard it in my youth in Tweeddale where, I was assured, men had passed it down mouth to mouth over the generations from one who had had it himself from the lips of Merlin. Be that as it may, nothing that I have learned in my deep studies in the libraries of Rome and Naples, Salerno and Salamanca, Paris and Oxford, and here in Palermo, contradicts this version, at least not conclusively; and indeed, my deepest studies serve, to some extent, to confirm what I first heard from a wise man in Drumelzier, who had had it, he said, from a hermit in the Ettrick Valley.

When Lucifer, who is also Satan, and Father of all Evil, was hurled from Heaven to lie on a burning lake of pitch, it happened that a jewel fell from the crown which had been awarded him while he sat on the right hand of the Almighty, and which had been fashioned by the cunningest smith. This stone fell to earth and was found in Golgotha, the place of skulls, outside Jerusalem, where Christ was to be crucified. And this is credible for Golgotha is hard by Gehenna, one of the entrances to the Underworld which Christians term Hell.

No one knows who found this most precious jewel, but it was brought into the presence of the most glorious King David, father of Solomon who built the Temple in Jerusalem. That task was denied to David, since he had innocent blood on his hands, but when he received this jewel he ordered it to be carved into a vessel of great beauty which he wished to dedicate for use in the Temple that his son should build. So it remained in the Temple, a thing of wonder, till the Jews were carried off to captivity in Babylon; and at that time it disappeared.

Many generations later it came – none knows how, but by the will, as we may assume, of the Almighty – into the possession of one Joseph of Arimathea, a rich merchant of Jerusalem, who prized it for its beauty, being a great lover of fine jewels.

This Joseph heard the word of Christ, though he declined baptism, and presented the dish to Jesus, who drank from it in that Last Supper he ate with his apostles. Then, when he was taken, being betrayed by Judas, called the Iscariot, and crucified, Joseph stood by the Cross and caught some drops of the Redeemer's blood in the vessel, the Grail, henceforth called Holy, as the blood streamed from the wound which the centurion's spear had made in his side.

So it was believed that from this day on the vessel was endowed with magical powers, for it was written: 'Whoever looked on it, even though sick to death, would not die; whoever gazed long upon it would escape the ravages of age, for his cheek should not grow pale, neither should his hair turn white.'

Now Joseph, as is related, carried the body of the crucified Christ from Golgotha to the Garden where he laid him to rest in the tomb; and when he rose from the dead the Jews, alarmed and angry, declared that Joseph had spirited him away. So they took him and threw him into prison where he languished for a year and a day without either food or drink. Yet, because Joseph had the Grail with him, of which they were ignorant, he came to no harm.

Many years later a certain Emperor – some say Vespasian and others Hadrian – heard the story of the Passion and of Joseph's part in it from a knight who had come to Rome from the Holy Land. He sent to seek for the truth, for he was desirous of securing some holy relic. And this was because his son Titus – if the Emperor in question was Vespasian – or his lover Antinous – should it have been Hadrian – was sick, some say with leprosy, others with a profound melancholy.

The knights in time returned and told the Emperor what they had learned from Pilate, the Roman governor who had washed his hands of Christ's fate. They brought with them too an old woman, by name Veronica, who had wiped Jesus's face with a napkin on which was imprinted his likeness; and she carried the napkin with her and the likeness was vivid as the rising sun. The Emperor pressed it on the face of Titus (or Antinous, as the case may be), and the young man was instantly restored to health and vigour.

Then they sought out Joseph and found him in the prison, still chained to a pillar, but yet well and strong. So he was released, but fearing the vengeance of the Jews, whose Temple Titus had in wrath destroyed, fled with his sister Eugenia and her husband Brons across the sea, till they came to Massilia, which is now Marseilles, and there they rested, till one of the company of their disciples committed a grievous sin. And this occasioned a famine – or, as some report, a plague – in the land.

Joseph then sought to discover who was guilty and he invited the disciples to sup with him, on a great fish which he had caught that morning. Eleven took their seats and gazed on the Grail which he had placed in the centre of the table. Then when the twelfth disciple, whose name was Moses, seated himself, his guilt was manifest, for the earth opened and swallowed him, and so delivered him, it is supposed, straight to Hell. The properties of the Grail are truly miraculous.

Subsequently Joseph fell into debt, as many do in Marseilles even now, and so he prudently fled his creditors and came to Britain. He brought the Grail with him and settled in Glastonbury, where he planted a sliver of the Cross on which Christ was hung. It grew into a rose tree and blossoms every year on Christmas Day. For this reason Glastonbury is holy and a place of pilgrimage. Some of the native people were converted by Joseph, or rather by his example, for he never preached his faith. But this was many years before the great Emperor Constantine saw the cross floating in the air as he was about to give battle at the Milvian Bridge over the Tiber, and conquered in its sign. So the Christian community at Glastonbury endured persecution in the reign of the Emperor Domitian (but others say Diocletian) and was extirpated. Some historians, however, relate that they escaped thanks to the properties of the Grail, which Joseph had bequeathed to them, but others maintain that the last believer, before being put to death, consigned the Grail to the depths of the lake called Avalon, that it be not taken and desecrated by the heathen – for so they considered even the Romans. And if any question why the Grail did not save these believers from their unhappy fate, then one must reply that the ways of the Almighty are inscrutable and that he fashions his work in mysterious manner, so that what at first seems bad often serves a longer and beneficial purpose; and, of course, vice versa.

This is the version of the origin of the Grail as disseminated also by the Abbot of Glastonbury and his monks, whom some accuse of having devised it to magnify the importance of their house . . . Another version of the tale is as follows.

A famous knight, by name Titurel, the heir to great estates bestowed on his grandfather by the Emperor Vespasian as a reward for his endeavours and exploits in the Jewish war, spent the early years of his manhood engaged in warfare against the Saracens, and won many battles and much booty. This he gave either to Holy Church or to the poor (who made better use of it). His fame spread through many lands and it is written that his courage and prowess in war were equalled only by his virtue and his humility.

One day while he was walking in the hills of Galilee, he was met by an angel, who hailed him by name in a voice of surpassing sweetness, and told him that he had been chosen to be the guardian of the Holy Grail, which he would find upon a certain mountain called Montsalvat.

Greatly honoured, Titurel returned to the camp. But he was also puzzled for he knew no mountain of that name. And indeed, to this day no one since has discovered which it be or where it is, though some say it is Mount Etna here in Sicily and others Mount Gargano, which is the chosen abode, on his earthly visits, of the Archangel Michael, and which is also, as you may remember, according to some the place where Arthur's grandfather, the Emperor Marcus, was conceived. So it is probable that Montsalvat and Mount Gargano are one and the same.

Titurel waited many days for a sign, and at last a long white cloud appeared in an azure sky and Titurel was guided by it on a long journey, which took him through deserts and forests and across the sea till he came to the base of a mountain that was shrouded in mist. Notwithstanding the danger, he ascended it and on the summit the mist, through which the white cloud had moved, leading him on, miraculously cleared and shimmering above him he saw the Grail, which was held as if by invisible hands. He fell to his knees and prayed that he might be worthy of this charge, and a voice came from Heaven ordering him to build a temple fit to receive the holy vessel. Then the vision of the Grail was withdrawn from his sight.

So Titurel summoned his knights and many masons and workmen skilled in fashioning precious stones. The building of the temple took many years, for it was larger and more glorious than Solomon's, and there was a chapel for each of his hundred knights, who from this day on were denominated the Knights Templar. When the building was finished and consecrated, the knights formed a procession and marched round it singing psalms and swinging censers. Then the eyes of all were drawn to the altar, for there, on a beam of white light, came the holy vessel, moving silently through the air. All then seemed as if struck dumb as they gazed in wonder; and at that very moment a choir of angels took up the song of praise and continued singing till Titurel reached out his hands and took possession of the Grail. He raised it high, and all fell to their knees and worshipped.

So for many years, supported by the Grail, Titurel and the knights were victorious in battles against the Saracens even when outnumbered twenty to one. For when they fought in defence of the Grail they were invulnerable.

But in time Titurel grew old and frail and, his son being dead, it was this son's son Amfortas who assumed the office of Grand Prior of the Order. He too was a mighty knight, but one of quick temper. So, one day, thinking himself slighted because the King of France had stolen from him a favourite page, he so forgot the rules of the Order as to make war on a fellow Christian. In this battle he was wounded by a lance, the point of which had been dipped in poison, and it was with difficulty and in sickness that he repaired to the temple. Though he did not die, his wound never healed and he suffered grievously.

So Titurel prayed that Amfortas be freed from the pain that made every day and night a torment to him. And when he opened his eyes from prayer he saw that the Grail was illuminated, and he read there a message that a knight, pure in spirit and ignorant of the flesh, would one day ascend the mountain and enquire the cause of Amfortas's suffering. At this question the evil spell that held the land in misery would be broken, Amfortas would be healed and the pure knight would be hailed as guardian of the Holy Vessel.

It was then the custom of Arthur to hold a great Feast for all his knights at the time of Pentecost, but this year he was unwilling to do so. He was disconsolate and sunk in melancholy. There was no one in whom he could confide. Gawaine and Lancelot were still absent, and those closest to him, on account of their position at court, were the old knights Kay and Bedivere, who had never loved him and whose advice he had so often disregarded.

So all was unsettled and many questioned whether the feast would be held or not. Some of the young knights also were out of temper. One, by name Mordred, of whose origins all were ignorant though I have already revealed them to you, had recently been admitted to the Order and, though as a newcomer it was proper that he kept silent, speaking only when addressed and then modestly, yet soon found himself in favour with the disaffected. He had a sharp tongue and an insinuating smile. Those who talked to him readily discovered that he was in full agreement with them, sympathised with their misfortunes or grievances and was quick with a jest at the expense of authority. Yet at the same time he was careful. He always spoke respectfully of Arthur; but when he had left off speaking, his audience felt that the King was diminished in their eyes.

'Of course,' he said, 'the King is well rid of that Cal. Or so I'm told. My mother used to say that he was always eager to try to corrupt the King, for instance, by slandering the . . . virtuous . . . Guinevere, or introducing some blue-eyed stable boy to his bedchamber. Of course, the King would have none of it. And yet, she said, he had an affection for this Cal because they had been strolling players together in their youth. I can't believe that, of course, and nor, I'm sure, did she. It's just the way women talk, even the best of women, such as my saintly mother. Still, I'm very glad not to have known this Cal. I'm certain the court is a cleaner place without him. By the way, have you heard . . .'

And he would then retail some salacious gossip.

When he was in the King's presence, however, no one could have been more humbly dutiful, more respectful, more adept in subtle flattery than this Mordred. Yet his manner was such that those disaffected knights who had lent their ear to his conversation could not but suspect that he was delighting in his own performance and his ability to practise dissimulation.

When Arthur understood the mood of his knights he roused himself of his lethargy, condemned himself for having given way to low spirits and ordered the great feast to be prepared. He did this the more willingly because Sir Gawaine had returned to

Camelot and brought news that Lancelot was being healed of his madness.

So on the day of Pentecost they assembled in the Great Hall of Camelot and took their seats at the Round Table. But there were two empty chairs, one of which was covered with a silk cloth.

When they were ready to eat, Sir Kay approached the King and said, 'Sire, if you eat now, you will be breaking the rule of your custom, for at this feast you have never eaten till you have seen or heard tell of some great adventure.'

'That is true and a good custom,' Arthur replied, 'and yet I fear we must depart from it today, for no adventure offers itself and the knights are seated, and eager to eat and drink.'

At that moment a squire approached, knelt before the King and said, in a voice that trembled with dread or excitement, 'Sire, I have seen something truly marvellous.'

'And what is that?' said Arthur, smiling for the first time in many days.

'I was walking by the river and I saw there a big stone . . .'

He hesitated, and some of the knights laughed and mocked him, till the King ordered them to be silent.

'And this stone', the squire said, 'was as big as mounting block, but it did not sink under the water, but floated on the surface. And that's not all. There was a sword sticking out of the stone.'

Hearing this, Arthur thought of Merlin and of the sword that he himself had pulled from the stone, and for a moment he feared that this marvel which the squire spoke of was of ill omen.

But he smiled again and said, 'Truly that is a great marvel. Let us go see it, and then we may eat and drink.'

So all left the castle and went to the river bank, and there they saw the stone floating with the sword stuck in it just as the squire had said. The stone was of red marble and on the pommel of the sword was written: 'No man shall draw me hence save he by whose side I ought to hang and he shall be the best knight in the world.'

At first all were eager to try to draw the sword and clamoured to be the first who should make the attempt.

Then one called out, and men say it was Sir Mordred, 'Let the King draw the sword, for surely he is the best knight in the world.'

Arthur smiled and said he had drawn one sword from a stone and by this act he had been acknowledged as King; but it was not fitting that he should draw this one. If Sir Lancelot had been with them, he said, he would invite him to make the attempt, for surely all recognised him as the best knight in the world.

'When he's not mad, that's as may be,' someone muttered and Arthur's brow darkened.

So he asked Sir Gawaine to be the first, but Gawaine said, 'No, I know I am not worthy. I'm a plain man, my Lord, and there are better knights than me. Besides, I recall that you yourself defeated me in battle. So how can I pretend to be the best, seeing as Lancelot also has unhorsed me?'

Then an old man, dressed all in white, whom no knight had seen before, stepped out from the trees that stood by the river bank and said, 'You are well-advised, Sir Gawaine, to decline the challenge' – at which words Gawaine blushed from very shame – 'seeing as it is written that whoever tries to draw this sword and fails will one day be wounded by this same blade.'

When they heard these words, all the knights drew back, save a young knight whose name was Parsifal, who knelt before the King and said, 'My Lord King, I do not pretend to be the best knight in the world. I am young and untried. Yet last night I dreamed that I should perform some mighty exploit, but what it was escapes me. Nevertheless, on account of that dream, I beg you to grant me leave to make the attempt.'

Arthur said, 'But didn't you hear what the old man has just said, that if you fail, you shall one day be wounded by this same sword?'

'Indeed yes,' Parsifal said. 'And that makes me afraid. On the other hand, he said "wounded", not "killed", and men recover from all wounds that are not mortal. Therefore I beg you grant me leave.'

Arthur looked on the knight, who was scarcely more than a boy, slight of build, with a pale face, grey eyes and a smooth skin. 'Your reasoning is as sound as your courage is evidently great. So I grant you leave.'

Parsifal stepped forward to the cheers of the knights, but Mordred plucked at his companion's sleeve and whispered, 'You see how easily a pretty youth can win the King's favour' and his companion, whose name was Tyryns, sniggered. Parsifal drew on the sword, but he could not loosen it from the stone, and so turned away downcast and fearing that he had made himself an object of ridicule, for being so presumptuous as to think his dream meant that he would prove himself in this way. Indeed, some knights did begin to laugh and cry out in mockery, but Arthur silenced them with an awful look and said, 'Do you who did not dare to make the attempt for fear of failure and the wound which in time to come this sword would give you dare to mock this lad who had the courage to risk this hazard? I tell you, he has proved himself a brave and worthy knight, and in token of his courage and as a mark of the favour he has won in my eyes, he shall sit at my right hand at the feast tonight.'

Many were abashed, and even ashamed of their laughter. They fell silent. Then all returned to the castle. Sir Mordred plucked his companion by the sleeve and whispered, 'It is just as I said. A sly boy, that Parsifal. We must watch him.'

The evening sun shone through the open door of the Great Hall and lit up the banners of the knights that hung from the roof. The tables were covered with fine linen, and gold and silver dishes, and the jewels placed in the back of the knights' chairs – or sieges as they were properly called – sparkled. The feast was of an equal richness. There were great barons of beef and whole lambs turned on spits, and pies a foot deep filled with game and wildfowl. Great fish, salmon, pike, carp, glistened on ashets and were surrounded by shellfish, lobsters, prawns, crabs, crayfish and shrimps. There were bowls of fruit and nuts, and many jellies, creams, junkets, cheeses and almond tarts. The wines came from Bordeaux and the vineyards of Hampshire, now flourishing again as they had in the time of the Roman peace. And on every table also stood great jugs of beer, cider and mead. Truly, the abundance of the fare testified to the prosperity of the land and the peace which Arthur, by his prowess in war and wisdom in administration and even-handed justice, had restored.

Two sieges remained unoccupied when all the knights had taken their place. One was reserved for Lancelot and many wondered as to whether he would appear. The other, which was still covered with a silken cloth, was designated for no knight as far as anyone knew, and many were the speculations as to whether the King would surprise them by dubbing a new knight and granting him this siege.

Arthur, however, seemed unconcerned. Neglecting Sir Kay who, as the senior knight present, sat on his left, he directed his conversation to the young Parsifal. Some wondered at this, but in truth, for no good reason. Arthur had known Kay for many years. There was nothing they could say to each other that had not been said many times before. Besides, they had never been good friends. Kay could not forget that, before Arthur was recognised as the son of Uther Pendragon, he had regarded him as being of no account, while for his part Arthur recalled the kicks and cuffs Kay had dealt out in those years and the bad advice given him so often since. In any case it is a melancholy truth that, even had they been closer friends than they were, they would in all probability have exhausted their conversation by now. Much is said in praise of friendship and with good reason. Many philosophers of high repute, from Socrates onwards, have told us that friendship sweetens the bitter reality that we come naked from our mother's womb and go naked into the cold earth. It imparts warmth to our existence and comforts us in our essential solitude. Yet the effect is transitory. All but the closest friendships crumble and are seen in the end to have offered only an illusion of community. Perhaps even the greatest cannot escape this fate. Had Christ escaped the Cross, the day would have arrived when he looked on even John the Beloved Disciple with an indifferent eye. So now Arthur found the fresh enthusiasm, even naivety, of the young Parsifal preferable to the conversation that Kay or Bedivere might have offered.

While they were thus engaged in talk, of a sudden the doors and windows of the hall shut of their own accord. And when they were closed a great wind blew through the hall and extinguished the candles. Yet, to their wonder, the hall was not darkened, but a white light shone through it.

Then an old man, whom none remembered to have seen before, stood in the doorway, though none had observed him enter. He had with him by his side a young knight, in crimson armour, but bearing no sword nor shield, though an empty scabbard hung from his belt.

The old man said, 'Peace be with you, fair lords and knights' and he led his young companion up to the high table where Arthur sat, and said, 'My Lord King and Emperor, I bring you here a young knight, of royal lineage and the descendant also of that saint, Joseph of Arimathea, who carried the body of the crucified Christ to the garden tomb, Gethsemane; and this is he who shall accomplish great marvels.'

Arthur graciously bade him welcome, and watched as the old man led the young knight to the Siege Perilous, where no knight had dared to sit. There he lifted the silken cloth that covered it and revealed the legend: 'This is the siege of Sir Galahad, the high-born Prince.'

So the young knight, Galahad, settled himself there, and all were amazed that no harm befell him and that it seemed that the siege was his by right. And yet he appeared but a boy whose beard had not yet grown so that his downy cheeks had not felt the razor. He sat there as one unconcerned by the stir he had caused and spoke to no one, nor did he drink wine or eat meat.

Then the hall was dark as the blackest night of winter, and the wind that passed through it was from the north and cold as the December winds that carry snow. All shivered and many drew their furs about them, and the teeth of several knights were heard to chatter. Fear seized them and they could find no words to express it, but all sat in amazement wondering what great wonder might next appear.

And with the wind came the crack and roar of thunder so loud that the palace shook and it seemed as if it would break in pieces and the roof fall on them as they sat there. It was still dark as the blackest night of Hell and cold as the Devil's touch. Many knights thought of their sins and the wrongs they had done, and would have confessed them had terror not put a lock on their tongues.

Then all was still, the wind fell away, and through the darkness shone a sunbeam, though it was now night, and that sunbeam was seven times brighter than the sun's rays at midsummer. Floating in the air, halfway precisely between floor and roof, they now saw the Holy Grail, covered in white samite, and yet the covering was transparent. It was there but for a moment that lasted no longer than the time that a swallow might fly through the hall, and then it vanished, so speedily and completely that afterwards there were many who wondered if it had been but a dream and others who questioned the evidence of their eyes.

Arthur raised his hand to demand silence and then said, 'We have been vouchsafed a great wonder and we ought now to thank our Lord Jesus Christ for what he has shown us this day of Pentecost.'

And Gawaine, deeply moved, said, 'Surely it is a great wonder, and yet there is one thing missing: that we did not truly see the Grail, it being covered with a cloth of samite, as I think. Wherefore I swear a vow that tomorrow at first light, I shall set forth in quest of the Grail, and that I shall not abandon this Quest for a year and a day.'

His words inspired many others to leap to their feet and swear the same oath, and chief among them were Lancelot, though he had come late to the feast and was still pale from his sickness and weak of frame and ailing, and his cousin Bors; and the two young knights, Parsifal and Galahad.

Arthur himself was sore perplexed. On the one hand he was proud of his knights and of the zeal which they displayed, but on the other hand he was assailed with foreboding. Tears started to his eyes and his face was grey, and he sighed deeply. 'For', he said, 'I fear, Gawaine, that by taking this vow you will have deprived me of the fairest and truest body of knights that was ever seen in any kingdom in all the ages of man. For when they depart from thence, I am sure that we shall never all meet again together in love and friendship, and that many will be slain in the quest and that our glorious fellowship will be dissolved.'

With these words he retired to his chamber and wept.

VIII

How long the Quest for the Grail continued, no man surely knows. There are many stories of the Quest and to distinguish those which are true from those which are false is a task to puzzle the Recording Angel himself.

For instance: in the course of his journeying Parsifal came on a lady in chains, led by a knight who seemed to take pleasure in tormenting and torturing her. Obedient to the knightly code, which taught that it was his duty to come to the aid of any lady encountered in distress, he challenged the knight to combat and unhorsed him. Well, this was very proper, but it transpired that the knight he had unhorsed was the husband of a lady whom, on his first journey to Camelot, Parsifal had found asleep and had then awakened with a kiss. (For his mother had enjoined him that he should kiss every fair lady he met.) The lady had been first angry, then, when she had gazed on Parsifal, less angry and then contented, inviting him, indeed, to kiss her again and again. So it was for her dalliance with Parsifal that her husband had punished her and now Parsifal wondered whether he should himself feel guilt, on account of having been the cause of the lady's torment. He raised the fallen knight and, apologising for the wrong he had doubly done him, urged him in future to treat his lady wife tenderly and so rode away.

Again, it is said (by some) that Parsifal came to a castle where a King lay sick of a grievous wound, or (alternatively) suffering from a wasting disease, in consequence of which the land lay waste and was afflicted with famine. The Queen greeted him kindly, for in every arrival she sought the one who would put the question that would release the King from his sickness and restore the land. So she set Parsifal by her at the high table, though in truth (if there be any truth in the tale) the fare was meagre.

Then the King in a faint voice ordered that Parsifal be presented with a sword of the most exquisite workmanship, the hilt decorated with amethysts, beryls, rubies and sapphires, and (doubtless) other precious stones too numerous to mention. At that moment the doors of the hall were thrown open and a servant appeared bearing before him a lance, all bloody at the point; and this he paraded round the hall while the company sighed, groaned and wept. He was followed by a beautiful maiden, clad from head to toe in black silk, and her face masked. She carried a shining vessel, and this she placed before Parsifal, and the murmur ran round the hall that it was the Grail.

From the Grail there now streamed forth a quantity of fine food and rich wines, and all the company partook. Yet, though their hunger should have been appeased, they ate in silence and sadness, and Parsifal wondered at the meaning of it. At last the King rose and, leaning heavily on two squires – sturdy youths fit to bear burdens – gazed for a long minute on Parsifal who, knowing not what to say, remained silent; and then the King, with many groans and sighs, withdrew. The knights looked now angrily on Parsifal, as if he had failed them; and some addressed harsh words to him; and they departed and he was alone.

A servant approached and indicated that Parsifal should follow him. He obeyed and took the opportunity to question the servant concerning the meaning of what had taken place. But the old man shook his head, and opened his mouth and showed Parsifal that his tongue had been torn out by its roots, and that he was dumb. He led him to a chamber and its walls were hung with tapestries, of great art and rich design. One showed a knight, who much resembled the King, being cast to the ground by a spear thrust into his side so that the blood flowed. Seeing this, Parsifal was eager for enlightenment and resolved that he would put the question in the morning.

But when he woke he found that he was alone and all the doors were barred save one that led into the courtyard, where his horse stood saddled and bridled. It was a grey morning with a sky the colour of slate and the wind in the east. He looked around, but all was deserted as if those who had been his companions of the night had been spirited away.

So he mounted his horse and rode off, but hardly was he clear of the castle, than a voice spoke to him from the Heavens, cursing him for having left undone a great work for which he had been chosen.

And as he rode over a barren plain, he asked himself whether he had indeed seen the Grail or whether he had dreamed of doing so.

Now this is the essence of stories of the Grail: that whatever appears at first to be solid melts and dissolves on reflection, till, like a castle one sees in the distance at noon, it vanishes as night falls.

So, for instance, while I raise the suggestion that Parsifal himself wondered if his vision had been but a dream, there are scholars who assert that not only did he indeed see the Grail, but was appointed its guardian.

And hence this story is told.

By the power of the Grail, Parsifal, now grey and weary after many years of wandering and much unhappiness, found his way back to the castle of the ailing King, where the same ceremony was now repeated. This time Parsifal, mindful of what had happened before, prayed that he might pass the test that he now knew had been set him. So it was that when he opened his eyes, the figure of the Archangel Michael, glorious in crimson armour, stood before him. Whereupon, hearkening to the angel, Parsifal enquired of the King what ailed him. At these words the spell was broken, and the King restored to health.

It was on account of this act that Parsifal was installed as the guardian of the Grail and married Conduiramour, the King's daughter. They had two sons, the elder Kardeiss, of whom nothing is known, and the younger Lohengrin.

When Lohengrin had come to man's estate, a silver bell that hung in the innermost sanctum of the temple where the Grail was kept (guarded night and day by worthy knights, obedient to Parsifal) was heard to peal; and this was a sign of urgency.

The knights foregathered to learn its meaning and writing appeared on the Holy Vessel which declared that Lohengrin had been chosen to defend the rights of an innocent assailed by great evil, and would be guided to his destination by a swan. Immediately, therefore, he put on the silver armour of righteousness long preserved in our temple till looted by the King of France, accursed of God, and bade farewell to his mother and sisters. But Parsifal accompanied him down the mountain to the lake where a swan sailed, drawing after her a little boat.

Parsifal gave his son a horn to sound when he arrived at his journey's goal and reminded him that as a knight of the Grail – that is, also, of the Temple – he was obliged to reveal neither his name nor where he came from; but if the question was put and he should answer it, he must return straightway to the holy mountain where the castle stood.

He kissed his father goodbye and boarded the vessel, and to the sound of flutes and trumpets, was carried to the black river that ran out of the lake.

There was a lady, by name Else, a princess and orphaned, very beautiful and desired by many men, chief among them her guardian Frederick of Telramund, whom, however, she detested; and with reason, for he was cruel, coarse of manner and stank of rotten fish. Nevertheless, she was hard put to hold him off and retain her much-prized virginity.

One day she dreamed, as she lay in a forest glade, that a beautiful young knight had come to her and given her a silver bell, with the command that she ring it should she require a champion. She woke from her dream and saw a falcon hovering above her; and when the bird saw that she was awake, he came and settled on her shoulder. Then she observed that a little bell was attached to his jesses, and she unfastened it and kept it by her.

Frederick, meanwhile, had grown weary of her refusal to wed him and, since he was greedy for the lands she had inherited, resolved to win them by another way. So he seized her and cast her into prison, till she consented with many tears to marry him unless a champion came to rescue her before the moon was full. He laughed, and gave orders that the boundaries of the land be closely guarded so that no such knight could approach. The lovely Else, weeping in her cell, was near despair as the moon waxed. Then she remembered the little bell which she had tied to her rosary and rang it. The tinkle was faint as a sparrow's cheep, and Else fell into deeper despair for she could not imagine that so faint a sound could be heard by any beyond her narrow cell. Yet it floated out of the window and was carried many leagues to the castle of the Order of the Temple, and it was on account of its echoing ring that Lohengrin knew the command of the Grail.

The day for combat was appointed and no champion appeared. The sun rose in the sky and passed its zenith, and still Frederick sat his horse in the lists and smiled, for his frontier guards had assured him that no knight had passed them by. The heralds sounded a last call for the champion and Frederick gazed on Else with lust. He was on the point of leaving his station to take possession of her when the swan boat glided up the river and Lohengrin leapt to the shore and blew his horn.

When he saw Lohengrin Frederick's face was black as a thunder cloud, and he charged madly at him, forgetting the science of battle. Lohengrin was young and had never fought in earnest till now, but he was armed with the certainty of righteousness and protected, as he believed, by the Archangel Michael. He parried Frederick's wild blows with ease, or avoided them neatly; and the longer the combat lasted, the more furious and careless Frederick became. Then he swung a huge blow that would have cut Lohengrin in half, but he stepped inside it and thrust his sword into Frederick's neck, and he fell to the sand, blood gushing from his mouth. The crowd cheered and minstrels straightway began to compose songs in honour of the Swan Knight.

Else was so delighted to be free of her persecutor that she immediately determined to marry her rescuer, even though she was ignorant of his name. Lohengrin did not refuse her, but instead cautioned her that she must never ask what he was called; and no doubt this mystery further inflamed her passion. On the other hand she soon learned that there were many saying that he concealed his name only because he was guilty of some terrible crime; and so one day, before all the court, she pressed him to say who he was. At this question, all colour fled from Lohengrin's face. But he could not tell a lie. So he spoke his name and added that he was the son of Parsifal, the guardian of the Holy Grail. But, he said, by breaking her vow and enquiring of him what was his name when he had cautioned her not to, she had also broken the bond that held them together; for, he added, 'love cannot live without faith.' Therefore he must leave her and return to the holy mountain.

With these words he raised his magic horn to his lips and blew three long notes, while the air around him grew chill and the sky darkened. Then the notes of the horn were echoed by faint music and the swan appeared, pulling the little boat. Lohengrin embarked and was never seen again by Else.

Now, while there are some who advance mundane and indeed scurrilous explanations for his conduct, the truth is simple and has been revealed. He was the servant of the Grail, which is also to say the servant of the Christ who demands of all who have faith in him more than sensual and sinful man is ready to give, more, indeed, than most are capable of giving.

What, then, is the truth of the Grail?

Nobody knows.

I have enquired of wise men and philosophers wherever I have journeyed. I have listened to poets and troubadors telling the Grail stories to amuse ladies, and have sometimes heard wisdom, even in their foolishness.

A certain rabbi whom I knew in Spain – he was a native of Cordoba but I encountered him in the libraries of Salamanca and subsequently spent many nights in deep discussion with him in the city's taverns where he drank wine for his stomach's sake – said this to me, 'Your Grail is but an idea. It has no form. Were it otherwise it could not be perfect. The food and wine which in your idle tales flow from the Vessel are not to be vulgarly understood as material things. They are the bread and wine of life, spiritual, not fleshly, sustenance.

'Those who search after enlightenment seek initiation into the great and Heavenly Mysteries. It has been so in all ages. And at the heart of the mystery rests Spirit, which is the Pure Intelligence; and it is this that your Grail signifies. Moreover, it is for this reason that it can never be grasped: for of the Pure Intelligence we mortal men can glimpse only the shadow, never the perfect form. And yet we seek it because to abandon the quest is to live like unclean animals, even pigs, and wallow in sloth and filth all the days of our life.'

That was his opinion. I give it you as he spoke, and you should ponder these words, my Prince . . .

Concerning the Quest of the Grail, the stories are many.

Too many, you say, my Prince?

The Grail bores you?

You think it's fanciful, all made up?

You want me to get on with the story of Arthur, your forerunner as Emperor?

You want to hear about his relations with the Pope?

That's easy. Being a true Emperor, he did as he pleased and told the Pope to obey him. The Pope flourished that document called the Donation of Constantine, which proved that Constantine, on departing to build the New Rome in the East, had conveyed to him (as lawyers say) imperium over the Empire in the West. Arthur said the document was a forgery and told the Pope – to use a vulgar expression which I heard on your lips yesterday, and for the use of which I should have rapped your knuckles or tanned your buttocks, but I was laughing too much, convulsed with laughter, on account of the circumstances – where was I? Yes, he told the Pope to stuff the Donation of Constantine up his arse.

That's what you'd like to hear, isn't it, and it may be true.

Nevertheless, before I leave off recounting the stories concerning the Grail and return, as you wish, to the true history of Arthur, there is yet something to be said.

In the legends the sighting of the Grail is attributed to divers knights, and you will not be surprised to learn that prejudice determines which knights were successful in the Quest.

So, for instance, the Scots and the Welsh declare that Gawaine, being their hero, was the brave knight who overcame many dangers, and was rewarded with the vision of the Grail. Likewise the Germans award the palm to Parsifal, whom the Knights Templar declare to have been the founder of their Order. But the French will have none of this and swear that it was Sir Bors, a knight of Aquitaine, who on account of his unsullied virtue was permitted the holy vision. This claim is mocked by the Bretons who are certain that Lancelot alone succeeded in the Quest; and they justify this assertion on the grounds that he was recognised by all as the finest flower of chivalry, so that it would be ridiculous to suppose that others might succeed and he fail.

There is also a consensus among those who hold to no particular allegiance that Galahad, who so daringly occupied the

Siege Perilous, and who is said to have been the only knight without sin, alone saw the Grail, and that only after years of fasting and penance, whereupon his soul was straightway borne to Heaven. This version is supported by many churchmen, who are eager to demonstrate the efficacy of prayer, fasting and penance. And indeed, it is true that Galahad plays no other part in the history of Arthur and was never seen at Camelot again after he set forth on the Quest of the Grail. But it may be merely that he was slain in some obscure encounter, as has often been the fate of even the bravest and most accomplished of knights.

Finally, you are to consider the theory that from that appearance in the hall of Camelot on the occasion of the feast of Pentecost, the Grail was an illusion created by papal agents to divert the knights and break the unity of the Round Table, and so render more difficult, even impossible, Arthur's purpose, which was to re-establish imperial authority and reduce the Bishop of Rome to his proper subordinate status.

There are two things to be said for this theory.

First, it was what Arthur himself came to believe.

Second, this was indeed the consequence of departure of so many knights on this chimerical Quest.

In short, however noble their ambition to achieve the vision of the Grail, the Quest diverted the knights from their proper duty, and foreshadowed the tragedy that was to befall Arthur and cause darkness to shroud the Age of Gold which he had promised to renew.

IX

When the knights departed on the Quest of the Grail, Arthur, as I have said, was dismayed. He could not prevent them. He would not have prevented them had he been able. He recognised that the challenge was one such as no true knight could have resisted without shame. And yet he saw it also as selfish. He had never had a high opinion of those who, pleading a vocation, withdrew from the world to make their souls. Moreover, though Arthur's name is indelibly, and for as long as men care about such things, associated with the word 'chivalry' – a concept admirable in itself – yet he had little but contempt for what is called knight-errantry. That too often appeared to him mere self-indulgence.

This is why, in the many tales of Arthur and his knights, you will find that poets and storytellers dwell more on the exploits of the knights than on Arthur himself. Indeed, often, after the account of how he drew the sword from the stone and established himself as ruler of the kingdom, it seems as if he is of no interest to the tribe of romancers, until he returns to the story in its last sad chapters.

I must admit that one exception is the pseudo-historian of whom I made earlier mention, Geoffrey of Monmouth. Though an imbecile and a liar, he does at least try to tell the story of a king and his reign. Unfortunately he is interested only in wars and battles, which are certainly important, but which are not the main matter of a true king and emperor. Furthermore, the wars and battles which Geoffrey narrates are for the most part mere inventions of his own disordered fancy. He has, for instance, Arthur fighting a long war against the Emperor Lucius, and his account is detailed (if not very exciting, because he wrote so badly). As it happens, this Emperor Lucius never existed. I have searched the annals and records stored in the papal libraries and in the libraries of the universities of Salerno, Bologna, Salamanca, Oxford and Paris, and found no trace of him.

Therefore this history is worse than useless.

It is, of course, the duty of a king and emperor to make war when this is necessary, and so some monarchs conclude that war should ever be their first business. But a true and good king such as Arthur understands that war is not what a certain sophist called it: the extension of politics by other means. Or, if it is that, it is so only by default, for war is ever the consequence of the failure of politics. It has taken the world a long time to understand this, even though the greatest of emperors of Rome – Augustus, Tiberius and Hadrian – all arrived, by experience and meditation, at this conclusion. Arthur too: he believed, as I would wish you, my Prince, to believe, that the essential problem of politics is how to get beyond war, to create a world in which war is neither necessary nor desired; in short, to outlaw war.

The true business of a king, and therefore of politics, is administration, and especially the administration of justice. Arthur, throughout his reign, strove to establish peace and the rule of law. In his own words, his intention was that 'the key shall keep the castle and the bracken bush the cow'.

But, though it is necessary, my Prince, to impress this on you, it is not the stuff in which romancers delight. Nevertheless, Arthur gave Britain what it had not known since the departure of the legions: peace, prosperity and security. The robber barons were called to order or suppressed. I suppose Arthur derived peculiar satisfaction from bringing his old persecutor Sir Cade and his infamous father to stand trial in his court on charges of murder, extortion and sodomy, but I am equally certain that they would have received the same trial and exemplary punishment if he and Cal had not suffered at their hands.

This trial sharpened the distress he felt at having been persuaded by Guinevere to drive Cal away and, in the melancholy mood which now took possession of him in the absence of so many of his most favoured knights, a mood that was deepened by the coldness that persisted between him and Guinevere, to whom he was bound only by honour and duty and not affection, he sent to seek where his old friend might have found refuge. But his messengers returned to report that they could find no trace of him.

When Sir Kay learned of this he sniffed and muttered that the court was the better place for the absence of that intriguing pervert; a view with which Eugenius the Archbishop of Canterbury agreed.

Arthur, however, was disconsolate. Lonely, in poor health, often suffering fevers and aching in his joints, he sighed for the days of his youth.

Nevertheless he applied himself unremittingly to business, and to holding courts of justice in all parts of the kingdom. 'Justice', he said, 'is the important thing. Where there is no justice, virtue is smothered.'

One day in October he held his court in York, which the Romans called Eboracum. He tried many cases and retired weary to the bishop's palace where he lodged, for there was then no habitable castle within the city walls. The bishop received him coldly. He was displeased because Arthur had dismissed a case in which an old woman was charged with being a witch. He quoted to him the Biblical text: 'Thou shalt not suffer a witch to live.'

'I have heard it often,' Arthur said.

'And yet you set this woman free.'

'I was not persuaded of her guilt. Witchcraft depends on the existence of a pact, either tacit or expressed, between the accused and the Devil. Is that not the teaching of the Church? I found no evidence of such a pact, merely an old woman who claimed to be able to cure cattle or make them sick according to her will. A silly old woman, perhaps a nasty old woman, but one in league with the Devil? I think not.'

The bishop flushed. 'You are too trusting,' he said, 'too credulous.'

'Credulous?' Arthur said.

'With respect, Your Grace, yes. You are too ready to place trust in human nature, and you do not appreciate how active the Devil is in his efforts to suborn and take possession of simple people. The fear of the Lord is the beginning of wisdom and, again with respect, you lack that fear. Therefore you do not understand how against the moral and sacramental system of Holy Church, which is appointed for the redemption of souls, there is erected a monstrous will, powerful, malevolent and intelligent. This is the will of the Devil. And what, I ask you, is Satan's motive for enticing people to his service? It is to offer the greatest offence to the Divine Majesty by usurping to himself a creature who is, or ought to be, dedicated to God, and thus more surely to secure his disciple's damnation, which is his chief object. And when you dismissed the case against that woman, poor, ignorant and wretched as she may be, you did the Devil a service, for you released her to work for the corruption of other souls.'

Arthur sighed. The bishop's words carried him into unfamiliar territory. He felt their harshness; he had an intuition, as it seemed to him, of their essential wrongness; and yet, given the premises on which the bishop built his argument, he could not dispute his conclusion.

Seeing him hesitate, the Bishop renewed his attack. 'There are evil angels,' he said. 'Now it is established that the angelic and the human essence are entirely distinct from each other, and good angels respect these holy limits. But not so the evil angels. A surge of matter passes through the hierarchy established in the infernal regions, and so they seek the bodies of men and women; they desire to become flesh, to penetrate human flesh, for malice only. So they create a kind of body that is not a true material body and in this false body enjoy intercourse with men and women, who are themselves, as it were, intoxicated by this experience and freed in their disordered minds from the moral law, and so commit themselves to the Devil. And some so committed wear the mask of true religion, and are for this reason still more dangerous, more given to malice.'

'But I was not persuaded by the evidence that this old woman was a witch,' Arthur said.

'She was accused of witchcraft and tested for witchcraft, and if the evidence seemed insufficient to you, then that itself is evidence of the wiles of the Devil, that it should appear that a witch might be innocent.'

'If what you say is so,' Arthur replied, 'then there is no true judgement and justice itself flies out of the window.'

So he broke off the argument.

Later that night, as he was preparing to retire, his squire came to him and said that a certain man, who would not give his name, had come to ask for an audience. Arthur hesitated for he was fatigued to exhaustion. Then the squire said, 'He told me that if you did not grant his request I was to repeat this verse to you:

> My love, he loves another love –
> The winds now wester blow –
> My love plays false as fairy dice,
> Alas, why does he so?

When Arthur heard this it was as if the years had been ripped away and his youth restored. His heart raced and he told the squire to bring the man to him without delay. 'Is it really you, Peredur?' he thought. 'Brought back to me when I thought you dead?'

The man who entered was stocky, running to fat in the face and belly, and very different from the spritely boy of Arthur's imaginings. But the black eyes still sparkled and, looking at him, Arthur knew that it was indeed Peredur and that he himself was not the smooth-faced youth he had been when they were together, but a weary man with careworn features. It was impossible that either should now desire the other and yet affection flowed between them as the sun's rays may of a sudden lighten a room. So they fell into each other's arms and embraced.

Peredur said, 'When I heard that you were coming to York I told myself that I would not dare approach you. I thought also that there would be no purpose in our meeting, for we are not what we were, and what we were is so far behind us that we might as well be people who had never known each other.'

'How could you think that?' Arthur said. 'There is scarce a day when I have not thought of you.'

In saying this he did not speak the truth, but for the moment supposed it was indeed as he said.

Peredur smiled, shook his head and laughed. 'You have changed less than I feared,' he said, 'for you were ever ready to make more of me than I was and to allow your fancy to gild reality.'

Arthur himself now laughed, for he recognised a line from a

comedy they had played – indeed, the one they had played that night at the inn where Arthur first lay with Morgan le Fay.

So for a little they talked of old times and of the Goloshan and Cal, and the adventures they had been engaged in, and they drank the good wine of Bordeaux, though Arthur's physician had forbidden him it.

Then Arthur said, 'Why did you leave me? Why did you ever leave me?'

'It was not of my will. Though I confess that I have never been capable of constancy in love, on account of the flightiness of my nature, yet I loved you as truly as I was capable of loving anyone. But Merlin came to me and upbraided me, saying that I was a cause of shame for you and made you an object of mockery to your knights. I could see that was indeed so. Yet still I could not have brought myself to leave you. Merlin understood this and argued with me fiercely, and I supposed that he was arguing in your interest. Yet still I resisted. So he cast a spell upon me, or wove a spell round me. Perhaps he gave me a love potion, I don't know exactly. The upshot was that I found myself unable to resist his advances, horrid though they were. He forced himself on me and abased me, and though I shudder now to think on it, this gave me deep and unholy pleasure. When with his dirty hands he slowly stripped the garments off me, my lust matched his. And so I submitted, even to pain, joyfully. That disgusts you?'

'It frightens me,' Arthur said.

'It disgusts me to remember it,' Peredur said and smiled. 'I don't recall how long it lasted. It was as if time was consumed. I was overtaken, I see now, by madness. But Merlin and his caresses and the rough usage he dealt out were all that mattered. Even his stink excited me. And then he vanished from my life, and the madness passed and I was restored slowly to sanity.'

'Poor Peredur,' Arthur said. 'Poor Merlin too.'

'It was odd, the way he vanished. I never saw him again. I suppose someone killed him. Of course, later, when I thought about it in my right mind, I knew that for him I was a substitute, that he made me what he had never had the courage to make you. An unhappy man, don't you think?'

It had never occurred to Arthur, but now he thought, 'Yes, Merlin was wretched.'

'And then?' he said.

'I wandered and in time arrived here in York and married the widow of a rich mercer and prospered. We have three lovely daughters. I've been fortunate. I suppose I'm a happy man.'

They drank more wine and then Peredur said, 'That woman you set free today. She's the sister of my wife's mother, a nasty old thing.'

'But not a witch,' Arthur said.

He saw that Peredur was sweating, though the room was cold. 'Perhaps not,' Peredur said, 'but there are stories. She has certainly been active in certain proceedings, consorted with . . . I don't know exactly who. But the dealings frightened her, that's how I came to hear of them. And – this is what I must tell you – they were aimed at you. There is a certain great lady, I don't know her name, who seeks or sought to win your love. She went to a priest and brought him gold, promising more if he would help her by holding what is called an amatory mass . . . I don't know all the details. Such as I do know are horrid. She – the great lady – disrobed and lay on the altar, naked. The priest laid the chalice on her belly or between her legs. The priest proceeded to say the Mass. Then, at the moment of the Offerings of the Elements, a child was brought forward, laid on the altar and its throat cut. It was a boy child, seven years old, blond, with blue eyes and fair of face. Its blood gushed forth and was caught by the priest in the holy vessel. Then flour was added to the blood, a paste formed and a wafer made, in sacrilegious imitation of the Body of Christ. I'm a Christian myself now,' Peredur said, 'and the thought of what they did and what it signifies fills me with horror. Then the priest, as I'm told, knelt before the altar and said, "Ashtaroth, Asmodeus, Prince of Darkness and desire, I call on you to accept the sacrifice of this innocent child, and in exchange grant what I now ask of you: that the love of the King may be returned to me . . ." He spoke, you understand, on behalf of the Great Lady or in her person, or it may be that it was she herself who uttered this obscene prayer. My wife's mother's sister was confused in the telling, for even she was afraid of what she had witnessed. Then the priest and the lady drank of the child's blood which had not been employed to make the wafer. And later, but I don't know how much later, when it seemed as if the invocation had failed – as you will know better than I that it did – there was another Mass, but this time it was the Mass of Death, and it was your death that was demanded.'

'Death comes to all men', the King replied, 'at the appointed hour. But as you see it has not yet laid its icy hand on my shoulder.'

But, though his words were bold and he seemed calm, Peredur felt him tremble as they embraced; for Arthur understood, with no need of words or further evidence, that the Great Lady of whom Peredur spoke was Morgan le Fay, whom he had cruelly discarded for reason of State, and he felt pity for her and fear for himself.

In the morning he sent for the old woman whom he had set free, now wishing to question her further and privily, as Peredur had advised him. But she could not be found in all the city. A few days later she was discovered hanging from the branch of an oak tree in a grove at the opening of a valley that led to the high hills. Many said she had killed herself, but others maintained that she had been murdered by her fellow witches.

Arthur would have kept Peredur with him from this day on, but Peredur would not, though he was sore tempted, on account of the love he still bore the King. But he said he had a duty to his wife and daughters, and especially to his wife who had freed him from the sins of lust and despair, and brought him into the Faith. So Arthur gave him gold, that he might have a dowry for his daughters, and rode away in sadness. The next day the bishop preached a sermon on the text 'Thou shalt not suffer a witch to live' and he wrote in cipher to Eugenius the Archbishop to inform him of what Arthur had done and of how, by setting free a witch, he had proved himself unworthy and no true Christian monarch. When Eugenius read the letter, he called the young knight Mordred to him and they spoke together of these matters.

X

When Arthur left York, he dismissed his companions and rode on alone till he came into the hills that now serve as a frontier between England and Scotland. The air was keen, clouds were banking in the east, and a wind moaned around the bare tops and up the valleys. A skein of wild geese were flying south. A grey dog-fox – for the hill foxes are grey, not red – watched him warily from a patch of bracken, and Arthur caught its scent borne on the strengthening wind.

He turned up a dark valley that grew narrow as the track climbed. It was a desolate place, with no sign of human habitation. A pair of buzzards hovered in the sky below the tops of the hills and seemed to mark his progress, and, as the light began to fail, there came the screech of an owl. But except for that, and the sound of his horse's hooves, there was silence and he might have been alone in the world.

Arthur knew fear, and did not reproach himself, in that dark place where his horse slipped on the scree and the grass was scant as a leper's hair. Then the track levelled and he was on a little plain or plateau, where there stood a few trees, hawthorn, alder, birch, all bent double by the force of many winters' winds. It began to rain, that thin rain which in Scotland we call mirk, rain scarce to be distinguished from enveloping mist, but cold, chill, unwelcoming. And then, rising out of the gloom, he saw the tower.

It was a squat, ugly building and it seemed deserted, but he banged on the iron-studded door with the pommel of his sword. He knocked three times and in the deep silence could hear only his own breathing.

Then the door creaked open and a dwarf stood within and enquired of him what was his business. 'If you're a traveller,' he said, 'you'll find neither meat nor drink here, but there's an ale house in the next valley.'

'We are all travellers,' Arthur said, 'at different stages in our journey from birth to the grave, but if you take this ring' – which he withdrew from his finger – 'to your lady, she will offer me a less surly welcome than you have given.'

'That's as may be,' the dwarf said, 'should I choose to deliver the ring, but I'm no greatly minded to do so' and with these words he made to shut the door, pausing only when Arthur offered him gold.

'There's little use for coin here,' he said, taking it nonetheless, 'but if you'll bide a wee, I'll see whether your ring will serve. I'll no guarantee it, mind, for we're canny folk here and quiet, whae dinna look wi' ony favour on the wide warld.'

So saying, he shook his red head, and shut the door between him and Arthur.

It was the length of a Mass before he opened it again, and ordered Arthur to dismount and tie his horse to a hawthorn tree that grew some feet from the door. When Arthur asked if there was not one who could tend to the beast, he shook his head again and said, 'I misdoubt you'll be here lang enough for the cratur to need stabling. Follow me.'

Then, hobbling at speed, he led Arthur up a staircase that turned widdershins, and admitted him to a chamber high up in the tower. It was lit by three wax candles in a branched holder and a heavily veiled lady sat by a spinning wheel.

'Here's the mannie that ettles to see you, my Lady,' the dwarf said. 'And I'm bound to say he seems a civil enough, well-spoken chiel. But you'll judge for yoursel, as you aye do.' With these words and a sharp laugh, he left them alone.

Arthur said, 'Will you lift your veil, Lady, that I may be certain it is indeed Morgan le Fay whom I am addressing.'

'And do you indeed require to see my face to be certain of that, since I received the ring which I once gave you in token of our love?'

'Yet I should still wish to see it once more.'

'And if you saw it as it is, ravaged by grief and misery, and bearing the marks and deep lines inflicted on it by the tedium of life, would you recognise it?'

'I believe I should,' Arthur said. 'I did you great wrong. I have come here to tell you so.'

'We did each other great wrong,' Morgan said and her voice was suddenly soft. 'But it was not of our own volition.'

Saying this, she raised her veil, and Arthur saw that she was an old woman, the eyes glittering in the dancing light of the candles, the mouth twisted and the cheeks hollow. Little remained of her beauty and yet, as he gazed on her, there was still a trace of it, like the echo of a song dying in the night.

'So – do you recognise Morgan whom you loved? Do you recognise your sister?'

'Sister?'

'Yes,' she said, 'sister.' And for the first time she smiled. 'Truth can't be concealed for ever. It will come to the surface like oil.'

For the moment he could think of nothing to say. He was the King and Emperor who must never be at a loss for words.

'We have different mothers,' she said, 'but Uther Pendragon fathered both of us.'

'Half-sister, then,' he said, as if this made a difference.

'When you married the Saxon woman,' she said, 'I was tempted to tell you. But what would you have done? Sent me to a convent? Blinded me? Torn my tongue out?'

'None of these things. I could have done none of these things. Did you know from the start?'

'Not at the inn when I thought you merely the player-boy.'

Were there words that could be spoken? Arthur was overwhelmed and paralysed by the truth. He couldn't remember why he had come to this tower, only how with hand, lips, his whole being, he had explored her body, discovered its delights.

'And later it was of no importance to me,' she said. 'The old gods practised incest. So, Merlin told me, did the Ptolemy kings and queens of Egypt. Why should I care? I have never been a Christian.'

'Merlin told you?'

'Who else? Who else but he who ordered my life from early childhood and malformed it?'

The wind howled round the tower. It alone seemed to keep them company. 'If it weren't for the wind,' Arthur thought, 'I could imagine us dead. But perhaps the wind will sigh and howl audibly over our graves?'

'Merlin,' she said. 'Merlin the cold-hearted, who saw himself as the master pulling the strings of puppets dancing to his narrative. We had a child, you and I, conceived that night at the inn.'

'Conceived in love, then.' He spoke almost dreamily.

'Conceived in ignorance and born a cripple. Merlin took him from me to rear. But I recovered him and sent him to Camelot, to plague you and serve as my instrument of revenge.'

Did she say that? Did he afterwards imagine it? He couldn't tell, but often it seemed to him a speech from one of the plays in which he and Peredur and the Goloshan used to act.

'His name is Mordred,' she said. 'Some say it means the bitter one . . .'

Then he spoke to her of her other sons. Or so he later recalled, wondering, however, if he remembered not what he said, but what he should have said. He spoke of Gawaine's nobility and resolution, of Agravaine's intelligence, of the desperate courage Gaheris displayed in suppressing his effeminacy and conquering his fear.

'I'm told', she said, 'your Saxon cheats you, bedding your knights, especially Lancelot. That makes you wretched?'

He sighed, made a vague gesture with his hands as one pushing something unwelcome away. 'I have failed her,' he said, not denying now what he had never before admitted. 'Not that it matters,' he added.

A bell, far distant, began to toll, its notes heavy, dark, ominous in the empty night.

'For years', she said, 'I thought you would return to me. Often I dreamed that you had done so and lay beside me.'

He had come to accuse her of all that he had learned in York. She had risen up evil in his imagination. Now he experienced tenderness; she too was one of the defeated. She had sought to compass his death? She couldn't wish for it more longingly than he did himself. The priests said that too was a sin.

She said, 'I know why you came. It was not necessary. It is finished.'

He looked her in the face. For an instant, the duration of an exhalation, the twisted mouth seemed to relax, almost into a smile; and then she lowered the veil. 'Merlin is dead,' she said, 'and everything he sought, foolish man, to make.' She laid her hand on a skull placed on the table by her side. 'I have to remember we too must die,' she said.

BOOK FOUR

I

'Time's long corrosion, what does it not infect?' The line, quoted often by Merlin, who had it from the Emperor Marcus, whose consolation in old age was Horace, sounded like a muffled drumbeat in Arthur's head as he sat at the high table in the hall of Camelot. Gawaine was absent, none could say where; Lancelot also; Parsifal long gone, married, some said, dead according to others returned from distant lands; Galahad vanished as if he had never been, perhaps to ethereal realms, perhaps lodged in a grim monastery.

Meanwhile the minstrel-bard chanted a warrior-poem, harsh, discordant, Gothic, dull to Arthur's ears.

Guinevere too had withdrawn from the court, retired to a convent whence she sent a letter (dictated, for she had no skill in writing herself) demanding an annulment on the grounds, she claimed, of his sterility.

From the end of the table Gaheris looked at him, seeking affection. He was pale, thin, exhausted as one who had held fear at short arm's length from boyhood. His eyes searched Arthur's face and what he saw there caused him to turn away to hide his tears.

Months had passed since Arthur rode back to Camelot. Winter was loosening his grip, Easter approaching. The Archbishop Eugenius chewed on a marrowbone, and talked of sin, vice and the need for penitence. That afternoon under a rainy sky, flagellants had scourged themselves in the sight of God and the King, calling for mercy on a land beset by enemies.

The wild tribes of the North were in motion. Saxons, Jutes,

Angles, sailed up the eastern rivers, burning and looting. There were murmurs of war from the Saxons already established in Britain; now refusing to pay tax or supply the King with troops. Even the petty chieftains of the Cambrian mountains raided the lowlands, carrying off sheep and women.

These were the months of Mordred's ascendancy. The young knight, devout son of the Church, favourite of the Archbishop, butter-mouthed and skilful in flattery, set himself to be the advocate of reform. He said nothing against Arthur and left all whom he spoke to thinking less of the King.

Gaheris, plucking up his courage, came to Arthur and told him Mordred was conspiring against him. Arthur smiled, thanked him, assured him of his love and did nothing. The truth was he could not look on Mordred without shame, now that he knew he was his son, born of his incestuous union with Morgan. Moreover, because Mordred was also a cripple, he pitied him. 'Cripples have a right to be cankered,' he said to Gaheris.

But, though he did not act on this warning, Gaheris's concern roused him from the weariness of soul that had afflicted him since his visit to Morgan in her tower.

He collected his army, a small army, smaller than in the days of his prime, for many of his most valiant knights were dead or missing, or like those heavy veterans, Kay and Bedivere, whose stolidity in earlier years had won battles while their caution had too often deprived them of the fruits of their victories, were now too old, too stiff, too aching in body, for the fight.

But Arthur in these months was wonderful to behold. He seemed no longer the King-Emperor weighed down by responsibilities, but rather the young prince restored. He wore, men said, his long boots once again, and he whirled his little army up and down the valleys, over the hills, striking blow after blow. He threw back the invading Irish with great loss of life and their lamentations were heard across the seas. He fell on the Saxons as they spread out from the estuary of the Humber. When their King sent to demand that he surrender to them the land they had occupied, he answered that the only land he would grant him was 'six feet of British earth'; and before night fell on the flat lands, the Saxons had been scattered as the winds of autumn strip the red leaves from the trees, and the river ran with their blood all the way to where they had moored their ships. Then he turned on the Welsh and sent them screaming and gibbering in disarray back to their high mountains. And, lastly, he descended into the plains and engaged with the rebel Saxon King whose name was Cynewulf, and defeated him soundly in five great battles, till Cynewulf confessed his treason and begged mercy. This Arthur granted him, saying that mercy is the prerogative of the victor and of all high princes.

Which indeed it is, as I would urge you, my Prince, never to forget; but when you have vanquished your enemies, to remember Arthur's word.

All men marvelled at Arthur's deeds that summer; but Mordred gazed on them with dismay that approached despair for, he thought, the Lion is roused again and I have much to fear from his wrath.

That summer was the last time Arthur knew joy in battle. Concerning which, there is much to be said. Some theologians maintain that war is evidence of original sin and that, if we were without sin, as we shall be in Paradise, there would be no war or occasion for war. This is as may be, though there was war in Heaven itself when Lucifer, who is also Satan, and the rebel angels challenged the power of the Almighty.

Yet, however this may be, it is also evident that fighting and therefore war are as natural to man as making love, or indeed eating and drinking. For there is no nation that has not made war and no people that does not honour the heroes of war above all others. Furthermore, the act of war may be, and often is, exhilarating in itself, as exhilarating and life-enhancing as the act of love. We recall that the greatest hero, Alexander, wept because there were no more worlds to conquer.

Even the strictest theologians agree in formulating the concept of the Just War, and though there may be argument as to whether a particular war is just or not, the fact of this agreement is undeniable. And if war is just, there is no reason not to take pleasure in it.

It is undeniable, on the other hand, that war is also cruel and occasions much suffering. For this reason no prince should embark on it without good cause. But all men must die, and death in battle is acclaimed as the noblest and most honourable of deaths, save for martyrdom, which is granted but to the chosen few.

And this is why the poets have all sung of war, which gives men the opportunity to display whatever virtue is in them: courage, devotion, magnanimity.

These virtues may be recognised in the story of Arthur, as in the tales told of Achilles and Aeneas, which have delighted the generations of men.

In the course of this summer Arthur, in the absence of Gawaine and Lancelot, made Gaheris his confidant, who acted also as his chief of staff. This was a role for which he was well suited, better fitted than leading men in battle, being highly intelligent but cursed also with an imagination that caused him to feel pain before he experienced it, the pain of others as much as his own. For this reason he suffered failures of nerve which men took for cowardice.

Arthur took pleasure in his company and spoke to him as he could now speak to no other.

The King said to him, 'There is no responsibility without guilt. When my ancestor Aeneas had sailed from Troy and come to Italy as was his destiny, he was compelled to make war on a people called the Etruscans. He was engaged in battle against their King who, fearing for his life, ran away. Then the King's son, a young man called Lausus, came forward as if to the rescue of his father. Aeneas warned him to keep away. "This contest will be too much for you," he said. But the young man persisted. They fought, and Aeneas stabbed him "through", as Virgil has it, "the tunic which his mother had woven with pliant gold". When the young man lay dead before him, his face pale and surprised, Aeneas was deeply moved by the sight. "Poor boy," he said, "what can I give you in recompense for so glorious a death? Keep the armour which was your pride; and I restore your body to your friends if that is any consolation." And so he lifted the body, carrying it in his arms, while the long hair stained with blood hung like a veil. In that moment, I am certain, Aeneas felt the burden not only of the boy's corpse, but of his own destiny, which forced war and killing on him. The image of Aeneas bearing the body of the dead Lausus is one that disturbs my nights when I lie between waking and sleeping. At the end of that great poem, with which I have lived since I was a boy, having it first from Merlin's lips, Virgil, himself perplexed by the demands that destiny or the gods make of men, cries out, "Was it really your will, Jupiter, that peoples who were to live together in eternal peace should clash in war?" How often have I asked that question myself, when I think of the wars in these islands and our Empire! Is it necessary that Romans and Britons should fight Saxons, that Romans should war with Goths and Germans, Franks and Vandals, that a new and greater Empire may be formed? I have won many battles and, if our poets be right, eternal renown, yet I tell you, Gaheris, that to be a ruler and conqueror is to be one who himself requires pardon and pity, on account of the cruelties with which he has burdened himself. Indeed, it seems to me, now as evening draws in on my life, that to be a victor and conqueror is a fate as terrible and awful, in many ways, as to suffer defeat and subjection. For the vanquished are acquitted by the very nature of defeat from responsibility for future action, while the victor is condemned to that. And I ask whether after all my victories the world is a better place than I found it when I was nobody?'

What could the tender-hearted Gaheris find to reply to Arthur in this mood of self-laceration? Nothing but platitudes, which spoke of his profound sympathy for the King's anguish, but brought no consolation.

II

The next year, with all Britain at peace, Arthur travelled through Gaul, which was not yet France, and over the Alps, and descended into the valley of the Po, and thence to Ravenna. Gaheris was with him, to act as his secretary, and a company of his knights, and also priests, monks and two bishops. These he carried with him to show that he journeyed in peace; and in truth, had any king or count through whose lands he passed chosen to attack him, his strength was too weak to resist. But his renown travelled before him, and all kings, princes, dukes and counts made him welcome. Moreover, in Milan he was hailed as Emperor, and when he attended High Mass in the cathedral, the Archbishop placed a golden diadem on his head, and this diadem had been donated to the cathedral by the great Constantine himself.

I mention this because some still assert that Arthur was no true Emperor, but merely King of Britain. They are ignorant men who say this, or liars; for I myself have read in the Archbishop's library the document which relates this ceremony in the cathedral. However, you must understand that this was not a coronation, for that no bishop or archbishop has authority to perform, unless by the will of the Emperor himself, guided (it is said) by Almighty God. Now in the document which I have perused closely, there is no hint that Arthur so commanded the Archbishop. Therefore I conclude that this ceremony represented a recognition or acknowledgement of Arthur's imperial title, which indeed he had inherited from his grandfather, Marcus.

One night he rested in his chamber in Milan, between waking and sleep, or in that light sleep in which thoughts and dreams may not be distinguished one from the other, but appear nevertheless to be more vivid, more urgent and more full of significance than the ideas we consciously formulate or the impressions that strike our mind in the hours of day; and this is, I surmise, because at such moments, which I call half-sleep, we are free of the body as we shall be in the grave. Therefore it may be that all the mental activity of the half-sleep offers us a foretaste of how things shall be when the body is given over to corruption, and mind or spirit released.

Be that as it may, it was in this half-sleep that Arthur found himself in converse with Marcus. He came to him white-bearded (which was how Merlin had recalled him when speaking to Arthur in his boyhood). He came as an old man in a dry month, when the land was parched and they were waiting for rain. And he spoke to Arthur as if Arthur himself were young still. Arthur looked to him for encouragement and at first found none, for Marcus, or the ghost of Marcus, or the image of Marcus that Arthur had conjured in his search for an equal who would understand the burden of Empire which he bore and which weighed so heavy on him now, spoke first of cheats and delusions, of how history, he said, deceives with ambitions, even those we dare only whisper in the dark hour before dawn, and guides us by vanity.

'So,' he said, and Arthur remembered these words clearly and in the morning recounted them to Gaheris, who wrote them down, and I have read his record which is preserved here in Palermo in the library founded (some say) by Archimedes of Syracuse. But I digress, or am in danger of doing so. Another time I shall instruct you in the wonders which Archimedes revealed. 'So,' said Marcus and his tone, Arthur remembered, was sorrowful, and he spoke as one who had endured more than a man should, which indeed, Gaheris thought and noted, was in his opinion Arthur's lot also.

'So,' Marcus said, 'signs are taken for wonders, and history offers such supple confusions that we can find no sure footing in the river of rushing time. Yet there is one lesson to be learned from history: that the task of the King or Emperor is always to repair the wall. And the wall is forever crumbling.'

In the morning Arthur spoke of these things to Gaheris and asked him whether he knew the story of the Sybil that was kept in a wine jar at Cumae. Gaheris replied that he did not, and Arthur said, 'They questioned the Sybil and asked her what she wished for, and she replied that she wished for death. Sometimes', he said, 'it seems to me that the Sybil speaks for all men. The rattle of the bones sounds in my ear.'

When he spoke in this manner, Gaheris understood not the words, but the meaning that lay beneath them. 'Truly,' he thought, 'the King is weary of all things. And yet the Empire is at peace and prospers, by reason of his rule.'

So he was puzzled and dwelt on these questions as they journeyed from Milan to Ravenna.

Ravenna was Marcus's birthplace, or rather he was born in a lonely farmstead a few miles beyond the city, in the marshes. It was to Ravenna also that his body was brought by a devoted servant after his death in that Roman tavern and, respecting his renown and anxious to claim him as a faithful son of the Church, the bishop of that time erected a magnificent tomb, studded with precious jewels, to house his remains. An effigy of Marcus surmounted it. Arthur gazed long on the smooth brow, shadowed in the red light of a dying day, but ivory in its stillness. And the unseeing marble eyes ... how much, and what things, had the eyes that were not marble gazed upon?

Arthur swayed, thrust out his arm to clutch Gaheris and steady himself. 'The eyes in my dream,' he said, 'if it was a dream, were the colour of a dawn sea and as deep.'

To Ravenna came also, with all pomp and the circumstance of imperial greatness, the other Emperor, from the city of Constantine, to debate affairs of state with Arthur. He came accompanied by cavalry, a legion drawn from the sturdy mountaineers of Asia, a thousand courtiers in robes of gold cloth lined with ermine, the Patriarch of Constantinople, sundry bishops, priests, confessors, sixty eunuchs who served in his secretariat, musicians, dancers and jugglers, mistresses, catamites and a travelling menagerie. Gaheris had never seen such magnificence and luxury, and yet this Emperor, with his long beard dyed purple, approached Arthur and embraced him as his equal.

At first Gaheris was abashed, even shamed, by the contrast between the splendour of this Emperor Justinian's appearance and Arthur's, and he was angered when he heard some of the eastern courtiers make mock of Arthur's simplicity of dress and manner.

For an afternoon and an evening, and deep into the black night, the two Emperors were closeted together, while outside the palace, itself half-ruinous with owls nesting in crumbling towers, beyond its walls, the tents were drawn tight, horses stood at tether and the singing of the Anatolian mountaineers rose plaintive to a cloudy sky.

No man knows what the Emperors said to each other, not precisely, whether they talked of the grandeur that had been Rome and of how to restore it, whether they planned (as I believe) the reduction of the Bishop of Rome and the suppression of his pretended right to mastery of the Empire, which, you will remember, he asserted on the basis of that spurious Donation of Constantine. But it is certain that they recognised each other's greatness and swore to uphold the unity of the Empire.

This I assert on the evidence of the memoir written or dictated by Gaheris, who reports that he had never seen Arthur so serene as when the time arrived to take leave of his colleague and depart from Ravenna.

Furthermore, it is known that when word of this meeting was brought to the Bishop of Rome, he grew first pale with fear and his face was blank as a stone. And from that moment he resolved to destroy Arthur, in the manner which I must now, with pain and even anguish, relate.

III

Let me now, for your better instruction, my Prince, expatiate on this so-called Donation of Constantine, even though it is a tissue of lies from first word to last. And, before I do so, it is proper to observe that the reliance of the Bishops of Rome, over the centuries, on this document is evidence of fraud, impiety, arrogance, impertinence, duplicity and bare-faced mendacity.

It purports to be a letter dated the 30 March, in the year of Our Lord 315, from the Emperor Constantine to Pope Sylvester I. It opens with a narrative relating how Constantine came to be converted after the sign of the Cross appeared in the sky over Rome as he prepared to fight a battle that would win him command of the city. This apparition, being attested by other witnesses, may be taken as authentic. You should note, however, that those who wish to deceive you will often begin with a true statement, in order to secure the confidence of those they intend should be their dupes. The letter then tells of Constantine's baptism and, if anything serves to prove its falsity it is this; for it is recorded by sundry historians that, though Constantine declared Christianity to be the official religion of the Empire, he was not himself to receive baptism till he lay on his deathbed, and he did not die till twenty-two years after the supposed date of this letter.

The Emperor then, apparently, recalls how he was cured of leprosy at the intercession of the Pope Sylvester; but no authority that I know of, or have learned of in my deep researches, declares Constantine to have been a leper. So this too is a lie.

The document then records the Emperor's gifts to the Vicar of St Peter, and how he granted him pre-eminence over the patriarchal sees of Antioch, Alexandria, Jerusalem and Constantinople. And this the Patriarch of Constantinople disputes and denies to this day.

It records the gift to the Bishop of Rome of the imperial insignia and of the Lateran Palace, which, indeed, he occupies; and finally the transfer to the Pope of the imperial power in Rome, Italy, and all the Provinces of the West.

You may judge for yourself how improbable it is that Constantine, after waging many campaigns to establish his supreme and sole authority over the whole Empire, should wilfully surrender half of it.

Yet it is on the basis of this document, which I do not hesitate to call a forgery and fraud scarce paralleled in the annals of recorded history, that the Bishops of Rome have claimed primacy over your own imperial forefathers and it was on the basis of it also that the then Pope, one Hormisdas, subsequently canonised, now moved against Arthur and conspired to depose him.

I should add that, as a final act of impertinence, the author of this forgery states that, as a mark of the inviolability of his donation, the Emperor Constantine placed the document on the body of St Peter, which no man has seen since it was interred after his crucifixion.

Why, you may ask, did this Pope, this Hormisdas, this creature, a wretched monk, son of a peasant in the hill country behind Rome, wish to destroy Arthur, who had restored peace and prosperity, and was regarded by all good men as the prince of chivalry and the fount of honour?

The answer is simple: Arthur's greatness was intolerable to the monk. It made his pretensions appear ridiculous. Now the news that Arthur and the Emperor of the East had come together in friendship excited the Pope's fear and jealousy. Therefore he resolved on his destruction.

He wrote, first, to Eugenius, the Archbishop of Canterbury, once a fellow clerk in the Roman curia and so an old ally. He required of him two things: first, that he should supply him with evidence of sins or crimes committed by Arthur, and of any indulgence Arthur displayed to the old and outlawed religions of Britain as, for example, whether he had trafficked with sorcerers or witches. Second, he required Eugenius to supply him with the name of a 'noble prince' whom he might appoint King in Arthur's stead.

The Archbishop was happy to oblige.

Within weeks, while Arthur was still in Gaul, where he held courts of justice and received the homage of numerous princes, he set to work and soon supplied the Bishop of Rome, the self-styled Vicar of St Peter, with a list of Arthur's alleged crimes, sins and high misdemeanours.

These included – for I am honest and shall conceal nothing, even though I know that too many men give credence to the proverb that there is no smoke without fire and consequently tend to regard any allegation as proof positive, confusing what men say with what actually is:

That he had committed incest with his sister;

That he was guilty of the sin of sodomy with divers youths, among whom were named Peredur, Parsifal, Gaheris and Geraint;

That he had allowed himself, to his shame and pleasure, to be sodomised by Lancelot;

That he had delivered known witches from judgement;

That, taught by the wizard Merlin, he had obtained the kingdom by sorcery, drawing from the stone a sword that was embedded there by the arts of magic;

That, finding that his Queen Guinevere was barren, he had sought by witchcraft to enable her to bear a child;

That, this failing, he had resorted to the Black Mass for the same purpose;

That he had compelled or encouraged Guinevere to drink the blood of a dead child for the same purpose;

That he had suborned Lancelot to lie with the Queen for the engendering of a child and heir;

That, in the celebration of unholy and diabolic rites, he had kissed a cat's arse in mockery of the elevation of the Host;

That he had consorted with pagans, and broken bread with them;

That he had sold benefices for gold and was therefore guilty of simony;

That he oppressed the poor, giving their land to his knights;

That he had condemned barons to death without proper trial;

That he had imprisoned three clerks in despite of the benefit of clergy, which required that they be tried in ecclesiastical courts;

That he consorted with players, jugglers, courtesans, prostitutes both male and female;

That his court was a den of vice;

That he had insulted the Archbishop himself and denied his authority;

That he had declared that the Bishop of Rome had no more power over the Church in Britain than any other foreign (sic) bishop;

That he had practised alchemy;

That, to please the Evil One, he had spat on the Cross;

That . . .

Oh, the list of allegations was long. I haven't time, inclination, heart to record even a half of them. What I've written should be enough to make clear to you the intention . . .

When Eugenius had prepared his denunciation, he felt as he had never felt before. How to put it decorously? In a manner that won't shock anyone who reads this after you, my Prince? Shall I simply say, he felt like what he had never had? He felt like a man who has walked the streets consumed with lust so sharp that his loin aches and who has, late in the evening, fallen on another and discharged himself.

Satisfied. That's what he felt. Richly and rewardingly emptied.

He read it over three times and called for wine.

Then he sent an underling to summon Mordred to his palace.

He had had his eye on Mordred for a long time. He knew he was the man for what he had in mind.

Have I given you a clear picture of Mordred? I think I have. But you should forget it. It is no longer accurate.

That is because Mordred had grown up. He had learned to curb his tongue which had formerly, to his delight, struck out like the poisonous fangs of a serpent. He had learned that the man who exercises a spiteful wit at the expense of others may amuse his audience and lead them to think less of those at whom his barbed sneers are directed, but will not win their confidence or inspire them with trust. Each thinks that the same wit may be directed at him when he is no longer of the company. So Mordred now cultivated silence. And, because only the memory of his wit hung about him, men began to think of him as formidable. He revealed so little of himself that all supposed there were great qualities that lay concealed.

He made a show of his chastity. This was not because he saw

great virtue in chastity, but because he believed that by mastering desire he proved himself strong. Moreover, he feared that in making love he would surrender something of himself. And it may be that in truth he felt little desire, that his love was wholly concentrated on himself. I do not pretend to read his mind. But the consequence is certain. Men wondered at his self-denial, and at the same time it frightened them and so they looked on him with respect, even with awe.

Then he altered his appearance as he had changed his manner. Whereas when he first came to Camelot he had taken great care to dress in a manner which disguised his deformity, he did so no longer. And this was because he calculated – for all that he did was calculated – that his seeming carelessness of his deformity would impress those whom he intended to lead. For it is natural that we should seek to conceal our weakness and disguise whatever is ugly, and the man who disdains such pretence appears to us to be remarkable.

When Eugenius summoned him, he did not answer immediately, for that was not his way. He made the prelate wait, in order to demonstrate his superiority.

At last he allowed himself to be announced at the palace and was straightway escorted to the Archbishop's library. He found Eugenius at his ease, in a fur-lined dressing gown of yellow silk, and reading the invective which St Jerome directed against the Pelagians, whom he styled heretics. Mordred kissed his ring, courteously, and refused the wine which was offered.

After a few pleasantries, for you must know, my Prince, that it is impossible to enter into any discussion in Britain without some preliminary remarks about the weather, which in that sea-girt island is changeable as it is not here in Sicily and therefore occupies the minds of the natives to a degree which would surprise you – but I digress . . . So, after a few pleasantries, the Archbishop embarked on a speech which, Mordred understood, had been carefully prepared.

'For', he said, 'just as the Almighty has so arranged that the sun and moon shed a light so that the beauty of His Creation may be perceived by fleshly eyes at all seasons, so also, lest Man, the creature He has formed in His own image, should be lured and enticed into sin and thus endanger his soul, He has provided in the apostolic and royal dignitaries the means of ruling the world according to His divine will. If I, as your Earthly Father are to answer for you to your Heavenly Father on the awful Day of Judgement' – here he paused, to allow the significance of that thought to sink in – 'before the just Judge who cannot lie and is your Creator and the Creator of all that moves on land and sea, I now urge you to consider carefully how I must diligently provide for your salvation, and how you, my son, for your own safety, ought without delay or question to obey me in all that I may command, so that at the last you may enter into everlasting bliss.'

Mordred, whose eyes had not left the Archbishop as he spoke, now lowered them, bowed his head and seemed to give himself to deep reflection.

Then, in a low voice that spoke of his profound humility, he said, 'It must, my Lord, be as you say and as you instruct me.'

Not by the slightest tremor of the voice or flicker of his eyes did he so much as hint at the pleasure which he took in such abject hypocrisy. So he continued, 'It must be as your Lordship says, for what is a prince but the sword obedient to Holy Church.'

'Would it were ever so, as it should be.' The Archbishop sighed deeply, as one whose mind is sad or disturbed. Then, saying that he understood that Mordred, unlike so many of his fellows, had mastered the art of reading, he handed him the document which he had drawn up listing the charges which Arthur was to answer.

Mordred read it slowly, very slowly, for he wished to give himself as much time as he could to determine the best response, and when he had finished he threw himself on the floor, and chewed the rushes and howled like a deserted dog. Eugenius watched him in silence, and still said nothing when Mordred, now on his knees, shook his head and moaned, 'Is it possible? Surely it is not possible that the King should be so wicked?'

Eugenius laid his hand on the young man's bowed head and said quietly, as if sorrowfully, 'Alas, it is as I have written, to the last word.'

Then, now speaking clearly and with energy, he said, 'When King Saul sinned against the Lord and disobeyed His command-ments, the Prophet Samuel, High Priest of Israel, pronounced judgement against him and anointed the shepherd-lad David to be King in his stead. Arthur is Saul, I am Samuel and you, my son, are my David.'

He took a flask of consecrated oil, and poured it over Mordred's head and said, 'My child, I have consecrated you the servant of the Lord God Almighty, by virtue of the authority vested in me by the Holy Father, the Vicar of the Holy Apostle Peter, and I call on you to be the instrument of his vengeance, and to bear the Sword of Justice and the Shield of Truth against his enemies, heretics, sinful men, blasphemers, and especially against the renegade and tyrannical Arthur, now put down from the High Places and, according to the Bull to be published by the Holy Father, excommunicate. And may the hearts of all turn away from him and the hand of every Christian man be raised against him.'

And then he knelt by Mordred and they prayed.

IV

I find I must say more of this Mordred whom I have presented to you, my Prince, so far only in flashes.

He was, as you will remember, the youngest son of the lovely and unfortunate Morgan le Fay, fathered, as she believed and asserted, by Arthur himself when, as a strolling player in his tender youth, he delighted her eyes, was lured to her chamber where both enjoyed a night of love.

This I have already related.

It may well be as she said.

Yet there are those who question her account.

In the first place, they say, Morgan and Arthur were alike paragons of beauty, while Mordred was ugly. This, they say, is against nature: a fine stallion and a lovely mare will not give birth to an ill-formed and common foal. And indeed, all who have engaged in the breeding of horses, or dogs or cattle, confirm this observation.

Secondly, they find in Mordred no resemblance of character as of appearance to his supposed parents, for Morgan's misfortunes arose from the warmth and impetuosity of her character, but Mordred was cold, sly and cautious; while Arthur, as I have abundantly shown you, was a compound of all virtues.

Yet this argument is less cogent, for it is well-known that noble parents may spawn ignoble children, the philosopher-emperor Marcus Aurelius, for example, being the father of the vicious and intemperate Commodus.

So, though many deny that Arthur could have fathered such a son as Mordred, I do not hold the denial proven.

Be that as it may, none can doubt that Morgan accepted Mordred as her son, even though he bore no resemblance to his brothers or half-brothers Gawaine, Agravaine and Gaheris, in looks, manners or morality. Nevertheless, some suggest that the infant was a changeling, substituted by fairies, or perhaps by a corrupt midwife, for the child she gave birth to; and among those who make this claim, some assert that the true son of Arthur and Morgan, thus spirited away, was that Sir Galahad who sat in the Siege Perilous and was granted the vision of the Grail, while others believe that true son was Parsifal.

But of this there is no evidence and therefore I cannot advise you to believe it. I mention it merely in passing.

What is certain, as I have already told you, is that Merlin removed the infant Mordred from his mother, to rear him according to his method.

This was itself remarkable, for there was nothing to recommend the boy. He had been born with a full head of teeth, with one shoulder raised above the other, so that some thought him a hunchback, and lame in his left leg. Yet it is fair to add that Merlin soon discovered him to be possessed of a keen intelligence; and indeed, he proved an adept student. He learned to read and write, to know the ways of nature and the properties of plants, becoming skilled in herbalism. He was entranced by mathematics and acquired a deep knowledge of astrology. He assisted Merlin in his alchemical experiments and, at the age of fifteen, was wise beyond his years.

Gratitude was an emotion foreign to his twisted nature. Far from revering his learned master, he grew to detest him. Why, I cannot tell, merely surmise that he resented Merlin's understanding of his true nature. He therefore sought to plague him. One day he abstracted a love potion which Merlin had concocted for a Great Lady whose husband was blind to her charms (preferring to them the nubile daughters of his tenants) and slipped this into Merlin's evening mead, then arranging that when he woke he should set eyes first on a slut called Barbara, the daughter of a swineherd in the forest and stinking of her father's pigs. Merlin was seized with a lust so violent that the girl feared him and fled into the recesses of the forest where she was either eaten by wolves or spirited away by the fairies, or joined a band of witches and became the Devil's darling (for all these stories are told of her). Merlin meanwhile roved the fields and woods moaning lust and frustration, till, maddened by the impossibility of finding the slut, he fell to his knees and ate grass like a second Nebuchadnezzar. And this pleased Mordred greatly.

I have already told how subsequently, when Arthur took Guinevere as wife and, though with many tears, dismissed Morgan from the court, she, in the spirit of revenge which may take possession even of noble natures should they be high-mettled, sent to seek out Merlin and had him bound and thrown into a dungeon; and then had Mordred brought to her also.

Now at first Morgan wished merely to give herself the pleasure of the company of this son who had been taken from her as a child; and I believe she hoped tenderly that she would find in him the qualities she adored in Arthur, so that he might comfort her in her loneliness. But she soon discovered his malicious character and, though in her generosity she tried to excuse this as being the consequence of his deformity and also of his education by the detested Merlin, it was before long more than she could tolerate. He spread calumnies about her maids of honour, of whom she was very fond, and caused her sorrowfully to dismiss two of them; and there was reason to believe he had raped another. So her first enthusiasm turned to disappointment, then to disgust.

At the same time the initial grief she had experienced when Arthur rejected her turned to resentment, which festered, till her judgement was consumed in bitterness and the true love she had felt was transformed into hate. For sure, love and hate, being both founded in passion, are, as it were, brother and sister to each other. So now, when Morgan despaired of regaining Arthur, she thought to destroy him. Therefore she determined to send Mordred to the court and gave him a letter to deliver to Arthur – 'himself, in person' – in which, with honeyed words, the writing of which gave her deep satisfaction, she commended the young man to the King as his true and only son.

'Truly,' she said, 'they deserve one another.'

Mordred rode to Camelot with his hopes high. He was not yet absolutely vicious. He retained something of the ardour natural to youth; it may be even something of youth's idealism. Certainly he was ambitious, but that is proper in young men. He was conscious of his deformity which, as I have said, he sought in those days to disguise, for it shamed him to know how inferior he was in strength and agility to the most ordinary of knights; but he also knew that he was possessed of intellectual gifts that made him superior to his fellows. The combination is an unhappy one, which can be accepted with equanimity only by the virtuous. Mordred was not such a man and for this he is to be pitied.

He took his mother's letter to the King. Arthur read it and flushed. He did not doubt what Morgan wrote. He could not. Yet it was unwelcome. He was agitated, pained, displeased. He had often dreamed of a son, longed for a son, and had painfully reconciled himself to not having one. And now one was presented to him, a bastard, the product of a love he could not regret, but at the same time a son who was deformed and whom he could not acknowledge without giving pain to Guinevere; and this he was loth to do, precisely because he knew he no longer loved her.

Mordred looked at him and read rejection in his eyes. From that moment he determined to be revenged.

Arthur knighted him, treated him with respect, admitted him to his council. He accorded him the same privileged access to his person that Gawaine, Agravaine and Gaheris enjoyed. In private he spoke to him as his son, but he would not do so before the court, and he would not, as Mordred had hoped, nominate him his heir. For years Mordred sought to win his favour by flattery; in vain. He came to see that Arthur felt only pity for him and he resented this, all the more so because it appeared to him that this pity was expressed in condescension. His pride prevented him from disclosing his claim to others; yet he could not refrain from dropping hints or from speaking of himself, obliquely, as one disinherited and cheated from what should have been his by right. Gradually, he drew to himself all those knights who for one reason or another were disaffected, bored, thwarted in their ambitions, ripe for rebellion.

He cultivated the clergy. His attendance at Mass was regular. He confessed frequently. He allowed himself to be observed poring over commentaries on the Scriptures. So he acquired a reputation as an upright, God-fearing young man. It wasn't entirely false. Indeed, his religious zeal was far from insincere. He really did fear God. He practised an extreme devotion to the saints. Nothing delighted him more than to be given some holy relic. When, on some festal occasion Eugenius, who understood, and despised, this peculiarity of his character, procured for him a rosary made of ebony which had, he said, been fashioned by a Coptic hermit on Mount Lebanon, Mordred's eyes glittered and his joy was boundless. The hat which he customarily wore was garnished with little leaden images of saints and martyrs, and others dangled even from the helmet which he wore in battle. In conversation, when asked for an opinion, he would frequently kiss one of these images before replying; and it was observed that he did so with the more obvious devotion when about to say what was untrue or calculated to deceive.

Yet only a few people, his half-brother Gaheris among them, called him a hypocrite; and indeed, they may at the deepest level have been mistaken. His intelligence was such that he could not pretend to himself that his ways were not wicked and his fear of Hell was intense. Therefore, since he could not or would not change his ways, he looked for insurance from piety, or, in my opinion, from the grossest superstition.

Eugenius himself, as I say, despising the cult of relics, which he knew to be worthless, nevertheless saw in Mordred the qualities that he needed. He recognised and admired his lack of scruple, his ambition, his ruthlessness. He believed, however, that, with the advantage of age, he would be the master in their association. In this he deceived himself. Mordred recognised no man as his master.

V

So Eugenius pronounced the excommunication of Arthur, calling on the authority of the Pope 'able to bind and to loose in Heaven, acting on the authority of St Peter whose vicar he is, and therefore likewise able here on earth to bestow and take away empires, kingdoms, principalities, duchies, marquessates, countships and the possessions of men. For if he judge spiritual things, is he not entitled to judge all earthly things; and as St Peter judges and rules over angels in Heaven, so here on Earth his Vicar rules over even the proudest prince, as surely as that prince over his slaves . . .'

This was the first example of the employment of the powers of excommunication and deposition claimed against all reason by the Bishop of Rome, powers which have wrought great distress, provoked rebellion and war, and been the cause of much shedding of blood.

So now, on a bright March noon with the wind blowing snell from the east, Eugenius declared Arthur put down from the throne of Britain and installed Mordred in his place. He sat him on the sacred stone, which some call of Destiny and which, it is averred, served as Jacob's pillow on the night when fleeing the wrath of his brother Esau, he reposed in Bethel and before dawn wrestled with an angel. Whether this be true or not, it is known that this stone was carried by certain of our ancestors out of Egypt and brought to Britain, where it has been long revered. It is of sandstone and greyish-yellow in colour.

During the ceremony it was reported that Mordred seemed impatient, eager to have it over and be free to act as King. And yet it was important to him. It seemed like the fulfilment of his destiny. And he made a curiously imposing figure. The raised shoulder, the twisted mouth, the deepset black eyes, all spoke to onlookers of his will.

It was not long before the world, or rather the country, felt its force. He had prepared the ground carefully. Now he dispatched some of the young knights who had committed themselves to him to seize the coastal castles and disarm their garrisons. He issued a proclamation declaring Arthur and any man who sought to aid him to be outlaws, who might be summarily killed without penalty or guilt. He set himself to inflame the minds of the people, stirring them up against foreigners, and calling for the delivery to the officers of his Iron Guard (the body of special forces which he had formed) of all Jews, heretics and witches. Some of them were burned in London, Winchester, York, Caerleon and even Camelot itself, to the consternation or delight of the populace. Two legions were quartered among the Saxons settled in the south-east of the country, and the taxes demanded from the Saxon earls and ealdormen were trebled. If a landowner protested that he could not pay, his teeth were extracted till he confessed where he had hidden his treasure. If such persuasion – this being the term officially approved – was insufficient, then first his fingernails and then the nails of his toes were extracted.

At Easter, with the approval of the Church, a week of penitence was decreed. The city streets resounded with the shrieks, sobs and imprecations of troops of flagellants. Mordred himself set an example by submitting to be scourged on the steps of St Peter's Basilica in York, while on Easter Day itself he wielded a knotted whip so fiercely on the back and buttocks of a canon of the Minster that the wretched man would have died had not an angel descended from heaven to stay the King's hand; and this was attested to by divers witnesses who affirmed, moreover, that the angel then bestowed a golden crown upon Mordred and kissed him three times, once on the hand, once on the brow and once, as a token of the esteem in which he was held in Heaven, on the lips.

So enthusiasm drove reason from men's minds. A few were appalled; more were exalted and of these the bolder spirits gave themselves over to an orgy of cruelty, in which the Jews were the chief sufferers, though, by Mordred's express orders, the most painful deaths were reserved for those accused of sodomy, whether active or passive, onanism and other practices denounced as sinful.

Fear from the first suppressed any danger of rebellion, while those who were given licence to persecute grew ever stronger, more arrogant and more ardently committed to Mordred. For he understood that nothing binds men more closely to tyranny than giving them the liberty to oppress others and indulge whatever propensity to cruelty they might have.

He sent soldiers to seize Guinevere in the convent to which she had retired, but the Queen, alerted to the danger that threatened her, had herself let down from the tower in a basket, which procedure was hazardous, for she had become very fat, being a glutton who ate more the more she felt herself to be miserable or ill-used. However, she made her escape and, with the help of a young knight, by name Beaumains, who had long adored her (from a distance), she reached the coast where the captain of a vessel was engaged to carry her to Brittany; and there she was reunited with Lancelot. Honour compelled him, though such love as he had been able to feel for her had died; and he gave her refuge.

When Mordred heard of her escape, he was both angry and afraid; angry because he had been thwarted; afraid because he had been certain that, with Guinevere in his power, Arthur would not dare to make war in an attempt to regain his kingdom, lest she come to greater harm or be put to death. And in this he judged wisely, as was his wont.

He also had his mother Morgan arrested, and put on trial for witchcraft. Of all his evil acts none is more horrifying than this. Yet this evidence that he was altogether lacking in natural feeling impressed many. 'Let them hate provided they fear,' he said, a line first, to my knowledge, attributed to the Emperor Tiberius. Moreover, it pleased Eugenius and the bishops. They preached sermons in praise of the King's holiness and devotion to true religion. Eugenius himself, or his clerks, drew up the charges against the unfortunate Queen of Orkney. When they were read out in open court, Mordred wept to think that such wickedness was possible. Of course, he already knew the charges and had suggested some of them himself; so that his tears were a comedy. Yet, even in this instance, his hypocrisy was not absolute. His fear of witchcraft was very great and perhaps he really believed that his deformity was the consequence of his mother's trafficking with the Devil. When superstition takes possession of a man, reason is annihilated and there is no end to the nonsense he is ready to believe.

Yet at this point his nerve failed him. He would not consent that his mother be put to death according to the sentence pronounced when, after torture, she confessed to everything of which she was accused. He said, again with tears in his eyes, that he could not have her death on his conscience; and perhaps he was sincere. It may be that some trace of natural affection still lingered. Who can tell? Who can with certainty fathom the depths of a man's nature or understand what moves him?

It is said that he sent messengers to her with poison, that she might choose to escape the terrible and dishonourable death to which she had been condemned. But she disdained the gift.

So the sentence of death was commuted and she was imprisoned in a high tower in a remote valley where she was attended by eunuchs whose tongues had been torn out, that they might not communicate with her. Some historians declare that she was blinded, but I do not know if they speak truly. It may be that they are confusing her fate with that to which superfluous members of the imperial family are commonly condemned in Byzantium.

Finally Mordred searched out all those who had been friends or allies of Arthur, and who had not deserted him and joined his party.

Among the victims was the aged Sir Kay. Though Kay had frequently grumbled about Arthur and obstructed many of his designs, and though he often spoke fondly of the days when Arthur had seemed only a poor boy to be cuffed and kicked and subjected to Kay's discipline, yet the old knight had sworn the oath of allegiance to him and was possessed of an obstinate sense of honour. Therefore he would not submit to Mordred's usurpation, but tried to escape across the sea to join Arthur. His flight was arrested even as he was about to embark. He was dragged out of the little boat and his head was rudely hacked from his body on a muddy beach.

Peredur, too, was hunted down and brought to Camelot where, though an honestly married man for many years now, he was condemned to death as a sodomite and necromancer, and suffered the penalty of burning at the stake, to the great satisfaction of Eugenius and, as was declared, to the Greater Glory of God.

VI

So Britain suffered under a reign of terror, and many lifted their eyes to the heavens and asked when Arthur would return to redeem the land. Most put the question silently, in their prayers, for Mordred's spies reported any who mentioned Arthur's name without appending a curse to it. Such were seized and confined to prison or held in camps where they were subjected to what was called 're-education'. Those who proved intractable had their tongues pulled out, for then, as Eugenius's chaplain said in a sermon preached at the Basilica of St Paul in London, they could not abuse the Lord's gift of speech by uttering the name of one excommunicate from the Church. But the high sun of summer sank and there was neither sign nor word of Arthur. The leaves turned red and yellow, and fell from the trees, and with them the hope of many also fell away. Cold winter gripped the land with frost or throat-choking fog, but Arthur did not come. Some said he was dead, others, sadly, that he was afraid. Only a few continued to believe that he would return with the spring; and so the number of those loyal to him dwindled, and many thought it expedient to accommodate themselves to the New Order, which was how Mordred chose to describe his regime, and enter into collaboration. Some did so sorrowfully and reluctantly; others, having long delayed to change their complexion, now displayed the fervent zeal of converts. So, week by week, Mordred grew stronger and his mastery of Britain was complete.

Meanwhile Arthur was at Lyon, which the Romans called Lugdonum, when he learned that he had been excommunicated and deposed, and that his bastard son had usurped the throne. It came to him as the day of wrath which shall dissolve the world into ashes; and he fell to the earth in a swoon. A feather held to his lips did not move and at first they thought him dead. In truth, he passed many weeks hovering between life and death, as one who knocks at the portal of the underworld but is not admitted. His doctors bled him and he weakened. They rubbed his body with precious oils and he did not respond. And even the closest of his followers despaired of his recovery.

But Gaheris heard of a learned doctor in Germany, who had studied the hermetic texts and was deeply versed in the Cabbala, and caused him to be summoned, sending as evidence of good faith a ruby the size of a pigeon's egg. This man, whose name was Jacob Kuhnrath, sent word that he would come and sent also, by the messenger, his emblem, which showed a philosopher bearing a lantern through a forest and following the footsteps left by Nature. This seemed foolishness to the doctors attending the King and they would have denied Jacob access to their patient. But Gaheris prevailed; and, since he was hitherto thought to be a man of weak will and even frivolous, men wondered at the authority he now assumed.

When Jacob arrived, he first cast the King's horoscope and assured the doctors that if they persisted with their treatment Arthur would surely die, but if it was entrusted to him, then the stars indicated that the King would regain his strength. 'For', he said, 'though man's destiny is written, yet it is not written which path he shall certainly take.' Which some thought nonsense, arguing that what is destined must be and cannot admit of choice or alteration.

Then he sent his boy into the fields and woods to gather herbs, and instructed him to select among them those with divers properties, some of them if ingested by themselves noxious and venomous. 'For', he said again, 'the spirit and the body are alike disordered, and we seek to restore harmony.'

While his boy was absent on this mission, he drew certain mathematical or geometrical figures around the bed where the King lay pale, cold but also sweating; and these, he said, imitated the hieroglyphic characters which are written by Divine Will in the universe; and, since all were ignorant of these, none could deny him. Then he called for the music of flutes which, as he asserted, are the instruments that most closely echo the music of the spheres; and he burned sulphur as the music sounded about him.

When his boy returned, he approved the herbs and made a dish of them stewed in fine oil, and held this to the King's nostrils that he might inhale their odour. At which moment Arthur, for the first time in seven months, opened one eye. Jacob, speaking in an undertone, very low and indistinctly, for he knew the enterprise was of great danger, now muttered an incantation in the Babylonian tongue. Then he lit a fire of olive twigs and took an egg, which in esoteric studies symbolises the universe, since life emerges from it, and held it over the fire till the shell cracked. And at that moment Arthur opened his other eye, and his lips moved and he spoke. But none could understand his words. And Jacob passed his hands over the King's face, and gave him of the dish of herbs to eat. And when he had done so, he rose from his bed with his strength renewed, though his hair had turned white.

All marvelled at what they saw and many were afraid, for it seemed to them not natural that Arthur who had appeared dead should rise in this manner. So some spoke of witchcraft and departed from the city. Jacob himself disdained to account for what he had done though, when pressed privily by Gaheris, from whom he accepted gold and jewels, he relented to assure the young knight that there was nothing to fear in what he had done. 'Some will speak of magic,' he said, 'but they use the word ignorantly. There are four kinds of magic, you must know. There is divine magic, which is beyond our understanding, and theurgy, which is religious magic that frees the soul from the contamination of the body; there is goetia, which is witchcraft, and natural magic, which is the science of nature. Judge by the results which magic I have performed, and know that of these four kinds of magic, only the third, goetia, is wicked.'

Gaheris thanked him and Jacob then said, 'If you choose, believe that I saw the King surrounded by a wall of fire and, when I came nearer, I saw that the wall moved, for it was but a procession of many angels who walked there. And these angels were there as my guides and also as the guardians of the King, so I knew that my medicine would prevail.' Then he took his fee, and returned to Germany and his studies.

And from that day Gaheris believed in and was assured of

Arthur's immortality. But he kept his counsel for fear of what men would say if they heard him speak in this manner.

VII

It was a long time before Arthur regained his strength and indeed, it never fully returned. He could not mount a horse unaided and to ride for longer than the light lasts in a northern December wearied him. His mind also was unsettled. He gave orders and rescinded them. He could not fix on a course of action. Some secretly declared him senile. Others thought the time ripe to slip away, cross to Britain and make their peace with Mordred. It was well known that he extended a welcome to any knight who had deserted Arthur.

Even those most devoted to him could scarce conceal their anxiety. Gawaine and Gaheris talked through the dark hours, and their subject was ever the King's state of mind. At first, they kept from him the worst of the reports they had of Mordred's tyranny, for fear lest they precipitate the recurrence of his illness; they could not forget how he had swooned when word came of what they called 'the rebellion'. But this could not last. 'We cannot treat the King as a child, to be protected from knowledge of what is happening,' Gaheris said to his brother. But it was in both their minds that the King was entering on his second childhood.

'But Guinevere at least is safe?' He put the question haltingly.

'So we understand. Fled to Lancelot.'

'That is some comfort,' the King said. 'I have done the poor woman much wrong.'

Again, both thought of how, in the world's eyes, he was dishonoured because Guinevere had sought refuge with the man reputed to be her lover rather than with her husband. But they kept this thought also to themselves.

By the spring Arthur was stronger. He rode into Brittany, land of salt marshes, the shrines of saints, and squat castles. He sent messengers to Lancelot seeking his aid, but was too proud to command it as was his right. They returned to report failure.

Gaheris had never admired Arthur more than at the moment when he received this unlooked-for word. His face was a mask. None could discern the pain he felt. Lancelot had offered no explanation; merely given this curt refusal. Gawaine was furious. He rode off at once to speak with Lancelot, his closest friend, the knight whose superiority he had acknowledged with all the force of his generous nature.

'I would have prevented him had he told me of his intention,' Arthur said to Gaheris.

'But why? We need Lancelot and it is his duty to serve you. My brother means to recall him to his duty. Is that wrong?'

'Duty,' Arthur said, 'such a heavy word to ring down the years. As for needing, why, the fewer men, the greater share of honour. I remember saying that once before. It made more sense then.'

'Yet', Gaheris said, 'what else is there in the end?'

'There was an old knight I knew once,' Arthur said, 'who talked to me of duty and said, "At my age, it is no reward. What was my duty now seems to me worn out, exhausted, too old, the sort of thing you do and then find it has no meaning. It has lost the significance it had for me." I have often thought recently of that old knight.'

Gaheris thought that the old knight was Arthur himself.

The King said, 'Last night I dreamed of Camelot. There is no greater sorrow than to remember the happiness of yesterday in the hour of present misery. And yet we must to Britain.'

So the King mused on the transience of his glory.

Meanwhile Gawaine rode up to Lancelot's castle of Joyeuse Gard, blew his trumpet three times and demanded to speak with Lancelot. For a long time he was kept waiting, then the drawbridge was lowered and he entered.

Lancelot received him in a little chamber high up in a tower. He was dressed not as a soldier or a knight but in a tunic of red cloth girdled at the waist; and he had slippers on his feet. They embraced, and Lancelot poured wine and said, 'Gawaine, my sworn brother' and sighed. 'How I wish I had prevented you from coming, or refused to admit you.'

Gawaine was pleased to hear him speak in this manner; it

suggested to him that Lancelot was ashamed that he had not immediately answered the King's summons.

And indeed, Lancelot was ashamed. But, as Gawaine discovered, he was also resolute. 'The Queen', he said, 'came here in great distress. She escaped capture, trial and what she is certain would have been ignominious death. She had been deserted by Arthur, abused by Arthur.'

'I am sure', Gawaine said, 'that the King ever treated her with propriety . . .'

'Propriety?' Lancelot rolled the word round in his mouth as if it were wine and then, as if the wine had turned sour, spat it out. 'Propriety? Is that what a woman wants, Gawaine? The King married her without love . . .'

'All kings do that. So do most barons and knights. We marry for advantage . . .'

'And should we? We talk of chivalry. We make a great parade of chivalry and of our devotion to our mistress. But it is all words, empty words. We abuse women because we will not grant them what they most require . . .'

'These are foolish words, Lancelot. It is the way of the world.'

'Indeed it is, the bad way of a bad world. Arthur abused the Queen. I too – may God forgive me – abused her. Because I am so constituted that I cannot give myself fully in love, I took what she offered and could not be faithful to her. Yet she came to me in her distress. She came, fearing that I would reject her; and yet she came. Too proud to ask my pity, she sought merely my protection . . .'

The fading light of the winter afternoon cast Lancelot's face into shadow. Indeed, it seemed to Gawaine that he had so positioned himself that his face could not be read. 'These are fine words,' Gawaine said, 'and no doubt do you credit. But what have they – what have the Queen's fears and feelings – to do with the summons you had from the King? A summons you are obliged by the oath you swore to obey.'

'I have sworn other oaths,' Lancelot said, 'too many perhaps. And the most recent is the oath I swore the Queen: that I would not abandon her but would be guided by her in all things.'

'So is it then the Queen who prevents you from joining the King? Is it she who holds you back? And for what reason?'

'It is her will that I should not go. I have submitted to her will and in that submission I find peace.'

Gawaine swore and his fist crashed on the table. 'Peace? This is no time to babble of peace. We are at war.'

Lancelot shook his head. 'It's impossible that I should make you understand.'

'On the contrary, I understand all too well. You are grown soft or you are afraid. What will the world say when it learns that Lancelot, the greatest of all the knights, is sheltering behind a woman's skirts when his King has need of him?'

'The world may say what it will. The world says many foolish things.'

'Lancelot . . .' Gawaine's voice took on a note of pleading and he told of all they had learned of Mordred's tyranny. He spoke well and at length; he, who had never had a gift for language, spoke better than he knew.

But Lancelot would not be moved. For the first time he smiled and said, 'My poor Gawaine – and does it really matter? Mordred may be all you say, and worse. But Arthur is old and weak. He will soon be dead whether he wins this last battle or not. And then what? The pernicious race of vermin that we call men will resume their wars and quarrels and persecutions. There will be a second Mordred and a third. Much blood will be spilled and nothing gained.'

'You cannot believe that,' Gawaine said. 'You cannot be serious in speaking in this manner. You, like me, have known Camelot. You have seen there what life can be, you have seen how a well-ordered state can secure order and peace . . .'

'And men's happiness . . . my poor Gawaine, it was all but a dream. Even at Camelot there was jealousy and malice, ambition and greed, arrogance and cruelty, fear and hatred . . . When for what they call "reasons of state", Arthur married the Queen, did he not in that moment brutally destroy your own mother?'

'Not brutally . . .'

'Brutally or callously or for the highest motives – what does it matter how we describe it? You know what he did and what the consequences were. Arthur had many virtues, but he was first and last a man of power, and power knows no laws but those it finds for the moment to be convenient. No, Gawaine, no. I shall not move from here again. I am weary of war. Now it's enough for me to cultivate my garden – and such virtues as I may possess.'

'And if I call you "coward"?'

'I shall be content to leave you to your opinion.'

VIII

By the spring Arthur was stronger in body and spirit, though not in men and material. He had to hire ships from the Count of Picardy, few in number for his army was small. He crossed from the mouth of the River Somme and landed near the town now called Pevensey. There are shorter crossings, such as that made by Julius Caesar, but Arthur hoped to be able to raise more troops from among the South Saxons. He had learned how they had been oppressed by Mordred and knew their fighting spirit. Some joined him, but most of the great men held themselves apart, some because they resented his treatment of Guinevere, others because they saw how small his army was, judged that Mordred would defeat him and so concluded that their condition would be worse if they fought by Arthur's side than if they stood aloof. Moreover, the years of peace which Arthur had enforced on them had caused many to lose the appetite for warfare. They had become farmers, and farmers will ever care more for their crops and cattle than for affairs of state. One ealdorman said, 'It matters not a whit to us who calls himself King of Britain, so long as we can find a market in London for our beeves and corn.'

In Arthur's camp counsels were divided. Every man had an opinion and every man was certain that his neighbour's was folly. Some were for standing their ground and challenging Mordred to attack them in a well-fortified camp. Some were for striking at London. 'Who holds London holds the key to the kingdom' – that was Gawaine's view. Others, Gaheris among them, were for marching to the West where, they thought, they could be sure of support. Arthur temporised, unready to commit himself to one course, though all, if discordantly, urged action upon him.

But he had sent out scouts and awaited their report. Till he could glean Mordred's intentions, he would not move. His reasoning was sound; he had established a base, which could be supplied with provisions. He said to Gaheris, 'Your half-brother has never commanded an army. When he moves, he will move slowly.' He sighed. 'On the other hand he has experienced knights with him. They have already secured the line of the Thames and we are too weak to breach it.'

Word came that Mordred was hesitating. Arthur therefore sent a detachment of knights on the road to London. 'Let it be known that you are the vanguard,' he said. This was a feint, designed to draw Mordred into London.

(Look, my Prince, I have drawn you a map, a better one, I warrant, than the poor thing available to Arthur. Indeed, his own best map was his memory and the eye for country acquired in twoscore campaigns. Once, when someone asked him how he had trained himself in generalship, he replied, 'When riding in country I don't know, I have always tried to guess what lay on the other side of the hill.' This is advice which you yourself would be wise to follow in preparation for the day when you command an army.)

Mordred did as Arthur hoped, perhaps expected. Scouts reported that his whole army, but for garrisons left at forts on the Thames, was being drawn into London.

When he got this news, Arthur at once advanced north, to be free of the marshes, which lay between his base and the West, and then headed in that direction when he was beyond the marsh country. His intention was twofold. First, having given Mordred the slip, he aimed to draw the usurper after him. He was certain that Mordred's army was ill organised and that, in a rapid march, many would fall away. Second, he looked for reinforcements in the West where he had always been popular.

Gawaine expressed relief, though his own plan had been rejected. 'The King's mind is working again.'

Now Arthur moved rapidly, covering forty miles in three days. Then he halted, concealing part of his army behind a ridge, and waited for the pursuit. He attacked and threw Mordred's line of march into disarray, then called off his knights. 'We have gained two days,' he said. Now he hastened along the old Roman road that runs from Salisbury to the Bristol Channel and it was on that road, just where it leaves the Ridge Way, that he camped, awaiting fresh troops from the west, and Mordred from the east. 'We have need of a sharp battle,' he said, 'to discourage the enemy.'

Then it started to rain, the warm, heavy rain of a British summer in which – you will scarcely believe this, my Prince, when you gaze out on golden-yellow tawny Sicily – there is no colour but green beneath the sky, except for the flowers that bloom luxuriantly. An Italian friend of mind – a learned doctor, well-versed in literature and philosophy, went some summers ago to Oxford to lecture in the schools. He wrote to me: 'I cannot credit this country. It is like living in the middle of a salad.' And so, indeed, it is. Moreover, there are summers such as that in which Arthur fought his last battles when the air is never dry, so that even when it is not raining it is wet. So the valleys flooded, the rivers were too full to ford, horses feeding too richly on the too rich grass foundered or suffered colic, swarms of flies tormented all. Some fell sick of dysentery, others caught fevers. Many grumbled. Some deserted.

No doubt Mordred's army suffered likewise, even more severely. Yet because it was so much larger, and because he lavished the gold he had commanded from the Saxons, comman-deered from the monasteries, extorted from the merchants of London, stolen from widows and orphans, who were the King's wards, he was able to recruit mercenaries from among the Scots and the wild Irish, and from across the North Sea, Danes and Jutes, big yellow-bearded warriors wielding mighty battleaxes, pagans assured of honour, fame, feasts and virgins, should they be slain in battle.

The egregious Geoffrey of Monmouth tells us Mordred's army numbered 80,000 men. This is absurd, typical of that lying fantasist. It were impossible to provision such an army in those days. Even in the great days of Rome armies never attained that size. Divide the figure by ten and you come near a truer estimate. But that number was still four times larger than Arthur's little army.

Arthur now stood to fight. He had chosen his position well, with a line of retreat through the hills should the day go against him. His troops were drawn up in and around a ruined settlement, a farmstead that in the high days of Empire had been a rich Roman's villa. It stood atop a ridge, so that Mordred must attack uphill.

His knights advanced at a brisk trot, though they squelched and slipped on the wet ground, so that their charge became disordered and lost impetus. Arthur had ordered many of his own knights to dismount and to hold a position protected by a dry-stone dyke, broken in places, but nevertheless a sufficient defence-work. They thrust with their lances against Mordred's cavalry, wounding many horses and causing them to unseat their riders. Some were slain where they fell, others scuttled off down the hill, impeding as they did so a second charge and several being trampled underfoot.

This second charge was repulsed in like manner and this time, without waiting for the command to advance, many of Arthur's knights leapt over the dyke and attacked the disorganised enemy, forcing them back down the slope. When they saw this a detachment of mounted knights took it on themselves to engage and turned the check which Mordred's cavalry had received into a rout.

But then, at the very moment when they thought the victory was theirs, they were confronted by the shield-wall of Danes and Jutes, swinging their mighty battleaxes and doing great execution. Mordred's reserve cavalry then took them in the flank and it was with great difficulty, and only on account of their courage, marvellous to behold, that Arthur's men were able to extricate themselves and, resisting the attack as they gave ground, to regain the sanctuary of the defence-work. That they were able to do so showed how skilfully Arthur had selected the ground on which to fight the battle.

So that day's encounter ended in stalemate and, under cover of darkness, Arthur contrived to withdraw his army and resume his march to the West.

The battle had been fierce, and many noble knights were slain. Chief among them, lamented by all, was Gawaine, the fearless one. He was commanding the rearguard when he fell, an arrow, fired from the crossbow of a mercenary, in his throat. It was the first time Arthur's men had encountered that terrible weapon and it surprised them, for the scouts had failed to report Mordred's recruitment of these Italian professional soldiers, said to be Lombards.

When Arthur was told of his nephew's death he said, 'I would rather my right arm had been cut off than have lost Gawaine. He was the bravest of the brave, the most truthful and honourable of knights.'

And indeed, this was true. No unworthy act stained his reputation and there was no challenge he ever refused or duty he ever shirked.

It is to Mordred's eternal shame that when he learned of his half-brother's death, he had the battlefield scoured for his body and then, instead of giving it the honourable burial that was Gawaine's due, had the head cut off and stuck on a pole, and paraded round his camp that men might see that the great and terrible Gawaine was no more.

And when scouts reported this in Arthur's camp, Agravaine and Gaheris, the dead hero's full brothers, cut their cheeks and drew blood, and smeared it on each other's brows and swore that they would be avenged on Mordred, for Gawaine's sake and in his memory.

IX

That rash charge had cost Arthur some five hundred men, and the army he led into the West was bruised and battered in body but still resolute in spirit. No man who has written of this last campaign questions this and it is not recorded that any now deserted Arthur. But, though Mordred's army had suffered still greater losses, Arthur had been compelled to yield ground and so Mordred was accounted the victor. Furthermore, holding London and being rich in treasure, he was able to make good his losses, and other mercenaries, long contracted for, now arrived and joined themselves to him, so that within a few days of this first battle he was stronger than he had been before it; and his new recruits were fresh and eager to prove themselves.

And still it rained, as if the Heavens were weeping to see how the realm was in turmoil, and for pity that Arthur's glory should now be tarnished. It turned cold too, with the wind shifting into the north-west, so that the rains fell icily, though it was still by the calendar high summer.

Men now hesitated to join themselves to Arthur, for those who will willingly rise to aid one who seems destined to defeat are ever few. So now Arthur found even castles which he himself had caused to be built shut against him, denying him refuge or strongholds from which he might defy Mordred. And he was now too weak to lay siege to them. Gaheris, unknown to Arthur, sent again to Lancelot, telling him of Gawaine's death and beseeching him, even now, to come with all his knights for, 'Unless you respond to my appeal,' he said, 'then I fear the King is lost and the Round Table, that noble fellowship of which you were once proud to be esteemed the chief glory and the finest ornament, will be destroyed.' And he signed this letter, 'for the love of Gawaine, for the love I have ever borne you, and for the love you formerly professed for me and for the King'. But he did not speak of this letter to Arthur for he knew that the King's pride would condemn it.

So they were encamped at the head of a valley behind which lay the western sea. They were short of food and there was no wine, and when night fell, the darkness that gathered around them seemed to Gaheris to cover the whole land of Britain and lie upon it like a funeral pall.

One night, after word had come that Mordred's army, though advancing slowly on account of its large baggage train, was within two days' march, an old man presented himself at the outposts stationed to give word of its approach. He was dressed as a pedlar, in a yellow robe, and carrying a staff cut from an ash tree in his hand. His beard was grey and his face scarred, and he moved as one who was very weary, which indeed he was, for he had travelled many miles in rough country to be there, and had known much hardship.

He asked to be taken to the King. The sentry to whom he addressed this request hesitated, fearing that this seeming pedlar had been sent by Mordred either to spy out their nakedness or perhaps even to murder the King. But the old man spoke insistently, though gently, and at last the sentry called for his captain, who questioned the old man closely. But he would not reveal his name or the purpose of his visit, so the captain, puzzled and scratching his head, sent him under guard to Gaheris, that he might examine him.

Gaheris himself had been wounded in the battle: a lance thrust in the thigh, nothing serious, merely a flesh wound. He was dressing this when his page came to say that a sentry was outside his tent with an old man who sought an audience with the King. 'What manner of old man?'

'He looks a pedlar. Wrinkled, dirty and stinking like a billy-goat.'

The boy, an impudent saucy youth whose spirits remained high despite the danger of their position, giggled and held his nose as if in disgust. 'He might be mad,' he added.

'Might he, indeed? And are you a judge of madness, Will?'

'As good a judge as the next man. His eye wanders as if the world was strange to him.'

'In our present circumstances it might be that it is strange to all of us. Well, if he is mad, it will at least be a diversion.'

'That's as may be. I'll fetch him then, shall I?'

The old man shuffled in, the page behind him and brimming with curiosity. 'If your boy had not told me you were Gaheris,' the old man said, after long scrutiny, 'I would not have recognised you.' He leaned heavily on his staff, his eyes continuing to search Gaheris's face. 'Well,' he said, as Gaheris maintained silence, 'we are none of us what we were and I see you do not know me either. I had not expected that you would.'

'You have the advantage of me,' Sir Gaheris said, 'for at least you know my name. What, then, is yours, old man?'

'No,' the old man said, 'you are not the pretty youth that I remember. Then you looked like the King as he was when I first knew him, still a boy himself. As for my name, I have travelled far and been known by divers names in different lands, but when you knew me and I resided at Arthur's court, I went by the name of Cal, though the King would have knighted me and given me some higher-sounding name, but I would have none of it. Have you forgotten Cal, my pretty boy – for that's how I have ever thought of you.'

Gaheris was embarrassed. His page, Will, standing behind the old man, caught his eye and giggled, no doubt because the old man spoke in so ridiculous a fashion.

Gaheris did not immediately know what to reply. So, to give himself a moment to collect his thoughts, he told the page to fetch them wine.

'Willingly,' the boy answered, 'if there was wine to be fetched. But there is none and you know that for I told you so myself yesterday.'

'Then beer or even mead, and some bread and cheese if you can find that, for I am certain our guest has not eaten today and indeed, I am hungry myself.'

So the boy left them and Cal said, 'Will the King see me?'

'Why not? It might rouse him from his lethargy. You know that our position is hopeless?'

'So I had heard. It is why I have come, though for years I swore

I would never return, even if Arthur begged me or sent treasure to lure me back. And neither of these seemed likely.'

Gaheris went first to apprise the King of Cal's return. He found him lying on a pallet bed in his tent, being weak in body and distressed in spirit. He made no reply but his lips seemed to tremble as if he were trying to form words and sweat started on his brow.

Then Gaheris brought Cal in to him and without a further word left them alone together.

Arthur turned his head and tried to raise himself on the cushions that supported him.

For a long time they gazed on each other.

Arthur said, 'Have you come to scorn me in my extremity? If so, you are justified. Or have you come to reproach me for the wrong I did you? There, too, you are justified. Or have you come in pity? Then I reject your pity . . .'

Cal smiled, for the first time since he had come into the camp. 'You still talk foolishness, then, do you? Man, you look in near as poor a state as you were when I came on you in that stable in Old Stoneface's infernal castle. Did you ever, I've often wondered, bring him and his brute of a son to justice?'

'To what passes for justice in this poor world of ours, that I did.'

'Well, that's some good you've done at least, and it will have spared many a lad like that page of your nephew's, for instance, the suffering we endured. I've never found that suffering ennobled the character as the fools of priests sometimes tell us, but I'll say this for our experience at the hand of these monsters, that nothing that has happened since has been as bad. And there's been a lot of it bad enough, that's for sure. Why are you lying on that bed like one who has given up the struggle?'

Arthur smiled, for the first time in weeks. 'As I remember,' he said, 'you were the one who was always near to despair, ready to pronounce that we were all doomed.'

'Aye, and you would say, "This is not the worst so long as we can say this is the worst," or something like that. I never knew what you meant by it, but it fair used to annoy me.'

For a long time they talked of the past and Arthur relaxed to escape the present. Then Cal spoke of his travels: of how he had visited Constantinople and Jerusalem, 'where they tried to sell me bits of the True Cross and, if you ask me, there's enough of it to have made crosses for a whole legion of Roman soldiers' and other relics. 'Did you know', he said, 'that St Peter had more than a score of fingers, not counting, I suppose, those that were nailed to his Cross.' Of how he had been taken prisoner by Greek pirates and escaped only because the captain's son had fallen in love with him, 'which is something that never happened to me before or since, so it was near enough to make me believe in miracles'; of how he had journeyed into the wastelands of Rus, and formed a partnership with a Jewish merchant, Abraham ben Ezra, to sell furs to the imperial palace in the city of Constantine: 'They're canny folk, the Jews, and so Abraham liked to keep in the background and push me to the front of any dealing which we were engaged in – and that meant that when things went wrong, as they did, I landed in the shit, and he made off with what gold we'd got. Aye, canny folk, the Jews, but clever with it. I liked him too, in spite of the turn he served me.

'And so,' he said, 'they tell me your Queen has ditched you.'

'Not precisely,' Arthur said, remembering how it was at Guinevere's instigation that he had banished Cal from the court and kingdom. 'But tell me what happened with the Greek captain's son? Is he still your companion?'

'That's changing the subject,' Cal said. 'As it happens, no. You'll recall, perhaps, that I always had a horror of the flesh. Once the thing got beyond imagining, that is. So I couldn't satisfy him, and in any case the little tart soon found himself a rich protector within a few days of our arrival in the capital. Guinevere told lies about me. You know that, don't you?'

'Poor woman, she couldn't do otherwise. She was jealous, then.'

'And a Saxon. I never knew one that wasn't a liar.'

Arthur sighed. 'I did you wrong.'

'We all do each other wrong, mostly. I wanted to be the only one who told you the truth, the one you could rely on and trust before all others. That was vanity. Or conceit. Or fear. I don't know.'

They fell silent. But it was now a warm silence, a silence of old friendship renewed.

Arthur said, 'Pride. That's been my undoing. I have always allowed pride to come between me and things as they are. Now, it's only pride that prevents me from surrendering to Mordred.'

'From what I've heard – and seen as I journeyed through Britain – he's one as is right to be fought. It's a wasteland, where men won't look you in the eye.'

'Did you ever hear of the Grail?' Arthur said.

'Oh, that.'

'The best of my young knights went in search of it. Few returned.'

'A fool's errand, from what I've heard tell.'

'It may have been,' the King said. 'Who can tell? You might say that of life itself. Indeed, Merlin did. Or was it the Goloshan? Can't remember. "A long fool's errand to the grave," he said, whichever of them it was. He was quoting a poet, I think. It seemed a foolish remark itself. Then.'

'Not now?'

'Now? I don't know. I know very little. Do you remember a dream I had once, which I must have recounted to you; how I was in the fields, in a pleasant meadow, rich in flowers, and it was full of animals – fine horses and white cattle with their sweet breath, and the beasts that prey on others, lions and tigers and wolves; and yet there was neither fear nor fierceness but all was peace and gentleness and tranquillity. And then the sun rose in the cool of the morning and all the beasts raised their heads to it, in adoration or worship. There were dragons there and serpents, but they also offered reverence. And the world was very beautiful and still. That dream returned to me last night, and I woke when it was still dark and was happy.'

'Aye,' Cal said. 'I have often thought of that dream you dreamed. And longed for it to be true, but knew it for but a dream of things as they might be but are not.'

'It seemed to me', Arthur said, 'that I held out my hands to the beasts and they pushed their wet mouths towards me and nuzzled my fingers as dogs do to their masters. And then I fell asleep again, and dreamed again. And this time in my dream I saw the four horsemen whom we encountered riding through that desolate place that had once been a city . . . do you remember?'

'War, Famine, Pestilence and Death. And the last had no face.'

'And I woke sobbing and cold, as if I had lain on a bare hillside in winter. And I shivered to think of that dream and what it meant. It seemed to me in my anguish that the first dream represented things as they might have been and the second the world as it is; and I thought that I had been appointed to make the first dream reality, and had failed, so that all I had done was to summon up the four horsemen and let them loose.'

Cal looked at the King, his friend who had been and was again, and he seemed to hear the rattle of chains and the scrabbling of rats' claws, and he found that he had no words to speak.

X

When Cal left him, Arthur composed himself for sleep, easier in his mind than for a long time. And at first he slept soundly for some hours, but then woke in the middle of the night, and all around was darkness and silence. He was very cold and it seemed to him that it was the cold of the underworld, that land that lies beyond death, which assailed him. But he called for his page to come and rub his feet to warm them; and then he slept again.

This time he dreamed, and in his dream he saw himself sitting on a chair, which was fastened to a wheel and this rested on a scaffold. And he himself was dressed in the richest cloth of gold as in the days of his glory. But when he looked down from the chair, to which, he now saw, he was bound by ropes, he saw under the scaffold, far away, a hideous deep black water, which was stagnant and stank of all unmentionable things. And it was full of worms and serpents, and all manner of foul and noxious creatures. Then the wheel turned and he was cast, still bound to the chair, into this pool among the serpents, and every beast seized him by a limb. So in his great terror he called out for help and his page came in and comforted him again. But for a little Arthur knew not where he was, nor, truthfully, whether he was alive or dead.

His page sat by him, cooling his brow, for he was now sweating freely, till the King lapsed again into a half-sleep. Now it seemed to him that Sir Gawaine approached in the company of a number of fair ladies.

Arthur said, 'Welcome, nephew, doubly welcome, for I had feared that you were dead. But who are these ladies that you bring with you to my sickbed?'

Then Gawaine said, or seemed to say, 'These are all ladies for whom I did battle when I was alive and, because their cause was righteous and I fought for their right, they have been granted leave to bring me here to you to warn you that if you fight with my half-brother Sir Mordred today, then you will surely be slain. But if you send to him and ask for a truce to last for a month, then you shall prevail and the kingdom will be preserved and right triumph again. For in that month of truce Sir Lancelot will come with all his knights to battle on your side and assure you of victory.'

The King woke from his half-sleep and found he was alone but for his page. 'Is it light yet?' he said. 'Has the day broken?'

'Truly,' the page said, 'it is now morning, and I heard the cocks crow in the village down the hill some time ago. Yet it is no more than a half murky light and the rain still slants through a yellow mist.'

'That yellow', Arthur said, 'will be the sun regaining his strength.'

So he sent his page to rouse Gaheris and Agravaine, and Cal, and bring them to him.

While he was waiting for them, he nibbled some dried apricots to sweeten his saliva and the foul taste in his mouth, and composed his thoughts.

They came as he had commanded, and he told them of this second dream, but kept the first to himself.

'Mordred will be a fool to consent to a truce,' Gaheris said, 'for he has us at his mercy now.'

'Yet it is worth trying, for that very reason,' Agravaine said. 'I am ready to make the attempt. When we were children Mordred admired me, or so he once told me when he had come to court. I confess I was puzzled because he did not know me then, seeing that Merlin removed him from our mother's care. Nevertheless, precisely because our position is so desperate, I shall go to him, with a small escort of knights, and propose a truce, as the ghost of Gawaine has advised. I do not think Gawaine would come from the grave to offer you bad counsel.'

So it was agreed.

Now there are several versions telling what then ensued and I shall give you two of them, with reasons to support my belief which of them is true.

Some say that Agravaine and Mordred, and their attendants, met in open ground between the two armies. Mordred brought wine and they drank together as they talked. Agravaine proposed that Arthur should promise to cede to Mordred the counties of Kent and Cornwall, and should also name him as his heir to the whole kingdom. (You will note that in this version there is now no talk of a truce, but rather of a peaceful settlement.) Mordred, it is said, agreed and all was going well when an adder appeared out of a thornbush and stung one of Agravaine's knights in the heel. This knight then drew his sword to kill the adder, intending no other harm. But when both armies saw the flash of steel, they thought that the two parties were about to fight, and so horns and trumpets were sounded, and the battle was joined.

Now this story makes little sense and does not stand up to examination, though it is favoured by the poets. Neither army was standing to arms that morning. So battle could not have been joined immediately. In any case it would have been clear to the knights engaged in negotiations that this other knight had drawn his sword merely to kill the snake and (doubtless) sheathed it once the snake was dead. So it is only a pretty story.

You may ask, then, my Prince, why so many choose to repeat it. I have two answers. First, there are many who like to think that wars are started and disasters ensue, only on account of some mishap or misfortune. They believe in chance rather than malignity. This view of things is encouraged also by the poets and makers of romances of chivalry, the spirit of which is founded on generosity and self-denial. So in their view the magnitude of the tragedy that unfolded, and its pathos, are alike enhanced if the malignity is ascribed to Fortune or Destiny rather than to mortal men. Moreover, this dignifies all that befalls those engaged. It is doubtless for this reason that the poets of old, telling of (for instance) the Trojan War had the gods and goddesses of the ancient world, whom the True Faith deems false and chimerical, acting as partisans, and so depriving the human actors of Free Will, making them the mere playthings of malignant Fate.

It may be also that this version of what happened has been spread by those who adhered to Mordred's party, or their descendants, anxious to acquit themselves, or their forefathers, of all guilt and responsibility for the destruction of the noble Order of the Round Table.

Be that as it may, the true story is very different, more horrible and more shameful.

Agravaine took an escort of only seven knights, enough for dignity, too few for protection. He had instructed them to polish their armour and see that their horses were well-groomed, that they might make a brave show and not betray the sad straits to which the King's army was reduced.

Gaheris watched his brother ride through the rain and watched still, even after the red plume on his helmet had been swallowed up in the clinging mist and the jangling of the harness had died away.

There is no full account of what was said between Agravaine and his half-brother, not even of what the former actually proposed. They were closeted together alone, except for the presence of two of Mordred's Danish bodyguard stationed by Agravaine and ready to seize him. Barbarians, they did not speak Latin, the tongue in which the brothers conversed. It may be that Mordred dismissed the proposal of a truce out of hand. Certainly he had nothing to gain by a cessation of hostilities. If he had heard rumours that Lancelot was at last preparing to come to the King's aid, then the sooner he struck the better; it were folly on his part to think of truce. That much is clear.

Some say that the quarrel broke out when Agravaine rebuked Mordred for his harshness towards their mother Morgan le Fay. That may be true; of all the sons, Agravaine cherished an especial devotion to her.

But others say the cause was an argument over Mordred's collusion with the Archbishop in declaring Arthur and his chief knights excommunicate. Certainly Agravaine resented that; he was a pious man and dutiful in his religious observances.

But the truth is that no one knows what was said, or what passed between the brothers, till the moment Mordred emerged from his pavilion, crying 'treachery' and brushing his bloody dagger on the skirts of his tunic.

He was, men remembered, white-faced as the snow that lies on the mountains, and his eyes were black as the gates of Hell. In a harsh voice that quivered with the intensity of his feeling, he ordered his Danish bodyguards to seize the seven knights who had ridden with Agravaine into his camp and who were now sitting at wine with knights who, in happier days, had been their comrades.

So this was done and the seven knights were hanged from the pine trees that stood beyond the western gate of his camp. In the morning, when the mist cleared and the sun cast dark shadows on the pale grey-green sea-grass, Arthur's men, looking down from their camp, saw the bodies dangling motionless in the still air.

But they had not yet learned the worst.

Mordred was followed from his tent by one of the Danish Guards, carrying Agravaine's head by the long auburn hair that had been his pride; and in the black of night that followed a horseman carried it up the hill and hurled it over the rude stockade and earthwork that had been thrown up round Arthur's camp, so that it was found there at first light, the blood clotted and the eyes staring wide.

All were dismayed and some said, 'The sun shines on what will be our last day.'

Yet no man rode out to Mordred, deserting Arthur.

XI

Gaheris could not bring himself to tell Arthur of Agravaine's death; he was consumed by grief himself. So Cal assumed the duty.

'Spare him the worst,' Gaheris said between sobs.

But when Cal broke the news, as gently as was possible, Arthur, with a great effort, rose from his bed, looked his old friend in the face and said, 'Tell me all. Spare me nothing.'

Then, when reluctantly and with many hesitations Cal had disclosed the full horror as he knew it, Arthur fixed him with his blue eyes from which it seemed the clouds had fled away, and which were to Cal once more the eyes of the boy he had known and loved so many years before, blue as a northern morning in winter. 'Mourning would become us, but there is no time. The world's but a broken bundle of mirrors, and each fresh catastrophe but a fractured reflection of all that we have already known. Cal, command my page to fetch my armour.'

Then he stood very still, in the stained gown he had worn since he took to his bed, and Cal heard him murmur:

'What thou lov'st well remains,
The rest is dross
What thou lov'st well shall not be reft from thee . . .'*

---

*The reader may be surprised to find Arthur quoting from Ezra Pound's *Pisan Cantos*, and yet this is an exact literal translation of Scott's Latin which here seems to be verse. Since I cannot suppose that Pound had access to the original manuscript in the Bibliothèque Nationale, the more so since the learned archivist, M. Albert Saniette, assured me that there was no evidence it had been read by anyone in at least forty years before Lord Clanroyden discovered it, and by no one since he had had it copied, I therefore surmise that some Italian or Provençal poet of the thirteenth century was acquainted with it, and took these lines and made a poem of

Arthur called for a tub to be filled, and removed his stained nightgown and sat in the tub and washed himself. He did this vigorously, scouring his body with pumice stone. Then he stepped out and rubbed himself hard, so that his body was red where the rough towel had pulled hard against it. (Cal was shocked to see how thin his arms and legs were.) Then his page brought him his garments and he dressed himself, and then put on each piece of his armour with care. And that day his armour was black, for he knew his doom had come upon him. But because he had so wasted away it hung loose on him. He called for a glass and examined his face, and the pallor of death lay on it. So he called for rouge to disguise his condition and so that no man should think him afraid.

When he was dressed and armed, Cal saw that his eyes sparkled as in days of old and, mindless of the page, he leaned forward and kissed the King first on one cheek and then on the other; and he held him close. 'God – whoever He may be – be with you,' he said.

Then Arthur buckled on his sword, even Excalibur, which Merlin had given him, and called for his horse to be saddled.

There was but a pitiful remnant to man their defences. Many were weak, new recovered from dysentery or the fever, and others sickening for it. All were hungry; for two days they had eaten little but oatmeal mixed with water drawn from the well by the chapel around which they had made their camp. The sea lay behind them, far below black rocks which ran down to a level beach of grey sand. A twisting path led from the camp down to the beach, at the corner of the camp where the rocks had fallen away. It was a beach up which Lancelot, if he had come as was rumoured, could have run his ships, but there were no vessels on the sea and no sight of sail.

Below them on the landward side they could see the enemy deployed and they heard the cheers when Mordred rode along his lines. Some of Arthur's men shouted curses, calling him traitor,

them on which Pound drew from memory in his Pisan cage. Alternatively, Michael Scott may have annexed them from some troubadour. This may be more probable. He was, as readers will have gathered, something of a magpie. A.M.

coward and murderer; but the most part saved their breath for the fighting.

Yet the sun rose in the sky and Mordred made no move. It passed the zenith and there was no sign of any advance.

Arthur too moved among his men, speaking words of comfort and encouragement, though more than once he swayed in the saddle, all but overcome by his weakness, so that Gaheris who rode with him had to thrust out a hand to steady him and keep him from falling to the ground. But no words passed between them and indeed, Gaheris had spoken none since he had sent Cal to Arthur to tell him of Agravaine's murder and asked him to spare the King the worst. But later his page, Will, said his master had been 'fey' that day. 'There was a wild unearthly look on him such as I've never seen, nor wish to see on any man's face again.'

And often Arthur's eyes turned to the bodies of the seven hanged knights where they dangled from the pine trees. Then the mist came down again and closed in on them, chilling them to the bone. But there was no battle that day.

Cal said, 'He knows how weak we are and how every day we grow weaker.'

The next morning a cold wind blew from the east, dispelling the mist, and the sky was slate-grey, threatening snow, though it was still summer by the calendar.

Towards noon came the sound of trumpets and drums, and they saw Mordred's army begin to move against them. The hired crossbow-men advanced, nimbly, in loose formation before the mounted knights. They loosed their arrows and did much execution. One arrow struck Arthur in the leg, pinning him to his horse, and, to ease alarm, the King leaned forward and broke off the arrow, leaving its tip embedded. But because it was so embedded, the blood did not flow.

The first wave of cavalry struck the defences with a mighty shock, but was repulsed, with much loss of life on both sides. They withdrew in disorder and Arthur's remnant raised a cheer to see the back of them. And this was repeated three times, and each time they fell back.

Mordred now sent forward his Danish axe-men under cover of a volley of arrows from his Lombards. They were fearful to behold as they advanced in close order up the hill, chanting a war song which went like this:

> Teribus ye Teri-Odin
> Sons of Thor by him begotten.

The shield-wall behind which they advanced, to guard against any missiles hurled by the defenders, looked like a wave of the ocean at the time of the spring tides and their song sounded like the mighty roar of thunder. They swung their axes either in great scything sweeps or in a sharp hacking motion, and many a noble knight and gallant soldier fell to their terrible blows. Yet the defence-work held, and Arthur's men used their spears and lances thrusting under the swinging axes and the shields, so that the Danes were pushed back till, losing heart, they turned and fled.

Seeing this, some of Arthur's knights broke out of the barrier and gave chase. But they lost order and went too far, and were taken in the flank by a body of Mordred's knights and cut down to a man, no quarter being given or indeed, asked for.

So, though each attack had been repulsed, each had done much damage, and Arthur's men were now few in number and many of them wounded. No one performed more valiantly than Gaheris, and those who had formerly thought him soft and effeminate were amazed by his courage and the deeds he did that day.

There now came a lull in the fighting. A herald was sent forward by Mordred calling on Arthur to surrender for, he said as instructed, 'you cannot conquer this day and unless you yield you shall all be surely slain'.

Arthur said, 'For my part, I shall fight to the death, and I do not fear that. But I must tell you, my noble knights and gallant men, that a voice came to me in the darkness when sleep was denied me, warning me that this was my last battle and I should not live to see another dawn. And now that we have fought so bravely and yet the enemy is still strong and able to come at us again while we are so weakened, I fear that that voice spoke truth. Therefore, if any man-at-arms or knight wishes to take advantage of this offer and so to yield, he may do so with my blessing and my thanks for all that he has already done on my behalf today, which have indeed been mighty deeds such as will be remembered with wonder as long as men are men and speak in praise of noble feats of arms. And he may do so without shame, for shame belongs to none who has fought by my side today.'

When they heard these words, all were abashed and amazed, and most were resolute to die with their King and be received as heroes in the world beyond the grave.

Yet a score or so, despairing and thinking themselves not ready to depart this life, threw down their arms and rode out or clambered over the earthwork to surrender. Mordred had given orders that they be received with honour, for he saw that this would advantage him and weaken the resolve of Arthur's remnant. But they looked on the departed with sorrow as men who had failed their last and greatest test, preferring life and shame (despite the King's assurance) to death and glory.

So fewer than a hundred men now remained to Arthur and all commended their souls to whatever gods they believed in. Cal who, with the page-boys, had busied himself tending to the wounded, now saw that all was lost and took a broadsword in his hand and his place on the earthwork.

Thus, like the Spartans at Thermopylae, they stood their ground, obedient to the laws of honour and determined still to sell their lives dearly.

The sun already lay low in the sky above the ocean when they saw the last attack being mounted, and it shone blood-coloured on the Danish shields which wavered in a wall that was no longer regular, such had been the execution, such was the fatigue even of the axe-men. But they came on and this time the defence could not hold, being too thinly manned. So Arthur's remnant was pushed back and then cut up, separated into small groups, with all order lost and hope dying with each man that fell. For, though all those who still stood by Arthur had accepted the certainty of death, nevertheless man's disposition is such that hope lingers long after reason has bid it be gone.

And now the knights were among them too, no longer pushing with their long lances but slashing with their swords; and the air resounded to the screams of the wounded, the groans of the dying, and the oaths and commands that have lost all meaning – for who in the press of battle can obey them?

Arthur still sat his horse and for a moment Cal saw him clearly, and he looked as if a spectator in the theatre of his own tragedy. Then he glanced away, the dead eyes were restored to life, and he saw Gaheris assailed by two brawny knights, and unhorsed and pinned to the ground. So Arthur, settling lance in rest as in the lists at Camelot, spurred his horse forward and drove his lance hard through the neck of the knight who, dismounted, stood over Gaheris ready to dispatch him. Then Arthur drew his sword, even Excalibur, and brought it down hard on the sword arm of the second knight, and the sword fell to the ground, the arm dangled broken, and the knight with a shrill yelp pulled on his horse's reins and fled.

Arthur leaned over and took the lance on which Gaheris was impaled, and shook it free, and held out his hand to help his nephew rise. Now they were pushed back to the extremity of the camp but still would not yield.

The sun dipped below the water, and the gold faded and the sky paled. At that very moment of the dying sun an arrow, loosed at random, struck Arthur in the neck, just below the jawline of his helmet. He swayed in the saddle, leaned forward and seized his horse's mane, but would yet have fallen had not Cal held out his hand to steady him. His horse, misunderstanding the signal the King had given it, now started, reared and then took off at a gallop, clearing the little wall and making for the forest that here came up close to the sea cliff. Gaheris and Cal and the two page-boys who had kept in close attendance on the King all day long, followed. Gaheris, looking back, saw that all was now still, the battle over, for not another man of Arthur's army remained on his feet. So he turned away and they followed Arthur into the wood where the light had already failed.

They found him fallen from his horse in a little clearing beside a pool, and his horse crashed through the undergrowth beyond. They raised Arthur's head, and fetched water from the pool and bathed his brow. He coughed twice and a gout of blood spluttered from his mouth. They saw that the arrow had passed clean through his neck and was held there fast. It could not be removed without tearing open his throat. He coughed again: more blood. He moved his lips as if he would speak. Gaheris and Cal knelt by him, each holding him by the hand, and Gaheris mopping his brow with a wet napkin. His wandering eyes seemed to search their faces, but they could not tell if he knew them.

Far away they heard the song of the Danish axe-men rising in triumph to their gods:

> Teribus ye Teri-Odin
> Sons of Thor by him begotten.

And a breeze carried the smell of the sea to them. The page-boys now did not try to conceal their grief but wept freely, and Cal's eyes were also blurred. But Gaheris, though wounded himself and in pain, was dry-eyed as he looked on Arthur, as if this refusal to give way to grief were the last service he could render the King.

Then it seemed as if Arthur formed words; and afterwards when they had collected their thoughts and arranged their memories they gave words or rather names to his muttering: 'Gawaine, Parsifal, Agravaine, Kay, Nestor, Peredur . . . Merlin old fox . . . wait for me . . . in the Elysian Fields.'

His body was shaken by a convulsion and blood spurted from his mouth, nose and ears; and then he was very still and was dead, and the risen moon shone in his eyes.

So they knelt by him and prayed for his soul while the moon lay silver on the waters of the pool and the owl that is the bird of Minerva cried to the echoing night.

'What thou lov'st well shall not be reft from thee,' Cal said. 'Come, let us carry the King's body to a place of safety that it may not be found by Mordred's men and despoiled.'

XII

What's that, my Prince?

You say it's not how the poets end the story?

So you've been reading these poets, have you? On the sly?

Well, there's no reason why you shouldn't have. I'm not angry, not really angry. Read them if you like, so long as you don't believe what they write. Poets are liars. Like Geoffrey of Monmouth. Some of them are even worse liars than Geoffrey. So don't trust what they say. As best it's what they call 'poetic truth'. The only exception I would make is Virgil. Believe everything that he writes. But not Ovid. He's a liar, just like our modern ones. Entertaining? Certainly.

Geoffrey himself has a different version from mine. He writes that 'Arthur, with a single division in which he had posted six thousand six hundred and sixty-six men, charged at the squadron where he knew Mordred was. They hacked a way through with their swords and Arthur still advanced, inflicting terrible slaughter as he went. It was just then that the accursed traitor was killed and many thousands of his men with him . . .'

This is nonsense, my Prince. It's a rotten account of a battle too – compare it with mine.

Later he admits that Arthur was mortally wounded, but he still has him winning the battle before 'handing over the crown of Britain to his cousin Constantine'.

You will note that I make no mention of this Constantine. That's because he didn't exist. Geoffrey invented him.

One of these poets whom you admire has a story about Arthur ordering one of his knights to take his sword Excalibur and throw it into the lake. At first the knight tells lies, pretending that he has done as the King asked, though really he hasn't because he coveted the jewels on the hilt and thought it shame to throw such an object away. But Arthur upbraids him and sends him off again, and this time he obeys, and a hand or arm comes up from the lake – mystic, wonderful, your poet says – and catches the sword and draws it under the water.

Well, it's a good story and you may, if you please, believe it, but only if you accept that it is a metaphor.

A metaphor for what? you ask.

Work it out for yourself.

Geoffrey tells us too that Arthur was carried off to the isle of Avalon, so that his wounds might be attended to.

Since he has already told us that the King was mortally wounded, this seems superfluous.

But the poets like this story and have made much of it.

One (or more) of them has the King carried to a barge in which six Queens, dressed in black and heavily veiled, are waiting to take charge of him. According to some versions, one of these Queens was his half-sister, Morgan le Fay. Well, you know from my account what had befallen her and that she was kept close prisoner. So you will see that this story is poetic nonsense.

What's that? How do I know that my version is the true one? You say it's only one among several and not as finely imagined as some of the others? Well, of course it's not 'finely imagined'. Things which are true are not imagined, finely or otherwise.

How do I know? you say. I think you are teasing me again, as Arthur himself was wont to tease Merlin.

Still: I know because I have documentary evidence.

You remember the two page-boys. Will and . . . I forgot to give the other, Arthur's page, a name; it was Christopher, which means Christ-bearer, or, by some interpretations, truth-teller.

They survived the battle as you know, and escaped Mordred's vengeance.

Gaheris then sent Christopher to Lancelot to tell him what had happened. He hoped that Lancelot would now bestir himself to cross to Britain, and make war on Mordred and remove the usurper, whom Gaheris hated intensely (though hatred was foreign to his gentle nature) on account of his treachery and the murder of Agravaine. So Christopher either carried with him a written narrative of the last days and death of Arthur, or composed one subsequently in Brittany.

Lancelot was horrified, consumed with guilt, when he learned what had happened. He blamed Guinevere, he blamed himself. (Guinevere, by the way, took a different line. She said that if Arthur had treated her as he should, none of this would have happened. So he had brought disaster upon himself and it was nobody's fault but his own. This, my Prince, will not surprise you when you know more of women than you do now. Nothing, you will then discover, is ever the woman's fault.)

Gaheris had expected that Lancelot would leap to arms. He miscalculated. He should have known Lancelot better. The great knight, the paragon of chivalry, did what he always did in an emotional crisis. He went mad again. This time he fell into a religious mania and had himself scourged twice a day, for seven months, till he recovered. Meanwhile Guinevere was disgusted. She sat for some time in her boudoir eating sugar plums and drinking the sweet white wine of Bordeaux, and then she left him. She later married a German King with a fine castle on the Rhine, who had a passion for fat women – and also for the sweet white wine of Bordeaux. She lived to a great age and, when this King died, married another much younger than herself. Actually, he was her stepson and so young his beard had scarcely grown.

Lancelot recovered from his mania, by which time Mordred's tyranny was so well-established that there was no possibility of overthrowing him. In any case Lancelot had acquired a horror of war, killing and even tournaments; the memory of his own prowess and renown was painful to him. Some say he became a monk, but this is not so. He continued to reside in his castle of Joyeuse Gard, cared for by the boy Christopher who, like so many others, had fallen in love with him at first sight. His love survived Lancelot's mania and endured. They spent the days playing draughts – Lancelot now abhorred chess, which reminded him of war – making music and writing bad poetry to imaginary mistresses.

Christopher also wrote all this down in a long rhyming narrative, full of grammatical errors, in very bad Latin. I discovered it in the library of the monastery of Mont-St-Michel and copied it faithfully, even though the style made me wince.

So what I tell you is history and much stranger than poetry. Fiction, my Prince, is at best but a pale shadow of fact.

As for the other characters you have encountered in the story, they may be quickly disposed of.

Mordred reigned for ten years and was then killed by one of his Danish house carles, who was drunk and believed himself to have been insulted. Then the realm of Britain fell apart, exposed to wild sea-wolves and internal dissension.

Morgan le Fay eventually escaped from her prison and was never reliably heard of again. Some say she retired to the Orkneys and there practised witchcraft, ineffectually. There is a story that she was burned as a witch on the steps of the cathedral in Kirkwall, which is the capital of Orkney. In Tweeddale when I was young there was a legend about a beautiful bad Queen who lived in the remotest reaches of the Ettrick Valley and every spring spirited some young shepherd lad away. But those who tell this story confuse Morgan with the Queen of Elfland.

Gaheris and Will travelled to the Holy Land and did battle with the Infidel. They were taken prisoner, enslaved, escaped and, after many adventures, arrived in Ethiopia where they disappear from history.

And Cal? Cal kept his head down and resumed his trade of merchant. He used to say, 'I take no part in any man's quarrel but I'm aye mensefu' that men hae need of gear.' He had no time for honour which, in his opinion, led to homicide and affray, but only for trade which was the business of honest men.

Envoi

So it was as I have written. Arthur died of the wounds received in that last battle in the West. Though there is no mention of burial in that document I discovered at the monastery of Mont-St-Michel, yet it is reasonable to suppose that Sir Gaheris and Cal, with the help of the page-boys, laid him to rest. No tomb was raised, no grave marked. This has puzzled some commentators; unnecessarily. The burial was secret, hurried, the work of anxious or frightened men, aware that Mordred's cavalry were searching the country around for any of Arthur's knights who had escaped the field, and doubtless with particular zeal for the King himself. Moreover, keeping the grave secret was politic. Without Arthur's body to display, Mordred could not sit easy on the throne. There would be those to claim Arthur was still alive.

Nevertheless, the King had died. Yet he was not dead. He is not dead. Wherever you go, wherever songs are made and histories recounted of the heroes, there Arthur lives. You may dismiss this as memory or legend. Yet it is certain that in men's imaginings – and, indeed, in women's – Arthur is still a real presence.

He is celebrated in the halls of castles by poets, cunning and elaborate craftsmen. But he retains a deeper life than poets can grant him. When I was a boy in Tweeddale – where certainly poets abound, though rude bucolic rascals many of them are – it was yet common knowledge that Arthur sits with his knights at his Round Table in a grotto in the Eildon Hills, whence he shall ride forth at some unknown time to redeem the land. No one doubts this and I have myself spoken with an old man – a fellow of transparent honesty, as it seemed – who averred that he had himself when but a boy climbed, greatly daring, the hill, descended into the cavern, the entrance to which was hidden and to some extent protected by whin bushes growing as high as a man's head, as he put it; and there seen Arthur feasting with his knights, one of whom, he assured me, had urged him to drink wine with them. 'The whilk,' he said, shaking his head from side to side as one who would deny his own memory, 'the whilk I wadna dae, nor wad hae daen, though it were the Archangel Michael himsel that had tempted me, and no a scapegrace loon o' a knicht wha went by the name o' Persfil, or summat siclike.'

But likewise in the West of England they will point to a cave in the hills above Glastonbury where it is said Joseph of Arimathea planted a piece of the True Cross that grew into a rose tree that blossoms on Christmas Day, and tell you that it is there that Arthur and his band of paladins await the summons to rise again and save the land from peril.

And again he is known by some to wait the call in the depths below either the castle or cathedral of Winchester which, after his time, became the capital of England. This version of the story is sedulously advanced by the monks there resident, who thus acquire renown, and receive many rich and rare gifts, by reason of their association with the great King.

Throughout the forests of Britain, now divided between the kingdoms of England and Scotland, there have been many sightings over the centuries of Arthur and his knights. On certain days at noon, when the air is still, and also in the first silence of night, broken only by owls and vixens, and at the time of the full moon, a cavalcade of knights is seen hunting the deer with dogs and sounding their horns. And those who dwell in the forest swear that these are the followers and household of Arthur.

Why, my Prince, even here in Sicily Arthur is known. A few years ago he appeared on the slopes of Etna which, in the old tongue, is Mongibel. It happened that a groom in the service of the Bishop of Catania had gone there in search of a runaway horse that had thrown him. He tracked the beast over difficult and dangerous country, and his fear was great as darkness fell. Then the boy found a narrow path that led through a cleft of the rock, and he followed it and came upon a plain, in the middle, as it were, of the mountain, and there he happened on a palace of a beauty and magnificence such as he had never seen. He entered it cautiously and saw Arthur reclining on a couch. In halting language, for he was much afraid, he explained how he had come upon the palace and, as soon as the reason for his journey was known, his master's horse was returned to him. Arthur then asked him to commend him to his master and said that for many centuries since ancient times he had resided there. He had been ill for a long time, since every year the wounds he had received in the last battle against Mordred opened again.

How to account for this? For this persistence of memory? It is not enough to argue that the legends of Arthur and his Knights of the Round Table breathe the spirit of the chivalry of our time and thus naturally appeal to the bards, poets and troubadours who express that spirit in verse. This is obviously so, yet insufficient as explanation.

We must delve more deeply. Then we shall find that Arthur is Arthur the renewer, the heir of Aeneas, the father of Empire, and of Augustus who established a new age of gold in the realm where once Saturn reigned (as the great poet has it); that in the twilight of Empire the torch was carried, as I have already told you, by Marcus, and now, most gloriously, by Arthur, who conquered even in defeat, the vanquished victor.

It is the idea of Empire that he incarnates, that Empire which, as Jupiter promised Aeneas, was without bounds of either time or place; that Empire necessary for mankind, that Empire which through war bestows the blessings of peace and justice.

And that Arthur was destroyed, as I have related, by malevolence and the malignity of that perverter of Empire, the Pope, gives his story all the beauty of pathos.

Finally, in Arthur we see the promise renewed, broken, but never utterly destroyed. Hence he is known as the once and future King, for in him the hopes of the world congregate.

And as Arthur was heir to Aeneas, Augustus and Marcus, so too, as I shall show you, may God give me strength and life long enough to conclude my task, was Charlemagne Arthur's proper heir or reincarnation. And so also, my Prince, may you be.